Cupid
Painted
Blind

MH

Cupid Painted Blind
Copyright © 2016 Marcus Herzig
Cover Illustration Copyright © 2016 Andrew Yuuki

ISBN: 978-1-5377-0486-9

Marcus Herzig
244 Madison Avenue
New York, NY 10016-2817
U S A

www.marcus-herzig.com

For awkward teenagers everywhere

Chapter One

One day I'm going to write the next Great American Novel, with intriguing characters, a unique, original plot, and a killer opening line.

This is probably not it.

Call me Matt.

Most people call me Matt. When someone calls me Matthew, I know I'm in trouble. Most of the time I manage to stay clear of trouble though. I'm not particularly prone to drama or tragedy. I'm just a regular guy, and my name is Matt, and I'm gay.

Zoey knows all this, apparently.

I didn't know she did. I thought she only knew my name.

I didn't know she knew that I'm gay.

Aghast, I say, "You knew?"

She smiles and shrugs and says, "Kinda."

Zoey is my sister.

She's a junior at Brookhurst High School. I, as of today, am a freshman. A proud and anxious freshman.

It is a bright warm day in September, and the clocks are striking seven-and-a-half. It is the best of times, it is the worst of times and all that crap. I'm excited to start high school for an infinite number of reasons, not the least of which being that it's a major step toward adulthood. Adulthood means freedom and independence and driving and plenty of passionate, steaming, red-hot sex.

Or so I'm told.

Yet at the same time I'm anxious about starting high school because starting high school means meeting lots of new people.

Meeting lots of new people means plenty of opportunities to make a first impression.

I don't know that I'm good at first impressions.

What if my first impression makes people also *kinda* know I'm gay?

"How?" I say.

Zoey pushes her glasses up her pointy, freckled nose, takes a bite out of her apple, and says, "I don't know."

She doesn't know how she kinda knew.

Like most things in life, I find that profoundly confusing.

I think I know how I know most of the things I know.

"You love show tunes," she offers.

"Oh please," I say, hating how I'm such a cliché. "Not everyone who loves show tunes is gay."

"You binge watch *Modern Family* on Netflix."

"False positive," I object. "Again."

She looks at me. "How so?"

"I'm not watching it because of the gay couple."

"I know. You're watching it because you have a crush on that dopey kid. What's his name again?"

"Luke."

"See? You even know his name off the top of your head."

If I should ever write a book about my sister, I will title it *The Girl Who Knew Too Much*.

"Look at your fingernails," Zoey says.

I look at my fingernails. "What about them?"

"They're pristine and never dirty."

"What's wrong with pristine fingernails?"

"Nothing," she says, "but have you ever looked at other guys' nails?"

As a matter of fact, I have. Not specifically at their fingernails, though. I find guys' hands in general rather worthy of inconspicuous visual inspection. I have a thing for handsome hands, especially long, slender hands with bony, spidery fingers.

Like E.T.'s.

I've once seen a YouTube video of some guy from Romania or Bulgaria or someplace with fingers so long and agile, he could solve a standard-sized Rubik's cube using just one hand.

I watched that video nearly a dozen times in a row until I realized how my subconscious self was imagining those long, spidery fingers touching me in inappropriate places. Forget about being gay; I'm a closeted arachnodactylophile and I should probably get therapy or something.

"There are other little things," Zoey says. "Like the way you flail your arms when you're really excited about something, or the way you look at other guys sometimes."

"I do not!" I protest, not because it's not true but because I always thought my surreptitious glances at cute boys were surreptitious enough for no one to notice.

"And now you're blushing. That's cute," Zoey says, and it makes me blush even more. "But don't worry. I don't think anyone else would notice. I've known you since forever, so maybe I know you a little better than most people."

"So when were you going to tell me?" I ask.

"That you're gay? I wasn't. I thought you already knew."

"No, I mean ... when were you going to tell me you knew?"

"I wasn't. There's a reason it's called *coming out* and not *being dragged out*, you know?"

"Right," I say with a wry smile. "Hey listen, not a word to anyone, okay?"

She squints at me. "You don't want to stay in the closet forever, do you?"

"No! I mean ... no. Of course not. But I want to get this right. And I want to do it myself if you don't mind."

"Yeah, whatever," she says.

With screeching brakes, a bicycle scoots past Zoey from behind and skids into a halt right in front of us, blocking our way. Startled, Zoey jumps and grabs my arm.

My big sister seeking my protection makes me feel all grown-up and manly.

"¿Hola, que tal?" El Niño says with that silly but adorable grin of his.

El Niño is my affectionate nickname for Alfonso.

Alfonso is my best friend.

His full name is Alfonso Alonso, because his parents have a dry sense of humor.

"Fonso!" Zoey shouts at him, placing her hand on her chest and taking a deep breath. "You scared the hell out of me!"

"Sorry 'bout that," he says and leans forward. Zoey lets go of my arm to give Alfonso a quick hug.

"Hey," she says.

"Hey."

Alfonso raises his right hand toward me. "Hey, Matty."

Matty is Alfonso's affectionate nickname for me.

I grab it and we do a quick shoulder bump. When he places his hands back on the handlebar I cast an inconspicuous glance at his fingernails. They're nowhere near as pretty as mine.

I still like Alfonso's hands, though. At first glance they may look a bit chubby, but when you shake his hand, what superficially looks like chubbiness turns out to be all muscles. That's because Alfonso is a fruit picker.

That is not a euphemism for someone who bullies gay people.

He is an actual part-time fruit picker, and he spent the entire second half of the summer holidays out in the fields, doing whatever it is fruit pickers do, which I assume is picking fruit.

Don't bother calling child protective services or immigration. There is nothing illegal going on here.

Alfonso's parents came to the U.S. from Argentina sometime in the nineties, and by the time Alfonso was born they had started their own fruit picking business and become U.S. citizens. Today Alfonso's dad is the fruit picking king of Brookhurst County with a couple of dozen employees and a son who's eager to volunteer whenever he can.

"So," he says, "what were you guys talking about?"

"Nothing," I hurry to say.

"Oh really?" he says, eying me suspiciously. "Geez, I could have sworn I've seen you talk about *something*, but I guess I must have been mistaken."

In my mind I perform a quick calculation that involves multiple variables such as the loudness of our voices, Alfonso's braking distance, and the wind speed and direction to gauge how much of our conversation Alfonso might have overheard. Meanwhile, Zoey smiles at me with an expectant look, but if she thinks I'm going to come out to Alfonso in passing on a public sidewalk during the morning rush hour and in front of a witness, she knows me a lot less well than she thinks she does.

"Nah, we were just ..." I say to Alfonso with a dismissive and hopefully not too camp wave of my hand, "... I was just saying how exciting everything is, first day of high school and everything. It is exciting, don't you think?"

Alfonso shrugs. "Yeah, I don't know. I don't think it's gonna be all that different from junior high, to be honest."

Alfonso turns his bike around and we take him in the middle as we continue our way down Vine Street.

"Matt doesn't like meeting new people," Zoey says, "because he hates making first impressions."

"I don't *hate* making first impressions. But let's face it, first impressions tend to stick. Just imagine, first day, first class, a bunch of new people, and you say or do something incredibly embarrassing or stupid. That's so gonna stick with you through high school, the entire four years. So I think I'm gonna try to keep a low profile."

Zoey shrugs. "Whatever. Just try not to be too much of a wallflower. Did you know that thirty-four percent of echo boomers marry someone they met in high school or college?"

Alfonso frowns. "What are echo boomers?"

"It's a fancier word for millennials," I say. "And I bet that's thirty-three percent college and one percent high school sweethearts."

Zoey sighs. "You need to work on your attitude, Matthew. For all you know you might meet your future spouse today."

I hate how she says *spouse* to make it extra-ambiguous. Then again, I should probably be grateful she didn't say *husband*.

"I think I can already see her," Alfonso says, flicking his head toward the other side of the street where Sandy Lauper is flailing her arms and calling out to us as she's waiting for a gap in the early morning traffic on Vine to cross the road.

"Guys, guys! Wait up for me!"

My affectionate nickname for Sandy Lauper is *Hurricane Sandy*.

For the record, I don't name all of my friends after weather phenomena, just Sandy and Alfonso. That's because they're forces of nature, both of them.

"Oh no, not the limpet!" Zoey says, rolling her eyes. "Can we just keep on walking and pretend we haven't seen her?"

"That would be so rude," I say and stop. "She knows we've already seen her."

"He's got a point," Alfonso says and puts his feet on the ground, prompting Zoey to stop as well and turn her back toward Sandy, crossing her arms in silent protest.

When she makes it to our side of the street, Sandy first flings her arms around my neck, squeezing me as if she hasn't seen me in a hundred years and yanking my body left-right-left.

"Matt!" she squeals. "I've missed you so much! I haven't seen you since the last day of school. Did you go on vacation? It's so good to see you! You look so cute! I love your T-shirt, is it new? O-M-G!"

Her vanilla scent tickles the inside of my nose, and I don't have time to say anything else than "Hi, Sandy," because she's already let go of me and is throwing herself around Alfonso.

"Alfonso! I've missed you! O-M-G, look at you! Have you lost weight? You look awesome! I met Alfredo the other day, he said you were picking fruit again. Is that true? Have you taken over your dad's company yet? I mean, L-O-L!"

"Yeah, no, not yet," he says, but Sandy is already moving on to Zoey who leans in to her, her arms still crossed.

"Oh my God, Zoey! I missed you! Cute glasses! And I love your hair! What have you done with it? You have to tell me!"

"Hello, Sandy."

With Sandy hanging around her neck, Zoey crosses her eyes, sucks in her cheeks and moves her lips like a fish out of water which cracks Alfonso and me up.

Sandy, bless her, takes our giggles as a sign of joy that we're seeing her.

Finally letting go of Zoey, she looks at all of us. "O-M-G, you guys! First day of high school! I'm so excited, aren't you? I was so excited last night, I couldn't even sleep. First I was texting with Laura until she dozed off at like one a.m. and then

I've been on Twitter and Instagram until two or two-thirty or I don't even know. Good thing I know so many people in Europe and Australia and everywhere because everyone from around here was already asleep, obviously."

"That's great, Sandy," Zoey says, not even trying to conceal the snark in her voice. She never does when she's talking to Sandy.

Not that Sandy ever notices.

"I know, right?" She squeezes herself between Zoey and me and grabs my arm as we continue on our way. "But honestly, guys, it's so exciting, isn't it? I mean, it's the first day of freaking high school and everything! I can't even!"

"Yeah, I don't think it's gonna be all that different from junior high," Alfonso says, slowly rolling along to the left of me, his hand on my shoulder to keep his balance.

It's nice to have a friend lean on you.

"Yeah, no, I know," Sandy says, clinging to my arm. "But it's still exciting to meet new people, don't you think? And make new friends? And all the new teachers too! My sister says the teachers at Brookhurst High are really good. So what are your electives? There were so many to choose from, I didn't even know where to start!"

Over the summer, my mom has been asking me the same question about two hundred times. Alfonso always had his mind set on business management and—because he's a lazy bum when it comes to academics—Spanish. I took forever to make up my mind between drama, creative writing, literature, photography, filmmaking, and about half a dozen others. I handed in my picks—literature and creative writing—two hours before the deadline.

Not that Sandy will ever know, because she's already moving on.

"But you know what? You guys are so not going to believe what I'm about to tell you. I actually signed up for Chinese, can you believe it? Because Chinese is going to be so freaking important in the future, like, for real. Because my dad says there are, like, two billion Chinese, and they basically own us now because of all the debt America has. We owe, like, trillions of dollars to the

Chinese. And remember how during the financial crisis the banks foreclosed on millions of homes because the homeowners couldn't pay their mortgages anymore? My dad says that could totally happen to America. Like, if we can't pay off our debt to the Chinese they could just walk in here and foreclose on all our resources and our infrastructure and whatnot and just say, 'We'll take this, fēicháng gǎnxiè.' That means 'thank you very much,' by the way. My dad says we better prepare for when the Chinese claim all their money back, so I figured the best way to prepare for that is to learn the language so we can, you know, like, talk our way out of it when they knock on our door and want to ship all our bridges and national parks and everything to China. I mean, that would be better than starting a war with them, right, because they have nukes and everything. Honestly, though, can you imagine me speaking Chinese? Ching chong chow mein chop suey. I mean, L-O-L, right? It's gonna be so freaking hilarious!"

"It already is," Zoey says with a pitying smile that I'm sure looks genuinely nice to Sandy. "It already is."

Ahead of us, some reckless shop owner sweeps waste water out of his store right into the middle of the sidewalk. I'm about to step around it when I hear screeching bicycle brakes again, and someone shouts, "Watch out!"

I turn around and make a step back, stumbling over my own stupid feet and landing butt-first in the puddle. As Sandy and Zoey jump and shriek, Jack's bike comes to a halt inches in front of me while I feel dirty water seeping into my butt crack.

"Jack!" Sandy exclaims in half-hearted outrage.

"Hey, girls," Jack says.

It's not that he's greeting just Zoey and Sandy while ignoring Alfonso and me. Whenever he meets just the two of us, he always calls us girls just the same.

Jack is the kind of person who thinks that's hilarious.

My affectionate nickname for Jack is *Jackrabbit*, by virtue of his rather prominent front teeth.

Come to think of it, it's not really that affectionate.

Also, I would never dare call him that to his face.

While I rub the seat of my shorts to assess the water damage, Sandy throws herself around Jack's neck, her outrage from two seconds ago all but forgotten.

"Jack! Oh my God, I've missed you! How have you been?"

"All right," says Jack with a broad grin at me and my soaked butt crack as he rubs Sandy's back with one hand.

"We were just talking about our electives. I'm taking Chinese, can you believe it? So what are your electives, Jack?"

"Yeah," Zoey seconds the question, "what *are* your electives, Jack? Bullying and tomfoolery?"

Smiling a condescending smile, he says, "Those are classes that I teach, honey, not take," he quips, which makes Sandy shriek with laughter.

"O-M-G, Jack, you are so funny!"

Jack's broad grin is widening as he indulges in Sandy's appreciation of his unspeakable wit.

Alfonso rolls his eyes at me, and I just shrug. I'm the last person anyone could accuse of cutting Jack Antonelli too much slack—he's been my archnemesis for the better part of my life—but I do appreciate a good riposte.

Some people can always come up with a snappy remark when the situation requires it, and I can see why many find this an endearing quality. Sadly, that kind of talent usually isn't bestowed upon the most deserving individuals. I usually think of sharp, witty responses a few hours after I need them, and I have this theory that the world is in the sad state it's in because all too often, people tend to succumb to the charm of the bully.

"Anyway," Jack says and looks at his watch, "if you girls don't wanna be late on the first day, you better hurry up. Wanna catch a ride, Sandy?"

She shakes her head and grabs my arm again. "That's okay, I'll walk with my homie Matt here."

Jack shrugs. "Suit yourself. I'll see you later, girls!"

We watch him take off, and still wiping my butt crack, I say, "So how bad is it?"

Everyone takes a close look at my butt which is the last thing I would have expected—or asked for—on my first day of high school, and from their restrained reaction I can tell it's probably not looking great.

"To be honest," Alfonso says, "it looks like a pretty bad case of diarrhea."

"Great," I say. "Talk about making a splash on the first day of school."

Chapter Two

The entrance hall of Brookhurst High School is abuzz with a throbbing mass of sneakers and backpacks, of T-shirts, hoodies, jeans, and skirts as a couple of hundred freshmen anticipate their first of roughly seven hundred days in high school with nervous excitement. As soon as we enter the hall we lose Sandy in the thick of it as she endeavors to hug everybody (and I do mean *everybody*) and tell them how much she's been missing them over the summer. Streaming into the hall, the jumbling crowd crystallizes into eight semi-orderly queues, each one lining up for one of the tables set up against the wall opposite of the main entrance, and for a moment I'm not sure whether we're starting high school or auditioning for *American Idol*.

I sure hope it's not *American Idol*, because I can't sing to save my life.

As Alfonso and I line up for one of the tables, he's kind enough to stand about two inches behind me to shield the mud-streaked seat of my shorts from the prying eyes of my future fellow students. It takes us only about five minutes to realize that we're standing in the wrong queue. Each of the tables caters to a range of letters, and neither Dunstan nor Alonso falls into the N - Q range we're lined up for. We have to split up and each go to our assigned queues, so I'm standing alone in my queue now, moving forward at an agonizingly slow pace as my butt feels more self-conscious than ever and my ears miserably fail in their desperate bid to ignore the whispers and giggles. I can't wait to get to my classroom so I can finally obscure my dirty behind from people's view simply by sitting on it.

Somewhere behind me someone bursts out laughing. When I look, heads quickly turn away, and I continue to let my eyes roam, pretending that whatever they were laughing about, it wasn't me. Over in the K - M queue, Sandy is—I presume—trying out her rudimentary Mandarin skills on the bemused looking Korean dude in front of her. The guy standing right behind Sandy is wearing a black T-shirt that has the word *Larsenist* printed on it in big, bold, white letters. Aghast at this heinous act of orthographic deviancy yet intrigued by the audacity to put it so shamelessly on display on one's first day at a new academic institution, I cannot help but take a closer look to find out what kind of person would be so daringly rebellious.

The linguistic rogue in skinny jeans and black Chucks is tall and handsome. Around his suntanned neck a silver necklace is glistening in the bright halogen light of the entrance hall. On his head he's sporting a tousled mop of strawberry blond hair that looks as if he's come straight out of bed. He is—and I find this fact impossible to ignore—absolutely gorgeous.

Also, he's staring at me.

The moment I look at his face I catch him staring at me with piercing, ocean-blue eyes and the subtlest of smiles. It's a widely accepted and adhered to social standard that when you're caught staring at someone, you immediately look away as if you were just looking at them by accident, so that's what I do. I quickly, bashfully look away like some intimidated little puppy, my heart pounding in my chest, and my mind feeling like a tumble dryer.

After a few seconds I turn my head to seek him out of the crowd again. His queue has moved forward, but when I finally find him he's still staring at me, and when our eyes meet again he winks at me!

What the heck is wrong with this guy?

"Next, please!" I hear someone bark in my direction, and the guy behind me in the queue taps me on the shoulder. "That you."

"What?" I turn around, and to my surprise I look into the face of a middle-aged Asian man wearing a grubby gray jacket and a trilby hat. His face unshaven, his thick, black hair flecked with gray. He looks distinctly out of place here, and it suddenly occurs to me that all of this is probably just one of those bizarre dreams people keep having about school where weird and embarrassing things happen to them.

I look at myself to check if I'm actually naked.

Turns out I'm not.

"You next," the man says with an unnecessarily polite smile as he points at the table where a middle-aged woman is impatiently tapping her pen on a stack of manila envelopes.

"Oh, right," I say and step up to the table.

The woman bears an uncanny resemblance to Kim Davis, the county clerk from Kentucky who recently rose to dubious national fame by denying marriage licenses to gay couples, citing her religious opposition to same-sex marriage.

She looks at me over the rim of her glasses. "Name?"

"Hi, I'm Matt."

"That's great," she says with no discernible expression on her round face. "And do you also have a last name, or are you just Matt?"

"Oh," I say, feeling like a stupid freshman.

"Sorry. Dunstan. Matthew Dunstan."

"Dunstan," she repeats and starts leafing through her stack of envelopes. When she finds the one with my name on it, she opens it and pulls out a few sheets of paper and a small plastic card the size of a credit card with my picture on it that was taken when I enrolled at the school a couple of weeks ago. Her eyes bounce back and forth between the picture and my face until she's satisfied that I'm actually who I claim to be.

As if someone would actually try to con their way into high school.

"Bad hair day?" she finally asks.

I nervously scratch the back of my head. "Yeah, I … got a haircut just before that picture was taken, and it didn't quite come out the way—"

"No, I mean today."

My hand stops scratching, and I wonder if a pair of red-hot glowing ears can actually set off the fire alarm.

That would be helpful.

I could just turn around and run.

But I can't, obviously.

I'm caught in a trap, and it must be the weirdest trap anyone has ever been caught in, with a strange, trilby-wearing Asian man standing behind me, a breathtakingly attractive guy probably still staring at my reddened face, hundreds of freshmen smirking at my mud-streaked shorts, and Kim Davis, her mouth moving and moving but none of her words reaching my burning ears, handing me a whole bunch of papers, one after the other, none of which, I assume, is a marriage license because even though gay marriage is now legal, God still hates fags.

"Hello?" she suddenly shouts at me, prompting me to snap out of my stupor.

"Sorry, what?"

"I said: do you have any questions?"

"Um," I say. "Not right now, I don't think."

"Good. Next!"

When I turn to leave, looking at the stack of papers in my hand, I bump into the Asian man behind me as he steps up to the table.

"Ah! Sorry, sorry," he apologizes overly politely and bows.

"Sorry," I utter absent-mindedly and scurry away in an attempt to not draw any more attention toward myself.

Making my way across the hall I look at the K - N queue, but the Larsenist is gone. I scan the crowd, but to my great disappointment I can't find him anywhere. Instead, I see Alfonso and Zoey standing by the glass door to the hallway, waving me over. When I reach them, Zoey raises her eyebrows expectantly.

"So?" she asks.

I frown. "So what?"

"So who's your homeroom teacher?"

"Oh," I say and start clumsily leafing through my stack of papers. I don't even know what they all are. Taking pity on me, Zoey plunges her hand into the sea of papers and pulls out my class schedule with impeccable accuracy. She looks at it.

"Mrs. Spelczik. English. Room 201. Second floor."

She pronounces the name *spellchick*.

With a wide grin I nudge Alfonso. "Awesome name for an English teacher, huh? Spell chick, get it?"

He looks at me with a deadpan face. "Dude, seriously?"

"Never mind," I say, making a mental note not to speak unless I'm spoken to first.

For the next four years.

"This way, guys," Zoey says, pushing the door open as I look back across the hall, hoping to catch another glimpse of the Larsenist. "If you're looking for the limpet, she's already on her way up."

I shake my head. "No, I was just … never mind. And could you stop calling her *limpet*?"

"And why would I do that?"

"Because she's not a limpet."

"Well," Zoey says, "she's certainly clinging to you like one."

"That's obviously not true, because then she'd be here right now, wouldn't she?"

"Aw," she teases me. "You miss her already. That is so sweet."

"I … what?! No! I don't miss her at all! What are you talking about?"

"Matt, it's okay. You don't have to be shy. I'm your sister, Alfonso's your best friend. You can tell us. You can tell us everything."

"Tell you what exactly?"

"I don't know, you tell me."

"You two," Alfonso says, absentmindedly shaking his head as he's scrolling through the Twitter feed on his phone. "I don't know what it is, but you're acting all weird today."

"We're siblings," I say. "We act all weird every day."

"Not like that, though."

When we've reached room 201, Zoey stops and turns to me. "Okay, this is you. I'll see you in four years. Have fun. And try to remain seated, because it really looks like you've pooped your pants."

"Thanks, Zoey," I sigh.

"All right," Alfonso says. "Let's do this."

I follow him into our classroom. Of the thirty or so desks, about two thirds are already taken by our new classmates. I recognize a handful of them, most notably Jack and his sidekick Steve Henderson sitting at the back of the room, reclining in their chairs, their arms crossed, watching us enter the classroom like I assume Roman emperors must have been watching Christians being led into the Colosseum before the lions were let loose.

I don't have an affectionate nickname for Steve Henderson. That's because I have no affection for Steve Henderson.

Alfonso nudges me with his elbow and nods toward a couple of empty desks in the middle of the room. As I take my seat, I hear Jack say, "Look at the panty pooper," prompting Steve to laugh like a horse. Trying not to die of embarrassment, I turn my attention toward the front of the room where Sandy and her new Korean friend enter.

"Sandy! Over here!"

I wave at her and point at the single empty desk on my right. Sandy and the Korean guy make their way over and then walk right past me to sit behind Alfonso and me, leaving my right flank exposed and vulnerable.

As the rest of our new classmates keep trickling through the door and filling up the remaining desks, the one next to me is one of the few that remain empty until the very last.

Nobody wants to sit next to a panty pooper.

All of a sudden, the Larsenist is standing in the door, setting off bonfires in my chest, and I find myself sitting up straight and trying to look as tall as I can without standing up.

After a quick scan of the room, he walks straight over to the empty desk next to me, drops his backpack on the floor and sits down. He turns to me, still with that subtle smile on his suntanned face, reaches his hand out to me and says, "Hi. I'm Chris Larsen."

Of course you are, I'm thinking. *You're also gorgeous. Can I sit on your lap?*

Trying hard not to make a complete fool of myself, I act all cool, shake his hand and say, "Matt. Matt Dunstan."

"Nice to meet you, Matt-Matt Dunstan," he says, and I'm melting away at the electrifying touch of his hand and the sound of his silky voice saying my name.

My name sounds really nice when a cute guy says it. I want him to say it again.

I want him to say anything to me, really, so I'm about to pay him a petty compliment on his T-shirt and how *Larsenist* is such a clever pun on his name, when all of a sudden a voice from behind cuts my pathetic attempts to suck up to what must be the most gorgeous guy in this school painfully short.

"Chris Larsen, is that you?"

We both turn around, and my heart sinks like a rock to the bottom of the Mariana Trench as I look into the pimply, beaming face of the Jackrabbit.

"Oh my God, Jack!" Chris exclaims with heartbreaking excitement. He gets up from his seat and walks to the back.

Meanwhile at the front, a woman in her forties enters the room. "Good morning, everyone," she says as she walks to her desk.

Chris briefly returns to his desk—or his former desk I should say because he's just come to pick up his backpack. "See you around, Matt-Matt Dunstan," he whispers and winks at me again before he gets back to the back of the room where he goes to sit with Jack.

"Made up our mind back there, have we?" Mrs. Spelczik asks in Chris's direction.

"Yes, ma'am," Chris says. "I'm all good."

As Mrs. Spelczik, after introducing herself, starts droning about school and classroom rules, about discipline and diligence, about homework, exams, and assignments, my thoughts keep drifting back to the boy who's sitting three rows behind me at the back of the room. Occasionally I cast a surreptitious glance at him, and whenever I do that I catch him and Jack whisper and giggle like a bunch of giddy little girls. At one point Mrs. Spelczik chides them for disruptive behavior, and for a moment I'm hoping she might break up the two chatterboxes and make Chris sit with me again, but of course I have no such luck coming my way today, and the two keep whispering and giggling, leaving me to wallow in my petty jealousy.

* * *

"Man, these are all crap," Alfonso says. He's sitting opposite me at a table in the school cafeteria, skimming the list of extracurriculars that Mrs. Spelczik handed to us, urging us to sign up for at least one of them because it'll look good on our college applications. "Model United Nations, Philosophy, Robotics ... I mean, come on!"

"No fruit picking?" I ask.

"Funny," he says with a wry smile. "Any idea what you want to go for?"

I shrug. "I don't know. Maybe journalism."

"Well, you do like writing, so that would be good."

"Yeah."

It will be especially useful when I apply for the position of Senior Gay Reporter at the *New York Times*.

Alfonso keeps going through the list until his face finally brightens up. "Hey," he says, "they have Entrepreneurship! That's about starting a business, not taking over an existing one, but still."

"Even if you take over your dad's business, you might still want to start a new one someday. Besides, it will look good on your college application regardless, if you want to study business management or whatever."

"I guess," Alfonso says. He puts the list aside and grabs the juice box from his tray.

"Hey, guys."

Sandy and her new friend approach our table, both holding their lunch trays. "Can we sit with you?"

"Sure," I say, and Alfonso nods, sucking on his straw.

Together they go to sit next to Alfonso on the opposite side of the table. "So guys, this is Jason Dong. Jason, these are Matt and Alfonso. We've known each other, like, since kindergarten."

"Actually, the name is Jisun," Jason says, "but most people call me Jason."

"Hi, Jason," I say with a friendly nod, and Alfonso shakes Jason's hand, still sucking on his straw.

Jason has an endearing permanent smile that turns his eyes into two little slits so narrow that I can't even tell his eye color. Then again, he's Korean so I guess it's probably brown, although I'm not sure if that is a racist thing to say. Or think.

"So Matt," Sandy says, sticking her fork into her salad, "have you thought about your extracurriculars yet?"

I shrug. "I don't know. I'm thinking maybe Journalism or something."

"Sounds great," Sandy says. "I'm thinking about Contemporary Dance maybe, or Cheerleading."

Alfonso looks at Jason. "What about you?"

"What about me?"

"Extracurriculars," Alfonso says. "What are you gonna go for?"

"Oh," Jason says, "I already signed up for Robotics and Track & Field."

Alfonso nods approvingly. "At least one person who knows exactly what they want."

"Yeah, well," Jason says and shrugs. "All you need is a goal, something you know you want to achieve, and then you just do the things you need to do to get there. Simple, really."

Alfonso looks at him. "So what kind of goal requires robotics and athletics? Building a robot that competes in the Olympics?"

Jason laughs. "Building robots is the goal. But it involves a lot of sitting on your ass planning, building, programming and whatnot. So it's good to have some balance. Something to keep my body active as well so I don't turn into a fat blob."

"That makes sense, I guess."

"Hi, girls," a familiar voice says, and when I look I see Jack, Steve, and Chris standing at our table, holding their lunch trays and looking for somewhere to sit.

I hurry to remove my backpack from the chair next to me, hoping that Chris will accept my silent invitation to sit with me, but Jack nudges Chris out of the way and slumps into the chair.

"Thanks, Maddie," he says.

Maddie is the Jackrabbit's affectionate nickname for me because he knows I hate how it sounds like a little girl's name.

I nod and discreetly cover my nose with my hand because Jack's breath reeks of cigarette smoke. So that's why they made it to the cafeteria so late. Jack and Steve had to satisfy their craving for nicotine. I can't help but wonder if Chris smokes. I wouldn't call it a deal breaker per se, but I find it difficult to see how anyone would ever want to kiss someone whose breath stinks like that of Jack.

Not that I want to kiss Jack or anything.

I'm just saying.

Hypothetically.

Steve sits down next to Jack—he never leaves his side— leaving Chris's only option to walk around the table and take the last remaining chair next to Sandy.

"Hey," Sandy says. "You're Chris, right? I'm Sandy."

"Hi, Sandy," Chris replies.

His smile is so brazenly adorable.

Sandy looks back and forth between Christian, Jack, and Steve. "You guys, this is Jason Dong." She doesn't have the time to add that Jason's name is actually Jisun and that everyone calls him Jason, and which extracurriculars everyone around the table is going for, because at the sound of Jason's admittedly unfortunate last name, Jack and Steve start braying with laughter like a pair of horses. Even Chris doesn't bother to conceal his grin.

"I'm sorry," Jack says after a while, wiping tears from his eyes. He looks at Jason. "No offense, dude, but that is one hilarious name. Dong!"

"Guys!" Sandy says like a disappointed mother. "You're not being nice!"

"Sorry," Jack says, still shaking with laughter.

Sandy puts her hand on Jason's arm. "Don't listen to them. They're just being silly."

"It's okay," Jason says in a low voice, shaking his head and digging into his lunch.

From one moment to the next, the mood around the table has noticeably changed from relaxed to awkward. Nobody says a word anymore. I'm sure none of us approves of Jack and Steve's asshole behavior, but apart from Sandy—bless her—nobody has the guts to stand up to them, because deep down inside we all share the lackadaisical mentality of all silent witnesses of bullying and name-calling and their selfish feeling of relief that at least this time the target was someone else.

With a feeling of sympathy mixed with guilt, I watch Jason eat his lunch in subdued silence. At one point his gaze meets mine, and sure enough his eyes are brown.

Chapter Three

After brushing my teeth and spending more time in the shower than would be required for general cleaning purposes, I go to my bedroom, open my laptop computer and log into Wattpad, the outlet for my creative writing endeavors. I have twenty-nine followers on Wattpad. The various stories I've been posting over the last year or so have a total of seven hundred and thirty-two views and eighty-nine likes. That's a far cry from the millions of followers and tens of thousands of likes other Wattpad authors accumulate, but hey, I bet there was a time when they had twenty-nine followers and eighty-nine likes.

The reason I started using Wattpad is because my stories are not safe for family consumption, due to their shameless expression of sexually explicit teenage fantasies. I don't want those stories lying around my house, ready to be discovered by nosy family members, so I started posting them to Wattpad. Because let's face it, I'm not a writer because I love the sound of my own writing voice. I want to be read. Just not by my family, or anyone else I know personally, for that matter.

The recurring main character of all my first-person stories is a guy called Matt, and that's not a coincidence. In writing, nothing should ever be a coincidence. The reason I didn't choose a different name is because it's the perfect decoy. If—God forbid—anyone who knows me should ever accidentally come across my stories on Wattpad, they'd never think it has anything to do with me, because nobody in their right mind would ever write semi-pornographic stories about themselves using their real name. Therefore, most readers will subconsciously think that whoever wrote this story, his real name is probably definitely not Matt.

Oh, the cleverness of me!

Without further ado, I crack my knuckles and start typing.

Mattoid2002

> Hi Wattpad, it's me. Today I have some bad news, some good news, and some ... other news for you. Let's start with the bad news to get it out of the way. There will be no new installments of Jules's Jewels. Yeah, I know, it's a terrible tragedy, and I'm sorry for your loss. But really, that story wasn't going anywhere, and to be perfectly honest, I was running out of naughty things for Julian and Matt to do, so I've decided to scrap the whole thing. But hey, here's the good news: today I am presenting you with the first installment of a brand new story in which your favorite hero and boy toy Matt, on his first day of high school, meets a gorgeous guy named Chris, and as you can imagine, he falls head over heels in love. Matt, that is. Not sure about Chris yet, because I'm making this shit up as I go along. So anyway, I hope you'll like it...

I take a moment to collect my thoughts, then I write down the story of my first day in high school, recounting everything from me soiling my pants to Chris winking at me to Jack being an asshole at lunch. Great literature it is not, but I'm reasonably happy with it and I need that kind of release. I need to talk about my most intimate feelings, and as long as I can't talk about them with anyone in real life, I'll have to share them with the entire Internet.

Once I'm done on Wattpad, I head over on YouTube to watch a handful of coming out videos, or, more specifically, videos of people recounting how they came out to their friends and family. I've probably been watching hundreds of them in the last couple of months, looking for inspiration. Alas, it turns out there are about a million ways to go about it, some of which work great for some people and not so well for others and vice versa, and the more of these videos I watch, the more confused I get over which might be the right way for me.

* * *

When I wake up in the morning I reach for my phone like every morning, and like every morning I'm too drowsy to remember that the charger is plugged in, so I accidentally pull the plug out of the socket that is two feet up on the wall and have it slam down on the hardwood floor. That's how I went through three chargers in the last year. Also, it makes enough noise to wake up Greg in the room next door, and he responds by throwing random items against the wall to express his discontent.

Not that I give a rat's ass about my brother's discontent.

First I check my emails. Of course there aren't any because everyone I know was sleeping through the night just like I was. Also, nobody uses email anymore, even during the day.

Next I open Wattpad. I have a number of new eyes on my stories, most of them on the new one, probably thanks to the not very imaginative but distinctly clickbaity title *Freshmen Love*. There are even a couple of likes and comments. Not to sound ungrateful or anything, but they're pretty generic and uninspiring. It's always nice when people take a moment out of their busy lives to drop you a little *Thank you* or *I like it, keep it up!* but the amount of useful and constructive literary criticism on places like Wattpad is woefully small. Most people simply don't care enough to be honest with you and tell you why a story doesn't work. I have a handful of fans on Wattpad—people who regularly comment on my stories—but there's only one who never shies away from honest, sometimes blunt criticism. She usually doesn't leave comments overnight though, and she hasn't today.

I get up, put on a fresh pair of boxers and a T-shirt, and I make my way to the bathroom, but Greg beats me to it by a second. He usually showers for at least fifteen minutes in the morning, so I go and use the downstairs bathroom. After brushing my teeth and taking a quick shower I go back to my room and put on a pair of jeans because my favorite shorts are soiled and in the laundry. Then I try on five different T-shirts, and in the end I go for a plain green one because I don't have any clever slogan T-shirts that could play in the same league as Chris's *Larsenist* T-shirt. I don't even have anything pink or rainbow-colored. God, I suck at gay pride.

Breakfast is a largely unspectacular affair, except for an empty milk carton in the fridge that Greg put there after he poured the last milk on his cereal. I'm not going to eat my cereal without milk, so Mom makes me a grilled cheese and tomato sandwich, and then Zoey and I leave for school.

As soon as we're out of earshot, she asks, "So who's Blondie?"

I don't immediately know what she's getting at, so I frown at her and say, "You mean the 70s band?"

"Don't play dumb, Matthew. I'm talking about the cute blond guy you've been eating up with your eyes during lunch yesterday."

"Oh, him," I say. "How do you even ... wait, have you been spying on me?"

"Spying is such an ugly word. I've been sitting two tables behind you, and I couldn't help but notice."

I figure there is no point in denying it, so I tell Zoey everything about Chris.

"You're totally smitten!" she says when I'm finished. "That's so sweet. So is he gay?"

"No, I'm not. And how am I supposed to know? I hardly even know him."

"Sure you are," Zoey insists. "And you could just ask him."

I snort. "That is so not gonna happen."

"Why not?"

"Because you can't just ask people intimate questions like that."

"Right. Well, then you better start getting to know him better. You know, spend time with him, talk to him, get to know him. And then take it from there."

"I have no idea what to talk about with him, though."

"That's why you need a plan. Spend time with him and get to know him. Once you know him, you know what his interests are. Come on now, it's not rocket science."

"No," I say and nod. "It's much more difficult than rocket science."

"No, it's not. Don't be such a wallflower."

"But how am I supposed to talk with Chris when the Jackrabbit is always around?"

"Forget about Jack. You're not trying to impress Jack, so why do you care what he thinks about you? Just ignore him."

"That's easy for you to say. For you it's easy to make new friends or to ignore people you don't like or who don't like you. I'm different. I'm too … self-conscious, and I'm always worried I might say or do something stupid."

Zoey nods. "Yeah, that's not the right mindset. You're so focused on not doing anything stupid that you end up doing something stupid. It's like a self-fulfilling prophecy."

"Self-fulfilling prophecy?"

"Yeah, no, I don't know. Maybe it's not the right word. What I'm trying to say is, the things that you focus on are gonna happen to you. It's how your mind works. It's how everyone's mind works. Here, let me show you something. Close your eyes and try not to think of a pink elephant."

"Why does it have to be a pink elephant? I mean, why pink of all colors?"

"Because it's a gay elephant," Zoey says, rolling her eyes.

"That's not funny."

"For crying out loud, just do it, Matt!"

I close my eyes.

"Good," she says. "Now try not to think of an elephant, no matter which color."

Naturally, I fail. Trying to focus on what not to think of makes me think of exactly that. I open my eyes again. "Oh."

"See?" Zoey smiles. "The more you think about not doing or saying something stupid, the more likely you will do just that because that's what your mind is focused on. You need to stop worrying about what people might think about you and just be yourself. This is high school, Matt. You're gonna make a fool of yourself one way or another anyway, so you might as well relax and try to enjoy it."

"Gee, thanks, I guess," I say, turning my head because a shiny, black Tesla Model S is cruising past us down Vine Street. It's the first time I've seen one in the wild. A few weeks back, at the beginning of the summer holidays, Dad took me and Greg down to the Tesla showroom in Newport Beach where he had a test drive scheduled. Dad is the biggest Tesla fanboy east of

Texas, and he keeps daydreaming of buying one. Mom isn't crazy about the idea, mostly because we don't happen to have seventy-five thousand dollars lying around, but she couldn't talk him out of having a test drive. Behind that wheel, Dad was the happiest I've ever seen him.

As we walk on, Alfonso catches up with us on his bike. He and Zoey immediately start talking about school, and I zone out because I'm not interested. I have other things on my mind, things in which high school is but a mere backdrop, just the setting of the story I'm being the main character in. I can't stop thinking about what Zoey has said. Not just the pink elephant, or how I should relax and try to be myself, but about having a plan. And the more I think about it, the more I realize she's right. I do need a plan. A brilliant plan. Or just any old plan, really.

"Guys," I say as we approach the school, "before we go to class, can we stop at the message boards and check the sign-up lists for the extracurriculars?"

Zoey and Alfonso look at each other and then at me as if I just suggested we defect to North Korea or something.

"Dude," Alfonso says. "Have you been listing? That's what I just said."

"Um … I know," I lie. "So what are we waiting for then? Let's go!"

As I increase my pace, Alfonso and Zoey exchange puzzled looks, trying to keep up with me.

* * *

There are about two dozen extracurricular sign-up lists, and although we have until the end of the week to sign up, they're filling up fast. Some of them are almost full already. I scan each list, trying to find Chris's name somewhere, but I don't even know if he's signed up already.

"Matt," Alfonso says and nods at one of the lists, "over here." I walk up to him, and he points at the list titled School Newspaper. "This is what you're looking for, right?"

"Yeah, um," I say. "Thanks. Maybe. I'm not sure yet."

"Oh? What else are you're looking into?"

"I … I'm not sure. There are so many." I laugh nervously.

Alfonso looks at me. He knows something is not quite right, but he doesn't pry. "You can always cross out your name later if you change your mind. There are only three spots left, so you better make up your mind quick."

"I guess." I scan the list. Chris's name is not on it, because that would have been too easy.

He shrugs. "Well, what are you waiting for?"

"Right," I say and pull out my pen. I'm reluctant to sign my name because I want to know what—if anything—Chris has signed up for. It'll look stupid if I sign up for the school newspaper only to cross out my name two minutes later when I find Chris's name on the Arts & Crafts list or whatever. Not that I hope that's what he's going for, because I really suck at arts and crafts.

I look over to Zoey to my left, and she silently motions me over. When I join her, she points at Chris's name. I love his handwriting. It's so much clearer and prettier than my scrawl—or that of Jack directly above his. I look at the top of the list. It reads Track & Field.

"Oh shoot," I say. It's a double whammy. Despite his physique Chris didn't really strike me as a jock, and the fact that if I were to join him in Track & Field I'd have to join Jack as well considerably curbs my enthusiasm.

"Well," Zoey says. "There you go."

"What am I gonna do?" I hiss at Zoey, making sure Alfonso can't hear me.

She looks at me. "What do you want to do?"

"Well, I most certainly don't want to spend another six or eight hours every week with the Jackrabbit."

Zoey shrugs. "Looks like they're only available as a pair."

"And I don't even know if I'm any good at track. Or field, for that matter."

Alfonso joins us. "Are you ready? We have to get to class."

"Ask him," Zoey says and shrugs again.

"Well?" Alfonso looks at me.

"Oh what the heck," I say and push past him to sign my name on the School Newspaper list.

"What's he signing up for?" Zoey asks Alfonso.

"School newspaper."

"Oh," Zoey says, and when I look at her I can see the disappointment in her eyes.

* * *

I sit at lunch with Zoey. Alfonso is lagging behind because he had to go to the bathroom before going to suck up to Mr. Estrada who's in charge of Entrepreneurship.

"So," she says, "School Newspaper, huh?"

"Yeah. I want to improve my writing. I mean, journalism and fiction writing are two different pairs of shoes, but still."

"So no Track & Field for you then, I guess?"

I sigh. "I don't know. I mean, I do like sports, and I enjoy running. But you see ..." I lower my voice and look over my shoulder to make sure nobody's listening in. "Track & Field never ever would have crossed my mind if it weren't for Chris, and I'm not sure if that's a sufficient reason. I mean, I don't even know if he's gay. What if he isn't?"

Zoey raises her eyebrows. "What if he is, though?"

"Exactly! Then what am I gonna do?"

"Then you're gonna hit on him, and then he falls for you, and you're gonna live happily ever after."

I snort. "I wish! But it's not gonna be that simple and straightforward, I'm afraid."

"Well, that's love for you."

"Not the L-word!" I hiss at her and look over my shoulder again. "And keep your voice down!"

"Sorry," she says, cringing.

"Don't you dare talk about love! We're getting way ahead of ourselves here. I don't even know the guy!"

"Well, that's what we're about to change, isn't it?"

"And then what? I mean, seriously, what am I gonna do?"

Zoey shrugs. "Tell him you're gay too."

"I told you to keep your voice down!"

"All right, all right," she whispers. "Jesus! Can't we mention the G-word either?"

"*Especially* not the G-word! Not as long as I'm still in the closet."

"Yeah, I was gonna ask you about that."

I frown at her. "About what?"

"About your official coming out. How is that coming along?"

My shoulders slump. It's a sore spot because I know that with coming out to Zoey I started something that I will have to finish somehow, some day. Except I have no idea how.

"Oh, I don't know. Of course I do want to come out, but I don't want to make a big deal of it."

Zoey shrugs. "Then don't. I mean, it's not the 1990s anymore. Nobody really cares if somebody's gay anymore, not in this part of the country, not in our generation. And it's not like we're evangelical Christians and Mom and Dad will send you off to conversion therapy or something. Nobody who cares about you will think any less of you just because you're gay."

With a thud, a lunch tray lands on the table, and Alfonso slumps down in the chair next to me. "Oh," he says, "are you talking about Chris?"

Zoey looks at me with her eyes wide open. Neither of us saw or heard Alfonso ninja his way to our table. I feel adrenaline tingling my lower back, prompting my body to a fight-or-flight response.

But I can't run away.

I can't beat up Alfonso either.

And so, since I don't know what else to do, I panic.

"What?" I exclaim a lot louder than I should. "No! What?"

Alfonso looks puzzled. "Um ... I don't know, I just heard the word *gay*, so I assumed you were talking about Chris."

I don't even know what Alfonso is saying or how to respond to it, so I'm glad Zoey is jumping in.

"Do you know something we don't?" she asks him, her eyebrows almost meeting her hairline.

Alfonso looks back and forth between Zoey and me. "Didn't you guys know? Chris is gay."

"Get out of here!" Zoey says, casting a side glance at me.

Alfonso shakes his head. "No, seriously. When he turned fourteen, his parents threw a big birthday party for him.

I mean, a really big party, with all his aunts and uncles and grandparents, and some thirty or forty people from Littlefield Junior High. And right in the middle of it, Chris grabbed the microphone and made the big announcement. For his family it was a jaw-dropping moment, apparently, but all his friends broke into spontaneous applause and cheers and everything, and in the end everyone from his family was really supportive as well."

Zoey looks at him. "And you know all this ... how exactly?"

"My cousin Alfredo went to Littlefield with Chris."

"Wow, so Chris Larsen is gay." She looks at me. "How about that?"

"No kidding," is all I can come up with.

"Yep," Alfonso says, digging into his lunch.

I shake my head. "I really wouldn't have thought ..."

"Why not?" he asks.

"I don't know. He just doesn't appear to be anywhere near as flamboyant and fabulous as you'd expect gay people do be, I guess."

Alfonso shrugs. "I wouldn't know. I don't know any gay people. I mean, personally." He looks at me a little too long for comfort, and I can't help but wonder if he suspects anything or if I'm just being paranoid.

Zoey shrugs. "Well, they can't all be Tyler Oakleys, can they?"

"Who?" Alfonso asks.

"Tyler Oakley."

He shakes his head. "I don't know who that is."

"He's a YouTuber," Zoey explains. "Pretty popular too. He's got, like, seven million subscribers or something."

"Eight million," I correct her. "And how do you even know Tyler Oakley?"

Zoey shrugs. "I don't know. How do *you* know Tyler Oakley, Matt?"

I want to strangle her for asking that question in front of Alfonso, but thanks to my reasonable knowledge of contemporary American literature I can come up with an innocuous answer without stammering. "He's friends with John Green."

"Oh, the guy from *The Fault in Our Stars*?" Sandy asks as she and Jason sit down next to Zoey. "I loved *The Fault in Our Stars*!"

My heart skips a beat because just like Alfonso earlier, I didn't see them coming.

"He's not 'from' *The Fault in Our Stars*," Zoey says, rolling her eyes at Sandy. "He *wrote* it."

Sandy shrugs. "Same difference. So what about him?"

"His friend Tyler is gay," Alfonso says.

"Aw," Sandy says. "Poor Tyler!"

"Whoa." Jason looks at her and frowns. "Why would you even say that?"

"Not that there's anything wrong with being gay or anything," Sandy explains. "I mean, it's not a choice, right? You're born with it."

"Wow, Sandy," Zoey says, "way to make it sound like a disease."

In a rare instance of quick-wittedness, Sandy replies, "Not at all. If I say you were born with brown eyes, does that sound like brown eyes are a disease?"

Stone-faced, Zoey concedes, "Fair point, I guess."

"So anyway," Sandy continues, "some people are born gay, and that's, like, totally fine, but if you had the choice, would you actually choose to be gay? Like, if right before your birth someone came up to you, like God or whoever is in charge of these things, and they asked you if you'd rather be gay or straight, would any of you actually say you'd rather be gay than straight?"

Sandy looks at every single one of us, waiting for replies that aren't forthcoming. I have to admit, it's a pretty good question. A question that I've never really thought about.

"See?" Sandy says. "I mean, gay marriage is now legal and everything, but there is still so much discrimination going on. So would you really expose yourself to that if you didn't have to?"

We're all still speechless, except Zoey who puts her hand on Sandy's shoulder, and says to her with a smirk, "Good job, Sandy. Way to cheer everyone up," which, ironically, cheers us all up and makes us chuckle.

"I'm just saying," Sandy says and shrugs.

I don't even know what it is, but somehow Sandy's rant flipped a switch in my head, so I get up and pick up my lunch tray.

Zoey looks at me. "Where are you going?" she asks and starts sucking the straw of her juice box.

"I changed my mind," I say. "I think I'm going to sign up for Track & Field after all."

In combination with the orange juice, that information is apparently too much to process for Zoey, and the juice spurts out of her nose. As Alfonso raises an eyebrow at me, Sandy hands Zoey a paper napkin and cheers me on, "That's awesome! Go Matt!"

Go me, indeed.

CHAPTER FOUR

As I make my way to the message boards, Alfonso's raised eyebrow keeps haunting me. He knows me. My prowess in PE has always exceeded my motivation, so my decision to sign up for Track & Field must seem utterly random to him.

When I turn the corner, the hallway in front of the message boards is deserted. I pull a pen out of my backpack and approach the Track & Field sign-up list. Just before my pen hits the paper, I'm having second thoughts.

I know I'm doing this on a whim.

I haven't thought it entirely through.

Actually, I haven't thought it through at all, but right now I just want to do something—*anything*, really— because it is a truth universally acknowledged that a single gay boy in possession of good looks must be in want of a boyfriend.

Before I have any more time to change my mind, I sign my name right blow Chris's, when the sound of a vaguely familiar voice suddenly makes me jump.

"Hey."

I turn my head, and it's speak-of-the-devil Chris. He must have been walking down the adjacent hallway—presumably on his way to the cafeteria—when he saw me and stopped. Now he comes walking toward me. His T-shirt reads *Just do it*, and I'm thinking, *Sure. If you let me.*

Meanwhile, my knees turn into Jell-O, which is great because I skipped dessert.

"Matt, right?" he asks.

"Right, Matt," I reply stupidly. "Chris."

Speaking of dessert, I want to eat his sweet face with a spoon. That's a pretty stupid thing to be thinking of someone, but here we are.

"So what did you sign up for?" Chris asks, looking at the lists.

My first impulse is to say School Newspaper, but that list is some six feet to the right, and he's already spotted my name on the Track & Field list.

"Track & Field! That's awesome! I'm doing that too!"

"Yeah ... I ...," I stammer. "Your name ... on the list ..."

"So what's your favorite event?"

"My favorite event? I don't know ... maybe the Olympics?"

Chris laughs. "No, I mean, what are your favorite track and field events? Like, high jump, long jump? The throwing events? Running?"

"Oh!" I say, feeling incredibly stupid. "Running. I like running. Yeah."

"Awesome, I'm a runner too. Short or long distance?"

I shrug, struggling to make stuff up as I go along. "I don't know. A little bit of both, I guess."

"Right," Chris says with a shadow of a frown on his face. "So what's your time on the mile?"

I'm so far out of my depth in this conversation, I feel like I'm drowning. I run forty to forty-five minutes every Saturday morning. Now if I knew the exact distance of my regular run, I could probably calculate my average mile run time with a reasonable degree of accuracy, deduct ten percent to account for the fact that I usually run more like six or seven miles and I'd likely be a lot faster if I ran only one and if I were actually running for speed and not just jogging for fitness. Sadly, I lack that knowledge and the mental capacity to perform such calculations on the spot, so in order to give Chris a quick answer, I just make something up.

"Um, I don't know," I say, nervously scratching the back of my head. "Six minutes or so?"

"Really?" He raises his eyebrows. "That's pretty good."

Oh boy. I hope I didn't just break the world record for fourteen-year-olds. Maybe I can salvage the situation with a figure that is more firmly based in reality, so I say, "Actually, I do kind of prefer the shorter distances. In PE in junior high I ran the one hundred meters in 12.5 seconds."

That one is actually true.

Chris nods approvingly. "My personal best is 11.89, but 12.5 is not bad. Not bad at all."

I'm tempted to try and break his record right here and now by turning around and running away as fast as I can, but I obviously can't do that, so I just say, "Awesome."

I have no idea what else to say.

I'm so starstruck, it's not even pretty.

Definitely nowhere near as pretty as he is with his bright smile and his soft, clean skin and his messy hair.

"Listen," he says and puts his hand on my shoulder, and at that point I actually stop listening, because his touch sends electric shock waves through my body that short-circuit my brain. I'm tensing up, causing my shoulders to rise. It's as if my body is trying to nestle itself into his big, strong hand that feels heavy and warm through my T-shirt. It's the crudest form of body language that my shoulder is awkwardly trying to speak, and I'm longing for some sort of response, maybe a little squeeze, a tender stroke of his thumb, or anything that would reveal something about him that I will forever be too scared, too embarrassed to ask. But it's not happening, and then, all of a sudden, it ends as abruptly as it began. He withdraws his hand, and it feels as if someone cut the ropes of my parachute and I'm falling out of the clouds, hurtling towards the hard, unyielding ground of reality. My brain finally gets to processes the information it has stored in the data buffer between my ears and my cerebrum, and I catch up on what Chris was saying to me.

"I'm running late for lunch, so I better be going. I'll see you later, Matt, okay?"

"Okay, sure, yeah," I hear myself say. "Cool. See you later. Chris."

I love saying his name. Even more so when he can actually hear it.

"All right then," he says. With a smile he turns around and leaves. Before he turns the corner, he looks back at me, still smiling. I raise my hand, but before I let myself get carried away into an awkward wave, I drop it again and just nod and smile back.

When he's gone, it feels as if I'm finally allowed to breathe again. I turn and lean back against the wall, all the tension leaving my body, and with my heart still pounding heavily in my chest and my hands and knees trembling, I feel a strange and oddly satisfying sense of accomplishment.

* * *

As we leave the school grounds, the closing bell still ringing in our ears, Zoey, Alfonso and I get on our phones to check the emails and text messages we've been getting while we were incommunicado. In my case, it's mostly useless stuff as always. A text message from Mom, letting me know that she'll be taking Zoey to the mall and that I am to make sure that Greg won't leave the house or watch TV until he's done his homework.

As if I have any authority over my little brother when nobody else is home.

Then two spam emails, and one to let me know that Tumblr have updated their Terms of Service, and one from the middle-aged widow of some African dictator who offers me a thirty percent share of the fifteen million dollars she wants me to help her get out of her war-torn country before her corrupt government seizes everything and she has to sell her six young children at the local slave market.

And finally, there's a notification from Wattpad that 2-b-pretty, my biggest and truest fan, has finally left a comment on *Freshmen Love*. I don't even bother opening the Wattpad app to look at it. 2-b-pretty's comments tend to be on the longer side, and they often make me chuckle. I don't want to draw any attention toward myself. Neither Zoey nor Alfonso are aware of the true nature of my literary endeavors, because they're too sexually revealing.

"Oh," Zoey says, still looking at her phone. "Mom wants to take me to the mall."

"Yeah, I know," I say. "She wants me to babysit Greg while she's out with you."

"Wait," Alfonso says, "I thought we were gonna hang out later."

"We still can. I just can't come to your place. Unless you want me to bring Greg."

"Hell no!"

"See?"

"All right, your place it is then. Should I bring the Xbox?"

"Yeah, sure," I say and shrug.

"Wanna play *Phantom Pain* or *Fifa 16*?"

I snort. "Does it matter? I'm gonna get my ass kicked either way."

"True," he says. "Anyway, I'll just drop off my books at home and grab the Xbox and I'll be right over, okay?"

"All right."

He hugs Zoey good-bye, fist-bumps with me and takes off.

"Oh my God, finally!" Zoey says as soon as he's out of earshot.

"Whoa," I say. "Rude!"

"Well, excuse you, but it's not my fault we can't talk about this in front of your best friend because you're too chicken to come out to him!"

"I'm not too chicken!" I protest. "I just haven't found the right moment yet."

"Well, you better find it soon, because I don't know how much longer I can do this. Sooner or later I'm going to blab, and it will totally be not my fault!"

"All right, all right. I'll do it soon."

"Good! So anyway, tell me already, did you do it?"

We haven't had time to talk yet, so she doesn't know, and just for the fun of it, I pretend I have no idea what she's talking about.

"Did I do what?"

"Come on, Matt, don't play dumb! Did you sign up for Track & Field?" She looks at me, and as much as I'm trying to conceal a stupid grin, I can't.

"Yeah," I say.

"That's awesome!" she exclaims and jumps up and down. "Well done, you!"

It's really heartwarming to see her so excited on my behalf, and I'm glad I can share this moment with her, so I hug her and jump with her like the giddy little girl that she is, and I say, "I know!"

Once we've calmed down, Zoey asks, "Okay, so now what?"

I know what she's getting at, and my excited smile freezes into a grimace. "I have no freaking idea!"

"You better come up with a plan. Don't blow this now."

"I know. Anyway, guess who came passing by just when I was signing my name on that list!"

She thinks for a moment, then she looks at me with her eyes wide open. "No way!"

I nod emphatically. "Way!"

"Oh my God! Did he see you? Did he say anything? Come on, Matt, don't make me pull it all out of your nose!"

So I tell her, making sure to include every little detail I can remember, especially the moment when Chris put his hand on my shoulder.

"Oh my God," Zoey says again. "Do you know what that means?"

I frown. "No, what does it mean?"

Zoey throws her arms up in the air. "How can anyone be so clueless? Yesterday he winked at you. Today he put his hand on your shoulder. Plus, you now know for sure he's gay. He's totally into you!"

"Yeah, no, I wouldn't read too much into that. I mean, you hug me all the time. Does that mean you're into me?"

"Eww," she says. "You're my brother! That'd be like incest or something! Besides, you're gay!"

I glance around. There are people on the other side of the street, and it doesn't look like they can hear us, but I still have to remind Zoey, "Keep your voice down, okay?"

"Yeah, yeah, sorry."

As we reach our house, Zoey's getaway car is waiting, engine running. Mom reminds me to look after Greg, then they take off. When I enter the house, I find Greg in the living room, watching TV, his feet resting on the coffee table.

"Have you done your homework?" I ask.

"Who?" he says without taking his eyes off the screen.

"You!"

"No, who cares?"

"Your mom cares!"

"You my mom now?"

"No," I say and walk up to him. "But Mom asked me to make sure you do your homework. If you don't I'll be in trouble, and if I'm in trouble you're in bigger trouble. Take your feet off the table."

When he ignores me I lift my foot and gently nudge his legs.

"Ow!" he moans. "Why are you kicking me, asshole?" He tries to kick me back but I take a step back and he kicks a hole in the air.

"Trust me, you have no idea what it's like when I really kick you, and you don't want to find out." I lean forward and pretend that I want to hit him in the face. When he raises his arms in defense I grab the remote control from his lap, switch off the TV and take out the batteries. I put them in my pocket and say, "You can have them back when you show me your homework."

"You're such a square!" Greg says and rolls off the sofa.

"Yeah. And you do your homework. Now!"

Pulling a silly face, he walks towards the stairs. On his knees, like a thirteen-year-old who's pretending he's eight.

In the kitchen I grab a bottle of juice from the fridge and make my way upstairs. When I pass the open door to Greg's room, he's sitting at his desk.

"Square!" I hear him say loudly.

I stick my head in his room and say, "Watch it!"

He grabs a piece of paper and waves it at me, his face feigning angelic innocence. "No, I'm doing my homework. Geometry. Lots of squares, you know?"

I let him get away with it, go to my room, and close the door. While my backpack is still on its way flying toward my bed, I slump down in my chair at the desk and fire up my laptop. I open Wattpad and navigate to my messages.

2-b-pretty

Oh my! Poor Matty having quite a day; coming out and staying in the closet at the same time; his clothes soiled by his arch nemesis. All this on his first day of high school to which I can relate as I myself start high school soon. Without preexisting enemies or friends, I must add. Matty has friends, but will they accept him even when they know his dark secret? Will his enemies hate him more? Questions that intrigue me while I wait to find the answers. But not as much as beautiful, handsome Chris. As he catches Matt's eye, and captures Matt's heart and mind from the beginning. And to the end, the happy end where wedding bells will send the two young princes off to a life of eternal love and bliss? One can only hope. Hopefully Matt didn't do anything irrational that he might later regret. Hopefully Chris turns out as the prince charming as which he is first perceived. Sorry for being such a delusional dreamer, pouring out uncontrollable thoughts as I express overly too much in my comment but it is necessary for me to do so for this is how much I LOVE your story. Your writing is very intriguing as always. I'll say no more until next time, Mr. Mattoid. If there will be a next time, that is. There better be, because the story MUST go on. I'm totally obsessed. Can't wait for the next chapter.

Leave it to 2-b-pretty to put a stupid grin on my face. I don't affectionately call her *My Biggest Fan* for nothing, although I don't even know anything about her. Her comments are always quirky and fresh and honest, but she never reveals much personal information in her comments—at least not intentionally. In fact, up until today I didn't even know her age, but since she's about to start high school, I guess she must be my age. Her unconventional use of English grammar and spelling makes me think she's probably not a native English speaker. She might be some fourteen-year-old girl from France or the Philippines or some equally obscure place. But who cares, really? Somewhere out there among seven billion human beings there is someone who truly enjoys my literary effusions, and I'm sure that whoever does that cannot be a bad person. And one true fan is really all it takes for me to aspire to become a better writer.

I need to reply to her comment. Our conversations usually stretch across several days because she doesn't get online more than once or twice a day, so I want to reply to her right away, because the longer I wait, the longer I'll have to wait for her response, but a sudden noise makes me jump. I hastily shut the lid of my laptop, but it's just the doorbell, so I go downstairs to let El Niño in.

CHAPTER FIVE

We're playing *FIFA 16*, sitting on my sofa, our feet resting on the coffee table. Technically, my sofa is not a sofa but a loveseat—a sofa designed to seat two people—but it feels awkward to think of it as a loveseat when I'm sitting on it with Alfonso.

Or anyone else, for that matter.

Alfonso is killing it at *FIFA*, scoring one goal after another while I can't get a foot on the ground, but I don't mind. I just enjoy spending time alone with him, having fun, and being close to him—literally, physically close. I never had a sexual or romantic interest in Alfonso—it would be pointless because he's the most heterosexual guy I know—but I've always enjoyed the snug feeling of getting physical with him, whether he was wrestling me on my bed when we were younger or we were fooling around in the pool in his backyard or sharing a sleeping bag when we were camping out. Or just sitting next to him and getting my ass kicked at *FIFA*.

It's still summer, we're both wearing shorts and T-shirts, and our arms and legs frequently touch. I love Alfonso's warm, smooth skin, even more so now than I did one or two years ago, now that oodles of testosterone are pumping through his veins and oozing out of every pore. It's moments like this when we're both alone and relaxed and having a good time and I'm feeling so close to him that I'm dying to just get it over with and tell him I'm gay. Yet at the same time I know that by coming out to Alfonso I would inevitably render these moments that I cherish so much a thing of the past, because I simply cannot see how once the cat is out of the bag we could

MARCUS HERZIG

ever wrestle in the pool again or just sit on my loveseat like we do now without feeling extremely awkward. The moment I step out of the closet I'll walk into a room with an elephant in it, an elephant that for all I know might never leave us be. It's the only sensible reason I can think of why I'm not ready yet to tell Alfonso I'm gay. I just want to stay his best friend a while longer before I become his gay best friend.

Alfonso heads the ball into the net, extending his lead to 5-0. "¡Goooool!" he jubilates. "¡El magnifico! El grande! El impresionante Cristiano Ronaldo ataca de nuevo! Goooool!" He tosses away his controller, and as if to prove my point he pounces on me, puts his arm around me, exuberantly gives me a noogie, and pokes my ribs with his finger.

"All right, all right!" I say, trying to writhe out of his rambunctious embrace.

He finally lets go of me and cackles. "And that was me trying to let you win!"

"No, it wasn't!"

"It totally was, but you're completely elsewhere with your thoughts. Everything okay?"

"Yeah, of course."

Alfonso looks at me for a few moments, and he clearly knows everything is not okay, but he doesn't say anything.

Greg comes walking through the open door. "The batteries," he demands, nudging my thigh with his foot.

"Have you done your homework?"

He sighs. "Yes, mother."

I ignore the tease and say, "Let's see it then."

"It's on my desk. Go have a look if you want."

Without looking at him, I say, "Dude, you want something from me, not the other way around."

He moans and scurries away.

"What's he need batteries for?" Alfonso asks.

"TV remote. I took them out. He's not allowed to watch TV until he's done his homework."

"Great parenting, Matt," he says as he picks up his controller again. "Another match? I'll be ManU this time. You?"

"Does it matter which team you're gonna destroy next?"

"Nope."

"All right, I'm gonna be a patriot then," I say and select the L.A. Galaxy from the list. Alfonso snorts, and by the time Greg returns with his homework, ManU is 1-0 in the lead.

"Here," Greg says.

Without bothering to look at it, I say, "Desk."

He walks over to my desk and picks up the batteries. I cast a quick glance to make sure the lid of my laptop is shut and Greg doesn't touch it. He steps back and looks at the TV. "Can I play?"

"No," I say. "Go away."

"You any good?" Alfonso asks.

"Better than this douche anyway."

"You wish," I say, not because he isn't but because I have to at least try and maintain my fraternal superiority. It's a natural law.

"I'll kick your ass anytime," Greg says, and before Alfonso gets to ask whether Greg means him or me, I hand him the controller.

"There you go then, dickwad."

Greg takes the controller and immediately starts playing. He climbs over my legs, scraping my knee with his sneaker which totally isn't an accident, and squeezes his skinny butt between Alfonso and me. It turns out my loveseat can accommodate three people if necessary, but it's not exactly comfortable, so I get up and go sit my desk. I open my laptop, and after thinking about it for a few moments, I start typing my reply to 2-b-pretty.

Mattoid2002

Hi, Miss Pretty! I'm glad you enjoy the new story. And don't worry, there's nothing wrong with being a delusional dreamer. Isn't delusional dreaming what fiction is all about, especially with a happy end? That said, don't get your hopes up too high. Maybe there will be no happy end. Or maybe there will be. Maybe I don't know. Maybe I do know but I'm not going to tell you because I want you to keep reading. I'm rambling, what is wrong with me? LOL. Anyway, we'll see how it all pans out. The next chapter will be up soon. I hope to see you around.
Thanks again!

By the time I close the lid of my laptop, the Galaxy have beaten ManU 5-4, and Greg is the king of smug.

"Woohoo! Bow down and worship your master, Alfonso!"

"Yeah, I don't think so."

"I totally destroyed you, though."

"You won 5-4 on a last minute goal," Alfonso says. "That's not exactly destroying someone. Besides, I let you win because you're a child."

"No you didn't."

"Sure did."

"Whatever," Greg says dismissively and looks at me. "So Matt, are you ready to get your ass kicked by your little brother?"

"No," I say. "Go away. Do something useful. Watch TV or something."

"All right then," Greg says, puts the controller on the table and gets up. "I'll leave you to your girls' soccer tournament."

As he leaves the room, I kick after him. It's a narrow miss. I close the door and sit back down next to Alfonso. Looking at him, I ask, "Did you really let him win?"

He snorts. "Please! I never let people win. The little twerp destroyed me fair and square."

Grinning, I pick up the controller. "Another one?"

"Sure. You want me to let you win?"

"Shut up," I say and nudge him with my elbow.

He laughs and selects Bayern Munich.

I feel stupid because I don't even know what that is.

* * *

Haha, you are such a tease, Mr. Mattoid! But happy end, ambitious end, unhappy end, I don't mind either way as long as the master writer can make it work. A good story being about a good story and not the readers sensitivities or satisfactions, happy ends are over-rated anyways, for their often unrealistic and contrived in my experience. A master writer such as your humble self will prefer creating art over pure entertainment. Not that there's anything wrong with entertainment. I would never say that, oh no, for I am not a snob like many! But good art always being entertaining, good entertainment alone will not always be art.

2-b-pretty

Mattoid2002

Ambitious, Miss Pretty? Did you mean 'ambiguous'? ;)

Sheesh! :P && What's with that smilie? Don't you have a nose, Mr. Mattoid? ;-)

2-b-pretty

Mattoid2002

Touché, Miss Pretty. :-)

* * *

Another chapter, another day of torment and misery for poor Matty; as he is desperately trying to fit in; in a world he doesn't seem to belong; trying to dissimulate himself into being something he is not; he is making a fool of himself. A endearing, charming fool, but a fool non the less. No one seems to notice still, apart from his loving and beloved sister, what Matty is up to. Maybe not even Matty himself. It is intriguing for me, as a humble but observant reader, to know what Matty

2-b-pretty

wants even if he does not. Will he achieve his goal and find his luck? I cannot wait to find out. Keep at it, Mr. Mattoid. I'll say no more until next time.

P.S. What's with your generic avatar? Won't you show us your handsome face, Mr. Mattoid? ;-)

Mattoid2002

Not sure what is more intriguing, and indeed more mysterious, Matt's behavior or your analysis of it. Why do you think he doesn't belong in the world he's trying to be a part of? And what do you think he's up to that he doesn't know?

P.S. I'm probably nowhere near as handsome as you might think.

You portray Matty as thinking himself as a loser when he is a seeker. Seeking acceptance more than seeking love. Thinking he want Chris, what he really want is acceptance from everyone, as in: parents, siblings, friends, enemies. But he doesn't want to come out. But he want to be gay. He will have to come up with something. His sister is right: he need a plan. If only he has a good friend, a best friend he could talk to. >.o

2-b-pretty

P.S. That is not for you to decide, Mr. Handsome. ;-)

Mattoid2002

But he has a plan! He's joining the track & field club so he can be close to Chris and take it from there. What else can he do?

P.S. I have to protect my identity because I'm still the closet.

That is not a plan! It's random unless he has a history of athletics. I think he should come out to his best friend.

2-b-pretty

P.S. So you are gay? Gay and handsome? >.o

Mattoid2002

He's not ready to come out to his best friend yet.

P.S. No. Just gay.
P.P.S. If you were a dude I'd totally fall for you. ^^;

Who is not ready? The author or his character? >.o

2-b-pretty

P.S. Just checking, Mr. Handsome. ;-)
P.P.S. I don't think so.

Mattoid2002

Oh be quiet! :P

I'll say no more until next time, Mr. Handsome. ^___^

2-b-pretty

Mattoid2002

Good night, Miss Pretty. <3

* * *

Thank you for posting the latest chapter. Despite my criticism, I really enjoy reading your story and I devour every new chapter like chocolate cake, just so you know. That said, Matty is still confused; not knowing what he wants; not knowing he doesn't know what he wants; thinking he has a awesome plan non the less which he doesn't. I like the many opportunities he has to come out to his best friend and his other friends and how he squander them one by one; being afraid to jump in the water; thinking he cannot swim; not realizing the water is only 3 foot deep. I feel for Matty and I root for him despite his sillyness. I also like Sandy. She has a good heart. It's sad that you choose to portray her as being ditzy, for she really isn't. Oh and I hate Chris, haha. I wonder what Matty see in him except a handsome boy. I also wonder: being in track & field club with handsome Chris, what will happen when they shower together? Will it be hot and steamy or awkward and hilarious? Being the great writer that you are, I can't wait to find out how you will handle this situation. >.o I'll say no more until next time, Handsome. xoxo

2-b-pretty

Mattoid2002

Thank you for still reading, Pretty. And for continuing to give me feedback on this train wreck of a story. I know it's probably not very good. I'm still learning. Anywho, I disagree. Matt isn't all that confused, I don't think. He knows what he wants. He wants to come out to the world, hook up with Chris and live happily ever after. He simply doesn't know how to do it, or in which order. I like your analogy of being scared to jump into 3 feet of water. Can I use it? I'm glad you like Sandy, she's an interesting character, and I didn't mean to portray her as ditzy, but she kinda turned out that way, Idk. Why do you hate Chris though? You're not supposed to hate Chris, he's the love interest of my protagonist! Is that why

you don't want a happy end? >.o
And OMG, showers! I have no idea how I will
deal with that. I guess I'll have to come up
with something. ^^;

Not knowing how to do it or in which order is
being confused. >.o Chris comes across as
arrogant. It happens when people are
attractive & popular and they know it. Chris is
very attractive. For now, that's all I know about
him. I don't know what kind of person he is,
because all superficial Matty seems to care
about is his looks. Maybe I'm wrong, Idk. Anyway, I don't trust Chris, but maybe that's just
me? And I didn't say I don't want a happy end.
I like Matty, I want him to be happy. If loving
a handsome guy with no personality is what
makes Matt happy then good luck to him. I'm
surprised you have no plan for a shower scene. I
thought the shower scenes were why you came
up with track & field in the first place. You bait-
ed me with the prospect of shower scenes! If
they don't happen I want my money back! >.o

2-b-pretty

Mattoid2002

You need to give Matt more credit! &&
All right, all right, I'll come up with a shower
scene! Jeez! >_>

Maybe if you give me a reason. >.o && Good!

2-b-pretty

Mattoid2002

Oh be quiet! :P

57

^_^ I'll say no more until next time, handsome. xoxo

2-b-pretty

Looking forward to it. Good night, pretty. xoxo

Mattoid2002

* * *

The usual early Monday morning chatter fills Mrs. Spelczik's classroom as people catch up with each other—as if they hadn't been texting and chatting with each other the whole weekend. While we're waiting for our teacher to show up and torment us with late sixteenth-century British literature—which is a fancy way of saying Shakespeare without mentioning his name—I covertly check my phone under my desk. I'm worried. I've been happily chatting back and forth with 2-b-pretty all week until all communications suddenly ceased on Friday night.

No word from her on Saturday.

Or Sunday.

The whole weekend I've been wondering, was it something I said that made her fall silent? And if so, what was it?

I've been going through our entire exchange multiple times, and I realize I still know next to nothing about her. Even most of the things I think I know are things I extrapolated from the little she told me about herself, so the possibilities of her fate are endless and confusing and scary, but none of it matters because no matter who she is or where she is or why she stopped talking to me, in the end I'm still here and I still have to deal with my shitty life.

The arrival of Mrs. Spelczik drags me out of my drifting thoughts. Usually, when she enters the room, the noise quickly dies down, but today the opposite is the case because she is not alone. Walking right behind her is a timid looking kid whose outer appearance prompts the entire class to a variety of audible reactions from gasps to giggles to whispers.

The boy is Asian, with thick black hair and brown eyes, but that's pretty much all that's normal about him. He's wearing a frilly white shirt that looks like it comes straight out of an eighteenth-century period drama, and it forms a stark contrast to his shopworn jeans and dirty, worn-out sneakers. Instead of the standard backpack or satchel a normal person would take to school, he's carrying a handbag—a fake Louis Vuitton by the looks of it—in one hand and a battered umbrella in the other, which looks strangely out of place in a Southern Californian city like Brookhurst where we haven't had a drop of rain in three months. And as if that wasn't enough to make him look like an alien from a distant planet, there's his face—his grotesque, misshapen, disfigured, and distinctly unattractive face with a nose that, even though it looks like it's been broken multiple times, cannot distract from his most prominent facial feature that I wouldn't wish upon my worst enemy's dead dog.

He has a cleft lip.

I turn my head to the left to look at Alfonso. He looks back at me with his cheeks blown up as if to say, 'Oh boy.'

Mrs. Spelczik drops her bag on her desk and turns to the class, putting her hands on her hips. "Guys," she says, "I don't know what the noise is all about, but it has to stop. And I mean right now." She waits until everyone's fallen silent before she continues. "All right, class, today I'm pleased to announce a new addition to our school and to this class." She turns to the boy who's standing next to her with the body posture of a question mark, clutching his umbrella and his handbag while timidly staring at his feet. "Philip, why don't you introduce yourself to the class real quick?"

The boy hesitates, and without looking up he finally opens his awry, asymmetric mouth and mumbles something in a low, nasal, and almost inaudible voice.

Mrs. Spelczik leans in to him and whispers, "Speak up a bit, will you?"

He nods timidly, swallows, licks his lips, and tries again. "My name is Philip Thongrivong."

Predictably, the name provokes more giggles, and behind me, Steve Henderson can't help himself and blurts out, "Thong!"

which draws a mixed reaction from the crowd. Some people laugh, others turn around and frown at the class clown. Meanwhile, the new kid is still staring at his feet, his head turning red like a fire hydrant. It's painful to watch.

"Quiet!" Mrs. Spelczik taps her wedding ring against the whiteboard, calling us to order. "Philip just moved here from Texas," she says. "I expect all of you to give him a warm welcome and to show him around and help him out if he needs any help. Understood?"

"Yes, ma'am," some students reply with little enthusiasm.

"Philip," Mrs. Spelczik says, "there's an empty desk next to Matthew. Why don't you go and take a seat?"

In a mixture of irritation and embarrassment, I blush. How dare Mrs. Spelczik mention my name in the same sentence as his and—even worse—make him sit next to me?

As Philip makes his way to his desk, there are more giggles behind me. When I turn around, Chris is reclining in his chair, his hand covering his grin as he's trying to avoid looking at the source of his amusement: right next to him Jack is holding a ruler in his hand, the end of it propped against his upper lip to make a dent in it in an obvious attempt to mock Philip's cleft. Everyone around him is trying to conceal their smirks, and even I have to grin because it does look funny. But then my gaze falls upon Sandy. She's shooting me a scolding look, and I quickly wipe my politically incorrect smirk off my face.

"All right, class," Mrs. Spelczik says, "moving on. I know it's still early days, but we're going to have to talk about this. Two words: term papers."

There are groans and moans throughout the room.

"I know, I know," she continues, "it's a terrible burden, and I feel for you, I really do. However, I urge you all to take this very seriously as your term papers scores will make up twenty-five percent of your final grade. Anyway, here's the good news: none of you will have to do it all by themselves. Each of you will team up with a partner, and—"

All around me, people immediately start whispering and murmuring and looking left and right in search of a suitable partner. I look to the left at Alfonso. He looks at me and nods.

Mrs. Spelczik raises her voice and taps her wedding ring against the whiteboard. "Guys, guys! Nobody said you could break into chaos." She waits for the noise to die down. "Let me get this straight, this assignment is as much about literature as it is about teamwork *and* individuality. You will do your research together, you will come to your conclusions together. Then each of you will present these conclusions in your own unique style in your papers. If done right, this will teach you a whole lot about retaining your individuality while still being a team player. Now here's how this is going to work." She stands in front of the row of desks directly by the windows. "You guys look to the right ..." Then she moves on the next row. "... you guys look to the left, and what you see are your partners. Same with the next two rows, you look right, you look left, these are your partners. And the last two rows just the same. There you go, quick and easy. You're welcome."

I turn my head to the right as I'm told, and Philip looks back at me like a wet puppy. When I sigh he turns his head away and looks at his desk. It's probably not a nice feeling to have someone not even try to conceal their aversion to you, but deep down inside the only person I really feel sorry for right now is myself.

Mrs. Spelczik passes around our assigned topics on sheets of paper. For Philip and me it reads, *Romeo and Juliet — Star-crossed Lovers Across the Ages*. I look at him. He looks back at me. I twist my mouth but then it occurs to me he might regard it as a mockery of his cleft lip, so I quickly say, "Bummer, huh?"

He just shrugs.

"Okay," Mrs. Spelczik says. "I'm going to let you guys put your heads together and discuss how you want to organize your project, do your research, and put a little twist on your papers that is going to sweep me off my feet. So get on with it, but try to keep the noise level down."

Around us, teams of two are putting their heads together. Philip looks at me, once again like a puppy, but this time like one at the animal shelter, beaten and battered and desperately looking for someone—anyone, really—who will show some mercy in spite of themselves and adopt him.

It's a heartbreaking sight all right.

But I don't even want a dog.

"I'm Matt, by the way," I say.

"Hello."

"So. How should we go about this?"

"I don't know," Philip twangs not very helpfully.

"I guess we should probably read the damn thing first."

"I've already read it."

"Me too," I say, "but it's been a while. Do you still have your copy?"

He shakes his head. "I checked it out from the library."

"Right. Well, we can probably get it online somewhere."

"I don't have Internet."

I frown at him. It's 2016, how does anyone not have Internet? My glance falls on his worn-out sneakers and his battered jeans. He probably doesn't even have a computer.

Noticing my prying looks, he says, "When I need to use the Internet, I go to the library."

"Right," I say. "The library it is then, I guess."

There is no reply, and I don't know what else to say either, so we both read Mrs. Spelczik's assignment notes in awkward silence.

CHAPTER SIX

The inaugural Track & Field training session is scheduled after the end of the sixth period. When I enter the locker room, my heart sinks and I feel painfully out of place among the twenty-five or thirty of my fellow athletes, most of whom are at least six inches taller than me and distinctly more masculine. I briefly consider turning on my heel and walking away, pretending that some terrible mistake has been made with the sign-up lists and that I should actually be in Home Economics or something, but before I have the time to properly entertain that option, I hear Chris call out my name from across the room.

"Matt! Over here!"

I force a smile and nod at him, and before I even know it, I find myself walking toward him, partly because there is nowhere else to go, partly because I feel drawn towards him as if by some invisible force. No, strike that. It's not an invisible force. It is, in fact, quite visible, because Chris isn't wearing a shirt and he's got the physique of a Greek god.

Apollo, probably, the god of poetry and music.

Unfortunately Ares, the god of violence and warfare, in his earthly incarnation as Jack Antonelli, is standing right next to him equally shirtless and, although decidedly less attractive than Chris, still more muscular and manly than scrawny old me.

Next to Jack, Jason is changing into his kit, but I'm not familiar with Asian deities.

"What the hell are *you* doing here?" Jack asks and sneers as I approach them. "The gymnastics club meets on Wednesdays."

I ignore him as Chris fist bumps me. "Good to see you, Matt." Turning to Jack, he says, "Actually, our little Matty here is quite a runner, or so I'm told."

"Oh, right," the Jackrabbit says. "Maddie has always been good at running. Especially running away."

To be fair, he's not lying.

I have a history of outrunning Jack whenever he wanted to beat me up in elementary school or junior high, but I'm not keen on divulging that information to Chris. Being able to outrun Jack might impress Chris. Being a coward—probably not so much.

"And this is why little Maddie is so fast," Jack says as I get changed. "No air resistance because he's basically a stick."

It's a relatively tame jibe by Jack's standards, so I let it slide.

We make our way out of the locker room and onto the running track where Coach Gutierrez ticks all our names off his list. He's a short, potbellied man who looks as if he's never done any sports in his entire life. He's wearing shorts, a red polo shirt, and a red baseball cap.

"All right," he says to every student he ticks off his list, "two laps to warm up, then stretching until we're complete. Off you go."

So off we go. We run our two laps in silence, Chris and Jack up front, Jason and I a short distance behind them. By the time we pass the bleachers at the beginning of the home stretch, Zoey, Alfonso, and Sandy have taken their seats close to the track. They cheer us on which makes me smile, and I wave at them. When we finish our second lap Chris and Jack follow me and Jason as we walk back to the bleachers. We do our stretching right in front of our audience and exchange a few quips with them.

"Woo, nice legs!" Sandy calls out to us. She's probably talking to Jason, but we all make a point of flexing our muscles just in case.

Not that I have a whole lot of muscles to flex.

"Dude, look!" Jack suddenly says to Chris and flicks his head toward the street behind the bleachers. We all turn our heads. Philip is standing by the roadside all by himself, his handbag

64

in one hand, the other holding his opened umbrella to protect himself from the scorching afternoon sun. He's standing there motionless, facing the street. Every time a car is approaching from the left, he turns his head expectantly, but they all pass him by.

"Hey, Viet Cong!" Jack calls out to Philip. "Catching a cab to Saigon?"

He brays with laughter at his own joke.

"Actually," I say, "I don't think he is Vietnamese, to be honest."

Jack scowls at me. "So what?"

I shrug. "I'm just saying."

"Also," Chris jumps in, "I think Saigon was renamed Ho Chi Minh City after the Nam war." He looks at me and winks.

Well, what do you know? He's not only cute, he also knows his world history, which, honestly, makes him even sexier.

Or more confusing, if you're Jack and you have no idea what he's talking about.

Jack turns to me. "Wipe that stupid smirk off your face, Maddie!"

Naturally, I do as I'm told.

A whistle coming from behind us is calling for our attention. By the finish line, Coach Gutierrez is flailing his arms, motioning us to join him and the others.

"We better go," Chris says.

"All right," the coach says as we reach the finish line, "let's get started. My name is Mr. Gutierrez. You will address me either as Mr. Gutierrez or as 'coach,' because I'm not your friend. I'm not your teacher either. I'm your coach. My job is not to make you like me, my job is to make you like track and field and to excel in it. Our ultimate short-term goal is the Brookhurst County Schoolympics that mark the end of the athletics season in early November. This school has always done a great job at the Schoolympics, and I have no intentions to see that change."

As Coach Gutierrez keeps droning on, my gaze wanders back to the bleachers and to Philip who's still standing by the roadside. At one point, Sandy gets up and walks over to him. After a brief exchange she returns to her seat.

"All right, what we're gonna do today is we're gonna have tryouts in a number of events, namely 100 meters, 800 meters, 1500 meters. Today is all about running. We'll do all the jumping and throwing next time. Anyway, we're gonna start with the 100 meters today. Those of you not taking part in that, get on your smartphones and check your MySpace or whatever it is you kids do nowadays. I don't flippin' care as long as you're not standing in my way, all right?"

Chris, Jack, and Jason are in it for the short distances, and I spontaneously decide that am I too. Coach Gutierrez wants to start with the juniors and seniors, so we have a few minutes before it's our turn. We make our way back to the bleachers.

"You gonna try out for javelin or discus?" Jack asks, looking at Chris.

Please say no! I'm thinking. *Apollo killed his lover Hyacinth when he accidentally threw a discus at his head!*

Chris shakes his head and laughs. "Yeah, no. I throw like a girl."

Oh thank Zeus!

"Right," Jack says, making no attempt to ridicule him, and I wonder if he even knows that his best buddy is gay.

Back at the bleachers I walk up to Zoey and look over at Philip who's still standing there under his umbrella.

"So what's with the freaky kid?" I ask.

"Nothing," Zoey says. "Sandy went over to him and asked if he's all right ..."

"And?"

"... and he said he's waiting for his dad to pick him up."

As if on cue, a run-down, twenty-year-old old clunker pulls up and stops next to Philip. Thick, white smoke is swelling from under the hood, and the car sounds even worse than its looks. As Philip closes his umbrella, opens the door and slumps into the passenger seat, a small man in his forties gets out of the car.

He's wearing a grubby jacket and a trilby hat.

The same hat he was wearing when he was standing behind me in the queue on the first day of school.

Now he uses it to fan the smoke away.

"Just look at that!" Jack says.

While everyone is looking, my gaze finds its way half a block down the street where a shiny black Tesla Model S is parked. Sales really must be picking up for Tesla. Unless it's the same one I've seen the other day. I didn't get a proper look at the driver the first time around, but the person I'm looking at right now has shoulder-length dark hair and is wearing sunglasses and a white tank top. Nothing out of the ordinary, except for the fact that she's sitting in her car in the middle of the day on a relatively boring street with not much to look at.

Like a freaking federal agent or something.

Special Agent Nicole Tesla.

On assignment to surveil closeted high school freshmen.

When the smoke has cleared, Mr. Thongrivong finally gets back into the car, but now the engine won't start. He gets out and opens the hood again, stooping over the motor compartment to figure out what's wrong.

Alfonso rises to his feet. "Do you need any help, sir?"

"No, no," Mr. Thongrivong says and waves his hand dismissively. "Is fine, is fine."

"Good luck, Mr. Thongrivong!" Sandy calls out to him. Mr. Thongrivong waves at her and smiles awkwardly.

Meanwhile, Philip is sinking deeper and deeper into his seat, and it's obvious he'd rather we left him and his dad alone. Which is exactly what I'm doing. I'm up for my 100-meter heat, along with Chris, Jack, and three sophomores. As we make our way to the starting line, I hear giggles and emphatic moans from the bleachers. When I turn to look I see Mr. Thongrivong jumping up and down with a painful look on his face, shaking his right hand. Apparently, he burnt himself when he touched the hot engine.

"On your marks," Coach Gutierrez's voice sounds from the loudspeakers at the end of the starting blocks. We get into position. I'm running to the right of Chris, Jack to his left. The three sophomores are on the outer lanes.

"Get set!"

As we all lift our butts into the air, there are more giggles from the bleachers, and I hear Sandy cheering Mr. Thongrivong on again, so I assume he's had another mishap. My heart pounding in my chest, I push all distracting thoughts aside. Endless seconds trickle by, and then, all of a sudden, I see Chris moving forward at almost exactly the same time I hear the starting signal.

We're off and running. After a few strides, Chris is already several meters ahead of me. His powerful legs keep pumping heavily, and subconsciously, my own legs synchronize their movements with Chris's.

Left, right, left right.

My eyes focus on the soles of Chris's running shoes.

They're red.

I don't see anything else around me. Most notably I don't see any of the other runners which must be a good sign, because it means they're not getting ahead of me. My legs keep pumping and I almost forget to breathe. Chris keeps pulling ahead, and I do my best to keep up. By the time he passes Coach Gutierrez by the finish line he has a lead of at least five or six meters. When I cross the finish line moments later, a quick look to the left and right makes me think that all the other runners must have stumbled and fallen, because I can't see any of them. We run out, and I finally allow myself to breathe again. Ahead of me, Chris slows down and stops. He turns around and smiles as he walks up to me. I stop as well, and he high fives me with a big, bright smile on his face.

"Awesome," he says hardly out of breath.

I just nod, stoop over and prop my hands against my knees, panting heavily.

The other runners have reached the finish line as well. Now they're putting their hands on their hips or behind their necks, catching their breaths. Coach Gutierrez walks up to us and we all gather around him as he looks at his tablet computer.

"All right, gentlemen," he says. He looks at Chris. "You! What's your name again?"

"Chris Larsen."

"Right, Mr. Larsen. This is the moment where in a proper competition you'd be disqualified due to a false start. You got out of the starting block five hundredths of a second before

the signal. Which would make you ..." He turns to me, "...
the official winner."

Now that's an unexpected turn of events.

Before the race, my biggest hope was to not come in last.

I need some time to process this, so I just nod, trying to
conceal a smug grin. At the same time I hear cheers from the
bleachers a hundred meters away, and I feel immensely proud,
but when I look back at Zoey and the others, they're not even
looking in my direction. They all have their heads turned
towards the street where Mr. Thongrivong is taking a bow,
waves awkwardly, and finally gets into his car and takes off.

"However," the coach continues, turning back to Chris,
"this was not an official race, so you're first, Mr. Larsen. Good
time too, 12:21."

"Thanks," Chris says.

"As for the rest of you, gentlemen, great race. Photo finish
for third place, although I think it was probably you, Mr. ..."

"Jack Antonelli."

"Right, Mr. Antonelli."

Chris walks up to Jack and high fives him. I'm tempted to
do the same, but Jack would probably find it patronizing and
offensive, so I don't.

"All right," the coach says, "those of you who want to do
the 800 or 1500 meters, stick around. The rest of you get out
of here!"

Chris walks around high-fiving the rest of the runners,
and being the good sportsmen that we are, Jack and I follow
suit. Then we walk back to the bleachers. When we get there,
Zoey and Alfonso come walking toward me. At first it seems
they're excited about my excellent result, but it turns out
they completely missed it.

"So how did it go?" Zoey asks, "Were you any good?"

I'm struggling to maintain my smile. This was probably
one of the proudest and most exciting moments in my school
career, and my sister and my best friend completely missed it
because they were watching some stupid Asian driver fix his
stupid car.

"All right," I say. "I came in second after Chris."

"That's awesome," Alfonso says and pats my shoulder as Zoey flings her arms around my neck. I'm trying to appreciate their joy, but it has a stale taste to it. They shouldn't even have to ask me how it went. They could have seen it if only they'd bothered to look.

This is so not fair.

Just like it's probably not fair that I truly hate Philip, his ugly face, and his stupid dad's stupid car from the bottom of my heart for taking this moment away from me.

Screw fairness, though.

And Screw you, Philip Thongrivong.

* * *

The afternoon drags on with more tryout heats and endless breaks in between. Chris, Jack, and I try for the 800 meters. I come in third in my heat, after Chris and Jack. It's another unexpected success for me, and it comes with a special treat. Right after we cross the finish line, Chris turns around and flings his arms around Jack. It's one of those extremely buff, sportsmanly hugs that male athletes around the world can get away with without raising any suspicions about their sexual orientation and that even someone like Jack can engage in with no reserve and no sense of irony. I'm standing right next to them as they hug, and after three powerful pats on Jack's back, Chris turns to me and throws himself around my neck. It feels extremely awkward and yet at the same time so exciting. Chris's body is hot, literally hot, and he smells of deodorant and fresh sweat. I enjoy his embrace a lot more than I probably should, so I make sure to break away from it after a quick pat on his back before my body starts reacting in an embarrassing way. Jack is standing right next to us, and I don't even know what I'm thinking when I turn to him with my arms stretched out. It's probably just a reflex, fed by an adrenaline overdose mixed with some strange desire to belong, but before the heat of the moment gets to carry me away, Jack takes a step back, scowls at me and says, "Don't you dare touch me, faggot!"

Heads immediately turn our way, and I walk away, pretending that I wasn't involved in whatever prompted Jack's outburst, but it's pointless because everyone around us has witnessed the situation. Angry, embarrassed, and confused, I just want to get out of here so I start walking back toward the bleachers, but Coach Gutierrez stops me. He grabs my wrist and drags me along as he walks up to Jack in the biggest strides his short legs can muster.

"You!" he shouts at Jack who is walking away, but he doesn't get far. "Hey! You! Antonelli! Get back here!"

Jack stops and turns towards us. When we reach him, Coach Gutierrez rises on his tiptoes and looks down on Jack. I don't know how he does it because he barely reaches Jack's size, but it almost looks as though he's towering over him.

"All right, listen to me, Mr. Antonelli! I will not tolerate any bullying, taunting, or aggressive behavior, homophobic or otherwise, on my watch. If I ever hear anything like that again you can go and find something else to do, knitting or ballet or whatever else, I don't care. Have I made myself clear?"

He's still clasping my wrist so hard it hurts.

"Yes," Jack says.

"Yes what?"

"Yes, sir!"

"Good! Now apologize to Mr. Dunstan!"

The coach yanks up my hand and offers it to Jack.

Meanwhile, I wish I were elsewhere. The far side of the moon seems like a lovely place. I appreciate the coach taking a stand against bullying and name calling, but apparently he doesn't realize that he isn't exactly doing me a favor by pointing out the homophobic nature of Jack's outburst, because honestly, this is more likely to make people think I'm gay than Jack calling me a faggot.

Jack reluctantly shakes my hand, giving it a strong, painful squeeze, and mumbles, "Sorry," without even looking at me.

"No, no, no!" the coach says. "Louder, and at least have the decency to look Mr. Dunstan in the eyes and say it like you mean it!"

"I'm sorry, Matt," Jack says with the darkest, most intimidating look in his eyes I have ever seen, and I've seen a few.

The coach finally lets go of my wrist. "Good," he says. "Now let's move on. Those in the 1500 meters stick around. The rest of you get the hell out of here!"

I don't need to be told twice.

* * *

I don't shower. I just rub my sweaty hair dry with my towel, quickly get changed and hurry out of the locker room. Just before I'm out of the door I hear Chris calling after me as he's coming in from the track.

"Matt! Wait!"

I decide I've had enough social interaction for the day, so I pull the door open and leave. In the hallway, Jason, who also didn't take a shower, is waiting and checking his phone.

"Hey," he says.

"Hey."

I pull my phone out of my pocket and switch it on. I want to text Zoey and Alfonso and tell them not to wait for me because I'm going straight home, but I'm distracted by an incoming Wattpad notification. 2-b-pretty finally sent another message! Excited, I'm about to open it when I hear Zoey's voice behind me.

"Matt!"

I turn around and see Zoey, Alfonso, Sandy coming down the hallway. I switch off my phone and slide it back into my pocket.

"Hey," I say, trying to act casually.

"What happened?" Zoey asks as they approach me. "What was going on there with Jack and the coach?"

I wave my hand dismissively and force a smile. "Nah, nothing."

"It didn't look like nothing to me, to be honest," Zoey keeps prying.

"It was nothing. Never mind."

Behind me I hear the door to the locker room open. When I look over my shoulder I see Chris walking toward us. He's taken off his sweaty shirt, but he's still wearing his track shorts and running shoes.

"Matt," he says.

I'm so sick and tired of hearing that name! Why can't everybody just leave me alone?

"Jack and I are going to the Korova for a milkshake or something, and I wanted to ask you if you want to join us."

"Thanks," I say, trying not to stare at his erect nipples, "but …"

"The Korova?" Zoey asks. "What's that?"

"It's a milk bar up on Madison, across from the mall. They have great milkshakes and pastries. Scones and cupcakes and stuff."

"Oh," Zoey says with a scheming smile and puts her hand on my shoulders. "Sounds great. Matt loves cupcakes. Don't you, Matt?"

I glare at her.

"Awesome," Chris says as if it's a done deal. "By the way, you guys wanna join us too? The more, the merrier."

Glances are being exchanged and shoulders are being shrugged, and in the end everyone is like, "Yeah, sure, why not."

I don't have an exit strategy. If everyone is tagging along, there is no way for me to drop out. Chris or not, if it weren't for the others, there would be no way I'd voluntarily spend more time with Jack this afternoon. Then again, with my friends in the majority, I hope I can avoid further confrontations.

"Awesome," Chris says again. He quickly pats me on the back and says, "Jack and I will be right out, just give us a minute."

"All right," I say with little enthusiasm.

When Chris disappears back in the locker room, Zoey turns to me. "So?"

"So what?"

"So are you gonna tell us what happened out there? Because it wasn't nothing."

I sigh. I wish Zoey would make use of her privileged position as my sister by asking me intimate questions like that in a private conversation and not in front of the whole world, but apparently her curiosity is getting the best of her.

"Look," I say before I even know it, "Jack called me a faggot, okay? The coach called him out on it and made him apologize to me. The end. Can we move on now?"

"Oh," Zoey says, finally realizing why I was reluctant to come forward with these details. But the cat is out of the bag now. I still can't believe I used the words *me* and *faggot* in the same sentence, or that I used the word *faggot* at all.

Sandy throws herself around my neck and hugs me. "Don't worry about it. Jack says all sorts of silly things all the time. We know you're not a faggot."

Alfonso chuckles at her naïveté. "Oh boy."

"What?" she says innocently. "He isn't, is he?"

"I think," Jason jumps in, "what he means is that you probably shouldn't be using that word. It's kind of … offensive."

"Well, I'm sorry, but I didn't call anyone a faggot, did I? I was merely quoting Jack."

"Right," Zoey says, "and if someone used the n-word and you were quoting them, would you spell it out too?"

"Hell no!"

Zoey nods and raises an eyebrow at Sandy. "Think about that."

"Well, with *faggot* it's different, isn't it? If I were to say *f-word* instead of *faggot*, it would be confusing. Some people would think that instead of *faggot* I might refer to … you know, the other f-word."

"Oh what the fuck!" Zoey says and throws her arms up in the air.

Sandy nods. "Exactly."

"Guys, guys!" I say. "Can we all stop saying all these words for eff's sake? I mean, Jesus Christ!"

"Right on!" Jason says, and everyone nods approvingly. Well, almost everyone. Sandy looks at me with big, sad eyes and says, "Don't use the name of the Lord in vain, Matthew."

Pinching the bridge of my nose, I let out a deep and desperate sigh.

CHAPTER SEVEN

The Korova's interior is modernistic but simple. Plastic and glass surfaces are refracting the bright lights from the rainbow-colored ceiling and making the room distinctly colorful. In contrast, the walls are decorated with larger than life black-and-white photographs, very artistic photographs of couples kissing or looking at each other with longing eyes.

Nothing wrong with that, but it's worth pointing out they're all gay couples.

Nothing wrong with that either, obviously, but it takes me by surprise. After the way my day has been going so far, I wasn't expecting to be taken to a gay bar—a gay milk bar but technically a gay bar nonetheless. Apparently I'm not the only person who's taken aback.

"Whoa," Zoey says as she looks around.

Alfonso looks at a particularly sexy photograph of two girls making out. Then he nudges me with his elbow and flicks his head at the picture. "How about that, huh?"

"Uh," I say, too stunned to come up with a more refined response.

Sandy and Jason glance around, their eyes the size of saucers. The only person who doesn't seem surprised, apart from Chris, is Jack.

Which, ironically, is very surprising.

The patrons are a colorful mix, both in age and gender. By the window, a lesbian couple is having milkshakes with their two pre-k kids, a boy and a girl. Back in the corner, two guys in their late twenties are looking at us, sipping coffee. In the next booth, two younger dudes are holding hands and looking at a music video on their laptop, sharing one pair of earbuds between them.

Behind the counter, a heavily tanned man in a white tank top who looks way too young to be bald is polishing glasses. When he sees Chris, his face brightens up and he says in an extremely camp voice, "Why hello there! If it isn't my favorite baby face!"

"Hi, Milo," Chris says.

"Hello, sweetheart. Oh, I love your T-shirt!"

It reads *Hug Dealer*.

If I were alone with him I'd ask him if I could have some. Except I wouldn't because I'm shy.

"Thanks."

"So who are your friends?"

"Just some guys from school," Chris says.

Milo turns to us. "Well, guys from school, don't just stand there! Come on in, don't be shy! Welcome to the Korova. Why don't you find yourselves somewhere nice to sit, and I'll be right with you."

Chris leads us to a booth by the window. It's a bit cramped for seven people, but we just about manage by squeezing Zoey, Alfonso, Sandy, and Jason on one side of the table and Chris, Jack, and myself on the other, with Chris serving as a safety buffer between Jack and myself. As soon as we're settled in, Milo leaves his place behind the counter and comes walking over to us—if you can call it walk.

He *sashays*.

"So, my little kitties," he says as he stands in front of us, clasping his hands like a proud mother. "What will it be? We have some glorious cheesecake, homemade by my lovely husband Hans. Between you and me, Hans makes the best cheesecake in the world. It's even better than my mother's, but don't tell her I said that or she'll disown me. I can't have her disown me, I want that Renoir. I mean, it's a fake Renoir, but even so. It's just so beautiful. So, who wants some cheesecake?"

After this deluge of words we're all gasping for air and when we don't shake our heads quickly enough Milo says, "All right, seven slices of cheesecake coming up. And what would you like to drink? You have to try our milkshakes. They're home-made by my lovely husband Hans."

"Does Hans ever get out of the kitchen?" Zoey asks.

"No, darling, I chained him to the oven. But that's okay, he likes it hot." He winks at her.

Zoey giggles. "I bet he does. So which flavors do you have?"

"We have them *all*, darling. Strawberry, lemon, orange, tomato and basil, you name it. If we don't have it, I'll take out the whip and have Hans make it especially for you."

"Oh my." Zoey pulls a face. "I wouldn't want to do that to Hans, so I'll have a strawberry shake."

"Excellent choice! Made with fresh local strawberries."

We all order milkshakes in various flavors, and when Milo turns to leave, Chris says, "Oh, and don't forget the special surprise!"

"Please," Milo says. "As if I could ever forget a single word coming from your pouty lips."

"Surprise?" Sandy says. "What surprise?"

Jack glares at Chris. "Please tell me you didn't."

The rest of us exchange bemused looks, but Chris remains silent and smiles.

After a few minutes, Milo returns with our milkshakes, plus a solitary strawberry cupcake with pink glazing, a burning candle stuck in the middle of it.

"So," Milo says, "who's the birthday boy?"

Without looking at Milo, Jack sighs and raises his hand.

"Oh, it's you, is it?" Milo says. He places the cupcake in front of Jack. When he leans in to plant a kiss on his cheek, Jack reclines and raises his hands. "Please don't."

"So shy," Milo says, clasping his hands again. "How adorable! Well happy birthday to you anyway, sweetheart. And many happy returns."

Jack doesn't look happy. "Thanks."

When Milo leaves to get our cheesecakes, Sandy looks at Jack. "I didn't know it's your birthday." She leans across the table, puts her arm around his neck, pulls him closer and kisses him on the cheek. "Happy birthday, Jack."

We all echo Sandy's congratulations. "Happy birthday, Jack!"

"Watch out, the candle!" I say.

"Oh my God!" Sandy quickly grabs her long blond hair and pulls it away from the flame before it catches fire.

"You better blow out that candle before we burn the place down," Zoey says. "But don't forget to make a wish."

Jack quickly blows out the candle, pulls it out of the cupcake and drops it on the table. Then he picks up the cupcake and takes a halfhearted bite out of it.

Leave it to Zoey to address the elephant in the room.

"So Jack," she says. "What was that between you and the coach earlier? Did he wish you a happy birthday?"

I shoot her an angry look and kick her leg under the table. Unfortunately, it's Sandy who cries out in pain.

"Ouch!" she says. "Who kicked me?"

I smile at her sheepishly. "Sorry."

"It was nothing," Jack says without looking up from the table.

"Matt said you called him names," Sandy says, retroactively providing a valid justification for that kick against her leg.

Jack takes another bite out of his birthday cake, chews, then shrugs and says, "I've been calling Maddie names since kindergarten, so what else is new? He knows how it's meant." He looks at me. "Right?"

I'm pretty sure all the verbal abuse Jack has directed at me in the last ten years was meant exactly as it came across, but I'm stumped by his simple yet impeccable logic; also, I don't want to rile him up any more than I already have today, so I just say, "Right."

We sit at the Korova for about an hour. After the slow and awkward start we talk about the Track & Field tryouts (though carefully avoiding Jack's verbal derailment), about everyone's extracurriculars, and about school in general. The atmosphere is getting more and more relaxed, and I'm actually beginning to enjoy myself when Jason looks at his watch and announces that it's time for him to go home and study.

"Yeah," Sandy says, "me too."

Zoey nods and nudges Alfonso. "Yeah, we should go too."

Alfonso looks a bit confused because he only just got started on his third milkshake, but Zoey's glare is unequivocal, so he shrugs and says, "All right."

Zoey gets up and looks at Jack. "Are you coming too, Jack?"

"I'll stay a while longer," he says, shaking his head.

Zoey looks at me and shrugs as if to say, 'I did what I could,' and I acknowledge her with a nod.

"Don't you have to go home and, like, celebrate with your family or something?" Sandy asks, but there is no reply. Jack just stares at the table in front of him, looking unusually miserable.

As Chris gets up to hug Sandy and Zoey good-bye, I jump at the opportunity to change seats. I slide into the vacant opposite bench, relieved to put a table between Jack and myself. That same table is now between me and Chris, which is unfortunate, but at least it's easier for me to look at him now without twisting my neck.

The others leave and take the relaxed mood with them. I'm left behind with Chris and Jack, and that feeling of awkwardness that has been lingering under the surface. We sit in silence for a while and slurp the rest of our milkshakes until Chris finally puts his hand on Jack's shoulder.

"Sorry if that was awkward for you," he says.

Jack shrugs, and I'm not sure if that shrug is just a shrug or a way to get rid of Chris's hand. "Never mind."

"I wasn't planning on bringing that many people along, you know? But then again, I didn't want you to spend the afternoon all by yourself."

I have no idea what Chris is talking about and I feel out of place, as if I'm eavesdropping on a private conversation that isn't meant for my ears. I probably should have taken the opportunity and left when the others did. Now I'm stuck here between my crush and my nemesis, unsure what to do or say, so I just try to blend into the furniture and pretend I'm not here.

"Don't worry about it," Jack says. "It's okay." Then he gets up and grabs his bag. "I need one now."

Chris nods. "Yeah, me too." He gets up too and walks over to the counter to pick up the check.

While I'm still wondering what 'I need one now' means, Jack kicks my foot. It's not a violent or aggressive kick by any means, just a way to catch my attention. He looks me straight in the eyes, for the first time since the coach made him apologize to me. "Are you coming or what?"

"Where are we going?" I ask.

"Outside."

I grab my bag and follow Jack and Chris to the door. As I pass the counter, Milo winks at me. I smile awkwardly and check if my shoes are still on my feet.

"Thank you!" Milo calls after us as we leave the Korova. "Have a nice day!"

Once outside, we turn left, then left again, and walk down the back alley behind the bar. Jack drops his bag on the floor next to a dumpster, leans against it and lets out a deep sigh. Then he takes a pack of cigarettes out of his pocket, opens it and pulls one out. Chris takes one as well, and then Jack offers the pack to me.

"Uh, no, thanks," I say, shaking my head. "I don't smoke."

"Come on," Jack insists. "Don't be such a pussy."

"Nah," I say, feeling very audacious to resist the temptation. "I'm an athlete in training, you know?"

I'm expecting them both to snicker and sneer, but instead, Chris pats me on the shoulder and says, "Right on, Matty," and even Jack just shrugs and says, "Suit yourself."

The two light up their cigarettes. Jack takes a deep drag, puts his head in his neck and lets out a sigh of relief. "God, I've been looking forward to that all day," he says, smoke coming out of his nose and mouth as he speaks.

"I know, right?" Chris says. "It's as if the smoke fills some void that desperately wants to be filled."

"Yeah."

"So how long have you guys been smoking?" I ask.

"Couple of months," Chris says.

Jack nods. "Steve's party. I was so drunk, and when his older brother offered me a cigarette I just thought, 'Why the hell not?' I mean, the world is going to the dogs and we're all gonna die anyway, so what does it even matter?"

"I don't know," I say. "I guess it'll matter a lot whether I die a slow and painful death from lung cancer, or—"

"Or," Jack interrupts me, "whether die you a quick and painless death in a car crash or in a mall shooting?"

I look at him. "I didn't know you were such a cynic."

"There's a lot of stuff you don't know about me, Maddie."

It's a surprising response that invites further prying. It's almost as if he wants me to ask what he means by that, as if he wants to share things that he's never told anyone before, but I'm not taking that risk. I might be misreading this signal, and I don't want to clash with him again. Not in the mood he's in today.

"I guess," I say.

"So Jack," Chris jumps in, "will you be celebrating with your family today?"

He shrugs. "Mom asked me what I want for dinner, so I guess we'll be having dinner, my mom, my sister and my step-dad. But nothing fancy."

"Right," Chris says. "So what will it be? Mac and cheese?"

"Shut up!" Jack says, but he smiles. "No, I asked for burgers and fries. My mom does awesome burgers." He looks at his watch. "Speaking of which, I better be going. I can't be late for my birthday dinner, can I?"

He takes a last drag of his cigarette and throws it into the dumpster. It seems a bit reckless, but since the world is going to the dogs anyway I guess he's not very worried about causing a conflagration. And right now I don't care much either, because for all I care the world could perish in a storm of fire and brim-stone—with Jack in it or not—as long as I get to spend a few minutes alone with Chris.

Jack picks up his bag and fist bumps Chris. Then he reaches his fist out to me, but before I get to fist bump him, he raises his hand and flicks my nose. Not very strongly, and it doesn't even hurt, but it's enough to remind me that in Jack's eyes I'm—if anything—the last among equals.

As I rub my nose, Jack cackles and leaves.

"Enjoy your burger!" Chris calls after him.

"Yeah, yeah." Jack waves his arm dismissively and turns the corner.

"Wow," I say when he's gone. It's the best way I know how to express my confusion over everything Jack said and did today.

"I know, right?" Chris takes a last drag from his cigarette, then flicks it into the dumpster. I find it even more disturbing—and, quite frankly, more disappointing—than when Jack did it, but again I choose to let it slide.

"So how do you know Jack?" I ask.

"Jack? We actually met at that party. Steve Henderson's party. My sister was dating Steve's brother at the time."

"Oh, I didn't know you had a sister. Or that Steve had a brother, for that matter."

"Yeah. Anyway, I met him out on the patio, and when I saw his cigarette, I wanted to bum one off him, but he had bummed it himself, so he shared it with me. We started talking, got along, and the rest is history."

"Right," I say.

"So what about you?"

"Me? I met Jack in kindergarten. We never talked about anything meaningful, we never got along. The rest is also history."

"You don't like him very much, do you?" Chris asks as we slowly stroll back to the main road.

I shrug. "He's never given me much reason to like him. Which is fine, you know? I don't expect everyone to like me. But I've never given him much reason to dislike me either, I don't think, yet for some reason he really seems to hate me. Like, what was that on the track earlier? When he came in second in our 800-meter heat, I was happy for him, I really was. And I just wanted to give him a pat on the back and say, 'Well done!' or something, just like you did. I thought he'd appreciate that, but I guess not."

"Jack can be an ass sometimes, but deep down inside he's a good guy, really."

I snort. "Must be very deep down inside. It rarely shows on the outside."

"Yeah. You know, I think he's very suspicious of people, and he's not exactly used to getting a positive response to most of the things he does. It has a lot to do with his family, if you can call it that."

"Why?" I ask.

"His mom and his step dad are both boozers, you know? And his stepdad has a pretty … shall we say unreserved attitude towards physical violence."

I look at Chris, unsure what he means.

"He hits them both," Chris explains. "Jack and his mom."

"Wow," I say. I had no idea. I've never thought much about domestic violence because it has never been an issue in my family, but I'm well aware that not everyone is so lucky. It makes me almost feel sympathetic towards Jack, which is a first, and it's very confusing.

Chris nods. "I know it's not an excuse. But it's an explanation."

"I guess."

When we reach the main street, Chris look left and right. "Which way?"

"Depends on where you want to go."

"I want to walk you home."

This has got to be the most romantic thing anyone has ever said to me.

"Right," I say. "Left then."

Chris looks at me with a puzzled smile. "Right, left?"

"Sorry." I laugh. "Left."

It's getting dark. Most cars have their headlights turned on as we walk down Mercer Street, and we flow along with the steady stream of the last people heading home from work, evening shoppers, and the first couples heading for a night out at the movies or at a restaurant.

"So what's your story?"

I frown. "My story?"

"Yeah. Everyone has a story. So what's yours?"

"I don't know," I say, and I'm not even lying. I'm just a guy, trying to settle into high school without attracting too much attention. That doesn't seem very exciting, so I pluck up all my

courage and decide to share one of my best-kept secrets with
Chris. "I write stories."

"You write stories?" Chris asks, raising his eyebrows.

Emboldened by his piqued interest, I add, "Yeah, well,
nothing big. I want to write the next Great American Novel
one day, but for now it's just a couple of short stories and
stuff."

"That's awesome! So what kind of stories are we talking
about?"

"Just stories ... about people," I say vaguely.

"Are they love stories?" He nudges me with his elbow.
"Come on, you can tell me. Don't be shy."

"Nah!" I lie, and I'm glad that in the evening twilight he
can't see how my face must be flushing. "I don't know what to
call it, really. Call it contemporary fiction, if you like."

"All right then. Maybe I can read some of your stories one
day?"

"Yeah, I don't know. They're probably not very good."

"I don't think that's for you to decide."

"All right then, we'll see," I say, eager to change the topic.
As if on cue, my phone chimes. I pull it out of my pocket and
quickly check the screen. It's a text from my mom, summoning me home for dinner. I quickly reply 'On my way' and
hit send. When I notice Chris peeking over my shoulder, I
quickly switch the phone off.

"Your mom?" he asks.

"Yeah. She wants me home for dinner."

"Right," Chris says, and when I'm about to slide the phone
back into my pocket, he adds, "Wait, I don't think I have your
number."

"Oh," I say and wake the phone again. "Let's see ..."

The sad and awkward thing is that I have no idea where on
my phone my own phone number is stored. I swipe and tap,
tap and swipe, browsing through the phone's settings, but I
can't find that stupid number. "Damn it!"

"Can't find it?" Chris asks with a smile.

"Apparently not. I know this is very embarrassing, but I
don't call myself very often, you know?"

"It's okay, don't worry about it," Chris says, but it's not okay. It's not okay at all, because I sure as hell want Chris to have my number. "Listen, I know my number, so why don't you just send me a text?"

Grateful for the lifeline, I say, "Oh, okay. That'll work. Give me a second ..."

I type a quick message, then I ask for his number.

Chris tells me the number. I punch it into my phone and hit send.

> Hello, it's me!
>
> Me

A few seconds later, his phone chirps. He looks at the screen, reads my message, and chuckles. Then he taps a reply into his phone and sends it. Moments later my phone chimes.

> Your cute!
>
> Chris

Oh no. He's one of those people who don't know the difference between *you're* and *your*. And I'm one of those people who find it too embarrassing to point out other people's embarrassing mistakes, so I just smile sheepishly and say, "Thank you."

We walk in awkward silence for a while. The sky is the darkest shade of blue by the time we turn into Vine Street.

"So how far is it?" Chris asks.

"Not far," I say. "Three blocks. You can almost see it from here, or you could if it weren't so dark."

"Is it before or after the intersection with Hill Street?"

"It's right on the corner, actually."

"Good. I have to turn into Hill Street to get home."

"Oh, okay."

We reach the intersection, and I walk Chris a few steps down Hill Street because our dining room is facing Vine, and I don't want to put on a display for my family as they congregate around the dinner table.

"All right then. I guess I'll see you at school tomorrow," I say.

Instead of a reply, Chris raises his arm, puts it around my neck and pulls me toward himself for a close, tight hug. His body feels soft and warm, and when he rubs my back, a tingle runs down my spine.

Fireworks.

Birds and flowers and rainbows and all that crap.

In my head.

"Oh," he whispers in my ear, "you smell nice."

Clearly, this is a blatant lie. I haven't taken a shower after Track & Field, so I must be reeking of sweat. Nevertheless, I accept the compliment because it's making me melt away, and I'm feeling dizzy because all the blood is rushing from my head to a lower part of my body where it is needed more.

"You too," I say.

I figure if he gets to lie about my odor, I'm allowed to lie about his. His shower gel smells nice all right, but the nicotine stench lingers. It's quite repulsive, really, but I'm not allowing myself the luxury to be picky.

When Chris finally retracts his harm and our bodies part, I nearly pass out. He smiles his wonderful, enticing smile and says, "Good night, Matty. I'll see you tomorrow."

Matty. How I hate that name! Except when Chris says it. When Chris says it, it sounds cool and manly and powerful, like waves breaking on the beach.

He is already walking away down Hill Street when I say, "Good night!"

He turns his head one last time and smiles.

I look after Chris for a minute until he disappears in the dark. As I turn back toward Vine, I see something move behind one of our upstairs windows from the corner of my eye. When I look, Greg's bedroom is dark, and he's nowhere to be seen.

When I open the front door, Mom is on her way from the kitchen to the dining room, carrying a steaming pan with sizzling pork chops.

"Oh, there you are," she says with a bright smile. "Right in time for dinner."

"Good. I'm starving" I say.

Nothing against cheesecake, but I really need something savory now.

"Go wash your hands."

I sigh. "Yes, Mom."

"Greg!" she calls up the stairs. "For the last time, dinner is ready!"

"I'm coming!"

But he isn't. When I make my way upstairs, I find him waiting for me on the landing. His back toward me, he's hugging himself, his hands caressing his own back, and he's making kissing noises. Blind with anger I drop my bag and push him against the wall.

"Not a word to Mom and Dad!" I hiss.

"Or what, faggot?"

The slur is enough to push me over the brink. I cover his mouth with my hand and wrestle him to the ground. As he's trying to writhe free, I twist his arm and he yelps in pain.

Attracted by the noise, Dad comes storming up the stairs.

"What the hell is going on here?" He says as he grabs my arm and yanks me away from Greg. Greg tries to kick me, but with his other arm Dad grabs him and pushes us apart. He looks at me. "Well?"

"Nothing," I say, panting heavily, avoiding Dad's angry look as I glare at Greg.

Dad turns to my brother. "Greg?"

"Nothing."

"Right," Dad says, "well, then nothing is what you two will be having for dinner tonight. Go to your rooms, both of you!"

"Thanks a lot, asshole!" Greg spews in my direction as Dad pushes him into his room.

"That's enough, Greg!" Dad scolds him, but the door already slams shut.

Dad finally lets go of my arm, and he's about to say something to me, but I'm not interested. I stomp into my room and slam the door.

* * *

Half an hour later, there's a knock on the door. I'm in a horrible mood, but I appreciate that even when there's a fight, my parents still respect territorial sovereignty.

"Yes!"

The door opens and Dad sticks his head in. "May I come in?"

"It's your house," I say and shrug. I'm sitting at my desk, reading 2-b-pretty's latest message. I was just about to reply to it, but this has to wait for now, so I close the lid of my laptop and go and lie down on my bed.

Dad closes the door and sits opposite me on the loveseat. He looks at me and says, "You want to tell me what that fight with Greg was all about?"

I shake my head.

Dad snickers. "Just what is it with siblings and their parents? You and Greg are exactly the same as John and I were at your age. We used to fight all the time, even violently sometimes, but whenever our dad broke us up and asked what was going on we would both always say, 'Nah, it's nothing.' It was almost as if despite our differences we would stand together against a common enemy."

I look at him. "So what did you guys fight about when you were younger?"

"You know what, I don't even remember."

"See, if you can't even remember it, you were probably right when you told grandpa it was nothing."

Dad smiles. "Well, it wasn't nothing at the time. Time changes your perspective, and you forget a lot when you get older, but that doesn't mean that they weren't things that really mattered to us. So I'm assuming whatever it was that you and Greg were fighting about was something that really matters to you at this point in time. Because it sure as hell didn't look like you were fighting over nothing."

"It was nothing I want to talk about," I say, staring at the ceiling.

"I see. Look, I know what it's like to have an obnoxious and annoying little brother who thinks he's smarter than you. Someone who keeps bugging you and teasing you and who is simply just a pain in the ass. But you see, if you don't want to talk about it, I can't help you. And I do want to help you if I can."

"Thanks, Dad. But I don't need any help."

Dad shrugs. "Suit yourself then. I for one would have loved to have been able to talk to a neutral person in a situation like that."

I turn my head and look at him. "Well, that's the problem right there. You're our dad, you have to be impartial. If I wanted to talk about it, which I don't, I'd want to talk with someone who's not impartial. Someone who's one hundred percent on my side."

Dad nods. "I understand. But just so you know, my offer stands, so whenever you feel like talking, I'll be there, okay? And I'm not just talking about any problems you may have with your brother. You know you can talk to me about anything that's on your mind, all right?"

"All right," I say. "Thanks."

He stands up and I hope he's finally going to leave me alone so I can get back on my computer and talk to 2-b-pretty. She may be a complete stranger, but at least she's one hundred percent on my side. But Dad doesn't leave. He comes to sit on my bed and looks at me.

"Everything okay with you, son?" he asks.

I frown at him. "Yeah, sure."

"Really? I'm asking because you seem a bit under the weather recently. Ever since you started high school, actually. Is everything okay at school?"

I shrug. "Yeah. I mean, everything is new and different and complicated, but it is what it is. Nothing I can't handle."

Dad keeps looking at me. He knows there's something else on my mind than just school, and for a moment I'm tempted to take this chance and come clean. Just tell him I'm gay and be over and done with it. He's probably as ready for it as he'll ever be.

Problem is, I'm not.

"All right," he finally says and puts his hand on my leg. "I'm gonna leave you be. Make sure you eat something before you go to bed, okay? Mom put your pork chop in the fridge."

"Okay," I say. Dad gets up and walks to the door. He opens it, and before he leaves the room, I say, "Dad?"

"Yes?"

"Thanks."

He just smiles and nods, and then he's gone.

I go back to my desk and open my laptop. To refresh my memory, I read 2-b-pretty's latest message again.

2-b-pretty

Hello, Handsome! Have you been missing yours truly? Sorry I couldn't write earlier, having been busy quarreling with my retarded brother and starting high school, and I don't know which was worse. But enough about me and my miserable life as Matty's life is so much more exciting. His awkward attempts to endear himself to Chris without making Jack or indeed anyone else suspicious are very funny. Just be careful though. Don't turn this into a Hollywood high school comedy for their usually terrible. Unless that's what your going for, but why would you do that. Sadly, no progress on the other front. Still no attempts to come out to his best friend, what is wrong with silly Matty? Something need to happen. Soon! Or otherwise Matty will create even more problems for himself that he doesn't need. Unless that's what your going for, which I think you are because you seem to enjoy tormenting your protagonist. Can't wait to read the next chapter! Yours truly, xoxo

Even though I've read this for the third or fourth time now, it still puts a stupid grin on my face. For some reason, 2-b-pretty's messages strike a chord in me. I think it's her silly quirkiness and also the fact that although she's never met me in person, she seems to understand both my hopes and fears surprisingly well, even though she doesn't even know they're actually my hopes and fears. She still thinks Matt is a fictional character. Either way, being understood is really all I want from people. I need people who understand but don't judge. People like my sister and Alfonso. I wouldn't mind having another person like that in my life.

Mattoid2002

Dear Pretty! I am SO relieved to hear from you! You suddenly disappeared all of a sudden, and I spent the entire weekend going through our previous conversation to see if it was something I said that may have offended you or put you off or something, LOL. So you have an obnoxious little brother too? Poor Pretty! Anyway, thanks again for your feedback. Yeah, I get it, Matt keeps procrastinating. That's because he is insecure, and also because he wants to take it one step at a time. The next step is trying to bond with Chris. The chapter is ready, but I still have to hammer it into the computer. I hope I can get it done before bedtime, so I better get on with it. I'm hoping to hear from you soon and I'm dying to find out what you make of the latest developments in Matty's hilariously miserable little life. Talk to you soon, Pretty. xoxo

I hit the send button, and I'm about to start typing the next chapter of Freshmen Love when there's a knock on the door. It's Zoey.

"Oh my God, I'm so sorry!" she says as we sit on the loveseat.

"Sorry? About what?"

"I was trying to get you some alone time with Chris when we left. I'm sorry I didn't manage to drag Jack away from you two."

"It's okay," I say. "We didn't stay that much longer anyway, and when Jack finally left, Chris walked me home."

"Oooh, romantic!"

"You have no idea." I tell her everything that happened, not leaving out any detail, from the back alley cigarettes to Jack's boozer parents to Chris's hug and the pork chop that's still waiting for me in the fridge.

"Wow," Zoey finally says. "You've had quite the day, huh?"

"Yeah."

"So what's next?"

With great confidence I look at her and say, "I have no freaking idea whatsoever."

"I mean, we know that Chris is gay, and he probably wouldn't tell you that you smell nice if he found you, like, totally repulsive, right?"

"Yeah," I say, "I get that."

"So when are you gonna tell him that you're gay?"

"I ... I don't know. I'll need to wait for the right moment, you know?"

"No," Zoey says, "actually I don't know. What's the right moment?"

"I mean, I will obviously want to be alone with him, and you've seen how difficult it is to get rid of Jack. And I'm sure as hell not gonna do it with Jack around."

"Fair enough."

"So yeah."

Zoey sighs. "If only you had his phone number or something."

"I do have his number actually," I say and immediately bite my tongue. I withheld that information earlier, and for a good reason, too.

"What? Since when?"

"He gave it to me earlier."

"Well, there you go then. What are you waiting for, you idiot? Call him right now and tell him!"

"Nah," I say. "I can't do that."

"Why not?"

"Well, first of all, I'm talking to you right now."

"Oh shut up! You're not gonna make me one of your convenient excuses."

"I'm not making ..."

"Damn right you're not!" She jumps to her feet. "Get on the phone right now and then ... well, get on the phone and call Chris. You can thank me later. Bye!"

She leaves the room.

I pick up my phone and hold it in my hand, one minute, two minutes, five minutes. I open my contacts and scroll down to C as in Chris. My thumb hovers over his number, then retreats.

Rinse, repeat.

Twice, three times.

The fourth time, my thumb inadvertently twitches, and the phone begins to dial. My thumb keeps hovering, and I'm about to tap disconnect but it's too late. Chris answers after the second ring.

"Hello?"

"Hi," I say.

"Who is this?"

"It's Matt."

"Matt who?" he says. "I don't know any Matt."

I'm at a loss for words for a few moments until Chris bursts into laughter.

"Sorry, I'm just messing with you! Hey, Matty, what's up?"

"Oh," I say and force a laugh, "you got me there. For a moment I thought ..."

"What?"

"You know, that you already forgot about me or something."

"How could I ever forget you, Matty?" he says, and I'm melting away. "So what's up?"

"Nothing," I say.

"Oh, okay then. Well, thanks for your call. Bye!"

"No, wait! Listen, I've been meaning to ask you something."

"Sure," Chris says, "ask away."

"It's ..." I have no idea where I'm going with this, or how to get there. "Look, you went to Littlefield, right?"

"I did."

"Right. So, my best friend's cousin went to Littlefield too, and ..."

"Oh yeah?" Chris interrupts me. "What's his name?"

"My friend? Alfonso."

"No, the cousin."

"Oh, right. Alfredo. Alfredo Salazar."

"Right! I remember Alfredo. So what about him?"

"Well, Alfredo says ... well, he told Alfonso about ... about your last birthday party."

"Did he now?" Chris says. "That's interesting. I don't even think he was invited, but hey, what do I know?"

"He wasn't, but ..."

"Yes?"

"I don't know, word got around I guess."

"And what word is that?" Chris asks. He knows exactly what I'm getting at, but he wants to hear it from me.

"That word would be … gay, I guess."

"Gay?"

"Alfredo says you came out to your friends and family on your birthday."

"Is that a question?" I hear him smiling.

"No, I guess my question is, is that true?"

"Yeah," he says, and for some reason my heart starts beating faster, as if I hadn't known the answer before.

"Oh, okay."

Chris snickers. "So, is that a problem?"

"Oh, no, no!" I hurry to say. "No problem. Not at all. I was just … curious, that's all."

"All right then."

A few moments of awkward silence. Then, before I even know it, I hear myself say, "Listen, um, I had a great time at the Korova today, so thanks for asking me along."

"No problem. I had a great time too."

"Yeah, it's just … it was a bit of a crowd, wasn't it? So I was wondering, um … I mean, maybe we could repeat it some time, but without the entourage?"

"Why Matty!" Chris says in a teasing voice. "Are you asking me out on a date?"

"Um … no, I was just thinking … you know, nothing big. Just a quick milkshake and a muffin or … or something."

"But just you and me?"

"Yeah."

Chris laughs. "Where I come from we call that a date, Matty."

"Oh," I say. "Well then … Yeah, I guess I'm asking you out on a date. So what do you say?"

And he says, "Sure. I'd love to."

"Awesome." There is more awkward silence, so I decide to call it a day before I blow it all by saying something really stupid. "All right, I guess I'll see you at school tomorrow."

"Sure."

"Good night."

"Nighty night, Matty."

I end the call, throw my phone on the bed, punch the air three times and sound my barbaric yawp over the roofs of the world.

"Shut up!" I hear Greg shout through the wall, but I really couldn't care less.

Chapter Eight

When the bell rings at the end of another of Mrs. Spelczik's classes, Chris, Jack, and Steve hurry out of the room like they always do at the beginning of lunch break.

"What's with these guys?" Sandy wonders. "Always the first out of the classroom and the last in the cafeteria. So weird."

With two fingers at his mouth, Alfonso mimics dragging on a cigarette.

Sandy frowns, then it dawns on her. "You mean they're smoking?"

Alfonso nods. "Behind the gym."

"That is so unhealthy." She puts her hand on my arm. "Please tell me you don't smoke."

"I don't," I assure her.

The day after our group date at the Korova, Chris had asked me to join him, Jack, and Steve for a smoke behind the gym but I respectfully declined. While I love spending time with Chris, the smell of cigarette smoke remains a major turn-off, and although there have been no further clashes with Jack, I'm still reluctant to give him more opportunities to be offended by my mere existence, so I try to stay out of his way if I can.

We are strolling down the crowded hallway toward the cafeteria, talking about our term papers, when Sandy asks, "So have you read Romeo and Juliet before?"

I'm about to answer when I realize she wasn't asking me. Her question was directed at Philip who is walking a step behind us like an ugly duckling.

"Yes," he says in a low, nasal voice.

"Great. Maybe you can teach Matt a thing or two about love," Alfonso says with a smirk. "He needs it."

I glare at him.

He shrugs. "What?"

"Why would you say that?"

"Why wouldn't I?" he replies. Then he puts his arm around my neck, yanks me into a headlock, gives me a noogie, and kisses my bruised head before he lets go of me again.

Seriously, how *do* straight people get away with that kind of thing?

At the entrance to the cafeteria, Zoey joins us. As we line up to get our food, Philip is about to leave us and move on to the table under the stairs in the corner where he usually spends his lunch break alone, but Zoey holds him back.

"Aren't you gonna get anything?" she asks.

He shakes his head.

"But you need to eat something. Aren't you hungry?"

"I'm fine," he says, skillfully dodging the question, but we all know he's not fine. He's poor.

"At least have some orange juice or something," Zoey says. "Would you like some orange juice?"

He doesn't say no quickly enough, so Zoey grabs a glass of freshly squeezed orange juice and puts it on her tray. "Are you sure you don't want to eat anything?"

"Really, it's okay."

Zoey shrugs, grabs her lunch and pays. Philip follows us to our regular table and reluctantly sits between Zoey and me.

"Oh, Philip," Sandy says, sitting opposite him. When he looks at her she bows her head at him and says, "Ni hao! Zuì jìn hào ma?"

While Jason next to her cringes, Philip looks at Sandy with an empty face. "I'm from Laos."

"Isn't that in China?"

Jason laughs, shaking his head. "Oh, Sandy!"

"Well, excuse me. I've never been good at geography," Sandy says and shrugs. "Sorry, Philip."

"It's okay," Philip says. "Laos is south of China, between Thailand and Vietnam."

"Oh," Sandy says. "Well, at least I wasn't a million miles off."

Zoey looks at Philip. "So you were born in Laos?"

Philip nods.

"And when did your family come to the United States?"

"When I was two."

As Philip keeps answering Zoey's questions sparingly like a witness in cross-examination, I see Chris, Jack, and Steve enter the cafeteria. They get their lunches and then come straight over to our table.

"Well, well, well," Jack says as he puts down his tray at the end of the table. "Who have we here? If it isn't Miss Saigon the Vietcong-Thong."

The reactions to Jack's trolling are pretty diverse. Phil lowers his eyes and sips his orange juice, pretending nothing's wrong. In pan-Asian solidarity, Jason also lowers his eyes and looks embarrassed on Philip's behalf. Steve laughs, Chris smirks, and Alfonso rolls his eyes and shakes his head. And Zoey doesn't deign to even look at Jack as she says, "That is so offensive, Jack."

"Besides," Sandy chimes in, "Philip is from Laos."

"Laos?" Steve frowns. "Where the hell is that?"

"It's south of China, between Vietnam and Taiwan."

"Thailand!" Jason corrects her.

"Yeah, that."

"See?" Jack says. "Vietnam, just like I said."

Now Zoey looks at him. "It's rude and insulting to call him … what you just called him."

"Well, what else am I supposed to call him then?"

"He's got a name, you know?"

"Ooooh!" Jack says, feigning sudden enlightenment. "Why didn't you say so? Hey, Thong, what's your name again?"

"Philip."

"Philip, huh? Well, that's a bit clunky, isn't it? We all have nicknames around here. Christian is Chris, Steven is Steve, Matthew is Maddie. So how about I'm gonna call you … Philippino?"

"He's not from the Philippines!" Sandy says.

"All right, all right," Jack says. "Fair enough. I'll just call him Lip then."

As Chris' smirk widens into a grin and Steve almost falls off his chair laughing, the rest of us are aghast.

"You're such an asshole, Jack," Zoey says.

Jack shrugs like an innocent choirboy. "Why? It's an affectionate abbreviation of his name. Isn't that right, Lip?"

I don't dare look at Philip because it's just too painful, but from the corner of my eye I can see that he's getting smaller and smaller until he's suddenly getting taller as he slowly rises from his chair, ready to walk away.

Somebody should tell him to stay.

Somebody should tell him to sit back down again and not pay any attention to the mean and offensive bullshit of some pompous jackass who has never had anything nice to say about anyone in his entire, miserable life.

Somebody should stand up for Philip, and I know it should be me even if it's for no other reason than that it would be the right and decent thing to do. But I can't seem to bring myself to do it, and it's making me feel awful.

I didn't want him to join us at our table in the first place. Everyone knows that if you feed a stray dog you're never ever going to get rid of him. It may be a cold and cruel way to look at things, but I have too many other things on my mind to take the weight of the entire world upon my narrow shoulders.

"Philip," Zoey says, "don't go. Don't listen to that jackass."

Philip shakes his head, puts on a forced smile and says, "It's okay." Then he walks away and goes to sit alone at his usual table in the far corner of the cafeteria.

Zoey glares at Jack. "Well done, asshole!"

"What?" Jack says and shrugs. "Not my fault if he can't take a little joke."

"Screw your little jokes, Jack. Just because your parents are both boozers and beat you up all the time it doesn't give you an excuse to take it out on other people!"

Despite the busy cafeteria background noise, the pin that drops on our table sounds like thunder. Everyone stares either at Zoey, who looks like she realizes she may have gone a step too far, or at Jack whose face is turning a dark shade of crimson.

Everyone except Chris.

Chris is staring at me, knowing this particular piece of sensitive information about Jack's family situation could only have come from me. Unable to stand his accusing glare, I look at my lunch tray and play with my peas.

I hate peas.

I hate them almost as much as I hate my life right now.

* * *

After the last period of the day, Chris and Jack are waiting for me outside of the classroom. Surprisingly, they're not waiting for me to beat me up for telling Zoey about Jack's parents, but to walk with me to the locker rooms. I appreciate the gesture, but I have something else to take care of first.

"I'll catch up with you guys, okay?"

While Jack scowls at me, Chris's facial expression is ambiguous. He neither smiles nor frowns. "Suit yourself," he says. I'm trying to detect any emotion in his tone but there seems to be none, and I have no idea if that's good or bad.

I make my way downstairs, run out of the building and turn the corner into Harper. There he is, standing by the roadside under his umbrella. My jog slows into a walk, and when Philip turns his head to look down the street in expectation of his dad's old clunker, our eyes meet. He holds my gaze for a moment while he seems to ponder if he should acknowledge my presence or not. In the end he turns his head back toward the street.

"Hey," I say as I reach him.

He looks at me, expressionless.

"I'm sorry about earlier."

"Why?" he says, which perplexes me. I didn't expect I'd had to explain to him what happened.

"Well, you know, the way things went down at lunch."

"You didn't even say anything, so what are you apologizing for?"

"Maybe I should have said something."

"Why?" he asks.

I shrug. "Because it wasn't fair to just sit there and say nothing when Jack was being mean to you."

Philip looks at the street. "Don't worry about it."

"No, seriously," I say. "Jack can be an ass. I've known him my entire life, and I've received my fair share of abuse from him, so I know what it's like."

"Do you?" He turns his face back towards me, and I'm pretty sure he does it to remind me of his cleft lip and that I couldn't possibly have any idea what it must be like to have a face like that and to have it made fun of on a daily basis.

"Look, Jack has a lot of issues, and he likes to take it out on other people. Just don't listen to him. It's not worth getting all worked up about it."

"I wasn't."

"I know. I mean, I'm just saying."

Again, he turns away, showing no interest in my plight whatsoever.

"Look," I say, "I'm making an effort here."

He looks at me. "Why?"

His question leaves me speechless.

Speechless and offended. I came to talk to him make us both feel better. Now I'm feeling worse, and Philip doesn't seem to have any feelings at all.

As Mr. Thongrivong finally pulls up in his old clunker, the voice of Coach Gutierrez sounds across the fence. "Dunstan! Get your ass over here right now or you're out!"

As I turn around and run, Special Agent Nicole Tesla is cruising past me in her shiny black car, thinking I don't notice.

* * *

Hello Handsome! I liked the new chapter. It was fun to see Matt excel in track & field only to have his proud excitement crushed by the Jackrabbit's homophobic outburst. But oh, such a nifty way to keep him out of the shower. Yes, I'm looking at you! Don't you think I don't know that it was you who weaseled your way out of that shower scene, not our hormone driven Matty. I'm letting you get away with it this time, Handsome, but you know you will eventually have to let it happen, yes? Anyways, so Matty is finally getting somewhere with his non-plan. Chris gave him a hug. I was hoping they will take it one step further and that there would be a kiss, just a little kiss, but no such luck. Oh well, maybe next time, yes? I'll say no more until then. xoxo

2-b-pretty

Mattoid2002

Thanks again for your feedback, Pretty! Please keep it coming. I'm sorry the shower scene didn't happen at this time, but it wasn't meant to be. You see, the thing is: my stories tend to develop a life of their own and then I just follow them wherever they take me, so I'm afraid I can't accept any responsibility for the canceled shower scene, or anything else for that matter. >.o Anyway, I got news for you: looking at Matty's whole situation, I don't see a quick an easy solution forthcoming. Things are way too complicated already, and they're getting more complicated every day. Speaking of which, I just posted another chapter. I hope you'll like it. Looking forward to your comments, as always. xoxo

Chapter Nine

My knees are shaking as I enter the Korova, mostly because I'm walking into a well-known gay milk bar in the middle of town, in the light of day. In this day and age that kind of thing should be a non-issue, and for most people it probably is. Then again, I'm not most people.

This is what it must feel like if you're some obscure sound editor walking the red carpet at the Oscars. It may feel as if the whole world is watching you when in fact nobody has any idea who you are, and they don't care much, either.

"Why hello, sugar!" Milo greets me with his hands on his hips, his head cocked sideways, a bright smile on his glistening lips.

I nod at him bashfully and look around. The booth in the corner where we sat the last time is empty except for a lonely, untouched strawberry milkshake on the table.

I look at my watch.

"Chris couldn't wait for you any longer," Milo says, "so he went to the restroom. If you know what I mean."

He makes an unambiguously suggestive movement with his hand in front of his crotch. Having no idea how to deal with lewd jokes appropriately, I react to Milo's remark the only way I know how: I turn my ears the color of a fire hydrant.

Pointing at the corner table I ask, "Is that his table?"

"It sure is, sugar. Can I get you anything?"

"I'll have what he's having."

"Of course you will," Milo says with a wide smile.

I walk to our table and sit. After a few moments Chris comes back from the restroom. He smiles as he sees me, and I smile back.

"Hey," he says and slides into his seat opposite me.

His T-shirt reads *Gay Bae.*

"Sorry I'm late."

"Are you?" He looks at his watch. "I just got here myself, so no worries."

With the new school year in full swing we were struggling to find a slot for our first date, and even the one we picked is sandwiched between other commitments. He has a dentist appointment later, and I have to meet up with Philip at the library, but Chris doesn't know that.

Milo comes and places my milkshake in front of me. "There you are, sugar. Enjoy."

"Thanks."

He blows me an air kiss, then he looks at Chris. "Just the two of you today?"

"Yeah, just us today," Chris says.

"All riiiight," Milo says with his eyebrows raised and a big grin on his face. "I'm gonna give you some privacy then. Threesomes are overrated anyway."

He turns and leaves. Chris looks at me. "You're blushing."

"I know! I'm blushing all the time. Don't rub it in. I'm not used to having all that sexual innuendo in my life."

"You'll get used to it."

I'm not sure if I can or if I even want to, so I just smile politely and suck on my milkshake.

"So listen," I say, trying not to look him in the eyes. "About earlier ..." I pause, waiting for him to preemptively shake his head or wave his hand dismissively and say something gracious like, 'Oh, don't worry about walking around and telling people about Jack's darkest family secrets that you're not even supposed to know. No biggie.' But although I'm sure he knows what it is I'm trying to confess, he's not doing me the favor of making it any easier on me.

"What about earlier?" he asks.

"You know ... about Jack. I mean, what Zoey said to Jack. About his parents. She knew that from me."

Chris nods, his bright smile waning. "I thought she might."

"We're really close, you know? She's basically my best friend. I tell her everything, and I didn't expect her to use that knowledge against Jack. She usually doesn't do that kind of thing. Blabbing, I mean."

"I see," Chris says. "Well, it was a pretty stupid move, but good to know. I guess in the future I'll have to be more selective about the information I share with my little chatterbox."

It's not exactly the kind of reaction I was hoping for. I was expecting him to be more forgiving.

"I'm really sorry," I say sheepishly.

"Yeah, well," he says, "let's not talk about it anymore."

Not to be nitpicky, but there's a subtle difference between forgetting about something and simply not mentioning it anymore. Chris isn't doing anything to alleviate my nagging feeling of guilt. In fact, he's doing the exact opposite, and I hate how he wants to move on when this is clearly something we should talk about. I'm beginning to think our first date couldn't have been off to a worse start.

"So your sister is your best friend, huh?" Chris says. "That's funny. I thought your best friend was … that Mexican dude."

"Alfonso," I say. "And he's Argentinian."

"Right." He says and shrugs. "Whatever."

"Anyway, they both are my best friends."

"Wait, but you didn't tell Alfonso about Jack's domestic problems too, did you?"

"Oh, no!" I hurry to confirm. "I … no, of course not."

"Good. I'd hate to run into the same awkward situation again."

I thought we weren't going to talk about this anymore. Apparently I was mistaken.

"So why not?"

I'm not sure what he means. "Hm?"

"If they're both your best friends then why did you tell Zoey but not Alfonso?"

"I don't know." I shrug. "Some stuff you share with some people, other stuff with others, I guess."

"I see." After a pause he asks, "So which one of them knows you're gay?"

I'm aghast. I know, I know. I'm sitting with an openly gay friend in an openly gay milk bar, but that kind of question still freaks me out.

"Why would you think I'm gay?" I ask and suck on my milkshake.

"I don't even know what it is, but it never even occurred to me that you're not gay, to be honest."

"But why, though? Do I flail my arms around when I talk? Do I sound gay? Do I walk like a gay person? I don't get it."

Chris grins. "You're no Albert Goldman, if that makes you feel any better."

"Who?"

He looks at me as if I'd just ask him who Harry Potter is. "Have you never watched *The Birdcage*?"

I shake my head and shrug. Chris pulls out his phone, taps the screen a couple of times and then shows me a YouTube clip of the late Robin Williams and an extremely effeminate guy who, as it so happens, isn't even a complete stranger to me.

"Oh," I say, "I know that guy! He's got a recurring role on *Modern Family*. I just didn't know his name was Albert Goldberg."

"Goldman. And his name is Nathan Lane. His character's name in *The Birdcage* is Albert Goldman."

"Right." I laugh awkwardly. "Sorry, I'm more of a book type. But I'm not anything like that Goldbergman guy, am I?"

"Yeah, that was my point," Chris says and puts the phone away. "But I don't know, you have certain mannerisms. Most people probably won't even notice it, so don't worry about it, but for someone with a functioning gaydar it's not too difficult to figure out. Remember how I winked at you in the entrance hall on the first day of school? You looked away and your head turned bright red. A straight guy would have reacted in a totally different way, so that was the first clue. And then the way you reacted when Jack called you a faggot, same thing. I didn't really have any doubts anymore after that."

"I see."

"So who else knows?" he asks. "I mean officially."

I shake my head. "Nobody. Just Zoey."

"Alfonso left out of the loop again, huh? So is he, like, your best friend for all the unimportant stuff?"

I feel tension rise in my body. We're moving on very thin ice here, both of us.

Under normal circumstances, anyone who dared to question my friendship with Alfonso or how important that friendship is to me would have a lot to answer for.

But these are not normal circumstances.

Chris is not a normal circumstance.

Our date was off to a bumpy start. I don't want to send it down the drain for good, so I will have to swallow my annoyance for the time being.

"I talk with Alfonso about all sorts of important stuff," I say, "but ... look, I've known him my entire life, and I love him. But only as a friend, you know? I'm afraid that if I tell him I'm gay ..."

"... he'll think you're hitting on him."

I nod. "You know ... there are some things, like ... when we haven't seen each other in a while we hug. I like hugging him. It makes me feel close to him, and there's nothing sexual about it. I don't want to lose that. But if I tell him I'm gay, I'm afraid things will change."

"Yeah, maybe you shouldn't tell him that," Chris says.

I frown. "What do you mean? Not tell him I'm gay?"

"No, you totally should tell him you're gay, if he really is the friend you think he is. What I meant is, you shouldn't tell him that you didn't tell him you're gay because you were afraid it would affect your friendship in a negative way. Because that's like telling him you didn't trust him, and that might be worse than telling him you're gay."

"I never looked at it that way," I say.

"Just tell him you're gay. If he's the friend you think he is, he'll be fine with it. And if he doesn't want to hug you anymore, then maybe he's not that good a friend after all."

I understand what he's trying to say, but I almost find it offensive to have him question the loyalty of my best friend. It's rude and presumptuous.

But he is so cute though, so I'm not saying anything, even though I'm dying to prove him wrong. Incidentally, the opportunity to do so presents itself sooner than expected.

My phone rings. After a quick look at the screen I answer it and say, "¡Hola!"

"¿Que pasa, Guapo?" Alfonso asks.

"Nothing."

"Wanna hang out?"

"Sure," I say, and I immediately bite my tongue. My reply was a reflex because it's what I always say when Alfonso wants to hang out with me. "Except not right now. I'm still busy with something."

Chris raises his eyebrow at being called *something*, but he also points at his cheek to remind me of his dentist appointment.

"How about in an hour?" I say.

"All right. Wanna come over to my place?"

"Yeah, sure."

"Okay then, see you later."

I end the call and place my phone on the table.

"Someone's pretty popular," Chris says.

"Not really," I say. "That was Alfonso."

"Speak of the devil, huh?"

"Yeah. He wants to hang out."

"Oh really? Good thing I have a dentist appointment, huh?"

"Yeah."

He reaches across the table and playfully slaps me on the head. "That was a trick question! There's nothing good about my dentist appointment! I hate dentists!"

"Right," I say sheepishly. "Sorry."

"So," Chris says and looks me right in the eyes, "are you gonna tell him?"

Shaking my head, I say, "I don't know."

"I understand it's a big step and I understand you're scared of his reaction, but that reaction is his to make, not yours to assume. You have to at least give him the chance to accept you the way you are. Or not."

"I know," I say, looking at my fingernails.

They're pristine, except for one torn cuticle.

"And besides, if you and I … I mean, if we're to spend more time together in the future, I want to be on good terms with your best friend. And that will be difficult if we have to keep hiding things from him. That's not good for us, and it's not good for your friendship with Alfonso. I mean, I'm not expecting you to climb on a table in the school cafeteria during lunch time and make a big announcement or anything. Whatever is happening between you and me is nobody's business as far as the general public is concerned. But your friends? I mean, come on."

Too many thoughts are zigzagging through my mind, and there are too many things I want to say or ask. I have to pick one, and it's, "What *is* happening between you and me?"

Chris shrugs and smiles. "Whatever we want."

"Right," I say.

He looks at me for a few moments, then he says, "I like you, Matthew Dunstan."

I swallow. My heart is pounding like a jackhammer, and I actually do want to jump on the table and shout it out to the world, but I'm a wuss, so I say in what is barely a whisper, "I like you too, Christian Larsen."

For a long moment, a very long moment, we look each other in the eyes. His smile becomes more subtle, his blue eyes deeper than the ocean. I want to drown in his eyes, in my thoughts, my feelings, my awkward, awesome feelings. I want to sit here forever and just stare at him, his eyes, his lips, his hair and everything else that's so perfect about him. I want to grab his hand, drag him out of this place and run, run out of the Korova, out of Brookhurst and run, just run to the end of the world. Leave everything and everyone behind, wrap my arms around him and never let him go again. Ever.

But this is not happening, at least not today.

We're not running anywhere today, except out of time.

When it's time to part, Chris plants an awkward kiss on my cheek. Then he runs off to see his dentist, and he takes all my euphoria with him, because the moment he turns the corner and disappears from my longing view, I fall out of my cloud-cuckoo-land and hurtle toward the stony ground.

Alfonso is sitting at home, waiting for me. Having someone sitting at home and waiting for you is a nice and comforting thing.

If you're fifty-five.

I'm fifteen, and my life is a mess. I said yes to a play date with Alfonso when I knew I already had a work date with Philip. It was a stupid thing to do, born out of my desire to show Chris how awesome my friendship with Alfonso is. And hey, it worked, didn't it? Except solving one problem created another.

I can't bail on Alfonso. He's my best friend.

I can't bail on Philip either. He's not my friend, but we have to work on our term paper together for the next few weeks whether we want to or not, and if I don't show up at the library for our very first work date he'll probably think I didn't come because his face freaks me out. It does, but that's not the reason why I can't come to the library, and I don't want him to think it is. And I can't call him to make up some flimsy excuse because he doesn't carry a cellphone in his fancy fake Louis Vuitton bag.

Alfonso doesn't have a Louis Vuitton bag, but he does have a cell phone, so I pull out my phone and speed dial his number.

"Hey," I say when he answers, "listen …"

"I'm listening."

"I … something came up. I can't make it today."

"What happened?" he asks.

"It's … I got grounded. Long story, don't ask."

"Oh, okay. You want me to come over to your place?"

"No!" I say way too loud and too quickly, so I tone it down a notch. "I mean, that would be awesome, but … I'm in solitary confinement. No visitors allowed."

"Oh boy. That sounds pretty bad. What have you done this time?"

Stop asking questions, goddamnit! I got no answers!

"Uh … like I said, it's a long story. I'll explain later, because I'm actually not allowed to use the phone either, so … sorry, I really gotta go now."

"Oh well, all right then, 24601. I guess I'll see you at school tomorrow."

24601 is the prisoner number of Jean Valjean in *Les Misérables*.

I made Alfonso watch the movie with me under the not exactly false but nevertheless ostensible pretense that it's a marvelous example of great storytelling.

The real reason was that I love show tunes.

And that I had a crush on Marius Pontmercy.

"See you tomorrow," I say. "Bye."

I end the call, and feeling even more miserable than the miserables in *Les Misérables* for having lied to my best friend, I make my way to the library to meet freaky-faced Philip.

CHAPTER TEN

When I arrive I find him standing in front of the library under his umbrella, his fake Louis Vuitton handbag hanging from the fold of his arm. Motionless like a sculpture by some obscure modern artist, he's staring at the street. He doesn't even see me coming, and for a moment I just want to walk past him and pretend that I have nothing to do with that weirdo.

But I can't do that, obviously.

"Hey," I say as I approach him.

With a blank look on his face he twangs, "Hello."

"So ..." I put my hands in my pockets, unsure how to proceed, but Philip just turns and walks toward the library entrance. I follow him like a clueless duckling. I don't like to be in that kind of position, not with someone like Philip, so on the stairs to the second floor I take two steps at a time and put myself in front of him. When we reach the landing, I stop and look around. Philip walks straight past me to one of the workstations and takes a seat. He waits until I've caught up with him. The seat next to him is taken, so I remain standing, lean into him and put my hand on the computer mouse.

"All right," I say, "I guess we best start with Google. That's a search engine. We can use it to—"

"I know what Google is," Philip interrupts me.

He looks at the screen and nudges my hand away from the mouse so he can use it. The moment he touches me I withdraw my hand as if from a burning candle.

He types 'Romeo Juliet character development' into Google. After a quick scan of the results page he quickly opens the second, third, and fifth search result in new tabs. Then he looks at me. "We should both do our research independently and then compare our results later."

"Right," I say, feeling like a stupid little kid. There's a free workstation opposite of Phil's, so I walk around the table and sit down. I'm about to start typing when out of nowhere someone kisses me on the cheek. Startled, I turn to look at ...

"Sandy!"

"Hi," she whispers with a smile. Then she looks at Phil and waves at him. He acknowledges her with a barely noticeable nod.

"Sandy," I whisper, "what are you doing here?"

"Urgh, don't ask," she says. "Last week our Internet died and Comcast is too stupid to fix it. And I've already blown my entire mobile data allowance for this month on YouTube, so I have to come here to check my email and stuff."

"Oh. Bummer."

"I know, right? So what are you guys doing here?"

"Nothing," I say. "Just working on our term paper."

"Oh, okay. You got *Romeo and Juliet*, right?"

"Yeah."

"Lucky you," Sandy says. "At least you got something romantic. Jason and I got freaking *Macbeth!*"

"Oh. A tale told by an idiot, huh?"

Sandy frowns. "I don't think Shakespeare was an idiot, Matthew."

"Uh, that was actually a quote from *Macbeth*," I say. "He calls life a tale told by an idiot. I was joking. Never mind."

"You are so funny and clever, Matthew!" she says, slapping my arm. "But anyway, I think the librarian lady is about to kick us out because we keep talking, so I better go."

"All right then, see you later."

"See you later guys," Sandy whispers, waves at an unresponsive Phil again and finds herself a workstation across the room.

I turn back to my computer monitor and start sorting through my search results.

On the other side of the table, Philip keeps typing and clicking and scrolling and scribbling things down on a

116

notepad. Behind both of our computer screens I can only see his eyes, his forehead, and his mop of thick black hair, and I catch myself thinking that if you ignore the cleft lip and the cauliflower nose, he's not even all that ugly.

When he catches me staring at him I quickly avert my gaze and look around the library. Apart from us there are maybe a dozen people around, most of them middle-aged or older. On a workstation by the window on the opposite side of the library, Sandy is typing away on her keyboard.

My phone buzzes in my pocket. I take it out and look at the screen. 2-b-pretty has left a comment on the latest chapter.

Congratulations to Matty on securing that valuable spot as third runner in the relay team. Best place on the whole track because once he's handed the baton over to Chris he can just keep running after him and watch him shake his booty.

2-b-pretty

It's not even all that funny, but for some reason picturing that scene cracks me up. Sometimes—especially when you're in a shitty mood to begin with—the silliest things can make you literally laugh out loud before you even remember you're sitting in that temple of silence that is a public library.

Instantly, a dozen pairs of eyes from all around the library are on me with piercing, accusing looks. I wince and place my hand over my mouth. Opposite me Philip scowls, and on the other side of the room Sandy is silently laughing at me and shaking her head.

"Sorry," I whisper to no one in particular, trying to withdraw my head between my shoulders like a turtle. As the reproachful eyeballs divert from me, I type a quick reply to 2-b-pretty.

Mattoid2002

Your comment about watching Chris's booty made me laugh out loud, and now the whole library is staring at me. This is all your fault! :P

I hit send and slide the phone back in my pocket. When I look up, I catch Philip staring at me, his head raised above his computer monitor, and something is off. It's not the infamous blank stare anymore. All of a sudden there is something in his eyes that I can't quite put my finger on, and I have no idea what it's supposed to mean.

"What?" I say.

"Are you done with your research?" he whispers.

I shake my head.

"Well, get on with it then!"

"Jesus Christ," I utter under my breath as his head disappears behind the monitor again.

A minute later my phone buzzes again.

"I have done no harm. But I remember now I am in this earthly world, where to do harm is often laudable, to do good sometime accounted dangerous folly. "
Now stop messaging me and get back to work or whatever else it is you have to do at the library!

2-b-pretty

Mattoid2002

Why is everyone so bossy today? I'm actually here because I have to work on this stupid school assignment with that freaky weirdo from my class.

I hit send again, and this time I place the phone on the table, hoping that 2-b-pretty is still online and will reply quickly. I turn my attention back to *Romeo and Juliet*, but I can't seem to concentrate. There's something about 2-b-pretty's last comment that tickles the back of my mind, so I pick up my phone and read it again.

I don't know why, I don't know what, but something is off. I've come to know—and indeed love—2-b-pretty for her occasionally quirky language, but this sounds too weird even by her standards. And why is she using quotation marks? Suddenly a strange suspicion besets my curious mind, so I put my phone back on the table and type the quotation into Google. The result knocks the wind out of me.

Macbeth, Act IV, Scene II.

Faster than I can think I jump to my feet and look across the room.

Sandy is gone.

Phil stares at me as if I've lost my mind.

Maybe I have.

"I have to go," I say.

He frowns. "What?"

"I have to go. Sorry, something came up. I'll see you tomorrow."

Without waiting for a reply, I grab my backpack, turn around and run down the stairs and outside. I look up and down Broadway, but Sandy is nowhere to be seen. I make my way to the corner of Broadway and Madison, but there's still no sign of her.

Does Sandy have a bike? If she has a bike she could be miles away by now. Or just half a mile if she went straight home. Without giving it much thought, I run. I run until I'm standing in front of her house, sweating, and panting like a dog. The garage door is closed, the windows are closed, there is no sign of life inside. Not even when I ring the bell and knock on the door. There's nobody here, which means Sandy's not here, but I need to talk to her, so I want to give her a call.

But where's my phone?

I check the front and back pockets of my pants, I check the side pockets of my backpack. I check the inside of my backpack even though I know there's no way I put my phone inside my backpack without remembering it. I know I didn't. I put it on the table at the library, next to the computer keyboard.

And I forgot to pick it up when I left in a hurry.

Damn!

I make my way back to the library and up to the second floor. It's been only about twenty minutes since I left, but my phone is not where I left it, and neither is Philip. I approach the librarian, a fifty- or sixty- or seventy-year-old lady with gray hair and a sky blue turtleneck sweater. When I ask her if somebody found a phone and left it with her, she glances at me over the golden rim of her glasses.

"You're not allowed to use your phone at the library, dear," she says, pointing at a sign on the wall. The sign is self-printed and laminated, and it shows a crossed-out, stylized cell phone with a tiny screen, a dedicated keypad, and a freaking antenna!

"Yes," I say, "but has somebody found a phone and left it with you?"

She shakes her head slowly. "No, dear, I'm sorry."

My heart sinking to the bottom of the deepest ocean, I turn around and walk back out into the scorching afternoon sun. It's way too hot for October, and I'm way too stupid to be alive.

How could I have left my phone on the table and just run away? Without my phone I'm deaf and blind. My only hope is that maybe somehow Philip noticed that I left my phone and picked it up, but I don't know where he lives so I won't know until I see him at school tomorrow. All I can do until then is … nothing.

I start wandering around aimlessly.

I don't feel like going home and telling my parents that I probably lost their four-hundred-dollar Christmas gift, and I think I could use a bit of fresh air to help me make sense of what just happened.

I mean, what happened just before I lost my phone.

Sandy?

Could it be that Sandy is 2-b-pretty?

Maybe I'm missing something.

Or maybe I'm seeing something that isn't there.

The quirky language in 2-b-pretty's messages doesn't sound like anything I've ever heard Sandy say. Then again, when I look at my own online personality I don't even recognize myself sometimes. 2-b-pretty's language might be Sandy's way of very skillfully trying to conceal her real identity. Heck, it might be *anyone*'s way of very skillfully trying to conceal their identity. In fact, it might be an FBI agent's way of very skillfully concealing their identity.

What if 2-b-pretty is Special Agent Nicole Tesla on assignment to investigate my violations of U.S. obscenity laws by way of distributing my teenage sexual fantasies via the Internet when I posted them on freaking Wattpad?

What if Special Agent Nicole Tesla is Sandy in a dark wig?

Wait, what?

This is getting out of hand, and it has to stop.

This impossible charade has to stop, and the only way to stop it is to confront Sandy head on. Now.

Well, maybe not totally head on and not *right* now. I don't have my phone, so I can't text her, and if I write to her on Wattpad, she won't be able to read it until after school tomorrow. I can't just walk up to her at school and tell her I know she's 2-b-pretty, because at school we'll have neither the time nor the privacy for the discussion that would inevitably ensue. And I don't want to go all in anyway, because of that minute 0.01% chance that I'm missing something, something really big and obvious.

What I could do, though, is to write to her on Wattpad and tell her I think I might know who she is, and then drop a few hints at school tomorrow. Yes! That way I'm not revealing anything that she might not know after all, and I'm leaving all my options open. Oh, the cleverness of me! I need to get on my computer before I change my mind and before I confuse myself even more by thinking about the whole thing too much, so I turn around and make my way back home.

CHAPTER ELEVEN

The sight of Philip standing on the sidewalk in front of my house, holding his umbrella in one hand and his handbag in the other, almost startles me, yet at the same time it rekindles my hope that maybe he found my phone after all. As I approach him he turns his head and looks at me, expressionless as ever. Before I can get to him, the front door opens and my mom steps outside.

"Matthew," she says, "can I have a word?"

"Give me a second," I say to Philip and walk over to her.

"Do you know this boy, Matthew?" she whispers.

"Yes, that's Lip ... I mean, Phil. I mean, Philip. The guy I have to work with on my term paper. Why?"

"I see," she says, casting a quick glance at him before leaning in to me. "He says he found your phone."

"Yeah, I left it on the table at the library. Thank God! I was hoping he'd found it. But why is he still here?"

"Because he didn't want to give it to me. He insisted on handing it back to you personally. He's been standing there the entire time."

I frown at her. "What do you mean, the entire time? How long?"

"Almost two hours!"

I look at my watch, and for a moment I'm not sure what stumps me more, the fact that I've been wandering around town for two hours or the fact that Philip has been standing in front of my house like a living statue the whole time.

"That's a bit weird, don't you think?" Mom says.

"Well, that's Philip for you. Let me talk to him."

I walk back to him, hands in my pockets. "So, I hear you found my phone?"

"Yes," he says, cradling his umbrella between his neck and shoulder, fishing my phone out of his handbag and handing it over.

"Thanks. You really could have left it with my mom, you know?"

"I thought maybe you don't want your mom to check your phone and read your emails and messages and everything."

For a moment I'm tempted to ask him if *he* read my messages, but for some reason he doesn't strike me as the kind of person who would do that.

"Right," I say. "But you really didn't have to wait here for me. You could have given it back to me at school tomorrow."

"It's okay. I didn't have anything else to do."

I notice how tired he looks, and he's probably dehydrated if the sweat patches under his arms are anything to go by.

"Well, thanks again. Are you all right, though? Have you had anything to drink?"

I look into his eyes and I can see how he's tempted to lie, but then he says, "No." And as if to emphasize his point, his stomach growls like distant thunder.

Mom, who has been hovering nearby pretending to check on the flowers lining our driveway, hears it too.

"Oh dear," she says, "are you hungry?"

Philip looks at me, desperate for a way out, a way to save his face and let us know he's perfectly all right when he really isn't. But there is no way out because his stomach unambiguously answers Mom's question by growling again, even louder than the first time.

"All right," Mom says, "why don't you step inside and I fix you a nice big glass of ice tea. And then we'll call your mom to let her know you'll be staying over for dinner. I'll give you a ride home afterward."

Philip takes a breath as if he were about to object, but then he exhales, a silent sigh of resignation and relief accompanied by a sluggish nod.

As we make our way to the front door, a car that's been parked half a block up the street since before I arrived starts moving. As I close the door behind me, it passes our house, and Special Agent Nicole Tesla looks at me from behind her dark sunglasses.

* * *

"Why are we eating so early today?" Greg asks as he enters the dining room, late as always. Then he sees Philip sit in the usually empty sixth spot at our dinner table and stops dead in his tracks. "Whoa!"

"Greg," Mom says, "we have a guest. This is Philip, a friend of Matt's."

I cringe at the word *friend*.

Philip is not my friend.

Philip is my school-appointed nuisance.

"Hello," Philip says in a low voice as Greg takes his seat next to me, and his unabashed reply is, "Wow."

We're having chicken fillets with potatoes and vegetables. Greg says he doesn't want any veggies, but of course Mom won't have any of it and scoops an extra serving of beans and carrots on Greg's plate.

He points at Philip who has only chicken and potatoes on his plate. "Why doesn't *he* have to eat veggies?"

"Potatoes *are* veggies," Zoey says.

"Philip doesn't like vegetables," Mom says as she hands Greg his plate, "and he is our guest. If you're invited to dinner at Philip's family I'm sure they won't you make eat ... raw squid if you don't like it." She sits back down and turns to Philip. "I'm sorry, Philip, I have no idea what people eat in ... your country."

"Laos," I help her out.

"Right, Laos." Mom laughs awkwardly. "Sorry, I'm not even entirely sure where that is."

"It's between Thailand and Vietnam," Dad chimes in. "Got battered pretty badly during the Vietnam War. It's roughly the size of Utah, I think, but we actually dropped more bombs on them than we did on the whole of Europe during World War II. They still have millions of unexploded bombs in the ground over there, some of them going off every once in a while." He looks at Philip. "Is that why your family left Laos?"

Philip shakes his head. "We came to America because I could get better medical treatment here."

After a few moments of awkward silence, because nobody expected Philip—or anyone, for that matter—to mention the elephant in the room, Greg finally remembers his role as troll-in-chief and chants, "USA! USA! USA!"

"Greg, please," Mom says.

Zoey looks at Philip. "You're American, though, right?"

He nods. "We're not illegals if that's what you mean. Nationalized citizens."

"Naturalized," I correct him. When he frowns at me, I add, "It's *naturalized* citizens."

I can see in his eyes how he wants to challenge me on that, but before he gets to it, Greg turns to me. "So Matt, how did your date go?"

I'm not too thrilled by his suggestion I was having a date with Philip.

"It was not a date! We were at the library working on our term papers."

It turns out that wasn't even what he was talking about.

Greg frowns. "Oh? That's weird. I thought I saw you sitting at the Korova with *someone* earlier."

The way he stresses the word *someone* reveals a thinly veiled threat: *be nice or I'll tell them it was a guy—the same guy you hugged the other night.* The only way to take the wind out of his sails is to flee forward.

"Oh, that," I say. "Yeah, before I went to the library I met up with Chris from Track & Field. We want to train together because we're both on the relay team for the Schoolympics, so we were discussing that."

"At the Korova," Greg adds helpfully.

Mom puts her hand on Dad's arm, preventing him from lifting the fork to his mouth. "Oh, did I tell you, honey? Matthew made it into the 100-meter relay team."

"Really?" Dad looks at me. "That's great, son!"

I smile. I like it when my dad is proud of me.

He puts a potato wedge in his mouth and says, "So what's the Korova?"

Mom scowls at him. "Don't speak with your mouth full, honey." Then she looks at me. "What *is* the Korova, Matthew?"

"It's a bar," Greg says, and I'm tempted to kick him under the table.

"It's a *milk* bar, downtown on Madison."

Dad swallows and says, "Never heard of it."

Mom looks at Dad. "I had no idea milk bars were still a thing. We should go and check it out some time, what do you think, honey?"

"Oh, you *definitely* should," Greg says.

I glare at him, contemplating which piece of cutlery I should stab him in the eye with, the knife or the fork.

"That'd be swell," Dad says.

Mom turns back to me and Philip. "But then you went to the library to work on your term paper with Philip, right?"

"Yeah."

"And did you make any progress?"

I shrug. "I guess."

"So what's the topic?" Dad asks.

"*Romeo and Juliet*," I say, not even trying to conceal the contempt in my voice.

Mom gets all misty-eyed. "Oh, I love *Romeo and Juliet*. It's so romantic."

"Actually," I say, "I think it's pretty boring, and not very realistic."

I look at Lip for approval, an affirmative nod, or any sign of support, but he just keeps on eating and pretending he isn't there.

"True love is never realistic, darling. Remember my words when you fall in love for the first time."

Both Greg and Zoey snicker, Philip casts a furtive glance at me, and I just want to crawl into a hole.

Mom puts her hand on Dad's arm again. "Do you remember how crazy it was when we fell in love, honey?"

Dad takes the fork with his other hand and puts food in his mouth so he doesn't have to answer. He just smiles at Mom and nods.

Turning back to me, Mom says, "So will you be going to the library again next week to work on your term papers?"

"Yeah," I say. "Philip doesn't have Internet at home, so he has to use the computers at the library."

Philip averts his eyes and focuses back on his food, trying to ignore the baby elephant that just entered the room. It's wearing worn-out shoes with holes in them, grubby pants, and a slogan T-shirt that reads *I'm poor. Get over it!*

Meanwhile, it doesn't take me more than a second and a puzzled look from my mom to realize my flawed argument.

"Well," Mom says, "we have Internet at home, so why don't you work on your assignment over here?"

"Thanks, but I think we'll be doing fine at the library."

Mom doesn't let go. "You'll be doing much better over here. Don't you have to discuss things about your assignment? At the library you're only allowed to whisper. That's no proper way to work on an assignment together. Isn't that right, Philip?"

"Mom ..."

Philip shrugs, struggling to find an answer. The one he eventually comes up with is, "I guess."

"Great," Mom says. "That's settled then."

Phil looks at me bashfully, his eyes begging for forgiveness.

* * *

After Mom and I gave Philip a ride home I get back to my bedroom and fire up my laptop. There is no new message from 2-b-pretty. Of course there isn't. Comcast still hasn't fixed Sandy's Internet at home, and she's exceeded her mobile data allowance, so she can only use the library to message me.

Sandy was at the library when I received 2-b-pretty's comment, and in her second comment 2-b-pretty even quoted *Macbeth* at me, just a few minutes after I talked about it with Sandy. There is no way this could be a coincidence. As crazy and unreal as it sounds, there is no way Sandy is not

2-b-pretty. I have no doubt. There can be no doubt. It has to be her.

My heart is in jackhammer mode, and I feel strangely exposed. Did she know who I was when she wrote her first comment about Matty getting to look at Chris's booty on the track, or did she only realize who I was when I told her the whole library scowled at me because her message made me laugh? Was that why she left? Because she was just as shocked to realize who I am as I am now? Or shouldn't she have realized it much sooner? After all, I use all our real names in my supposedly fictional story about Matt and Chris. Heck, she's even a character in that story herself! And what's with the weird, quirky kind of language she uses all the time? Is that really just an attempt to conceal her identity?

Too many questions, and it's time to get some answers.

Mattoid2002

Dear Pretty!
Sorry there's no new chapter today because my life descended into turmoil and I didn't have the time write anything. I hope you understand.
In other news: let's cut the BS. I think you know who I am, and I think I know who you are too.
xoxo

This is crazy and exciting.
Mostly crazy though.
Without further ado, I hit send.
So does Zoey, two doors down the hall.

Zoey

So how did it go with Chris?

All right, but I'm too tired now. I'll tell you tomorrow.

Mattoid2002

There is no reply from her, not even a simple 'OK' or anything.

Her silence is Zoey's way of letting me know she's pissed.

She's always ready to listen, and I appreciate that.

But I'm not always ready to talk.

She doesn't appreciate that quite as much.

CHAPTER TWELVE

"Sorry about last night," I say as we walk down Vine in the morning. "It was already pretty late and I wasn't really in the mood to talk."

Zoey shrugs, eating her apple. "Whatever. You don't have to tell me anything if you don't want to. It's fine."

Clearly it isn't fine. If it were, she'd be begging me to tell her all about my date with Chris, because I know she's dying to know. But her pride is getting the best of her at the moment, and so she's doing that passive-aggressive thing that girls sometimes do where in order to make you feel bad they pretend they don't give a shit about anything when the shit they actually do give is the size of that giant dinosaur turd Laura Dern digs her arms into in *Jurassic Park*.

And it's working. I am feeling pretty bad, but it's not having the effect Zoey is going for. She probably wants me to throw myself at her feet and tell her I'm ten times sorry, but I've got my own pride to cater to, and our natural sibling rivalry commands me to stand my ground on this one. It's not like she's the only one who's got a reason to be mad, and someone ought to let her know.

"Well, maybe I shouldn't," I say. "My date with Chris wasn't off to a great start, in case you're wondering."

"Oh yeah?" Zoey says, taking the bait. "Why is that?"

"He wasn't too crazy about your outburst at Jack. And it wasn't too difficult for him to figure out that the information about Jack's family situation could only have come from me, so ..."

"Oh, that. Yeah, well, Jack is an asshole, so my compassion for him is really pretty limited. He deserved to hear what I said."

"This isn't about Jack," I say. "I don't give a rat's ass about Jack. The problem is you made me look bad in front of Chris, because I told you something I wasn't supposed to tell anyone."

"Well excuse me, but how is that my fault? It's not like I waterboarded you or anything."

"No, but if you had kept it to yourself, Chris never would have found out."

"And if you had kept it to *yourself*, there wouldn't have been anything for him to find out in the first place. Sorry, Matt, but you can't pin that on me. Man up and take some responsibility. You're not twelve anymore."

"Wow," I say, stumped by her makeshift logic.

I sulk for a while until Zoey finally breaks the silence.

"So how'd the rest of your date go?"

"All right," is my extensive answer.

"Good."

"Yep."

Zoey sighs. Then she drops her apple core on somebody's front lawn and looks at me. "Look, Matt, I get it. You're mad at me because of what I said to Jack. But I was really upset and I wasn't thinking straight. I didn't do it to make you look bad. Not everything is about you. Get over it."

I look back at her. "This is probably the closest thing to an apology I'm gonna get from you, isn't it?"

"Pretty much. So can you forgive me? Just this once?"

"Well, I don't have much of a choice, do I?"

She shakes her head. "Nope."

"Oh well."

She grabs my arm. "You know what, it's that whole damn secrecy thing that will be all our downfall, I'm telling you. You still haven't told Alfonso, have you?"

"No."

"Well, what are you waiting for? He's your friend. He deserves to know."

I sigh. "That's exactly what Chris says."

"And he's exactly right. The longer you put it off, the harder it gets."

"I know," I say. "And it's not that I don't trust him. It's just awkward for me because—"

"Because he's a guy?"

"Yes! I mean, it would be a whole lot easier for me if he was a girl."

"Yeah well," Zoey says, "he isn't, and he's not gonna have a sex change to make things less awkward for you, so ..."

"Yeah, I get that. But even so, I'm just so scared that things will change between us because he might think I'm hitting on him or something."

"Well, are you?" she asks.

I scowl at her. "Hell, no! I mean, he's not unattractive or anything, but he's so totally not my type."

"You can tell him that now." Zoey nudges me with her elbow and nods toward the street corner where El Niño is waiting for us on his bike like a brooding storm, and he's not alone. Standing next to him is Hurricane Sandy.

"Not a word to Alfonso," I hiss at Zoey's we approach him.

Zoey snorts. "Please. Give me some credit."

"Maybe I would if you hadn't pulled that stunt with Jack."

"Oh get over it already!"

"¡Hola chicas!"

"Hi, guys!"

Sandy throws herself around my neck and kisses the air next to my ear while Zoey hugs Alfonso. Then Alfonso and I fist bump, and I immediately notice something's off. His eyes are fixed on me. Of course they are—he wants an explanation. He wants an explanation I don't have, so ignore his prying looks as we continue on our way to school and Sandy starts a major rant about the intricacies of the Chinese language—or, in fact, languages.

"O-M-G, guys, did you know that the Chinese speak like a million different dialects? Okay, maybe not a million, but they have like ten major dialect groups and each of them has like dozens of different dialects, and sometimes even people who speak different dialects from the same dialect group have no idea what the other one is saying, yet they all use the same writing system. Mrs. Li—that's our teacher—Mrs. Li says it's like if someone from New York and someone from L.A. had a copy of the New York Times, they could both read it, but if the person from New York were to read it out loud, the person from L.A. wouldn't understand a word of it, can you believe that? Oh, and don't even get me started on the tones! Words can have several completely different meanings, depending on how you pronounce them. Like, the word *ma* can mean *mother*, but it can also mean *horse*. That's so super confusing. Imagine getting the pronunciation wrong and accidentally referring to someone's mother as a horse!"

Sandy is clinging on to my arm, but she's mostly talking in Zoey's direction while Alfonso is holding onto my shoulder to keep his balance as he's rolling along on his bike at walking speed. As Sandy keeps rambling on, he squeezes my shoulder a little harder to get my attention and says in a low voice, "So you want to tell me what happened yesterday?"

"It's nothing," I say, shaking my head. "I did something stupid. I'll tell you later, okay?"

For a few moments it seems okay, but then Alfonso lets go of my shoulder, stops his bike and says, "You know what, actually no, it's not okay."

I stop and look at him.

"I don't know what it is, but something is clearly wrong. You've been acting all weird recently." He looks at Zoey, then back at me. "Both of you. Do you really think I don't notice when you're having an animated discussion about something, and the moment I show, up you fall dead silent? Look, if you want to have secrets like two little schoolgirls, fine. But at least have the decency to say so and don't treat me like some little kid who's too stupid to notice."

"Hey," Zoey says, throwing up her hands in defense, "don't look at me. I'm sworn to secrecy against my will, and apparently I've said too much already."

Alfonso turns to me. "Well?"

I'm taking too long to think of a reasonable reply, because such a reply doesn't exist.

"You must have done something pretty stupid to get yourself grounded."

"Woah, what?" Zoey takes a step back, purses her lips and stares at me.

And there's your classic dilemma. Do I admit to having lied to Alfonso or do I double down and draw Zoey into this and force her to play along with my lie? I can see in her eyes that this is not something she will appreciate.

"Look," I say to Alfonso, "I'm sorry about yesterday. I'm not grounded. Something came up but I couldn't talk, so I lied to you."

He stares at me for a few long moments before he says, "And?"

"And I'm sorry."

Apparently, my response fails to satisfy him.

"Right," he says. "Well, if you should ever feel like telling me what the hell is going, you know where you can find me."

He gets on his bike and dashes off.

Sandy, who has been following our altercation with her eyes wide open, looks at me and says, "Was it something I said?"

I shake my head and look her right into the eyes. "You have done no harm."

My cryptic reply seems to confuse her even more by the look on her face, which, in turn, confuses me. I was quoting 2-b-pretty quoting *Macbeth*, and no matter if she's aware that I am the person she has come to know as Mattoid2002 or not, surely there should have been some sort of reaction if she is, in fact, 2-b-pretty.

A twinkle in her eyes, a twitch in the corner of her mouth.

But instead, nothing. Just a befuddled frown as she says, "Right, um … okay. So what happened? Why's he so mad at you?"

"Because I royally messed up."

"Aw," Sandy says and rubs my arm with her hand. It's a clumsy gesture full of ignorant sympathy, but it's actually kind of sweet.

"Yeah, it's a long story," I say. "Never mind. I'm going to fix this."

"You better, Matthew," Zoey says, the look in her eyes grim and demanding. "You damn well better."

* * *

Fixing it—and that's not even coming as a big surprise—is easier said than done. Alfonso ignores me for the rest of the day, and he's doing an excellent job at it too. When I ask him for an eraser during geography class, he takes it out of his pencil case. I reach out my hand but he ignores it and slams the eraser on my desk without looking at me. When I want to return the eraser, he ignores me again. I offer it to him with my arm stretched out until the teacher finally says, "Just put it on his desk, Matthew."

During lunch, Alfonso chooses not to sit at our table. He sits at a table across the cafeteria, directly in my field of view.

"Where's Alfonso?" Sandy asks when she notices someone's missing from our regular line up.

"I don't know," I say.

Philip, who's sitting next to me, points at him and says, "He's sitting right over there."

As Sandy turns her head to look, I glare at Philip until he lowers his head to admire his lunch.

"Did your boyfriend break up with you, Maddie?" Steve asks and nudges Jack with his elbow to prompt him to laugh which he dutifully does. Albeit it not as heartily as he would have done before the Track & Field incident the other day. Chris doesn't laugh. He doesn't even smile or smirk. He just throws me a sad, almost pitying look. His cobalt blue T-shirt reads *Blue* in white lettering.

When I met him in the hallway before the first period he asked me, "How did it go?"

I had to hurry to class so I just said, "It didn't. I'll explain later."

Now that Alfonso is so obviously shunning me, Chris must think that my coming out to Alfonso didn't go too well. I have yet to tell him that it didn't even happen in the first place. It's not until Track & Field when Coach Gutierrez snatches Jack away to coach him on his starting posture that Chris and I finally have a brief moment of privacy away from the others.

"Okay, talk to me," he says, still out of breath from our last race. "What happened?"

I shrug. "Nothing."

He frowns.

"I mean, literally nothing. I chickened out."

"You chickened out? How? I mean, why? I mean ..."

"I called off our meeting because something else came up."

"Right," Chris says. "That's sort of a relief, to be honest. I thought he's mad at you because you finally came out to him or something."

"No, it never got to that. I told him I couldn't meet him because I was grounded. Then he found out I wasn't grounded, so yeah."

Chris groans. "Okay, no offense, but that was pretty stupid."

"Tell me about it."

"Honestly, I'm beginning to doubt how close a friend he really is. I mean, to you. First you don't want to tell him the truth, then you lie to him ..."

I sigh. Him—or anyone, for that matter—questioning my friendship with Alfonso is the last thing I need right now. "Look, I messed up, okay? No need to rub it in!"

Chris throws up his hands in defense. "Hey, I was just saying."

I have no further response, but I'm saved by the bell. Or by Coach Gutierrez's whistle, really.

"Let's go," Chris says. "We can talk later."

* * *

After Track & Field, I skip the shower—again. I'm still not comfortable with the idea of getting naked with Chris—at least not in front of an audience. I don't have a problem with my body or anything. I'm neither too skinny nor too chubby, and for my height all my body parts seem appropriately sized.

What worries me is how my body—or specifically a certain part of it—might react when Chris is standing in front of me in his birthday suit. On any given day it takes much less to give me a boner, and I simply can't take the risk of my dick taking my coming out in its own hands.

Figuratively speaking.

My dick doesn't have hands, obviously.

That would be hilarious, though—the thought that it could rub itself while I just sit back and relax.

Anyway, I wait until everyone's in the shower, then I quickly change into my street clothes and rush home. I still haven't heard back from 2-b-pretty, and it's beginning to worry me. Did I scare her off when I told her I think I know who she is? Either way, I need to get on my computer because I want to tell her about the disastrous twenty-four hours I've been having since we last spoke.

Mom pounces on me the moment I'm through the front door.

"Oh there you are," she says, her hands in dirty rubber gloves. "I need some help in the garden. Can you ..."

"Not now!" I snap at her and run up the stairs.

She scoffs. "Matthew!"

My phone chimes the second I enter my room, announcing the message I've been anticipating. It's very short.

My dear Mr. Mattoid,
you know me, but you don't know who I am. And I'm not sure if you even want to.
I'll say no more until next time. If there is a next time, as I hope there will be. Your story is too intriguing and must go on. Online or off.
xoxo

2-b-pretty

"Matthew!" I hear Mom call from down below. "Will you help me in the garden now?"

"I'll be down in a minute, mom!" I shout back over my shoulder. Then I look back at the screen and read 2-b-pretty's message again, trying to make sense of it. I know her, but I don't know who she is? What does that even mean? And why wouldn't I want to know who she is?

"Matthew!"

I slam my laptop shut and rush out of my room, down the stairs, past my perplexed mom, out of the front door and into the garage where Greg is oiling the chain of his bike. I grab it, jump in the saddle and dash off.

"My bike!" Greg shouts as if I don't know whose stupid bike it is.

"It's an emergency!"

"*You're* an emergency, asshole!"

I don't even have time to hate Greg for always having a good comeback on his lips. Setting a new personal record and possibly breaking the speed limit, I pedal the heck out of Greg's bike and make my way to the library. When I turn the corner to the library's main entrance I nearly hit the weird figure standing in the middle of the sidewalk. With screeching brakes I manage to stop just inches in front of him.

"Phil!"

Without a flinch he turns his head, looks at me, and says, "Yes?"

"What the hell are you doing here?"

"I've been working on my term paper. If you had told me you'd be coming I would have waited for you, but you said you didn't have time."

"I don't!" I say. "I'm not here to … never mind. Have you seen Sandy?"

"Sandy?"

"Yes! Sandy. Have you seen her in the library?"

He slowly shakes his head. "No?"

I dismount the bike and hand it to Phil.

"Hold this for me," I say and rush past him into the library. As always, the second floor is sparsely crowded. Maybe eight or ten people populate the computers and seating areas. None of them are Sandy. I look at my watch. Less than ten minutes have passed since 2-b-pretty messaged me from here. She must have left right afterward.

Disappointed and exhausted I make my way back down. Phil is still waiting by the roadside holding Greg's bike.

"Are you sure you haven't seen Sandy?"

"Yes," he says, "but—"

"Does the library have a second exit or something?"

"No, but—"

"But what?" I snap at him.

He looks at me. He looks at me for a long time, but it's not his usual blank stare. There is something in his eyes, something he wants to tell me, so why doesn't he just say it? Because I don't have time for this.

Then, out of nowhere, out of the blue, out of the blue nowhere that is left field, a terrible, horrifying thought occurs to me.

The username 2-b-pretty is not a description.

It's the expression of a deep-rooted desire.

"No," I say in a low voice, looking at him.

He keeps staring at me with his big brown eyes like a maniacal, psychopathic deer, and suddenly I know it's true. From one moment to the next everything is falling into place and making sense and tearing my whole world apart.

"No, please no! Say it ain't true!"

"You know it is," he says with his obnoxious, disgusting twang.

I guess that also takes care of my theory that 2-b-pretty is driving a Tesla. Which means that Nicole Tesla is probably a special agent assigned to surveil me after all.

I grab the bike. It's not that I want to go anywhere, but I need something to hold on to before my legs fail me.

"How ... how did you ... when did you realize it was me?" I ask.

"On my first day of school when I suddenly found myself in the middle of the story I'd been reading for a week. At first I thought maybe it was a huge coincidence, but then I started reading about myself, so ..."

I stare at the ground, hoping for a hole to open up that I can crawl into and pull in after me. In a flash I recall every single ugly thing I've written about him, thinking I was talking about him behind his back when I was actually saying these things right to his disfigured face without even knowing it. I'm dying of embarrassment, but at the same time I feel exposed and violated in my privacy.

I know I've been writing down my story for people to read. Just not people who actually know me.

"Besides," Philip continues, "you're using everyone's real names. Not sure why you thought that would be a good idea."

"Well, it worked great for me until you came into my life," I say, and I immediately regret it.

He looks at the passing traffic again.

"Sorry, that came out wrong."

He shakes his head. "Never mind."

"No, seriously. It was a stupid idea to use real names. I can't blame you for that."

Without bothering to look at me, he says, "I have to go."

Behind me I hear a car pull up. It's Mr. Thongrivong in his old clunker. Without another word, Philip gets into the passenger seat and they take off.

As I watch them leave, closely followed by a shiny black Tesla, my mind is a whirlwind of all sorts of thoughts and emotions hitting me in the face like hail in a hailstorm that I'm exposed to with no shelter and no clothes.

I turn my bike around and I'm about to take off when another cyclist is blocking my way. It's Alfonso, of all people. He glares at me and doesn't say a word.

"Oh, hey," I say.

"Hey," he replies with little enthusiasm.

"So listen, can we talk? I'm really sorry I lied to you, and I want to explain how that came about. Actually, there are several things I need to explain to you."

Alfonso sighs and looks at the handlebar of his bike for a few moments. Then he looks me in the eyes and says, "Not now, Matthew. I'm running an errand for my dad."

Not now doesn't mean *no*. It simply means *not now*. So he's actually throwing me a bone—albeit a tiny one—and it's almost embarrassing how I pounce on it like a stray dog that hasn't had a proper meal in days. "Okay, can I come over later then? I really need to talk with you."

Again he takes his time to reply. Finally, he looks at his watch and says, "In an hour maybe."

"Perfect!" I say. "Thank you."

He could have said an hour after midnight in the cemetery and don't forget to bring a dead cat, and it would have been just as fine with me.

Without another word he gets back in the saddle and takes off.

"See you later!" I call after him. He's shaking his head in response, knowing exactly how desperate I feel.

I make my way back home, and when I turn into our driveway, Greg is still in the garage. He looks surprisingly cheerful. That's probably because he's not alone.

"Matthew Elliot Dunstan!" Mom fires at me as I dismount the bike.

"Sorry, Mom. I just had to do something real quick. I can help you in the garden now."

"I guess you could," Mom says. "Except for the next seven days you're not going to leave your room unless you have to go to the bathroom, to school, or to attend breakfast and dinner."

"Mom!"

"Starting now, Matthew!"

"But Mom! I have to be over at Alfonso's in an hour. It's really important!"

"You can talk to Alfonso tomorrow at school. For now, you're grounded."

"Mom …"

"Matthew," she says with a tone in her voice that leaves no room for interpretation.

I hand the bike over to Greg, who isn't even trying to conceal the stupid smirk on his stupid face, and I make my way inside.

"I'm very disappointed, Matthew," I hear Mom call after me.

Slamming the front door shut behind me is the only response I can come up with.

I run upstairs. Being grounded usually also means a restriction of my phone and Internet privileges. Mom didn't explicitly mention it in the heat of the moment, but it's just a matter of time until she'll remember and confiscate my phone. Blocking my Internet won't be quite as easy. Mom and Dad are too technologically illiterate to block the WiFi just for me without cutting it off for the rest of the family. Greg and Zoey know how to block individual users in the router, but we have a mutual silent agreement to refuse assisting our parents in enforcing cruel and unusual punishments.

As soon as I'm in my room, I pull out my phone and speed-dial Alfonso's number. He answers after the third ring.

"¡Hola!"

"Alfonso? It's me, Matt."

"Yeah, I know," he says, and I can hear how he rolls his eyes. "Caller ID, you know?"

"Right. Well listen, I'm really, really sorry, but something came up, so I can't make it. I got grounded." I give Alfonso a few seconds to say something. When he doesn't, I add, "For real this time."

Finally a response. He snorts.

"I know this sounds totally stupid, but I literally got grounded a minute ago and I wanted to let you know before Mom confiscates my phone. I'll explain it all tomorrow, okay?"

I listen, but there's nothing to listen to. Alfonso's already hung up on me.

It probably serves me right.

I throw myself on the bed, curling up and hugging my pillow. The tornado that's been wreaking havoc inside my mind slowly dies down, the quiet after the storm revealing the damage it has caused. Being grounded sucks big time, but it's actually the least of my problems. What really gets to me the most is the fact that Alfonso hates me right now, and I have no idea what—if anything—I can do to make him unhate me. I need to talk to him. I should have talked to him a long time ago, but now that I'm finally ready to do it I can't. For now, the only way to talk to him is at school which sucks due to school's inherent time constraints and lack of privacy. So that sucks. And then there's 2-b-pretty, who is not Sandy, or any other girl for that matter, or anything like I imagined her to be.

Him.

Whatever.

The shock of that revelation is still eating away at me. How could this happen? How could I be so stupid? In my defense I have to say that Philip's online and offline personalities are diametrically opposed, and nobody in their right mind could ever have connected one to the other. And what are the odds of him coming across my Wattpad just a few months before meeting me in real life? The only way I could have prevented this whole mess would have been by not putting my story online—or by not having been born. Both were not an option. There is nothing I could have done differently. Therefore, I have no reason to be mad at myself.

Yet, I'm feeling mad.

Hey, I'm only human. I have to direct my anger at someone, don't I?

Philip.

How dare he?

How dare he weasel his way into my life pretending to be pretty despite his ugly face and giving me relationship advice when he doesn't even have any friends? That is my gut reaction. Then my brain butts in to remind me that at first, Phil thought what he was giving me wasn't relationship advice but a simple story critique. Because apparently knowing one stupid quote from Macbeth makes him a freaking literary critic or whatever.

Fine.

But then he realized that the story wasn't just a story. It was real life. It was *my life* he was messing with, and he knew exactly what he was doing! That's what infuriates me. From day one I felt a strange kind of connection with her/him/whatever, a closeness that I didn't even know where it was coming from, and everything he said to me seemed to make perfect sense. He was giving me sound, reasonable advice, well-intentioned and with Matt's best interests at heart.

My best interests.

How dare he? What made him think I needed help from a pathetic lowlife with no friends who sounds like a freaking duck when he talks? How did he even come up with all the smart-assed things he said? A smart person can fake being stupid, but how can a stupid person fake being smart? That doesn't even make any sense.

Or does it?

God, I hate him!

I hate him so much that I want to punch him in his stupid, disfigured face.

What I hate him most for is how he makes me think all those mean, ugly things about him when all he ever did was trying to be friendly. And then he had the audacity to not even flinch when I said the meanest, most vile things about him to his online alter ego. His behavior towards me didn't change one bit even though he knew exactly what I was thinking about him.

Now who's the pathetic lowlife?

I should be ashamed of myself, and I am. I'm so ashamed, I can never face him again, except I have to work with him on that stupid term paper about Romeo and freaking Juliet.

Screw you, William Shakespeare! Screw you and your stupid drivel about two teenagers in love who aren't meant to be together. Your story sucks!

My life sucks, too.

My life sucks in Shakespearean proportions.

I clench my fist and punch my pillow tree, four, five times. Then I take the pillow, toss it against the headboard, and bury my face in it, trying not to burst into tears. I lie there for a long while, trying to free my mind of anything that might upset me, which is everything. Eventually all my thoughts slowly ebb away and I doze off.

When I wake up it's nearly dark outside, and the tide of depressing thoughts is on its way back in. I don't want to deal with them again, not now, not ever, so I grab my laptop for some distracting entertainment. Maybe watching a couple of videos of natural disasters will cheer me up. I click on the YouTube icon in my browser's menu bar and … nothing happens.

My Internet is dead.

"Oh what the hell," I mutter, and at the same time there's a knock on my door.

It's Zoey. "Matt? Dinner!"

I catch up with her on the landing.

"Is your Internet working?" I ask.

"Yeah, why?"

Without a reply I storm down the stairs. Zoey comes rushing after me because she senses there's a show not to be missed. When we enter the dining room, Mom, Dad, and Greg are already sitting at the dinner table.

"Why is my Internet not working?" I ask no one in particular as I take my seat next to Greg.

"You know why, Matthew," Mom says. "It's part of being grounded."

"I get that," I say. "But since when do you know how to block individual users?"

With a smug smile, Mom shakes her head. "That's not important."

"Oh, but I think it is," Zoey says, looking at Greg. I look at Greg too, and so does Dad. Greg is the worst actor in the world, though, and the perfectly innocent look on his face is a dead giveaway. If he really were innocent, he'd be outraged to be accused of treason.

"Well?" I say.

Greg shrugs. "Well what?"

"Wow," Zoey says, seeing through his charade. "Who'd have thought you'd stoop so low? So much did they pay you?"

"Nobody paid nobody anything," Mom intervenes and turns to me. "And it would show some strength of character on your part if you could just gracefully accept your punishment."

"I do accept my punishment, but I think I have a right to know by what means it is enforced."

"I don't think you do, actually," Mom says.

I shake my head in disbelief. "In a democracy this would be a case for the supreme court. But this family isn't a democracy, I guess."

Dad raises his eyebrows at Mom as if to say, 'He's got a point, you know?' but he doesn't say anything.

"Stop whining already," Greg finally says. "If you hadn't stolen my bike—"

"I didn't *steal* your bike, I borrowed it. And I told you it was an emergency."

Zoey snorts at Greg. "I can't believe you unilaterally terminated a lifelong mutual agreement because of your stupid bike!"

"Whatever," Greg says and shrugs.

Dad looks at me. "What was so urgent that you had to borrow his bike anyway?"

"I had to meet someone at the library."

"Probably his boyfriend," Greg says.

"Shut the hell up!"

"Language, Matthew!"

"So who was it?" Dad wants to know.

I drop my cutlery on my plate. "It was Sandy, okay?" Technically that's not even true, but at the time I thought it was.

Mom and Dad exchange proud, sympathetic glances.

"Well," Mom says, "I'm sorry, but you can't just grab somebody's bike without asking and take off. There has to be some kind of punishment."

I sigh. "I already told you, I accept the punishment! Does anyone in this house ever listen to anything I say?"

"Was it at least worth it?" Dad asks. "I mean, did you meet your sweetheart?"

"She's not my sweetheart, she's just a friend," I say, rolling my eyes. "Anyway, no. She wasn't there."

"Bummer," Zoey says.

"Yeah, welcome to my life."

Greg snorts. "You don't even have a life."

"Greg, I think we've heard enough from you today," Dad says, and I can't help but add, "Or any day."

Under the table, Greg stomps on my foot and I yelp, perhaps a little louder than necessary.

"All right, Greg," Mom says, "as you're well aware, we don't tolerate physical violence in this family. You know what that means."

"But I didn't—"

"Yes, you did. And you're grounded for a week. That includes your phone and Internet privileges. Good thing I know how to block individual users in the router."

"Wow," Zoey says shaking her head. "Karma is such a bitch."

CHAPTER THIRTEEN

When we leave for school in the morning, Zoey doesn't waste any time to get on my case.

"Anything you want to tell me?"

I frown at her. "What are you talking about?"

"Come on, Matt. The limpet, seriously? You got yourself in this whole mess over Sandy when you just could have called or texted her? I don't believe that for a second. Who were you really going to meet at the library? Chris?"

I sigh, knowing full well that denial is futile. Zoey can see through my lies like through an open window. Besides, overnight—a night that was sleepless for the most part—I've finally come to the obvious conclusion that all my tactical lies were a big strategic mistake. I need a new approach, and that new approach is: speak the truth or don't speak at all. The latter not being an option with Zoey, I finally tell her about my fictionalized online version of events and about 2-b-pretty, my biggest fan and his real identity.

"Wow," Zoey says when I'm finished. "That's an interesting turn of events. You made a new friend. And without any help, too. Didn't see that one coming."

"Very funny."

"So Phil is gay too, huh?"

Although the answer to that has to be pretty obvious to anyone who watches him for five seconds, I say, "You know what, I don't even care. Why would I? I mean, just look at the freak. He annoys the crap out of me."

"You didn't find him that annoying before you knew what he looks like, though, did you?"

"What the hell is that supposed to mean?"

"Love looks not with the eyes but with the mind," she says cryptically. "And therefore is winged Cupid painted blind."

I scowl at her. "What?"

"Mrs. Spelczik was my English teacher too when I was a freshman, you know? My term paper that year was about *A Midsummer Night's Dream.*"

That Shakespeare dude is really starting to get on my nerves.

"That's a lovely anecdote, Zoey, but it doesn't have any practical application in my situation."

"Oh, I think it does. You said it yourself, Matt. You said at one point you were so fond of 2-b-pretty's comments that you were secretly wishing she were a guy. Why would you say that if not for the plain and simple reason that you were having a crush on her? Him. Whatever."

"Look," I say as we reach the corner of Vine and Harper. El Niño is nowhere to be seen. "I have more pressing issues on my mind at the moment, okay?"

"Right," Zoey says, gracefully following my lead into a different topic. "So what are you going to do about Alfonso then?"

I shrug. "What am I supposed to do? He obviously doesn't want to talk to me, and I can't even blame him. I mean, he should be here by now, but he isn't, so I guess he's taking a different route to school today. At lunch he's gonna sit at a different table ... I want to talk to him and explain everything. I really do. But—"

"There is no but, Matthew! You made this mess, you clean it up. And stop whining already. Alfonso doesn't owe you anything, so don't expect him to make this easy on you. Just because he's avoiding you right now doesn't mean he doesn't want you to keep trying or that he doesn't care. He does care about you, you know that. But if you don't keep trying, he'll think that you're the one who doesn't care. You don't want that."

"But how—"

"Look, I get it," she interrupts me. "He's sulking right now. Get over it, and get over yourself. Grab him over lunch and talk to him. And if he doesn't want to listen, make him listen and tell him the truth. The whole truth, everything."

I mull over her words for a few moments, then I say, "I'm so freaking scared."

"Man up," is her stone-cold reply.

* * *

I get a hold of Alfonso outside of our classroom before the first period. He doesn't say a word when I stop him. He just looks at me with an indifferent look on his face.

"Look," I say, "I messed up, okay? And I want to make it right. A million things have been going on in my life, and I want to explain it all to you. Everything. If you don't want to talk, fine. Then don't talk. But at least listen to me. Please."

"Take your seats, boys," Mrs. Spelczik says as she walks past us and enters the classroom.

Alfonso doesn't need to be told twice. He turns around and walks into the classroom, leaving me out in the cold, neon-lit hallway. Meanwhile, Mrs. Spelczik isn't giving me much time to mope.

"In or out?" she says standing in the doorway, her hand on the door handle.

Despondently, I walk through the door.

Mrs. Spelczik asks us to produce our homework, so I take out my notepad that has my homework in it somewhere. I turn over a new page and grab my pen. I'd rather be anywhere else than in class right now, but on the upside, Alfonso is here too, and he's got nowhere to go, so I scribble him a note.

> I'm gay!!! Do I have your attention now? Good!!! We need to talk, so stop running away!!!

I tear the paper out of my notebook, fold it up, and throw it on Alfonso's desk. He eyes it disdainfully, but before he has the time to pick it up and throw it back in my face, Mrs. Spelczik ninjas her way between us and grabs it. My face flushing, I look at the floor, hoping to find a hole I can disappear in.

Mrs. Spelczik unfolds my little letter and reads it silently. I keep my pencil clenched in my fist, ready to stab myself right in the heart as soon as she starts reading my note out loud.

But she doesn't.

Instead, she looks at me and says, "Never use triple exclamation marks. Never! Express urgency through words, not punctuation."

"Yes, ma'am," I say in a low voice.

"Are you sure you want him to read that?"

I look back at her. I want to say, 'I sure as hell didn't want *you* to read it,' but I don't have the balls to be so ballsy, so I stammer, "Y-yes."

She turns to Alfonso. "You can pick this up after class."

As she puts the note in her pocket and returns to her desk, I unclench my fist and put down my pencil, relieved I get to live another day.

At the end of the period, Alfonso jumps up at the ring of the bell, grabs his bag, and heads for the door. When he makes his way past Mrs. Spelczik's desk, she calls after him.

"Mr. Alonso?"

Almost out of the door, he stops and turns his head.

Mrs. Spelczik holds up my note. His empty gaze grazes me briefly as he walks up to her and takes the note. I try to avoid eye contact with Mrs. Spelczik as I make my way out of the room, but I fail. On her face I detect the faintest shadow of sympathy. It doesn't take away any of the embarrassment that came with her inadvertently outing me to herself, but at least she didn't go out of her way to make me feel even more miserable like some of my other teachers might have done in a similar situation.

Out in the hallway, Sandy is waiting for me. Not just Sandy, actually, but she's the first in line. Alfonso, however, is nowhere to be seen.

"Where is he?"

"Restroom," Sandy says. "Is everything all right?"

"Yeah. I mean, no, not really. But I'm working on it."

"Poor Matt." She rubs my arm. "Listen, I have to get to my next class. I'll see you at lunch." She gives me a peck on the cheek, and as she rushes off I find Phil standing in front of me.

"Hello," he says like a dork.

"Wha… yes, hello."

"We don't have to work on our term paper together if you don't want to," he says. "I talked to the teacher. She said we don't have to work together. We can both finish our papers on our own. It won't affect our grades, she said. So if you—"

"Oh shut up, will you?"

Taken aback, he shuts up.

"Next Wednesday at four. My place. You stay for supper. My mom will cook something Asian."

Philip looks puzzled. "But I thought—"

"No you didn't. Wednesday at four."

"All right, but—"

"Don't you have a class to go to?" I interrupt him.

"Yes, but—"

"Well, then what are you waiting for? Go!"

I turn to leave, but I don't get far because I literally bump right into Chris. We almost hit our heads together and laugh awkwardly.

"Oh, hi," I say.

He smiles his beautiful smile. "Hey."

"Sorry about that." I take half a step back although I don't actually mind standing so close to him. His T-shirt reads *Cute*, and I'm thinking, *No kidding*.

"No worries," he says, looking at Phil as he walks down the hallway. "Everything okay?"

"What? Oh, yeah, sure."

He looks at me. "So, have you talked to Alfonso yet?"

"No. I mean yes! I mean, well, I finally came out to him, and to Mrs. Spelczik too I'm afraid, but we haven't talked about it yet."

He frowns at me for a second, then it dawns on him. "Oh! You mean you came out to him by scribbling him a note in the middle of class?"

"Yeah."

He sighs. "Why would you do that?"

"Because he wouldn't talk to me. I needed to get his attention."

"Right," Chris says. "Mission accomplished I guess. But anyway, listen, what I really wanted to talk about: you're invited to Jack's birthday party."

I frown. "What?"

"Saturday next week. Can you make it?"

"I guess. I'm grounded this week, but next week should be okay. Probably."

"Okay, awesome," he says, sounding genuinely happy.

"How come he gets to have a birthday party anyway? I thought with his domestic situation and everything …"

"His parents are away for the weekend. His stepdad is taking his mom to Disneyland or something."

"Huh," I say. "But why would Jack invite me to his birthday party? I mean, me of all people?"

"Well, technically he didn't invite you. You're my plus-one. I asked him if it's okay if I bring my boyfriend, and he said yes. In fact, he's excited to meet you."

"You did what?!"

"I asked if it's okay if—"

"Rhetorical question!" I interrupt him. "I heard you. I just can't believe you basically outed me to Jack!"

"Technically he won't know until you show up at his party. And he thinks you're a fag anyway, so …"

"Jesus Christ!"

"I know, right? It's gonna be awesome," Chris says. "We can have a beer and make out on the couch."

Suddenly I'm beginning to think of ways to make Mom extend my detention so I have a reason not to go. Not that I would mind making out with Chris, but off the top of my head I can think of a million better places to do it than Jack's couch.

"Right," I say. "We'll talk later, okay? I'll have to ask my parents first anyway. And now I gotta get to class."

"Sure," Chris says.

I scurry down the hallway, but I still don't get far because just as I'm about to pass the restroom, Alfonso steps out of the door and into my way.

"Oh, hey," he says, which is a huge improvement on our previous situation, because apparently he's speaking with me again.

"Hey."

"I have to get to class," he says, looking at his watch. "Let's have lunch."

I don't have any time to reply, because he's already hurrying down the hallway. I have to make my way to class too, and I do it with a little spring in my step.

* * *

"I can't believe it," Alfonso says. We're sitting at the small table under the stairs in the cafeteria, the one where Phil used to sit before he joined our clique. Alfonso's assessment comes after I've told him everything, and I do mean *everything*.

"It's true, though. I'm gay."

"Oh, that I can believe," he says. "It's pretty obvious. I can't believe you created this whole mess because you were afraid to tell me. Me, your best friend! I'm hurt, Matthew. Hurt!"

"I know," I say sheepishly. "I'm sorry."

"So what else have you been keeping from me?"

"Nothing!" I hurry to say. "That's all, I swear. And all this only happened because I didn't know how to tell you that I'm … you know, gay."

"Well," Alfonso says, "I guess you could have said something like, 'Hey, Alfonso, guess what? I'm gay.'"

"How was I supposed to know that—"

"… that I'm open minded and that you can tell me everything and that I will always have your back? How were you supposed to know indeed? We've only known each other for, like, …", he looks at his watch, "… ten years!"

"Yeah, sorry. I thought if I tell you, you might think I want to hit on you or something."

Alfonso snorts. "Please. I'm not even your type."

"How the hell do you even know what my type is?"

"Because I'm not blind," he says, rolling his eyes. "I know the type of guys you look at when you think nobody's looking."

I'm blushing.

He laughs.

"Why are you laughing?"

"You're blushing!"

"No, I'm not!" I protest and blush some more.

"Hey!" he says, looking all serious all of a sudden. He wags his finger at me. "No more lies!"

"Right, sorry. Yeah, I'm blushing. I thought I was good at casting glances at cute guys without anyone noticing, but I guess not."

"To be fair, I don't think anyone who hasn't known you your whole life would notice where you look. Or care, for that matter."

"Phew!" I wipe my forehead with the back of my hand. "That's kind of a relief."

"So," he says, looking at me with a subtle smile. "Chris, huh?"

"Yeah," I say and glance over at our regular table. Chris is sitting with his back toward us, but I catch Phil staring at me. When our eyes meet, he quickly checks if his lunch tray is still in front of him on the table.

Alfonso shakes his head slowly. "I can see why you're attracted to him physically. But ..."

"But what?"

"Nah, never mind. I don't know him well enough, at least not as well as you do, so I was just wondering if his personality matches his looks."

"Well," I say. "I don't know. I mean, he's really really nice when we're alone together. Really, he can be the sweetest guy you can imagine. But ..."

"Here we go," Alfonso.

I frown. "What do you mean?"

"I knew there was a *but*. No pun intended. Never mind, keep talking."

"I was gonna say," I continue, "he's the sweetest guy you can imagine when we're alone. But when there are other people around it's almost as if he's a different person. Especially when Jack and Steve are around. Like, you know how they sometimes say really mean things to people?"

"Sometimes?" Alfonso says. "They say mean things to people all the time!"

"Exactly. And Chris thinks it's hilarious. It's almost as if he's got two different personalities. And I don't know which is the real Chris."

Alfonso thinks for a moment, then he looks me in the eyes and says, "Look, I don't want to pee on your parade or anything. I know you're on cloud nine at the moment, but be careful, okay? I don't want you to get hurt."

"Thanks," I say. "I appreciate that."

"But if you do get hurt, I'm gonna beat the hell out of whoever did the hurting."

Clasping my hands over my heart, I say, "My knight in shining armor!"

Alfonso scowls at me. "Dude!"

"Too much?"

"Yeah."

"Sorry," I say, and we both laugh.

It feels good to be laughing with Alfonso again.

* * *

My day is going pretty awesome, which is more than I can say about any other day since I've started high school, but being the little Miss Sunshine that I am, I'm expecting to hit a major roadblock any minute now. If my past experiences are anything to go by, I'll probably run headfirst into a closed door, drop my lunch tray in the middle of the cafeteria, or fall flat on my face trying to pass the baton to Chris during Track & Field.

In a curious turn of events, none of that happens.

In fact, things seem to keep getting better and better. All of a sudden I feel five inches taller, and I'm not sure if it's the cause or the effect of my new and improved self-confidence, but I'm feeling like I'm high on some kind of wonder drug that makes me think I can do anything.

In Track & Field we have the best training session ever. Jason, Jack, Chris, and even myself, we're all strong individual runners. The problem that Coach Gutierrez has been facing in the past few weeks was using the parts at hand to build a machine that runs smoothly and reliably. There are twenty-four different combinations to have four runners run a relay race, and I think we've tried them all except the ones that involve Chris as the anchor. You want the fastest runner to finish the race and squeeze that last hundredth of a second out of it, so Chris's position as our anchor was never in question. But all other positions were up for grabs. At one point the coach even put me in the starting position, and that worked great as long as we were the only team running. But against other teams it would always put us at a distinct psychological disadvantage because by the time I, the slowest in our team, passed the baton on to the second runner, we'd already be five meters behind the next team, and that wasn't doing a lot for the motivation of the other three runners. So Coach Gutierrez has been switching Jack and me back and forth between the second and third position, and we've been driving him insane because someone would always mess up the exchange. If we didn't drop the baton, we'd pass it outside the exchange zone, and if we did manage to do it inside the zone, it would take us too long. It was almost as if someone had cast an evil spell on our team.

Today, though, we run the perfect race.

Jason is off to an excellent start. With a two-meter lead he passes the baton to Jack who manages to maintain our lead until he passes the baton to me. I lose a meter on the next team, but my exchange with Chris is a work of pure beauty, and in the end Chris manages to win that meter back and not only win the race for us but win it in record time.

Coach Gutierrez waits for us to gather at the finish line. He looks at us, then at his stopwatch, then back at us.

"Gentlemen," he finally says, "if this had been an official competition you'd have broken the California high school 100-meter-relay record in your age group by two hundredths of a second. Finally! Finally you guys live up to the completely overblown expectations I've put in you. Keep it up, you little bastards!"

We're stunned. Under the applause of the entire team we celebrate, shouting and jumping up and down. Jack hugs Chris, and he high-fives Jason. Then he turns to me. I lift my hand for a high five, but instead of just high-fiving it, he grabs it and yanks my arm so hard that he almost pulls it out of its socket. It's painful, but I can bear it because for the first time ever, I can detect the faintest sign of respect in his eyes. He lets go, and then Chris is standing in front of me with the widest grin on his face. He puts his arms around me, lifts me up, and swirls me around a full three hundred and sixty degrees. When he puts me down again, I feel Jason's hand squeezing my neck and his other patting my head. High on adrenaline and testosterone, the four of us end up in a ginormously rambunctious group hug. When we break up, I turn around and cast my glance across the field. There, as always, Phil is standing on the sidewalk, holding his umbrella and his handbag, but today he's not facing the street as he's waiting for his dad to pull up in his old clunker. Today he's standing by the fence, looking in my direction. On any other day that would have freaked me out, but not today. Today it makes me feel proud to have someone—anyone—witness my success. I raise my hand for a coy wave, and Phil nods back at me, which by his standards is tantamount to an emotional outburst of unprecedented proportions.

I turn my head to look toward the other end of the track, and sure enough, there, behind the fence, Special Agent Nicole Tesla is sitting in her shiny black car, watching me from behind her dark sunglasses. When I catch her staring at me, she looks away and takes a drag from her cigarette.

"I have to go and celebrate," Coach Gutierrez announces, "and possibly draft my *High School Coach of the Year* acceptance speech, so get out of here, you little bastards!"

With the rest of the team, I ride a sweeping wave of inebriating pride back to the locker room, and before I even know it, I find myself getting undressed. Caught up in a moment I don't want to end and unwilling to let the others continue their celebration without me, I strip down naked in front of everyone as if I've never done anything else in my entire life.

And nobody even seems to notice—or care—except Chris.

When he sees me take off my undies, his eyes linger for a brief moment—on my face, not my private parts—and the faintest of smiles crosses his lips. On a bad day I would have taken this as a smirk triggered by some sort of amusement about my physical features, but this isn't a bad day. This is the best day I've had in a long time, and that makes me think of his smile as a genuine appreciation of the fact that I've finally found my place among equals. And it feels awesome.

Taking a shower with a dozen teenage boys is—who'd have thunk?—a pretty straightforward and uneventful affair if you ignore all the testosterone-driven teasing and sexual innuendo. It's all about soap and water and dicks and boisterous laughter.

As a large part of the conversation revolves around dick sizes, I turn and face the wall. I don't want to give anyone the chance to catch my furtive glances at someone else's private parts and point that awkward fact out to the others. I imagine getting pummeled to death by a naked, homophobic mob probably isn't a very joyous affair.

When facing the wall, only the two people standing directly next to me can sneak a peek at my privates. On my right side it's Chris, but he's not looking. I'm trying not to feel offended, although I find his apparent lack of interest in my body some-what disappointing. Then again, he's not looking at anyone else's junk either, which, if it's a deliberate restraint on his part, might be his way of making sure naked peers who know he's gay don't feel uncomfortable in his presence. Because when straight dudes look at your dick and express their unsolicited opinion, they're just guys being guys. If a gay guy does the same, he's probably hitting on you. So much for equality.

The guy standing on my left is obviously not gay, which might be why he doesn't seem afraid to eyeball me up and down the entire time. As if that weren't awkward enough, the person in question is no other than the Jackrabbit himself. And instead of facing the wall and turning his head to size me up, he's giving me the full frontal view and rubbing his soapy crotch as he keeps glaring at me. I try to ignore him by staring at the wall in front of me, but it's difficult to keep it up.

Try to ignore a train wreck.

Try not to think of a pink elephant.

It's nearly impossible, so I occasionally cast bashful glances to my left, and every time I look, I meet Jack's eyes and his disturbing smirk as he keeps running his hands over his reasonably attractive body. He is obviously taunting me, trying to provoke a reaction, a visible physical reaction of my body that he can point out and laugh at and use as a reason to call me a faggot again. I'm not going to let that happen, so I turn my head, face the wall, and listen to the steady patter of water mixing with the boisterous, puerile chatter of naked adolescent athletes.

Chapter Fourteen

I pull up a folding chair I brought up from the garage and usher Phil to sit. Sitting down next to him on my desk chair I say, "Shall we get on with it then?"

"Yes?" he says.

His answers always sound like questions, and I'm never quite sure if that's because he's unsure of his answer or if it's his way of saying he thinks it's a stupid question.

"All right," I say. "I've done some more research on our topic and I found this essay on *Romeo and Juliet* that might be useful. I suggest we read it and see if we can use any of it for our papers."

"Okay," Phil says, pulling a pen and notepad from his handbag.

There's a knock on the door. It's Mom, bringing a tray with two glasses of milk and a plate full of cookies.

"Would you like some milk and cookies?" she asks.

"Mom," I say, pinching the bridge of my nose. "We're not seven anymore."

Mom scoffs. "What's that got to do with anything? One can enjoy milk and cookies at any age. Besides, I wasn't even talking to you."

"If you weren't talking to me, who's the second glass for then?"

"Oh shush!"

Cumbersomely, she puts everything on my small desk between the computer, Phil's notepad, and all the useless rubbish that litters my desk. "Chocolate chip cookies," she says to Phil and smiles. "I hope you'll like them."

"Thank you."

Mom has barely closed the door behind her when Phil puts the first cookie in his mouth and grabs a second one.

"Hungry?" I ask.

He nods, and without further ado he leans in to my computer screen and starts reading.

The essay we have to read is only five pages, but it takes us forever. Philip is a slow reader. Every time I reach the end of a page I have to wait a minute or two for him to catch up before I can click through to the next page. Since I don't know where else to look while I'm waiting, I watch Phil from the corner of my eye. The view of his profile isn't even that unattractive, and from this perspective his deformity would hardly be noticeable if it weren't for his cauliflower nose. With his cleft lip not hogging all the attention for once, I notice—for the first time—Phil's other features. His thick, black Asian hair, his immaculate skin that has the color of very light coffee, his perfectly shaped ears. And then there's his smell that is clean and fresh and pleasant. Most importantly, it's natural, untainted by the artificial scent of shower gel or cologne. Just as I wonder if I can lean in closer without him noticing, he catches me staring at him.

"Sorry," I say sheepishly.

He shrugs. "I'm used to getting stared at, believe it or not."

It's a kind answer, kinder than I would have expected, and it prompts me to ask, "Does being used to it make it any less unpleasant?"

He thinks about it for a moment, then he looks me straight in the eyes and says, "No?"

There is no hint of anger or self-pity, which amazes me. I've probably witnessed only the tiniest fraction of abuse and rejection he must have experienced throughout his life, and I'm thinking if I were in his place I probably would have killed myself, or everyone else, or both, a long time ago.

"Can I ask you something?"

"About what?" he asks.

"You know …" I awkwardly point at my mouth.

"About your mouth?" he asks with a deadpan face, making me chuckle.

"No," I say. "About yours."

"Sure."

"You were ... born with this, right?"

"This is not something you suddenly catch when you're ten or something, you know?"

"Right," I say. "Sorry for being so ignorant. I've never ... met someone with a cleft lip before."

"It's okay."

"Have you ever thought about ... you know ... I mean ... can't you get, like, surgery or something to fix this?"

He nods. "I've had my fourteenth surgery this summer."

"Fourteen?!"

I'm aghast. If he's had fourteen surgeries and his face still looks like this, I hate to think how it must have looked when he was born. And one surgery for each year of his life? I have a million questions, but they're all written right on my face, so Phil offers the answers without waiting for me to ask them.

"It's not just the lip, it's also my palate and my nose. When I was born I had a gaping hole smack in the middle of my face. They had to close the gap in my palate, fix my gums and my teeth, and to do that they had to break my nose multiple times. That's why it looks the way it does. Anyway, it's complicated to fix something like that, and you can't do it in just one or two surgeries, so I'm having surgery every year. Usually during the summer holidays so I don't miss school. But this summer we moved here from Texas and we couldn't schedule my surgery any earlier, that's why I started school a week late."

A piece of the puzzle suddenly snaps into place.

"It's why you suddenly fell silent that weekend before you started school," I say. "You were using the Internet at the hospital when you first started writing to me. Then you went home and didn't have Internet access until you started using the computer at the library."

"Yes."

I look at him. "So what's it like? I mean, having to spend so much time in hospital?"

"I don't know. It doesn't make much of a difference if I sit in hospital with nobody visiting or I sit at home with nobody visiting. It's the surgeries that are difficult to deal with. Every time you get general anesthesia, there's a chance you won't wake up again. And getting surgery also increases the risk of getting a blood clot later that might kill you. It's a small chance, but it's there, and the more surgeries you get, the bigger the chance."

"So how many more surgeries do you think you will need?"

"I don't know," he says. "But I'll try to get as many as I can until I'm eighteen."

"Wait," I say. "Why until you're eighteen?"

"Because as long as I'm a minor, our health insurance will cover most of the costs. Once I'm an adult I'll have to pay for it all by myself. Surgery is very expensive, so I try to get as much done as I can before I'm eighteen and hope that after that I'll need just one or two more."

"How much does it cost?"

"Anywhere between five and ten thousand dollars."

"For one surgery?" I say. "That's a lot of money."

"I know."

"And no offense, but …" I pause because I don't know how to say it without sounding like an upper-middle-class asshole.

"… I don't look like I have that kind of money," he completes my sentence.

"Yeah. Sorry."

He shakes his head. "It's true, I don't. We don't. My family is poor. When we were still in Laos, my family owned land and we were doing all right. Laos is a poor country, so by Laotian standards we were almost rich."

As his words slowly sink in and I'm thinking about my own sheltered life and my carefree, privileged childhood, I'm beginning to feel a strange sense of guilt over how I let my own petty problems make me feel miserable when I've never really experienced true misery. I'm humbled as he keeps telling me about his surgeries, how he never went on vacation because they can't afford it and because he spends most of his summer holidays in hospital, year in, year out. Life has been hard on him but it didn't break him, it only made him harder and more thick skinned, and I'm beginning to understand why he sometimes seems cold and detached. He tells me a few stories of people who have been mean to him in his previous school, and he does so without any hatred or anger. I wonder how a person can be so forgiving, so I ask him that.

"I don't know that I'm forgiving," he says. "But I'm not an angry or bitter person by nature, and I won't let other people turn me into such a person because that's not how I want to be. I had no control over the way I was born. I have no control over the things people say to me. But if I didn't have control over the way I deal with things, then I'd have no control over anything, and that would be terrifying, wouldn't it?"

"I guess."

"Let other people be angry if they choose to be angry. I choose not to be."

I look at him for a long time, bewildered, confused, and in awe. He holds my stare until he finally says, "What?"

"Nothing." I shake my head. "I just wonder how you do it, that's all. I mean, cope with it all."

He shrugs. "I don't know. I try to channel it into something positive."

"Something positive? Like what?"

"Art?"

"Art?" I say, pretending I've never noticed him sitting in the schoolyard or the cafeteria, or even in class, his head bent over his sketchbook and the pencil in his hand flying over the paper. "That's cool."

He shrugs again. "I guess."

"So are you any good?"

He pulls a face, which is no mean feat given his condition, and says, "I don't think that's for me to say."

"Show me some of your work then."

Now he's the one staring at me for a while, then he shakes his head. "I don't know."

"Come on," I insist and poke my finger in his ribs. He winces and raises his arms in defense.

"Don't do that," he says.

I poke him again. "Come on, show me."

"All right, all right! But stop poking me already!" He picks up his bag and pulls out his sketchbook. As he hands it to me he says, "Don't expect anything special."

I'm not expecting anything, but when I open the book and turn the first page I immediately know that Phil was hiding his light under a bushel. The first sketch shows the semi-profile face of a teenage boy, a little older than us, maybe seventeen or eighteen. It's crude, just a quick sketch, but it's good. It's really good.

When I raise the sketchbook to get a closer look at Phil's delicate pencil strokes, a photograph slips out from between the pages and falls to the floor. We both stoop to pick it up, but I beat him to it. From the corner of my eye I notice Phil's discomfort, but he doesn't make any attempts to tear the photo out of my hand, so I take a look at it. It shows a young Caucasian woman wearing khaki cargo pants and a plain white T-shirt. She's got shoulder-length, dark brown, wavy hair, green eyes and an attractive smile. On her arm she's holding a baby. It's Phil, obviously, and it's a pitiful, almost revolting sight, because of that gaping hole in the middle of his face. He may still not look great today, but it's a vast improvement on how he used to look as a baby, because that baby looks almost … non-human.

"Who's that?" I ask.

Visibly uncomfortable, Phil says, "Me?"

"Really?" I say with a wry look. "You used to be a Caucasian woman before all your surgeries?"

Showing no sense of humor, he says, "No. That's my god-mother. Her name is Phyllis. She's American."

"She's also very pretty."

"Yes."

I look at the photo a few more moments until Phil takes it out of my hand and puts it the pocket of his shirt. I have a million questions, but it doesn't look like Phil wants to talk about it, so I don't pry and turn my attention back to his sketchbook. On the next page we have a young man in his early twenties. He's wearing a pair of jeans. No shirt, no socks or shoes. Like the boy in the previous sketch, he's staring into the distance, a melancholy expression on his face. I turn the page again. The same guy, this time fully nude, his private parts concealed by a towel he's holding in his right hand. As I keep turning the pages, I see more variations on the same theme. Boys and young men in varying stages of undress, always sensual, always pretty, and occasionally very sexy, but always alone. About halfway through the sketchbook I come across a drawing that breaks the pattern. Two boys kissing, both their faces obscured by one another. I look at Phil. He looks back at me and says, "What?"

"Who are they?"

He shrugs. "Nobody?"

"One of them looks like you."

"No he doesn't."

"He does too. I recognize the hair and the ears. Well, one ear."

"We should get back to work," he says, grabbing the sketchbook and putting it back in his bag.

As he leans forward and continues reading the essay on my computer, I pull my chair a little closer and pretend I'm still reading along while I take slow, deep breaths and inhale Phil's subtle but intriguing scent.

* * *

"So what happened to 2-b-pretty?" I ask, slumping on my bed. With my back leaning against the wall and my feet dangling over the edge of the bed I look at Phil. He's still sitting in his folding chair by my desk, his back straight and rigid, his hands in his lap as if he's waiting to be called into a doctor's office. I try to make my question sound casual and innocent, as if it's something that just crossed my mind. The truth is, I've been dying to ask that question ever since he stopped leaving comments on my Wattpad despite the new installments that I post daily.

"Nothing?" he says.

"Are you still reading along then?"

"Of course."

"I'm just asking because you haven't been leaving any comments recently."

"I know."

I give him a few seconds to elaborate on his answer, and when no enlightening details are forthcoming, I ask, "Why?"

"I don't know," he says. "Things have changed?"

"How have things changed?" I ask with a high-pitched voice, almost sounding agitated. "I mean, I know things have changed in that I no longer think you're some random girl from Indonesia. Or Sandy. But you knew I was me all along, so how has me knowing you are you changed anything for you?"

He shrugs. Again. When you talk to Phil he always shrugs so much, it's a miracle he hasn't developed rotator cuff syndrome yet.

"I'm not good at leaving comments. They take me forever to write up, and no matter how much time I take writing them and rewriting them and polishing them, they never feel adequate."

"For what it's worth," I say, looking at my fingers fiddling with the seam of the small heart-shaped pillow I keep on my bed, "I always enjoyed your comments, your analysis, and your suggestions, so ..." I let the sentence trail off because I don't know what more to say.

"Thank you. But now that you know who I am there's no need for me to take an hour to write a five-line comment when I can just tell you what I think in person, is there?"

"I guess. Except you're not doing that either."

"You didn't ask me."

I frown at him. "I never asked you to leave comments on Wattpad either. You still did it anyway."

"Sorry about that."

"Oh for crying out loud!" I say, throwing my hands up in the air. "Will you stop apologizing for everything? What is wrong with you?"

"Sorry," he says again, and before I even know what I'm doing, I grab the heart-shaped pillow and hurl it at his face. Come to think of it, it's actually kind of embarrassing that I even have a heart-shaped pillow openly lying around like a twelve-year-old girl, but it was a Christmas gift from Zoey two or three years back, and I actually kind of like it, so it wouldn't be nice to store it in the junk box under the bed.

The pillow hits Phil in the face before he catches it, and for a split second he musters a shy grin. The grin goes as fast as it came, and he puts the pillow back on my bed, but I sense a tiny little hole in the wall he seems to have built around himself, so I put my hand in before it closes again.

"Okay, I'm asking you now. What do you make of it?"

"Of what?" he asks.

"Of the whole situation. With Chris. And everything. You know."

He thinks for a moment, his expression calm and pensive. Then he looks at me. "Do you love him?"

I'm stumped by the question, at first by its simplicity, and then, after a brief contemplation, by its complexity.

Love?

What does that even mean?

I'm a twenty-first-century teen and—as the work on our term paper keeps painfully reminding me—clearly not as knowledgeable about matters of the heart as Shakespeare's precocious sixteenth-century Romeo, nor am I nearly as eloquent in expressing my emotional turmoils. How is one to recognize love if one has never experienced it before? Where does affection end, and where does love begin? And isn't it, in the end, all just hormones?

"I don't know," I finally say. "I like him. He's so cute and handsome. When he smiles at me he makes me feel all warm and fuzzy inside. So … I don't know. Is that love? Or being in love? Or just a silly teenage crush? I don't know."

"Do you want to get naked and do naughty things with him?"

The awkward way he poses his question makes me laugh at first, but when I look at him there's no smirk on his face, no silly, awkward grin. He means it, and he's not shy about it, which has to be a first. I grab the heart-shaped pillow again and continue fiddling with the seam. I'm the one who's feeling awkward now.

"I guess," I say without looking at Phil, and I feel my ears turning bright red.

"And do you think he'd want that too?"

"I don't know. He didn't exactly size me up when I was standing next to him in the shower. Then again, neither did I."

"Right," Phil says. "So what about Jack's party?"

I look at him. "What about it?"

"Will you go?"

"Oh God!" I say, tilting my head back and bumping it against the wall. "I really don't know. I mean, it's Jack and a whole bunch of Jack's friends, and I don't like any of them."

"You like Chris, though."

"Yes, but … I don't know. Jack doesn't even know I'm coming, and he's not exactly my biggest fan. What if I show up at his place and he just slams the door in my face? I really don't need any more run-ins with him or any more humiliations."

"There's only one way to find out."

"That's easy for you to say." I look at him again. "Would you go?"

"I don't go to parties," he says. "I never get invited to parties, and even if I did, I probably wouldn't go because if someone invited me to a party I'd always think they're probably only doing it so they can pour a bucket of pig's blood over my head or something."

I sigh. "Let me rephrase the question: if you were me, would you go?"

He ponders the question for a while, and I'm thinking he's probably finding it more difficult to put himself in my shoes than making the actual decision.

"I think if I were you and if I really thought he'd be the right guy for me, I'd jump at any chance to spend time with him. And maybe, if I declined his invitation, I'd be worried he'd feel rejected and he'd lose any interest in me."

"Damn," I say and I hug my pillow and drop myself on the bed, "I knew you were going to say that."

"If you knew what my answer was going to be, you already know what yours is."

"Yeah, I'm not sure I follow the logic of that."

With a subtle smile on his face he says, "Think about it."

* * *

Late in the evening I'm lying on my bed, hugging my heart pillow again and staring at the ceiling, trying to come up with arguments to refute Phil's logic and valid reasons for me to weasel my way out of Chris's invitation to Jack's party without appearing ungrateful or indifferent about his amorous advances—if that is what they are.

Phil, I have to admit, is right about one thing: things have changed between us. A mere week ago I never even would have listened to anything he had to say, let alone giving his weird views any serious consideration. On the other hand, I would have given 2-b-pretty's advice a whole lot of consideration, so whether I like it or not, I can't come up with any reason to easily dismiss Phil's suggestions other than that he's ugly.

And that's so stupid.

I don't want to be stupid.

I will have to go to that party.

Damn.

The mere thought of it makes my heart beat faster, and I don't know if it's the decision itself that excites me or the prospect that I'll be spending an evening with Chris in an entirely recreational setting that—given our host's reputation—will in all likelihood include alcohol, cigarettes, and possibly other perks usually reserved for adults. Either way, a fast-beating heart has to be an unmistakable sign that I'm alive.

I like being alive.

My heart skips a beat as the ringing of my phone startles me out of my thoughts. It's Alfonso.

"Hey," I say.

"¿Que pasa?"

"Nothing much. Just staring at the ceiling and contemplating my shitty little life."

"No kidding, dude, I've seen your ceiling, it looks depressing as frick. You need to get out more."

"I know, right?"

"Speaking of which, wanna sleep over on Friday? We can get burritos, play Xbox, and I can give you an erotic massage if that makes you feel any better."

I take it as a good sign that he's teasing me about my sexuality. He wouldn't do that if he had a problem with it.

"As enticing as that sounds," I say, "I can't on Friday. Chris invited me to Jack's party, remember?"

"I remember you got invited. I somehow must have missed your decision to go. What else are you keeping from me, Matthew?"

"Nothing," I say. "I've literally just made up my mind two minutes ago. Sorry, pal. Should have called earlier."

"You don't love me anymore ever since you turned gay. I'm disappointed, Matthew. Very disappointed."

"I've never loved you, Alfonso. You were always just a token Mexican friend to me. To make me appear more tolerant and cosmopolitan, you know?"

"I'm Argentinian!"

"Potato, tomato," I say, and we both laugh.

"So have you told your parents yet?" he asks.

"No. Still working on my road map out of the closet."

"That's not what I meant. I'm talking about the party. You think they're gonna let you go?"

"Sure," I say, "why not?"

"And extend your curfew?"

"Probably not."

"That's gonna be one hell of a party for you then, if you have to be home by eleven."

I haven't even thought about that. Chris told me to be at Jack's by ten. "Oh," I say.

"Yeah, oh! Great planning, Matthew!"

"Like I said, I only just decided I want to go to the party. I haven't had time to think about the details."

"You should have thought about the details before you made up your mind, stupid," Alfonso says, and I can hear his eyes rolling. "Okay, let me try again: how about a sleepover on Friday? We can have burritos and play Xbox and then you can sneak out the back door, go to your party, and sneak back in in the middle of the night, and your parents—or mine—will be none the wiser. Sound good?"

What he's proposing takes a while to register. "Are you being serious?" I finally say.

He scoffs. "You got five seconds, Matty. Four ... three ... two ..."

CHAPTER FIFTEEN

A broken rotary clothes line is lurking in the dark on the dry, brown front lawn like a dead spider. The small house looks run-down and scruffy. It hasn't seen a fresh coat of paint in ages, and in the dim porch light I'm not sure if that paint was white or pastel blue. Now it's just dirty gray with brown splotches. I climb the three squeaky stairs to a front porch that seems to be used mostly as a storage area. There's a broken fridge, its inside walls brown and grimy, the door torn off and leaning against its side. I smell the dead rat before I spot it behind the fridge. Half a dozen plastic bags with old newspapers and leaflets from grocery stores and fast food places fill up most of the small space on the other side of the front door. Loud music is hammering through the thin walls, and I'm surprised someone even hears the doorbell when I ring it. A moment later the door swings open and Jack stands in front of me holding two bottles of beer, one full, one half-empty.

It takes a few long moments for my presence to register with him, and when it finally does, he says, "The fuck are *you* doing here?"

"I ... sorry ...," I stammer, and I'm about to turn around and leave before he smashes a beer bottle on my head, but then Chris ninjas his way in from the side and says, "He's with me, Jack. My plus-one."

His bright red T-shirt reads *Keep Calm and Party On*.

Jack's eyes jump back and forth between Chris and me two or three times before he slurs, "Fucking hell." Then he thrusts the full bottle of beer against my chest. I grab it so it doesn't drop on the floor and he makes me clean up the mess.

"Thanks," I say, "but I—"

"Shut up, Maddie. My house, my rules."

He puts his own bottle to his lips and empties it, tilting back his head. When he's done he leans in to me and lets out the longest, loudest, and most disgusting burp I have ever heard.

"I don't give a shit what you two fags are up to," he says to both Chris and me, "but whatever you do, don't jizz on the carpet. Or the furniture. Or anywhere. Or I'm gonna make you lick it up."

He bursts into laughter as his hand slams down on my shoulder. Then he turns and walks away.

"Don't mind him," Chris shouts over the music and closes the door behind me. "He's already pretty wasted. Come on, I want you to meet a few people."

He grabs my hand and pulls me into the living room. After the bumpy start I'd rather turn around and run, but Chris's soft, warm hand feels too nice in my own, so I stumble after him without protest.

He drags me across the room to a group of people, three guys and a girl. They smile at us as they see us coming, and my heart starts beating faster when I suddenly realize that I know at least one of the guys, David, a tall boy with ash blond hair. He was a year above me in junior high, and toward the end of seventh grade I used to have a crush on him for about four weeks. Then the school year was over and he went on to Jefferson High which is why I have never seen him again until tonight.

"Guys, this is Matt," Chris says and they all say hi as he tells me all their names, but the music is so loud and I'm so nervous that I don't remember any of them except the one I already knew.

David, holding hands with his curly-haired hipster boyfriend, raises his eyebrows with a big, bright smile and says something to me but I can't hear him so I lean in and say, "What?"

"I remember you!" he shouts in my ear. "Brookhurst Junior High, right?"

"Yeah!" I say, feeling flattered that I left an impression on an older guy, someone I used to have a crush on no less.

"I used to watch you in the schoolyard with your Latino boyfriend. I always thought you were such a cute couple."

"Oh, no no!" I say, shaking my head emphatically and flailing my bottle-holding hand about. "He was not my boyfriend. Just a friend."

"Right," David says. His smile says, 'I don't believe a word you say, but whatever.' Then he raises his bottle of beer, chinks it against mine and says, "Anyway, good to see you again. Cheers!"

He takes a swig from the bottle, and since I don't want to appear rude, I do the same. The bitter taste of alcohol running down my throat makes me shudder, but I pretend that of all the beers I've had in my life, this is clearly the best.

Which, technically, it is.

Here's to alcohol, the rose colored glasses of life.

Half an hour later and halfway through my second beer, I've not only grown used to the taste, I've fallen in love with it and with the rest of the world around me. I've heard of parties with booze and funny-smelling cigarettes, but I've never been to any, so I had no idea what I was missing. Chris's friends all seem very nice. They do most of the talking, I do most of the laughing like a giddy little schoolboy who's finally allowed to sit at the grown-up table. When I've finished my second beer I get up to get a third. I know my way around the house by now, but on my way to the kitchen my bladder is calling for my attention, so I make a detour to the bathroom. When I turn the doorknob, the door doesn't open, and from the inside a female voice calls out, "Just a minute!"

So I wait a minute.

Two minutes.

Three.

I'm eventually joined by a guy with shaggy brown hair who must be sixteen or seventeen. He's wearing shorts and a T-shirt with a surfing monkey on it. In his right hand he's holding one of those funny-shaped, smelly cigarettes.

"You waiting?" he says, flicking his head at the bathroom door.

"Yeah," I say.

"Right." He takes a drag from his cigarette. "So you one of Jack's friends?"

Friend isn't exactly the right word, but the guy probably isn't interested in my life story, so I just nod.

"Cool."

"Yeah."

"I'm Tony," he says and holds up his hand for a bro shake. I shake it. "Matt."

"Right."

The sound of running water is coming from the bathroom. No flushing toilet, just the tap running. A minute later the door opens and a girl careens into the hallway, hitting her shoulder against the door frame in the process.

"Ouch!" she says and laughs. Making her way back into the living room, she hits her other shoulder against the next door frame.

"Do you mind, Matt?" Tony says. "I really gotta go."

"Sure," I say.

Before he enters the bathroom, he hands me his cigarette.

"Thanks, but I don't—"

"Can you just hold this for me? I need both my hands to hold my dick, and I don't want hot ash falling on it while I'm peeing."

"Right, sure," I say. Tony closes the door and I look at the reefer in my hand. Because that's what it is, isn't it? It doesn't look like a regular cigarette and it doesn't smell like one either. I carefully lift it up to my nose and smell its strangely intriguing, sweet smell. After a quick look left and right to make sure nobody is watching, I put the reefer to my lips and take a small puff. I don't feel anything except a strong, musty smell in my mouth. I take another drag, and this time I inhale the smoke deep into my lungs. It burns, it stings, but I manage to exhale it without coughing. A few moments later I feel lightheaded and exhilarated. Here I am, Matthew Elliot Dunstan, at my first party, drinking and smoking weed like a boss.

If only Greg and Zoey could see me, I'm thinking and I giggle.

Then I'm thinking, *If only Mom and Dad could see me*, and I cringe, and my cringe makes me giggle some more.

I take another drag.

"Matt!"

Startled, I have to I cough. I look in the direction of the voice and see Chris floating towards me.

That's funny. I didn't even know Chris could float.

"Oh, hi!" I say, and my smile feels like it's stretching from one ear to the other.

"I see you're enjoying yourself, huh?" Chris says, looking at the reefer in my hand.

It feels like two or three minutes until I can make sense of his words, then I say, "Oh, that! No. No, no. That's not mine. I'm just holding that for Tony. You see, he needs both his hands to hold his dick ..." I giggle, "... and he doesn't want hot ash falling on it." I giggle some more because it feels so nice to be giggling.

"Just holding that for Tony, huh?"

"Yeah! He needs both hands to hold his dick and ..."

Saying the word *dick* to Chris makes me giggle again.

"Just give me that!" he says. With one hand he grabs the reefer, with the other he playfully slaps the back of my head, which is totally hilarious. He takes a deep drag and inhales the smoke forever.

Again, I hear water running. No tap, just the flushing of the toilet this time. The bathroom door opens, and Tony comes floating out. "Dude," he says, "that girl left the biggest turd I have ever seen just floating there in the toilet." He grabs his reefer from Chris's lips and looks at him. "Thanks for holding that for me, Matt."

"No problem," Chris says. "Good stuff."

"Yeah."

As fascinating as Chris and Tony's conversation is, I really gotta go, so I turn and float into the bathroom. I didn't even know I could float, but apparently I can, and I'm really good at it too.

I'm a natural born floater, I'm thinking proudly as I hover over the toilet and unpack my dick to relieve myself. As my urine flows down the bowl, the world around me melts. The grimy bathroom tiles, the house, the music, Jack and Chris and

Tony and David, the house, the street, Brookhurst, my family, Zoey and Alfonso and Phil, the world, the entire universe and I become one conglomerated mess, a beautiful mess, the messiest, most beautiful mess I've ever seen. I'm overcome by a profound feeling of love for my world, my life, my everything. What's not to love? I have the best best friend in the world, I have a huge crush on a super sexy guy who seems to be really into me, and I'm out partying on a Saturday night, drinking beer and smoking weed. Screw strict parents, obnoxious little brothers, and stupid school assignments with weird, freaky-looking partners. This is my life, and I'm going to live it the way I see fit, and whoever doesn't like it can go wherever it is the devil resides these days.

Trump Tower, probably.

I don't know how long I'm standing there, contemplating life, the universe, and everything with my leaking dick in my hand. Time has long since lost all its defining properties.

Nothing was, nothing will be.

Everything just is.

I am.

I am floating back to the door, and when I open it, I'm not even surprised to see Chris gone and Jack standing in his place. Why would I be surprised? It's Jack's house, goddammit, and he can fricking well stand wherever he likes! He just happens to stand right outside the bathroom, and I'm genuinely happy to see him.

Curiously, so is he.

"Oh Maddie," he says and puts his arm around my shoulder. "I've been missing you."

As he leads me down the hallway, away from the buzzing living room and toward the stairs, he leans his head against my neck. His warm breath smells of beer and nicotine as he continues to slur, "I like you, Maddie. I really, really like you."

"Why, I like you too, Jack," I reply. It's not something I thought I'd ever say, but right here, right now it seems like a perfectly reasonable response.

I'm not sure who is supporting whom as we totter up the stairs. I prop up Jack but he's the one leading the way on unsteady legs.

"You're a good guy, Maddie," he says. "A really good guy."

"You think?"

"Of course! A really good guy."

"Right," I say and giggle. "I'm just asking because you have a funny way of showing that sometimes, you know?"

"Yeah, yeah." He caresses my cheek with his hand, gently, almost lovingly. "You know how it's meant, though, right? Right, Maddie? I love to tease, and I tease because I love. I love you, Maddie Matt."

I'm so baffled by this unexpected revelation that I can't help but reply, "Why, I love you too, Jacky Jack."

My response makes Jack giggle through his nose, and a drop of clear, watery snot is hanging from the tip of his nose as he says, "You say the cutest things, Maddie."

He removes his arm from my neck and opens the door to what turns out to be his bedroom. We go inside, but we're not alone. Chris, my candy crush Chris is sitting in a tatty armchair and staring at a clunky, twenty-year-old computer monitor on Jack's desk. For some reason he's taken off his T-shirt and shoes. Jack closes the door, shutting out the noise from the party below. I'm still hearing voices though, so I look around for other people, but the voices are coming from the video Chris is watching. Two guys, maybe eighteen, maybe twenty years old, buck naked, engaging in explicit sexual conduct with the primal sounds to match, drowning out the muffled party music from down below.

Suddenly, my mood changes. It almost feels like when I'm taking a hot shower and Greg turns on the hot water tap in the other bathroom, except that makes sense because Greg does it all the time and on purpose. Here, nothing seems to make sense. I feel dizzy and my legs give way underneath me. Heroically, Jack catches me before I fall, and assisted by Chris he leads me over to the bed where they sit me down.

"He's so wasted," Jack slurs in Chris's direction before he floats away.

Chris sits down next to me and puts his arm around me to help me keep my body upright. I lean my head against his shoulder, and since everything seems to be spinning around me, I close my eyes but the spinning doesn't stop. In fact, it gets even spinnier. I lean in closer to Chris, press my face against his strong, smooth, muscular neck.

He smells so nice.

As he's rubbing my back, he sniffs my hair and whispers, "You smell like an ashtray full of beer."

"I had one of them funny cigarettes."

He snickers. "Yeah, I know."

"Everything is spinning."

"I bet it is. You should lie down."

Our feet still on the floor, we both sink backward onto the bed.

His arm supporting my head, he puts his other hand on my chest.

"You got a jackhammer in there?"

"You smell so nice," I say.

He chuckles and plants a kiss on my forehead. On my nose. On one cheek, then on the other. On my lips. His tongue gently forces its way into my mouth, and I'm too weak to resist. I don't even want to resist. I've been secretly wanting to kiss him from the moment I first saw him. Rejecting him now would be stupid and render the last few weeks of love's labor entirely lost.

We kiss, maybe ten seconds, maybe ten minutes, who can tell? I keep losing myself in the comfort of his arms and his warm, wet mouth. Chris is kissing me like fire and ice, and I let it happen. I want it to happen. I've fallen for him, and I keep falling, ever so much deeper, ever so much faster, but I'm not scared. I'm feeling safe and warm in his arms, and I'm hoping this moment will never end.

As Chris's left hand is caressing the back of my head, his right hand starts wandering. First he rubs my chest, then my belly. He pulls my T-shirt out of my pants and slides his hand across my skin. My head in his hand, our tongues entwined, his fingers are fondling my nipple. A heat wave engulfs my body as he unbuckles my belt and unzips my jeans. Our kissing intensifies, and cold air is sending down shivers down my spine as he frees my grateful dick from the confines of my boxers, pulling them down with both hands while playfully pinching my nipple and gently pulling the hair at the back of my head.

Wait.

What.

Something's not right.

How many hands does he actually have?

I push Chris away, gently at first but he keeps pulling me back in so I push harder.

"Relax," he whispers. "Everything is fine."

He puts one of his way too many hands on my neck and pulls me closer, his lips once again seeking mine. But everything is not fine. Something is terribly, terribly wrong, because even though I may be drunk and stoned and my view of reality may be impaired, I'm pretty sure there is no way can he do all these things at the same time.

I open my eyes and see Chris looking back at me with a knavish smile. With the back of my hand I wipe his saliva off my lips, and when I lift my head to look at my crotch I see Jack kneeling right in front of me on the floor, admiring the proud flagpole that is my fully erect dick.

Overwhelmed by the nightmare I'm finding myself in, my head starts spinning, and I feel a tension in my body, rising from deep within my bowels. My body suddenly feels burning hot except for that small exposed spot between my legs that is tickled by a rush of fresh air. Leaning forward, Jack opens his mouth, and just as he's about to go down on me, the music abruptly grows louder, and a painfully high-pitched scream tears the whole universe apart.

All our heads turn toward the open door where Sandy is standing, both hands covering her mouth as her horrified gaze keeps jumping back and forth between Chris, Jack, me, and the flagpole.

This is too much.

With everything spinning, reality collapses in on me. My heart bursts into a million pieces, my head explodes, my guts churn, and before I even know what's happening, I'm emptying the entire contents of my stomach onto Jack's bed.

* * *

It's a chilly night for October, so I've buried my hands deep the pockets of my pants. I'm shivering, but the cold helps me to sober up. Which isn't necessarily a good thing, because the clearer my mind becomes, the more I'm horrified by what happened. Maybe I should have another couple of drinks and kill another couple of thousand brain cells. I wish the physical effects of alcohol would wear off more quickly than the mental ones. I'd rather be oblivious to tonight's events than be unable to walk in a straight line without stumbling over my own feet every other couple of steps.

Sandy is walking next to me, steadying my gait with one hand whenever necessary while working her phone with the other, trying to get a hold of El Niño.

"Fonso! Where the hell are you? Call me back, this is an emergency."

She groans and puts the phone back in her pocket.

"If he's on the Xbox, he'll be wearing headphones," I mumble. "That's why he doesn't hear his phone."

She looks at me. "Should I take you to his place now?"

"No!" I blurt out. Startled by the loudness of my own voice, I tone it down a notch. "No. Not yet. He can't see me like this. I need to sober up first."

"So where do you want to go? It's kinda cold."

I stop and rub both her arms. "Oh my God, Sandy, I'm so sorry! Are you cold? You want my jacket? I can give you my jacket. I don't mind. I don't want you to be cold!"

"Matthew," she says. "You're not wearing a jacket."

I look at myself. "Oh my God, where's my jacket?"

"Were you wearing a jacket when you got to Jack's?"

I think for a moment. "No?"

"There you go."

We keep on walking down the deserted street.

"I'm so sorry, Sandy."

"It's okay, don't worry," she says. Then she points across the street. "Looks like Milo's still up."

I turn my head. A hundred meters away, the Korova is brightly lit.

I can go a hundred meters in 12.5 seconds.

"Oh my God, coffee!" I say. "I so need some coffee."

Without further ado, I let go of Sandy, turn around and start crossing the street.

"Watch out!" Sandy shrieks, but by the time her shriek registers with me, it's already being drowned out by the screeching tires of a braking car. I turn my head and stare into its beaming headlights. Blinded, I take a step back, stumble, and fall backward. My butt hits the ground the moment the car comes to a halt just inches in front of me. Hyperventilating, my heart pounding heavily in my chest, I push my hands and feet against the ground, trying to get up, but I'm too drunk to coordinate that many limbs, so I just move backward three or four feet in an awkward crab walk before I collapse. I try again, but now Sandy is kneeling down next to me, and putting her arm around my shoulders, pinning me down.

"Matt! Oh my God, are you okay?"

I shake my head, but it's not in response to her question.

As my eyes are getting used to the glistening light, I realize why I didn't hear the car when I stepped into the street. It's the kind of car that barely makes any noise.

It's a Tesla.

Still shaking my head, I lift my arm and point. "No. No!"

The car door opens, and two heavy boots hit the ground. In them, legs clad in black cargo pants.

"It's … it's …," I stammer almost hysterically, still pointing.

"Matthew, calm down!" Sandy begs me.

I look at her, shaking my head. "Run," I say. "We have to run!"

But Sandy keeps holding me down as Special Agent Nicole Tesla approaches us with big strides and gets down on one knee in front of me, but I don't think she's going to propose.

"Good God, are you okay?" she asks.

I shake my head and point at her. "You! I know you!"

"You know her?" Sandy asks.

"She's been following me around! She's FBI or something, but I haven't done anything! They were only stories I posted on Wattpad!"

"What are you talking about, Matthew?"

Special Agent Nicole Tesla looks at her, frowning. "Did he hit his head?"

"No," Sandy says. "I mean, I don't know. I mean, I don't think so. He's pretty drunk."

"You have to run, Sandy. You can't save me, but you can save yourself!"

"Should I call an ambulance?"

"No amnulance," I slur. "It's a trap!"

Sandy shakes her head. "He's gonna be okay. He's just had too much to drink."

"Are you sure?"

"You have to run, Sandy!"

"Pretty sure," Sandy says.

Nicole nods. "Okay. We should get him off the road though."

I have little resistance to offer as Sandy and Nicole lift me up and put me back on my feet.

They walk me back onto the sidewalk, and Nicole says, "You really shouldn't be walking around town like that in the middle of the night. You want me to give you a ride home?"

I shake my head emphatically. "I'm not getting into a creepy stranger's car! My mom told me to never get into a stranger's car." I turn to Sandy. "Let's call an Uber."

"Matthew, that is literally summoning a creepy stranger to get into their car!" She looks at Nicole. "It's okay, we'll walk. It's only a couple of blocks. We want to get some coffee first anyway. It's kind of our regular place over there." She flicks her head at the Korova.

Nicole shrugs. "All right then. Just don't let him reel into the street again."

As we cross the street, Nicole gets back into her car and follows us at walking speed until we reach the Korova. Then she takes off, just like that.

That's your tax dollars at work. Law enforcement in this country is so inadequate.

As I watch Nicole's tail lights disappear in the distance, Sandy slams the palm of her hand against the glass door of the Korova. "Milo! Open up!"

Milo is standing behind the counter polishing glasses. When he sees us he shakes his head and mouths, "We're closed," but Sandy keeps slamming her hand against the door.

"Open up, Milo!"

Milo sighs, flings the towel over his shoulder and makes his way to the door. He opens the door and says, "Sorry, sweetheart, but we're already closed." Then his gaze falls upon me, his face aghast. "Oh dear! What happened to *you*?"

I must look pretty awful, but if I look only half as bad as I feel, I can't blame him for his reaction.

"Long story," I say.

"Can we come inside, Milo? Just for a few minutes. Please."

Milo sighs. Then he steps aside and motions us inside.

"Thanks, Milo. You're the best."

"Don't I just know it?" he says and locks the door behind us. He follows us to our booth, and as we slide into it he asks, "Coffee?"

"Double espresso," Sandy says. "No wait, make that a triple. Extra strong. And water for me."

"Coming right up," Milo says and scurries back behind the counter.

I grab the menu off the table. Not that I want to order anything, but I need something to keep my fingers busy. It has a calming effect, and I need something I can focus on because I really want to distract myself from what happened.

"How are you feeling?" Sandy asks.

"How do I look?" I say without looking at her.

"That bad, huh?"

"Yeah."

"Do you want to talk about it?" she asks.

I know that I don't, but I also know that I probably have to. I just can't let Sandy go home without offering some kind of explanation for what she's witnessed in Jack's bedroom, so I look at her and say, "Sandy, I'm gay."

She chuckles. "Yeah, I kinda figured."

"Right. I guess it was pretty obvious the moment you walked in on us."

"Oh, no no." She shakes her head. "I kinda figured you were gay a long time before tonight."

My shoulders slump. Will this ever stop? Why do I even put so much energy in clasping the closet door shut with my fingernails when apparently my closet has glass doors?

"Hey," Sandy says. "It's okay. There's nothing wrong with being gay."

"No, that's not it. It's just ... it seems that everyone I'm coming out to already knows I'm gay, and it's kinda ... depressing."

"Don't worry about it. You're way too sweet for a straight guy. Trust me, that's a good thing."

Milo comes and puts our beverages in front of us. "Listen, darlings," he says, "I'm gonna give you a bit of privacy. I'll be back in the kitchen giving Hans a handjo— ... I mean, giving Hans a hand cleaning up the mess he's been making all day. If you need anything or you want me to unlock the door for you, just give me a holler."

"Thanks, Milo."

"Sure," he says with a sweet smile and disappears into the kitchen.

Over coffee and water, we talk. I tell Sandy everything. Everything that's pertaining to my crush on Chris and my perennial feud with Jack, that is. I keep Phil and my coming out to Alfonso out of the equation to keep things simple and to the point. When I get to the moment right before she walked in on us, Sandy asks, "So do you think Jack is gay?"

I shrug. "I don't know. Given his attitude towards me and gay people in general, I find it hard to believe. Then again, tonight I found him getting ready to suck my dick. Not sure why he would do that if he weren't gay."

After thinking about it for a while, Sandy says, "I know it's a very clichéd thing to say it might be *just a phase*, but sometimes that's just what it is. Some people need more time to figure out their sexuality than others. And some people have a hard time accepting themselves the way they are. Maybe that's where Jack's at right now."

"Yeah, maybe. I don't know."

"You know what I really can't wrap my head around though?"

I look at her. "What's that?"

"I'm trying to make sense of Chris's role in this. I mean, the way you describe your relationship, he really seems to be into you, and he wants to be your boyfriend and everything. But if you're in love with someone or have a crush on them or whatever, why would you want to share them with someone else? Do you know what I mean?"

I know exactly what she means, but the implications are too devastating to consider.

"Was it the first time you and Chris were ... you know ... making out?"

I reply with a silent nod because if I were to open my mouth right now I'd probably burst into tears like a colicky infant.

"See," Sandy continues, "and that's what's confusing me. I mean, to go from a few kisses straight to a threesome seems like an awfully big leap."

I stare at the table, trying to avoid Sandy's prying gaze. The triple espresso helped me sober up just enough to realize that everything around me has started spinning again, and the bitter liquid in my stomach is making me feel sick. With my cold, sweaty hands I rub my tired eyes, and I sigh.

"I'm sorry," Sandy says. "I'm talking too much. I should probably shut up."

"No, no." I look at her, my vision all blurry. "It's okay. It's just ... too much. Everything is too much, and I'm still too drunk to make any sense of ... anything, really."

"I understand."

"Sandy," I slur, taking both her hands, "one girl is more use than twenty boys. I really appreciate everything you did tonight. Like, taking me out of there. Who knows what would have happened if you hadn't shown up. Good God, I don't even want to think about all the ways things could have turned even worse, you know? And thank you for listening. And understanding. And offering your own perspective. And not judging. And everything. It's ... it's really good to have someone to talk to when there's no one else to talk to. I don't even know if that makes any sense. Right now I'm just sitting here and I'm listening to myself and I have no idea where all the words that are leaving my mouth are coming from because

I'm still, like, totally wasted, and I'm so so sorry that you have to see me like this because I'm usually not like this. I've never been drunk before. Or stoned. Or feeling sick like that. Or all of the above. And I don't even know what I'm talking about, but—"

"Matt. Matt!" Sandy interrupts me, squeezing my hands. "It's okay. I understand you're pretty upset and still feeling sick and whatnot, but everything is gonna be okay."

"I feel so ashamed, Sandy!"

"No," she says. "You *think* you're feeling ashamed. You think you're feeling all kinds of stupid things because you're still drunk, and I think what you really need right now is a cold shower and a long sleep. I'm going to take you to Alfonso's now."

"Oh God," I say. "He's gonna kick my butt so hard, but I probably deserve it."

CHAPTER SIXTEEN

"Whoa!" Alfonso says the moment he opens the door and sees me. "Someone's had a few."

"Don' gemme started, Fonso," I say.

"Night, Matthew," Sandy says. "Go get some sleep."

I give her a hug, a little too tight, a little too long, because I've lost all sense of time and force. "Thank you, Sandy. I love you so much! I wish you could be a dude, you know?"

"All right," she says, gently pushing me away, "you go and sleep it off now. Things will look different in the morning."

I'm tempted to tell her that with the soft focus of inebriation removed, things will surely look worse in the morning, but my head starts spinning again and I'm still sporadically hit by bouts of nausea, so I decide to heed Sandy's advice. I pat Alfonso on the chest as I make my way past him and stagger down the stairs.

"A word, Alfonso?" I hear Sandy say before I enter Alfonso's basement lair and close the door behind me. I don't need to hear the story she's about to tell him.

Alfonso—bless him—has prepared the couch for me with a bed sheet, pillow, and blanket. As I sit down on the couch I topple over, sinking my face into the pillow. My initial urge to sit up again is quickly crushed by the intriguingly comforting feeling of snuggling my face up against something cool and soft. I don't want to move anymore, so I slip my shoes off my feet, swing my legs onto my makeshift bed, and hug my pillow. I need something to hold onto. My life, my world, my entire universe is spinning around me, tossing me up and tearing me down and hurling me around until I know no more whether I'm upside down or inside out.

Indescribable feeling, soaring, mumbling, freewheeling on a batshit crazy night, a voice is singing in my head.

And then I'm out. I don't know how long Alfonso was upstairs chatting with Sandy. I don't know if he let her walk home alone in the middle of the night or if he was being a gentleman and escorted her home. I don't know what time it was when he came back downstairs and tucked me in. I can only assume he must have done it at some point because when I wake up way too early in the morning, I find myself with the blanket pulled up to my chin. I open my eyes and see Alfonso lying in his bed across the room, topless and peacefully snoring away. And then I notice the elephant in the room—a big, fat elephant, gray and heavy like a storm cloud. It's sitting where my head used to be, and it's trumpeting in excruciating pain.

"Oh God," I moan, rubbing my eyes. A cautious attempt to move results in more dull, throbbing pain and the sobering realization that I'd probably be better off dead. And that's just the physical pain. Its presence wastes no time in dragging me out of my comforting state of sleep-induced amnesia. In the sluggish blink of a still sleepy eye, it all comes back to me, and it brings with it the embarrassment that turns out to be no less painful than the physical agony. I scan my memory for any sign that it was all just a horribly realistic dream after all, but no such luck. It's all true, and I have no idea how I'm supposed to live with the burning feeling of shame and guilt that comes with it.

I'm thirsty. My tongue feels like our front lawn in August, and it probably has the same color, too. In spite of my pain I manage to lift my head and look around for a bottle of water, a watering can, or a garden hose, but the only thing within my reach is a half-empty bag of potato chips. Slowly, I swing my legs off the couch and get on my feet. I look around and spot the mini fridge next to Alfonso's bed. Something cold would be nice, so I make my way to the fridge on unsteady legs like a patient after hip replacement surgery. When I open the fridge, bottles in the door compartment rattle and chink, way too loud not only for the delicate, hypersensitive hearing of someone who's experiencing their first hangover but also for Alfonso's light sleep. Within a second he's wide awake, glaring at me suspiciously.

"There's no booze in there, borrachiño," he says with a croaky voice.

I examine the contents of the fridge. Not only is there no alcohol, there's nothing to drink at all, only bottles and jars of salsa and guacamole. Nothing against Alfonso's delicious homemade awesomesauce, but it's not exactly what I'm craving right now.

"Seriously?" I say. "You got a fridge full of condiments but not even a bottle of water or anything else that's remotely suitable to wash away the foul aftertaste of the shittiest night of one's life?"

Alfonso yawns and stretches like a sleepy dog. "That bad, huh?"

"Worse," I say and close the fridge. "Hasn't Sandy told you anything?"

"Oh, don't get your hopes up. Sandy has told me *everything*." He sits up and leans back against the headboard. "Wanna talk about it?"

"Do I have a choice?"

He shakes his head. "Nope."

With a heavy sigh that matches the weight of the world on my slender shoulders I sit down on Alfonso's bed. "It was the most embarrassing thing that ever happened to me."

"What was? Having a threesome with two dudes, or being walked in on by Sandy?"

"Both," I say. "And it wasn't a threesome! Not that I'm an expert or anything, but a threesome is something that three people do voluntarily. I had no idea what was going on. I was totally wasted and making out with Chris, and then all of a sudden somebody opened my pants and …" I can't say it, and I probably don't even have to because I'm pretty sure Sandy didn't leave out any of the critical details. "I was basically assaulted. Sexually, I mean."

"Right," he says. "How wasted was he then?"

"Jack? I don't know. I'm pretty sure he's had more than me, but I guess he's also more used to it. He didn't really seem like he didn't know what he was doing."

Alfonso looks at me in silence for a long while until I finally say, "What?"

"Nothing," he says, shaking his head. "It's just …" He chuckles. "I can't get over the fact that Jack likes dick. Didn't see that one coming."

"Tell me about it."

"So if you had to choose between Jack and Phil, who would it be?"

"What?" I say, sounding more agitated than I should.

"What what? They're both into you. It's pretty obvious."

"That is so not gonna happen. Like, ever!"

"Why not?"

I look at him. "What do you mean, why not? Jack is an asshole, and Phil …"

Alfonso waits for me to finish my sentence, and when I don't, he says, "What's wrong with Phil?"

"What's wrong with Phil? Dude, have you seen his face?"

"Wow," Alfonso says, "that's probably one of the most offensive things you've ever said, and I'm gonna put it down to your residual blood-alcohol level. Are you saying we wouldn't be friends if I weren't such a handsome stud?"

"Of course I'd still be your friend. And you're not even that handsome."

"See? Now think about that."

"Whatever," I say, rubbing my eyes with the palms of my hands. "I need a shower."

"You sure do. And breakfast. With eggs and bacon and plenty of coffee." He pulls up his leg and gently nudges me off the bed. "Go get your shower. Make it a cold one. I'll fix us some breakfast. See you upstairs."

"Yes, Mother," I reply obediently and schlep myself to the bathroom.

* * *

I was supposed to go home on Saturday morning, but even after a long shower and a hearty breakfast I'm still not in a presentable state, so Alfonso makes an executive decision: he grounds me, and I spend the entire day and another night at his place. I feel awful most of the time, both physically and mentally, and Alfonso does his best to distract me from my misery. We play Xbox, we watch TV, we talk. Several times I'm hit by flashbacks that take me to the verge of tears, and then Alfonso will crack a silly joke or a silly smile, or he'll poke his finger in my ribs to tickle me and make me laugh and forget about the sad state of my world for another couple of minutes.

In the afternoon, Sandy texts me to ask me how I'm doing and if it's okay for her to come over. Who am I to say no? She's witnessed the most humiliating and embarrassing moment of my life, and she just grabbed my hand and we ran. I'll never be able to deny her any wish for the rest of my life, and that's fine with me. So Sandy comes over and she hugs me and she tells me I look terrible.

Alfonso says, "See?" and I tell them both to shut the hell up, but it's all just playful teasing and, as such, chicken soup for my battered soul.

By the time I return home on Sunday morning, I'm almost my old self again, and my family is none the wiser. To them I'm still the same person I was before I spent two nights at Alfonso's. In the afternoon I tell Zoey about the party and how I made out with Chris. I leave out all the juicy details that involve Jack. I hate that I can't tell her the whole truth, but I simply can't risk that in another lapse of self-control she publicly confronts Jack about something that has to be even more embarrassing for him than his boozer parents or incidents of domestic violence in his family.

Nevertheless, telling Zoey about making it to second base with Chris props up my bruised self-confidence, and deep down I feel like I'm all grown up now. I'm no longer a boy. I'm a man with one hangover and one nearly sexual encounter under his belt, and I'm beginning to feel on top of the situation. My own extensive reasoning, fueled by long conversations with Sandy and Alfonso, finally lead me to the firm conviction that I'm not

197

to blame for anything except getting wasted. Everything else was beyond my control, and in the cold light of day it seems undeniable that Jack has more to be embarrassed about and Chris has more to answer for than I do. I'm the victim here, and acknowledging that makes me feel surprisingly good and strong. It makes me feel pumped. It makes me feel ready to walk into school on Monday with my head held high, ready to accept their apologies.

By the time I walk to school on Monday morning, I'm peeing my pants. Not literally of course, but it's a miserable feeling nonetheless.

"Something wrong with you?" Zoey asks, being annoyingly perceptive.

Of course something's wrong with me. I'm scared out of my wits to run into Jack and/or Chris, and I'd much rather turn around and run home, but I obviously can't tell her that.

"It's nothing," I lie. "Just feeling a bit under the weather. I think I might be coming down with something."

"You're telling me now?" Zoey asks, taking two steps back and stopping us all in our tracks. "I have a date on Thursday! If I catch whatever kind of pestilence you're stricken with I'm going to kill you, Matthew, so you better stay away from me!"

And off she runs, leaving Sandy, Alfonso and me exchanging puzzled glances.

"Poor Matt," Sandy finally says, feeling my forehead with her hand. "Are you having a fever?"

"What? No?" I swat her hand away like an annoying mosquito.

Alfonso looks at me. "You haven't told her, have you?"

"No."

"Told me what?"

I sigh. "Not you, Sandy. I haven't told Zoey what happened. I mean, I told her I went to the party and made out with Chris, but not … the rest."

"Oh," Sandy says.

"Yeah. Anyway, listen, you guys, I really appreciate what you did for me in the last couple of days, but once you see either Chris or Jack coming my way, could you take a step back? I really feel I need to deal with this on my own."

"Of course," Sandy says, putting her hand on my shoulder. "Just so you know, we're very proud of you, Matt. Aren't we, Alfonso?"

"Sure. Go get'em, champ! And if they start pulling your hair, just shriek like a girl and we'll come a-running and tie Jack's nose hair and Chris's butt hair in a knot!"

Both Sandy and I glare at him, but he just shrugs.

"Hey, I'm just trying to be supportive."

* * *

The moment of truth comes when we're walking down the second-floor hallway on our way to class. Chris is standing outside our classroom, scrolling through his phone, his back and one foot propped against the wall. The way he's standing there he's the definition of cool, and he knows it. I'm finding it less and less endearing. His black T-shirt reads *Kiss & Tell*—in pink lettering no less—and it's hard to believe he's not wearing it on purpose, today of all days. It's almost as if he's taunting me.

"Hey," he says as he sees us coming.

"Hey," say both Sandy and Alfonso before they give me a silent nod and disappear into the classroom.

I don't say, 'Hey.' I don't say anything. I'm not even returning his annoyingly complacent smile. That's how tough I am this morning. Good thing he can't hear my palpitations.

"So how are you feeling today?"

"Good," I lie.

"Right," he says, followed by a chuckle. "Man, you were so out of it Friday night."

"And you weren't?"

He shakes his head. "Nah. I usually stay way clear of my drinking limit."

I rest my case. He knew exactly what he was doing, and he doesn't seem to think there was anything wrong with it.

"Good to know," I say and walk into the classroom. I sit down at my desk and take my notebook and pens out of my backpack.

"You all right?" Alfonso asks, and I nod.

Chris finally enters the room, and when he passes me on his way to his desk in the back, he gives my shoulder a quick, gentle squeeze, still smiling.

The audacity!

A few seconds after Chris, Jack enters the room, as always with Steve in tow. I can't look him in the eye, so I quickly avert my gaze. I assume he'll just ignore me as well, because everything else would be awkward, but as he walks past me he says, "Hey, Matt," and nudges my arm gently, with the back of his hand. I look up, and behind him Steve looks almost as puzzled as I feel. And because he's Steve and he can't let any friendly behavior toward me stand, he flicks my ear in passing and says, "Hey, Maddie!"

It doesn't even bother me anymore. It's the kind of thing I expect from Steve. What mystifies me, though, is Jack's unprecedented attempt to treat me like a human being, so I turn around and look at him. Our eyes meet, and as he holds my gaze for a few long seconds, I try to read his face. I'm not exactly sure what I'm seeing—is it remorse, shame, or even affection—but I know it's something I have never seen in Jack's face before, and I have no idea what it means or how to deal with it. I turn back around and my eyes meet Phil's who is just taking his seat next to me.

"Hello," he twangs, dorky as ever.

I reply with a grunt.

* * *

I somehow make it through the first half of the day. Chris keeps pretending that nothing out of the ordinary ever happened between us, and he chooses to ignore all of my pointed remarks. Jack, on the other hand, seems to go out of his way to feign a level of friendliness that has never existed between us.

When he takes his seat next to me during lunch, he accidentally kicks the leg of my chair.

"Oops," he says. "Sorry, Matt."

I stare at him in silence, still trying to get used to his miraculous transformation from wolf to lamb.

"Boy," he says, digging into his mashed potatoes, "I got so wasted Friday night, I don't remember a thing."

"Oh really?" I say. "That's funny, because I got so wasted too, and I remember *everything*."

As if someone's hit the firing button, glances start flying across the table like shrapnel, back and forth between Sandy and Alfonso, and between Chris and Jack. Jack turns to me and grins, and I'll forgive anyone for mistaking it for his signature smug and slightly derisive grin, but I've seen it too many times to be fooled. I can tell it's fake and laced with insecurity today.

"Who'd have thought," he says, "that one day you'd turn out to be such a cool dog?"

Steve bursts out laughing, and rightfully so, because this can't be anything but a sick joke. I can't take it anymore, so I push my lunch tray away from me and get up.

"Where are you going?" Sandy asks apprehensively.

"Restroom," I say.

I have to go pee all right, but while I'm at it I might as well put my head down the toilet and throw up because this whole charade is making me sick to my stomach. I leave the cafeteria and walk down the deserted hallway. Being all by myself for the first time today, the smell of Lysol and waxed linoleum feels like a breath of fresh air. With my eyes fixed on the floor I turn the corner and bump into a small Asian man in a shabby suit and a trilby hat.

"Ah! Sorry, sorry," he says with an awkward laugh, lifting his hat. Not only are his clothes from the 1950s, his manners are too, and I'm thinking, *One thing's for sure: Phil was definitely not adopted.* "Please, I look for principal office?"

"The principal's office? That's on the third floor. This is second."

"Ah! Third floor, yes? Thank you, thank you!" He lifts his hat again and makes his way to the stairway.

As I look after him, I wonder if Phil is in some kind of trouble because why else would his dad see the principal in the middle of the school year? I also wonder if I should just follow Mr. Thongrivong to the school secretariat and tell them I'm sick so I can go home and bail out of today's track session. Maybe I could be, like, really *really* sick and bail out of school entirely for the rest of the year. Maybe I should tell them I have the swine flu or chickenpox or lymphoma.

No, not chickenpox.

They'll see I don't have chickenpox.

Maybe Ebola, though.

Ebola sounds good, but in the end I have to dismiss this enticing idea because nature calls, loudly, so I continue on my way down the hall.

The restroom is just as deserted as the hallway, but I take a stall instead of a urinal anyway, because I like my privacy when I go about my business, and you can never know who walks in on you. It turns out to be the right decision, because when I shake off the last drops, I hear someone enter the restroom. I flush, and when I exit my stall, Jack is blocking my way.

So this is it. He's either going to come on to me and finish where he left off on Friday, or he'll threaten to kill me if I ever speak to anyone about what happened. I briefly contemplate whether I should dash past him and try to reach the door or turn around and jump out of the second-floor window.

"Hey," he says, his hands buried deep in his pockets, and when I don't reply he continues, "So listen, about Friday. That was pretty awkward, huh?"

This has to be a trick question with no right answer, so I decide to exercise my constitutional right to remain silent.

"Anyway, I think if word got around of what happened, it could be pretty embarrassing for both of us, so here's the deal: you keep my secret and I keep yours. It's a win-win. What do you think?"

I look at him. I look him right in the eyes, and suddenly it dawns on me. His weird behavior is beginning to make perfect sense. He's not so much embarrassed about what happened as he is scared that anyone might find out. He's scared out of his wits, and he's trying to pass something off as a 'deal' that really isn't, at least not for me.

"My secret?" I say, frowning. "What secret? You've been calling me a fag my entire life, so as far as your audience is concerned, this isn't much of a secret, is it?"

His shoulders slump. He's writhing because I'm squeezing his balls. Figuratively speaking, of course, not literally, but it's a great feeling nonetheless.

Beware; for I am fearless and therefore powerful.

"Come on, Matt," he says in a low voice.

A glare at him for a while—a long while, because I'm enjoying his desperate, begging look way too much—until I finally say, "Look, I don't want any trouble. I never did and I still don't. So whatever's gonna happen is up to you."

Then I walk past him and out of the restroom because I can't stand the tension any longer. Not only is my high horse so high I'm beginning to experience vertigo, it's also uncomfortably painful to watch Jack buckle under the pressure he's built up himself his entire life by being—or pretending to be—a homophobic bully. My head makes me almost feel sorry for him while my heart wants to jump at the unexpected and tantalizing chance to crush him like a bug.

CHAPTER SEVENTEEN

Looking over my shoulder, I see Jack running toward me, his legs pumping like pistons, his feet beating the ground like a drum. His face is tense, his eyes fixed on me as he is taking deep breaths through his nose and exhaling through his mouth so forcefully that he sprays droplets of saliva, brute and raw like an attack dog ready to pounce on his prey.

I better start running before he reaches me, so I get moving, slowly at first because I can't see where I'm going. As he keeps closing in on me, I gradually increase my own speed, occasionally looking ahead to make sure I don't veer off course. The distance between us is decreasing more and more slowly with every step, and when he's so close that I can hear his deep, ferocious breaths, he reaches out his right arm. At the same time, I reach out my own toward him, but our hands are still too far apart.

Six inches.

Five.

Four ...

"Come on!" I shout at him, my voice forceful and commanding.

Jack keeps pushing forward, toiling, agonizing, torturing himself, and as I'm looking at his face, I can pinpoint the exact moment he crosses the threshold of pain, accompanied by a deep, primal moan. Feeling the touch of the baton in my hand, I clasp my fingers around it, and the last thing I see before I avert my eyes is how the pain and tension recede from Jack's face the moment he lets go of the baton.

"That's what I'm talking about!" I can hear Coach Gutierrez shout from the sideline.

When we started out as a team I used to feel intimidated by the sight of Jack running toward me with that fierce look on his face. Today, for the first time, it's all different, and instead of intimidating me, that sight is only motivating me to push myself even harder. I stood up to Jack in the restroom during lunch, and here on the track I'm going to show him—and everyone else—what I got, so I pound my legs hard, my eyes fixed on the figure that's waiting for me in the distance.

I'm not looking Chris in the eyes, though.

His eyes are irrelevant. All they have to offer is distraction. What I need is focus, so I look at his hands, at his right hand that's already wriggling its fingers in anticipation of the baton.

Three or four steps before I reach the go-mark, Chris suddenly takes off.

What the hell is he doing?

As he's picking up speed, I push myself harder, because now I have a longer distance to cover. I've long since passed my own threshold of pain, and my thighs are on fire. Nevertheless, I keep pushing myself to make up the distance to Chris inch by inch, but to no avail. By the time he leaves the exchange zone, his left arm stretched out behind him, I'm still a good three feet behind him. I pass the end of the zone, then I slow down and stop. It would be pointless to keep running because if this were an official competition and not just a training session, we'd be disqualified now. I stoop over and prop my hands against my knees, still holding on to the baton and taking deep, painful breaths. Meanwhile, Chris has noticed what's going on, and as the other three teams finish the race he comes stomping towards me.

"What the hell is wrong with you?" he shouts, his fists clenched in anger. "Why do you stop?"

I'm not having this.

Not today.

Not from Chris.

"What's wrong with *me*?" I stride back to the end of the exchange zone and point at the tape mark on the track. "Just freaking look! Where did you want to do the hand-off? Ten meters before the finish line? You took off way too early, so don't you dare blame me for your cock-up!"

I throw the baton at his feet.

"Dude, screw the tape marks!" He shouts at me. "This isn't a competition, this is practice! Why do you stop running?"

"Because it's not my job to fix your stupid mistakes, so screw you!"

"Hey, hey, *hey!*" Coach Gutierrez shouts as he walks up to us, each *hey* louder than the previous one. "Shut up, both of you!"

Chris and I both turn our heads and look at the chubby little man who's about to blow up in our faces.

"You!" he shouts at Chris. "You know why the go-mark is where it is? Because when the kid passes the mark is when you go, not when he's still ten feet out, you get that?"

"Yes," Chris says in a low voice, putting his hands on his hips.

"I can't hear you! And put your arms down! Your attitude isn't doing anything for you right now!"

"Yes, coach!" Chris says louder, dropping his arms.

"As for you, kid ..." The coach turns to me, his voice softening but still no-nonsense assertive. "Never stop unless your coach or a judge tells you to stop!"

"But—"

"I know! It doesn't matter. It's not your job to make those decisions. Your job is to focus on your running, and nothing else. Never assume, and never give up. A judge might be distracted because he has to sneeze or he's thinking about his mortgage or whatever, and he might miss your screw-up. Don't do his job for him. You just keep on running until you've made the pass, got it?"

"Yes, coach."

"Good. Now shake hands and get the hell out of here!"

I shake Chris's hand without looking him in the eyes, then I turn around and make my way off the track.

As I pass Jack, he holds up his hand and says, "Good exchange."

Being gracious and a good sport, I high five him as hard as I can, making him shake his hand in pain.

* * *

I'm about to rush out of the locker room with my backpack hoisted over one shoulder. I'm not going to take a shower today, or ever, because I don't ever want to get naked in front of Jack again, let alone Chris.

"Matt, wait!" I hear him say behind me.

I look at him. "What?"

"Look, I'm sorry, okay?"

"Yeah, whatever." I turn to leave, but before I open the door he's caught up with me and holds my shoulder.

"Can we talk?"

I shrug his hand off my shoulder. "What's to talk about? You heard the coach. You took off early, I should have kept going. We're even."

"Not ... that."

"What else is there to talk about?"

"Friday," he says as behind him the other team members start trickling into the locker room.

"Not here," I say.

He glances over his shoulder, then he nods at me. "Yeah, not here. The Korova? Please."

I sigh, and apparently in Chris's universe that means yes.

"Awesome," he says. "Let me get changed real quick and I'll catch up with you."

Without another word I open the door and leave.

I want this talk. Of course I want it.

What I don't want is Chris to know how much I want it.

I think I might be enjoying this little betrayed-wife act a little too much. Keeping people on tenterhooks, first Jack and now Chris, gives me a feeling of power. It's an intriguing experience, but it's all too easy to get drunk with power, and the last time I got drunk with anything ... well, we all know how that ended.

"Why, hello there!" Milo exclaims as I enter the Korova.

"Hey, Milo."

"How are you, darling? You look so much better than ... well, than the last time I saw you."

"That doesn't really mean a lot, does it?"

"Oh stop it, darling," Milo says with a dismissive wave of his hand. "Even when you're drunk you still look more gorgeous than most people when they're sober."

"I'm not so sure about that, but thanks." I drop my bag in our regular booth. "Anyway, Chris will be here in a minute. Fix us two chocolate milkshakes, will you? I'm off to the boys' room real quick."

I know Chris likes strawberry.

Milo knows it too.

"Two chocolate shakes, are you sure?" Milo says, raising an eyebrow.

"Yeah," I say and walk into the restroom.

When I return, Chris is there. I slide into our booth, and Milo serves us our milkshakes.

"Thanks, Milo," Chris says and sucks on his straw. He looks at me. "Chocolate?"

"Is that a problem?"

He looks at me, and I can see how he's trying to make sense of the bellicose tone in my voice.

"All right," he finally says, pushing his milkshake to the side. "What's going on, Matthew?"

"I don't know, you tell me."

"Honestly, I have no idea. You got totally wasted on Friday, and you've been acting all weird ever since."

"Me?" I say a little agitated, causing Milo behind the counter to raise an eyebrow. "*I'm* the one who's been acting weird? Look, I may be new to that whole gay sex thing, but I'm pretty sure that if you like someone and you make out with them, you don't let some other guy get into your guy's pants!"

"Come on now," Chris says and shrugs. "We were just fooling around."

Wrong answer.

"Maybe you were." My anger giving way to the underlying hurt, I lower my eyes and my voice. "I wasn't."

After a few moments of silence during which I'm seriously contemplating to just get up and leave, Chris puts his hand on my arm and says, "I'm really proud of you, you know?"

209

I frown at him. What the hell is he even talking about?

"I mean, look, just because I'm openly gay and I seem to be handling it all right doesn't mean I don't know how hard it is. It's not like I woke up one morning and was like, 'Oh, I guess I'm gay. Well, that's all right then, what's for breakfast?' I know all the *Why me?* and *Why can't I be normal like everyone else?* and *What are people gonna think?* type questions. I had to go through all that, too. We all do. And for what it's worth, I think you're doing really well."

I snort. "Yeah, right."

"Well, you're doing a whole lot better than Jack, that's for sure."

"So he's really gay then, is he?"

Chris shrugs. "He is on a good day, but he doesn't have a whole lot of good days. I guess he's going through kind of a it's-probably-just-a-phase phase. When he's sober, he's trying really hard to convince everyone—including himself—that he's that really tough, manly guy who's totally into boobs and stuff. It's only when he's drunk or stoned that he can be himself and, like, go online and look at gay porn and whatnot. So yeah."

I lean back, my shoulders slumping. "Fricking hell."

"I know, right?" He sucks on his milkshake. "This is quite nice, actually."

"I know."

"So anyway, I'm kind of trying to steer Jack in the right direction."

"Meaning what?"

"Well, I'm not trying to get him drunk at any opportunity or anything. He doesn't need to be encouraged to drink anyway. But when he's drunk and he's in the mood for gay stuff, I kinda encourage that, because I think the more he does that, the more it will eventually spill over into his sober state or something. I don't know."

It's amazing how much sense things seem to make when Chris casually tells them like that, and you're so easily distracted by his handsomeness and his winning smile—until you're directly affected yourself and you've had a chance to look behind the pretty façade.

"That's very helpful of you," I say.

He smiles almost bashfully. "I guess."

"Does he want your help?"

"What do you mean?"

"I mean, did he ask you to help him come to terms with his sexuality? Or is that something you do for the sake of some greater cause?"

His face turns serious, and I bet I know what's coming.

"I want to live in a world where everyone can live the way they want to, a world where homophobic bullying is a thing of the past. And I think the more people chose to come out and be proud of who and what they are, the better for all of us."

"Right," I say, tempted to call him out on the irresponsibility to push someone out of the closet who has an openly homophobic stepdad with a history of domestic violence, but I don't really care about Jack at this point. I care about Chris and me, if there has indeed ever been such a thing as Chris and me. "So how do you do it?"

"How do I do what?"

"You said when he's drunk and in the mood for gay stuff, how do you encourage that? What exactly do you do? Go online and watch gay porn?"

He grins. "Sometimes."

"And then what happens?"

His grin widens. "Well, you know."

"He gets aroused?"

"Sure."

"You get aroused too?"

"Hey, I'm only human."

"And you help him relieve the tension?"

"Sometimes."

"Physically."

"How else?"

"When was the last time you did that?"

He shrugs, still grinning. "I'm not sure."

"Take a wild guess."

"Last week or something, I don't know."

I look at him for a long time. He holds my glare, but his expression slowly changes. His boisterous grins wilts and withers and eventually dissipates into a blank stare, empty and cold. Ironically, I find this pure, raw look much more attractive than his usual smug smile and the impish twinkle in his eyes. Deep down inside I still feel so many beautiful feelings for him. Looking at him still makes my mouth feel dry, my heart race, and the airplanes in my stomach fly in loops and spins. But I have to be careful as to not lose my focus on the issue at hand, so I avert my gaze and look at my hands and watch my fingers picking away at my cuticles. It's not that I don't want to explode in Chris's face. I do. I want to shout at him and pull his hair and scratch his stupid eyes out of their stupid sockets but—and this is where my tactical thinking kicks in—I don't want him to see me mad.

I want him to see me sad.

If I get mad at him he'll probably get all defensive and brush it off as me being hysterical—which would make me even madder and prove his point. If I want to find out if he cares about my feelings, I have to see how he deals with me being heartbroken.

"I'm just so disappointed, you know?" I finally say in the lowest and most miserable voice I can muster. "I mean, technically, this was my first sexual encounter. Call me old-fashioned, but I was expecting it to be less of an ambush and with a person of my own choosing."

"Come on, Matt," Chris says putting a hand on mine, and I hate how the touch of his soft, warm skin sends shivers down my spine. "I wouldn't call that a sexual encounter. Like I said, we were just fooling around. I'm sure your first real sexual encounter will be awesome and with exactly the person you want."

He squeezes my hands a little as he says it, undoubtedly suggesting that person could be him.

The audacity.

"Oh well," I say, withdrawing my hands. I grab my milkshake and take a few swigs. That kind of dismissive reply—minus the hand squeeze—was not exactly what I was going for, and it didn't do anything to alleviate my anger or my sadness, but this is probably as good as it's going to get so I decide to call it a day. I have a lot of stuff to think about, and I like to think that so has he. "Listen, I have to go. I got plenty of homework and whatnot."

"Oh, okay."

"Yeah." I slide out of our booth.

"You want me to walk you home?"

"No," I say, shaking my head and picking up my backpack. "I'll see you at school tomorrow."

"All right then."

I make my way to the door. As I pass Milo behind the counter I nod at him and say, in a final act of passive aggressiveness loud enough for Chris to hear, "He's paying."

CHAPTER EIGHTEEN

"Can I ask you something?"

I'm lying on my bed, reading the tattered copy of Romeo and Juliet that Phil checked out from the library. From the corner of my eye I've seen how he's been looking at me for a minute or two, sitting over at my desk, agonizing over whether he should say something or not.

"If it's about *Romeo and Juliet*," I say, "then I probably don't know the answer."

"No, it's ..." His voice trails off.

I lower my book and look at him. "What?"

"Have I done anything wrong?"

"I don't even know what you're talking about."

He puts his pen down and starts looking for words on my desk, on the floor, in the curtains, and in his hands.

"Well?" I push him.

"You haven't updated your Wattpad in a while," he finally says.

He's right about that. I've last updated it on Friday afternoon when I was excited to go to Jack's party. I haven't been following up on that, because after everything that's happened I'm grateful for every second I don't have to remind myself of the sights and sounds of that night.

"Oh, that," I say. "That's not about you, don't worry."

"Oh, okay." He turns back to his notes.

"It's just ... well, let's just say the party didn't go the way I expected it, and I've had a couple of really miserable days and I didn't feel like writing it down."

He nods staring at his notes. "Okay."

"I think this is the moment where you're supposed to ask me what happened."

"You don't have to tell me if you don't want to."

"Ask me already!" I say and throw the book at him. He catches it before it hits him in the face. There's a brief glimpse of a silly grin before he puts the book aside and looks at me.

"So how was your party?"

"Urgh! Don't ask!"

"Sorry," he says, averting his gaze.

The guy's got no sense of humor whatsoever.

I let out a deep, long sigh, sit up straight, and then I tell him. I tell him every dirty, embarrassing little detail about Jack's party, my weekend at Alfonso's, and the chat I've had with Chris at the Korova on Monday. Phil listens to my narrative intently and without interruptions. When I'm finished he keeps looking at me as if he's expecting more.

"That's it," I say.

He nods. "Okay."

"So what do you think?"

"I think you've had quite a weekend."

"No kidding." He keeps looking at me, and I have to push him for more. "Anything else?"

"What do you want to know?"

"What do you make of Chris's behavior?"

He shrugs. "I don't know. Nothing good. But I never liked him in the first place, so I'm not surprised."

"Wait," I say, frowning. "What do you mean you never liked him?"

"I don't know. There's something about him. Something disingenuous. Something fake. I don't trust him."

I look at him. "I don't get it. Right from the very beginning you've been encouraging me. Even on Friday, just before the party, you told me to go for it if that's what I want."

"Yes?"

"Why? I mean … why would you encourage me to pursue my love interest with someone you have such a low opinion of?"

"Chris seemed to make you happy. Or rather, the thought of being with him seemed to make you happy. I wanted you to be happy."

I frown. "Why would you want me to be happy?"

Phil picks up his pen again and leans over his notepad, almost theatrical, like Jimmy Fallon writing thank you notes. He pretends to write something, but even from my vantage point it's obvious he's just doodling. After a long while he finally says in a low voice, "Because I like you?"

I have to let that sink in. It's not that the substance of his revelation comes as a surprise. From the moment he started following me on Wattpad and reading my stories, he's been kind and supportive, almost like a friend. He wouldn't have done that if he didn't like me. I don't know him very well, simply because does such a good job at not being known, but I know him well enough by now to know he doesn't say things he doesn't mean.

"Are you finished?"

Startled, I say, "What?"

"We have work to do. Have you finished reading the play?"

I snort. "Very funny. I've finished reading the first act."

"And I thought I was a slow reader. So what do you make of it?"

"It's all right." I get up, walk over to the desk and sit in my chair. "I love the archaic language. It's so poetic, so full of colorful, lush imagery that grabs your soul and lifts it up and makes it soar through the sky, you know what I mean?"

He shrugs. "I wouldn't know anything about that kind of thing."

"Okay, wait," I say. I grab the book and leaf through the pages until I've found the passage I'm looking for. "Here, listen to this: 'If I profane with my unworthiest hand this holy shrine, the gentle fine is this: my lips, two blushing pilgrims, ready stand to smooth that rough touch with a tender kiss.' That's beautiful, don't you think? I wish I could write like that."

"I like your writing much better than Shakespeare's."

I laugh. "Thanks, but ... no."

"At least when I'm reading you, I understand what you're saying. Shakespeare's language is so convoluted and not straightforward at all. I mean, why not just say it like it is?"

"Because that would be boring," I say. "It would be like ... if I described one of your drawings as, I don't know, 'Two naked dudes in front of a tree.' It would be an accurate description, but it wouldn't do it justice, would it?"

"I suppose?"

"Because a picture is worth a thousand words. So by using that amount of imagery in his language, Shakespeare can convey the meaning of thousands of words in just a few lines, and I think that's awesome."

Keeping his eyes on the notepad in front of him, he looks the way I feel when a teacher asks me something I don't know and I'm waiting for the moment when they grow tired of waiting for an answer that will never come and they finally put me out of my misery by moving on and asking someone else so I can look out of the window again and continue watching that squirrel in the tree.

"Anyway," he finally says. "We should get on with it. We still have a lot of work to do."

I watch him closely as he continues scribbling words on his notepad, and I wonder if anything I've just said means anything to him at all. My glance falls back on the book in my hand, on the passage I've quoted to him, and suddenly it dawns on me.

"Is it about the lips?"

He looks up but still avoids my gaze. "I don't know what you mean," he says, blushing.

"The thing Romeo says. *My lips, two blushing pilgrims.* That's why you don't like the bit I've read to you."

"I give no care," he says, shaking his head.

I don't call him out on his obvious, blatant lie. Instead, I stare at him until he gets so annoyed that he finally looks at me and says, "What?"

"Have you ever tried covering it up?"

"Covering what up?"

"The ..." I awkwardly point at my mouth. "... thing."

He nods. "I once put a potato sack over my head. That worked pretty well."

I look at his deadpan face for a few moments until we both crack up and laugh.

"Hang on," I say, getting up. I leave the room and make my way down the corridor to Zoey's bedroom. I know she's not home—no one is—so I don't bother to knock. I head straight for her dresser where she keeps all her beauty stuff. Directly below the wall mirror, her lipsticks are lined up against the wall like soldiers of an ethnically diverse army, their colors ranging from very pale to very bright. I pick one from the middle. There's a compact mirror lying on the dresser, so I grab that as well before I head back to my room.

"All right," I say as I slump into my chair, "let's make those pilgrims blush, shall we?"

Looking at the lipstick in my hand, Phil shakes his head. "I don't think so."

"Sure you do." I lean in to him and remove the lipstick's cap.

"No," he says, leaning back.

"Why not?"

"Because."

"Come on," I say, nudging his leg with my knee. "Don't you want to know what it looks like?"

He hesitates. I know he's tempted, but he's also embarrassed and he probably doesn't trust me.

"I won't tell anyone. I promise."

"Only if you do it too."

"Fair enough," I say. My own curiosity to see if Phil's cleft lip can be covered up is stronger than the potential embarrassment of him seeing me wearing lipstick.

He exhales through his nose, his shoulders slumping. I lean in and lift the lipstick to his mouth. The moment it touches his upper lip, he twitches.

"Hold still!" I warn him and grab his chin with my other hand. His skin feels smooth and silky, his peach fuzz having never seen a razor. As I carefully apply the lipstick to his lips, Phil looks at me suspiciously with his warm, brown almond eyes. When I'm done, I lean back and look at the result.

"Wow," I say. His cleft is still there, obviously, but it's nowhere near as plain and in-your-face as before, and from twenty feet away he might even pass for an almost normal looking person.

"What?" he asks, apprehensively shuffling in his chair.

I hand him the mirror. "Have a look."

He takes the mirror and looks at himself for a long time. He squints, he frowns, he moves the mirror so he can look at himself from one side and the other.

"So what do you think?" I ask.

"I think your mirror is broken," he says. "That looks nothing like me. It's weird."

I raise an eyebrow at him. "Weirder than before?"

"No," he says, still examining himself in the mirror.

"It only looks weird to you because you're not used to it. You should do this more often. It looks good on you."

He takes one last look at himself, then he puts down the mirror and picks up the lipstick. "Okay, now you," he says and leans in to me.

Phil is very concentrated as he paints my lips, his look focused and wrapped up in his task. His grip on my chin is soft and gentle although his fingers remind me of Alfonso's. Their skin feels coarse and dry, as if he's doing hard manual labor all day, yet his hand is an artist's hand, deft and nimble, moving the lipstick across my lips like a paintbrush across the canvas.

"Done," he finally announces, putting the cap back on the lipstick.

I pick up the mirror and have a good look at myself. The contrast between the color of my lips and rest of my face is not as sharp as with Phil and his olive skin, but it's still obvious. Phil was right, this is weird, even when there's no cleft to cover up. I put the mirror away and look at Phil. We stare at each other for a long time. After a while, I can't help but start smiling.

"What?" he asks.

"We look so silly," I say.

He shakes his head. "You look pretty."

I feel compelled to return the compliment, but I'm not going to lie to him. "You look good."

"No, I don't."

"I think you do, actually."

We keep looking at each other, and all of a sudden I'm feeling dazed and confused, and before I even know what's getting into me I feel myself leaning in to him, slowly, cautiously, closer and closer until our lips finally touch and we engage in an awkward but tender, spine-tingling kiss. His lips feel lush and warm and surprisingly … normal. If I didn't know about his cleft lip, there would be no way of telling just from kissing him.

Losing myself in the heat of the moment, I gently pry his lips apart with my tongue. As our tongues touch and perform a clumsy mating dance, a dam breaks, and I'm swept off my feet and washed away in a torrent of tender passion. Phil exhales through his nose deeply, slowly, almost coming close to a little moan. It's possibly the sexiest sound I have ever heard, and in this unexpected upheaval of emotions I'm thinking the outrageous thought that on a scale from one to ten, where one is kissing a pig and ten is kissing Chris, kissing Phil is a twenty-two.

When after a minute or ten or an hour—who can tell?—our lips part and I open my eyes, we're both taking long deep breaths through our open mouths. My eyes are seeking his, but he seems to be looking at some imaginary point on my chest, his peachy pink lips glistening with our saliva. His hands are resting on his thighs. I reach out and touch one of them, very carefully because I'm afraid he might pull it back, but he doesn't. The moment my fingers touch the back of his hand he raises it, and our fingers interlace. It almost feels as if he's trying to pull me under again, and I'm willing to let myself go, so I lean in to him again for another kiss. Our lips touch again, and this time it's his tongue that's impatiently seeking its way into my mouth. Our second kiss, less clumsy and more passionate than the first one, is becoming a force of nature, a force so powerful as to shake, rattle and roll the world around us to the point where it makes the floorboards outside my room creak.

Wait …

What.

No.

No!

* * *

When I release myself from our kiss and turn my head, I look straight at Greg standing in the open door, holding his phone in front of his face, the camera lens pointing straight at Phil and me. Now that he has caught our attention, he no longer has to hold himself back, so he bursts out laughing.

Without even thinking about it, I jump up from my chair and rush towards Greg. He turns on his heel and runs, still laughing as I follow him down the hall.

"Get back here, you little piece of trash!" I shout after him, my voice cracking.

Taking three steps at a time, he tumbles down the stairs. At the bottom I've almost caught up with him. When I'm only an arm's length away from him he makes a sharp turn left into the bathroom. I hit the door just as he slams it shut and turns the lock. I pound the door with my fist while rattling the doorknob with my other hand.

"Open up!"

"No!"

"Gregory Joseph Dunstan, if you don't open that goddamn door right now, I promise I'll kick it in and then may God have mercy on your sorry little ass!"

"The joke's on you, asshole. There is no God!"

"Open the door!"

"The moment you come near me, the video will go out to two hundred Facebook friends and five hundred Twitter followers and then everyone will see what a faggot you are! I got my finger on the button, Matt, so you better back off!"

Irate, I slam both my hands against the door three times. "If you do that, I will destroy you, I swear to God!"

"Back off!"

Behind me, I hear Phil's footsteps coming down the stairs. When I turn to look, I see him hurrying toward the front door. Before he reaches it, the door opens and Zoey walks in. Phil rushes past her.

"Phil!" I call after him. "Wait! Phil!"

He's not turning back.

Zoey shuts the door and walks up to me, the look on her face puzzled and alert.

"What's going on?" she asks.

I pound and kick the bathroom door again. "Open up, Greg!"

"Piss off, Matt!"

I keep pounding the door. "Greg!"

"Matthew," Zoey says, pulling me away from the door. "Will you calm down a sec and tell me what the hell is going on?"

Panting heavily, I look at her. "The little vermin's got a video of us kissing, and he's threatening to post it online."

"Us?" Zoey says, frowning. "You mean—" She looks at the front door where Phil's just left, then back at me, "—oh, wow. That's an unexpected twist."

"I'll kill him," I say. "I swear to God, Zoey, I'll kill him."

"No, you won't. Calm down." She turns to the bathroom door and knocks. "Greg? It's me. Open up!"

"No way!"

"You can't stay in there forever. Mom and Dad will be home soon."

Greg remains defiant. "Fine," he says. "Can't wait to hear Matt explain to them why he's besieging the bathroom and waiting to pounce on me!"

Zoey turns to me, shrugging. Then her sympathetic look turns into a frown. "Are you wearing lipstick?"

"Long story," I say with a sigh.

"He snuck into your room and stole your lipstick!" it sounds from behind the door. "And then he painted his lips and made out with his retard boyfriend!"

"He's not a retard! You're a retard, you stupid little zitface!"

"At least I'm not a *faggot*!"

I'm about to kick in the door, but Zoey holds me back. "All right, you really need to calm down now, okay?" She tones her voice down to a whisper. "I get that you're upset, but this is clearly not working. He's never gonna come out as long as you're out here."

"But—"

"No *but*, Matthew. Get out of here. I'll try to get him to come out and talk some sense into him. You say he's got a video?"

I shrug. "I don't know. That's what he says."

"All right. Now go and let me deal with this."

With a deep sigh I turn and start walking up the stairs.

"Oh, and Matt?"

I stop and look at her.

"Nice color," she says, pointing at her lips.

"Thanks," I reply with a wry smile.

* * *

Returning to my room feels like a punch in the stomach that knocks the wind out of me. Seeing Phil's chair abandoned, the chair he was sitting on when we kissed just a few minutes ago, suffocates my anger at Greg under a thick, heavy blanket of anguish and despair.

I close the door behind me and throw myself on the bed. Burying my face in my pillow, I try to keep my head from spinning. What just happened?

I kissed a freak and I liked it.

I *loved* it.

But what is it about me and my sweet kisses turning sour within the blink of an eye? This isn't even like a roller coaster. It's more like a meteor that's being blown to smithereens by the very same forces of gravity and friction that make it briefly light up as a shooting star as it hurtles through the earth's atmosphere before it perishes.

Except, I still exist.

What also exists is a video of me kissing Phil.

All my self-pity aside, I'm feeling sorry for Phil. He trusted me. I made him feel safe enough to open up and do something he never would have initiated himself, and I ended up dragging him into a feud between me and Greg that has nothing to do with him. As if his life didn't already suck enough without me contributing to his misery. I don't know why I even care—or when I started caring, for that matter—but apparently I do.

Damn you, Phil!

Why do I suddenly like you? And why do I still not know where you live so I could at least come running after you and tell you I'm sorry about what happened and that I'll make sure Greg deletes that video so there's no need to worry about it. Which you probably won't do anyway, because you're weird like that.

I lift my head. The sound of two car doors slamming shut announces the arrival of my parents. I better get up and meet them downstairs before Greg does anything stupid. On my way down, I drop by Zoey's room and return her lipstick and mirror. Just when I get downstairs, Mom is opening the front door, carrying a humongous grocery bag and ushering in my dad who's carrying two more. Zoey is watching TV on the living room sofa in direct line of sight of the bathroom that Greg comes walking out of, his hands empty, the bulge in his pocket revealing where he's put his phone.

"Hi, guys, we're home," Mom says cheerfully as she closes the door behind Dad.

"A hand?" he says. "Anyone?"

Zoey and I both rush to Dad and take his grocery bags.

"Thank you, guys," he says, wiping the sweat from his forehead as we carry the bags into the kitchen.

Mom places hers on the counter top and asks, "Who's down for some lasagna?"

My mom's home-made lasagna is gourmet restaurant grade and usually very well received, but our reaction today is somewhat restrained.

"Wow," Mom says, "don't thank me all at once."

Zoey puts her bag down and plants a kiss on Mom's cheek. "Sorry, Mom. I'd love to have lasagna for supper."

"Me too," I say, forcing a smile, weary of Greg standing in the doorway, his hands buried deep in his pockets as he keeps glaring at me. I know his game. He's trying to tick me off. He wants me to blow my top and pounce on him in front of Mom and Dad so he can play the victim card. But that's not going to happen. Not this time.

"Much better," Mom says and turns to me. "Will Philip be eating with us?"

Zoey casts a glance at me as she's unpacking the bags, and I feel Greg's smirk in my neck. "No," I say, trying to sound as casual as I can, "he had to leave. Something came up."

Mom opens the cupboard to get the casserole. "Oh, that's too bad. Tell him he missed out on some really good lasagna."

There is something in her voice that makes me think she's not entirely unhappy that Phil's already left, and I try not to be offended by that, so I just say, "All right."

"Will you chop this up for me?" she says, placing a large Spanish onion in front of me.

"Sure." I take the chopping knife from the drawer, casting an unambiguous glance at Greg. He keeps smirking his stupid smirk.

As I chop up the onion, the inevitable tears start rolling down my cheek, and even on a good day Greg wouldn't be Greg if he didn't take that as an invitation to taunt me.

"Hey Matt, why are you crying?" he says in a whiny voice. "Did your *girlfriend* walk out on you?"

Before I get to lunge at him and very slowly stab him in the face twenty-seven times, Mom steps between us.

"Are you bored, Greg? You can help us, or you can get the heck out of my kitchen."

"I'm gonna leave you girls to it," Greg says, strolling toward the living room where he goes to watch baseball with Dad.

The family evening ends in a truce between me and Greg, simply because Greg has too much leverage over me, and I'm finally beginning to learn how to pick my battles. He's never going to delete that video if I beg him pretty please with a cherry on top, and I can't force him to do it without coming out to my parents, and that is something I want to do on my terms and when the time is right. Today it is not.

After supper I retreat to my room and call Alfonso. I don't want to be alone with my ugly thoughts of retribution and revenge, so I tell him everything that's happened minus the lipstick, because in the grand scheme of things it's really secondary how exactly I ended up kissing Phil. Secondary and, quite frankly, too embarrassing.

"Nice going," Alfonso says when I've finished.

"Uh-huh."

"So what are you gonna do?"

"The way I see it, there's only one viable course of action: sneak into Greg's room in the middle of the night, smother him with a pillow, and destroy the phone." When my game plan is met with dead silence, I add, "Dude, I'm joking."

"Funny," Alfonso says in a deadpan voice. "Seriously though."

I sigh. "I don't know, you tell me."

"I don't know," he says, "maybe you should just ... you know ..."

"Maybe I should just what?"

"Consider a preemptive strike. Come out to your parents."

"I want to come out because I want to, not because I have to. And besides, there's still a video of me kissing Phil. Even when I'm out, that's still kind of embarrassing."

"Why?"

'Because he's ugly' is the obvious answer, but for some reason I can't bring myself to say it. "I don't know, it just is."

"Right. Well, one thing's for sure: your options are limited."

I sigh again. "I guess."

We say our good-nights and hang up. I keep the phone in my hand and dial Sandy's number. I tell her the same story, again minus the lipstick, and she's ecstatic.

"You kissed Phil?" she shrieks. "That's awesome! I'm so happy for you. Both of you."

"Yeah, hooray," I say with a wry smile she can't see, "but that's not really the point here, is it?"

"Even so, you have to focus on the positive things."

"That's easy for you to say. What am I gonna do if that video gets out?"

"Do you really think your brother would do that?"

"You don't know Greg. He'd do anything to humiliate me."

"I'm sure that's not true," Sandy says. "But for the sake of the argument, let's say he shows that video around, what's the worst thing that could happen?"

"Are you kidding me? *Everything* would be the worst."

Sandy laughs. "No, it wouldn't. What I'm asking you is, would the situation be any different if it was a video of you kissing Chris and not Phil? And if so, why? I think you know what I'm getting at."

I know exactly what she's getting at, but I don't want to go there. Getting dragged out of the closet by your dipshit little brother is one thing, but it's probably not life changing if coming out is something I want to do sooner or later anyway. And the lipstick? Heck, I could probably survive the embarrassment of that, too. It's just lipstick. It's not like I'm wearing a skirt and fake boobs or anything. It all comes down to the guy I was kissing. I'm not sure I can handle the embarrassment of that. I'm too self-conscious, plain and simple. Even with Chris I always worry what people will think of us when they see us together, tall and handsome Chris and a distinctly average-yet-probably-perceived-as-less-than-average guy like me. I hate to imagine how the world would react to me having a boyfriend like Phil, how they'd probably be thinking I couldn't get someone better. But what does that even mean, *someone better*? Is someone who lets someone else get into my pants while they're making out with me better boyfriend material than a kind, sweet, considerate, freaky-looking weirdo? And if so, does that make me a superficial, self-pitying jerk?

"Matt?"

I snap out of my labyrinthine thoughts. "I'm here, I'm here. It's just … everything is getting too much at the moment. I think I'm getting a headache."

"You know what," Sandy says, "you don't have to answer that question right now. Sleep on it. The world will look different in the morning. It always does."

I sigh. "I guess. Anyway, thanks for listening, Sandy."

"Anytime. Night, Matt."

"Night."

I put my phone down and pull my pillow over my face. It feels nice not having to see anything and to have the noise of the world around you muffled, but it makes breathing difficult, and for a brief and silly moment I wonder if anyone's ever succeeded in smothering themselves with their own pillow.

CHAPTER NINETEEN

I wake up from the sound of Greg repeatedly bouncing a ball off his bedroom wall. On a normal day I would walk over to his room, grab the ball, and toss it out of the window, but this is not a normal day.

There are no more normal days.

I schlep myself into the bathroom for a shower and then down into the kitchen where Greg is already sitting at the table, unshowered like some feral creature, devouring his cereal. His phone is sitting right in front of him on the table, another deliberate violation of our house rules which I choose not to point out to Mom, because I don't want her to make Greg put the phone away and out of my reach.

"Good morning, honey," she chirps, hovering over the sink rinsing cups as I take my seat opposite Greg.

"Morning," I say in a raspy voice and pour Cheerios in my breakfast bowl.

I reach for the milk, briefly startling Greg because he thinks I'm making a move for his phone. Glaring at him, I pick up the milk carton but it's empty. "Mom," I say, "somebody left garbage on the table."

She makes a step toward me, takes the carton from my hand and throws it in the trash. Not the reaction I was hoping for, Greg knows, casting me a smug grin.

I get up and walk around the table to get a new carton of milk from the fridge. When I pass Greg, he makes sure to shield his phone with his body. Zoey joins us as I return to my chair and pour milk over my Cheerios. She takes her seat next to me, looks at Greg, then at his phone, then at me, and, bless her, she immediately knows what's going on.

"Where's Dad?" she asks casually.

"He had to be at the office early today," Mom says, drying her hands on a towel. "Some team meeting or something. Ugh, that towel smells funky. Greg, finish your breakfast. I'll throw the towel in the washer real quick, then we're good to go."

"Yes, Mom."

As soon as Mom's left the kitchen, Zoey gets up and walks over to the fruit bowl on the counter. She picks up a tangerine and turns around.

"Greg? Catch!" she says and throws the tangerine Greg's way. The moment he raises his hands to catch it, I jump up and lunge across the table, reaching for his phone, but Greg is quick. He grabs the phone before I can reach it. My hand grasps at nothing, I lose my balance and literally belly-land in my Cheerios, toppling over the bowl and soaking both the table and my shirt in sweet, sticky milk.

Sneering at me, his phone safely in his hand, Greg says, "Nice try, asshole."

Alerted by the noise, Mom comes rushing back into the kitchen. When she sees the mess, she throws her arms up in the air. "Oh for crying out loud! Can't I turn my back for a minute without you guys wrecking my kitchen?"

"Hey," Greg says, raising his hands in defense, "I didn't do anything."

Getting a rag from under the sink, Mom says, "Go get your backpack and meet me at the car. Matthew, go change your shirt, you'll be late for school. Zoey, help me clean up this mess."

Zoey shrugs at me apologetically. 'I tried,' her eyes say. I acknowledge her with a nod and make my way upstairs to change my soaked shirt, admiring how my day is off to a great start.

I make it to school just in time, and I manage to intercept Phil as he's about to enter our classroom. When he sees me coming, he averts his gaze and looks at the floor.

"Hey," I say.

He looks at me bashfully. "Hello."

"Look, um ... I'm sorry about yesterday. About what happened. It was—"

"It's okay," he interrupts me. "Never mind. I get it, it was a mistake. Let's just forget it ever happened."

"What?" I look at him, and it takes me a few moments to realize we're not talking about the same thing. "Oh, no. No, no. That's not what I meant. I'm not talking about ... what we did. I'm sorry my stupid jerk of a brother walked in on us and, apparently, took a video."

"Oh."

"Yeah," I say. "Sometimes he behaves like he has a turd for a brain. But don't worry, he's not gonna show that video around because he knows I'm gonna kill him if he does."

"No, you're not."

"What?"

"You're not gonna kill him over a video."

I pinch the bridge of my nose. "Of course I'm not really gonna kill him. It's called hyperbole, okay? What I'm saying is, he knows I'm gonna make him regret it if he doesn't delete the video. I already tried to get my hands on his phone to delete it myself but that didn't work, but I'll make him delete it today, okay? So don't worry about it, okay?"

"I don't."

"Good," I say. "And sorry again."

"Thank you," he twangs. "But it's not your fault."

"Well, it kinda is, isn't it? It probably wouldn't have happened if I'd just closed the door."

"It's okay."

I'm still not convinced that it really is, though. His face is so incredibly difficult to read, and I'm not sure if it's because of his cleft lip or his stoic personality. Either way, we're gonna have to figure out how life goes on after our kiss, because we can't just leave it at that, can we?

"Listen," I say, "I was wondering, maybe you want to hang out later?"

He frowns. "Hang out?"

"Yes. I mean, I have track practice after school, but I'll be done at around four, so I thought maybe we can grab a milkshake or something? I know a place—"

"I can't."

I frown at him. "Why not?"

"I have to do the laundry."

That's probably the weirdest excuse I've ever heard, but I have to accept it for now because Mr. Ulbright is standing in the doorway, his hand on the doorknob.

"Gentlemen," he says, "if you want to grace us with your presence, the time would be now."

Without another word Phil turns on his heel and walks into the classroom, and I follow him because I have nowhere else to go.

* * *

Things start getting weird when after the second period I'm on my way to my Biology class. I used to like Biology in Junior High School. In High School I've come to hate it because it's the only class I don't share with any of my friends because apparently everyone else was more interested in Physics. So I have to walk to my classroom all by myself, and I hate wandering the school corridors by myself because I'm too self-conscious and I constantly feel being watched. Except today I feel like I'm being watched even more than usual, and not just watched. Today people are unabashedly staring at me, smirking, covering their mouths with their hands as they whisper to their friends, and giggling as they pass. The strange behavior continues into the classroom, and I'm beginning to get a really bad feeling. Deep down inside I seem to know what this is about, but I spend the entire period trying to convince myself that I'm being paranoid and probably just seeing ghosts.

On my way to fourth-period Math the ghosts are blowing me kisses and openly pointing fingers. Marking the finish line of my gauntlet run are El Niño and Hurricane Sandy, standing outside of Mr. Singh's classroom, holding their phones in their hands and sporting concerned looks as they see me approach them. They don't have to say a word to confirm my worst fear when Alfonso hands me his phone.

On the screen, running in an endless loop, is a six-second Vine video posted by user Gregstan2k3. Two guys wearing lipstick, kissing. Then one of them notices he's being filmed, jumps up from his chair, and lunges toward the camera. Repeat. It's my most successful online appearance to date, with over four hundred likes, eighty-five shares, and rapidly approaching ten thousand loops.

"I'll kill him," I say matter-of-factly as I hand the phone back to Alfonso. "I'm gonna have to kill him."

"Calm down," Alfonso says.

"Oh, I am calm. And I'm gonna be perfectly calm while I rip his beating heart out of his fricking chest and eat it with fava beans a nice Chianti."

As Alfonso slides his phone back in his pocket and Sandy sympathetically squeezes my arm, some sophomore I've never even seen before walks by and says, "Hey, Dunstan! Where's your retard boyfriend?"

I lunge in his direction, but I don't get far because Alfonso and Sandy both hold me back, which is probably a good thing because I'm panting and drooling like an attack dog in kill mode.

"Come on Matt," Alfonso murmurs while Sandy yells at the sophomore, "He's not a retard! He's got a cleft lip, you ... you retard!"

While I throw death stares at the sophomore who walks on with his pals, sneering and laughing, Alfonso raises his eyebrows at Sandy's unprecedented outburst. She notices his look.

"What?" she snaps, and for a moment it looks as if she's going to pounce on him.

"Nothing," Alfonso says, trying hard to conceal his smirk. "We should go before somebody gets hurt."

"All right," Sandy says, and fighting the forces that still make me gravitate toward that sophomore jerk, they push me through the classroom door. It turns out, the situation in here is not much different. People are staring, smirking, sneering. The only person with a more or less neutral expression on his face is Jack, of all people. As I take my seat right in front of Jack, I hear Steve next to him make smooching noises. I look at Alfonso to assure him that I'm ready to ignore this provocation, when I suddenly hear Jack say, "Shut up, asshole!"

"Dude," Steve says, "since when did you become a fag-apologist?"

There is no reply. Instead, just as Mr. Singh enters the room, there's the crashing sound of a chair toppling over and a loud thud as a body hits the floor. I turn around and see Jack towering over Steve, fists clenched. Steve looks up at Jack, a bewildered look on his face. "What the fuck, dude?"

"Mr. Antonelli," Mr. Singh says, throwing his briefcase on his desk, "principal's office. Now."

"But Mr. Singh—" Sandy intervenes, jumping up from her chair. She's in a feisty mood today, but she doesn't get far.

"Would you like to accompany him, Miss Lauper?" Mr. Singh interrupts her.

"No, sir, but—"

"Good. Then sit down and be quiet." He flicks his head at the door. "Off you go, Mr. Antonelli."

With an angry grunt, Jack grabs his backpack and stomps off, briefly putting his hand on my shoulder as he passes me. I'm still trying to come to terms with the total transformation of his attitude toward me. Not that I'm complaining or anything. It seems that I currently need all the moral support I can get.

As Jack slams the door shut behind him, Mr. Singh turns to the class. His gaze rests on me a tad too long for comfort, and I'm imagining the thigh-slapping laughter in the teacher's lounge as they watch the Vine of me and Phil loop after loop.

"All right, ladies and gentlemen," Mr. Singh says, pulling a piece of paper out of his pocket and looking at it as he continues, "for some reason I'm being told to remind you that the use of cellphones during school hours is strictly prohibited. You all know this of course, and I'm sure you abide by this policy religiously, so I'm not sure why you need to be reminded of it, but here we are."

As he crumples up the note and throws it into the waste-basket, I sink deeper and deeper into my chair, trying to escape the furtive, nosy, oh-look-a-train-wreck glances of my classmates.

* * *

After Math, Zoey is waiting outside my classroom, holding her phone in her hand, but when she sees my face she can tell I'm already aware of what happened, so she quickly puts it away.

"I can't believe he did that," she says.

"Can't you? It's Greg, so what did you expect?"

"So what are you gonna do now?"

"I don't know," I say. "Kill Greg and take it from there, I guess."

Sandy and Alfonso cast Zoey helpless looks.

"Hey, Dunstan!" somebody calls out to me, and when I look I see a group of four or five boys, all blowing me kisses.

"Fuck off!" Zoey yells at them, causing them to burst out laughing. She turns back to me. "Has Phil seen it yet?"

"Oh my God, Phil!" I say. "I have to talk to him."

I start moving toward the cafeteria, Zoey, Sandy and Alfonso surrounding me like bodyguards to shield me from the vicious mob that keeps taunting me. When we pass the restroom I stop dead in my tracks, causing Alfonso who's walking behind me to bump into me.

"Dude! What the—"

"Guys," I say, "maybe I shouldn't be talking to Phil in the middle of the cafeteria with hundreds of people watching, so can you go and tell him to see me in the restroom?"

"Good thinking," Zoey says. "You want me to wait here with you?"

I shake my head. "Nah, it's okay. I'll just lock myself in a stall."

Another random guy comes walking by, talking in a louder-than-necessary voice to his friend. "Dude, if I were that guy I'd totally kill myself. Like, totally."

"Dude!" Sandy yells after him, "If I were you I'd have totally killed myself a long time ago. Like, totally!"

"All right," Alfonso says, putting one arm around Sandy and pushing me into the restroom with the other, "I think we better go and find Phil. Don't do anything stupid, Matt."

"Oh please," I say with a wry smile. "Me, stupid? That's the most ridiculous thing I've ever heard."

The restroom is empty. I walk into the stall closest to the window and lock the door. Sitting down on the edge of the broken toilet seat I pull my phone out and look at the Vine again, reading the comments and watching the loop count go up and up, each comment, each new loop a small jab at my self-confidence. After two or three minutes I hear the door to the hallway open and a pair of feet shuffling inside. I open the door of my stall and step outside.

"Hello," Phil says. By the blank look on his face I can tell he has no idea what's been happening.

"We have a problem," I say, handing him my phone. As he looks at the Vine, I add, "I'm really sorry."

"Oh, so that's what's different today."

I put my hands in my pockets. "I've been getting stupid remarks by random strangers all morning. I guess you have too, huh?"

"I'm getting stupid remarks from random strangers every day," he says with stoic indifference, still looking at the Vine. "But today people are also blowing me kisses. That usually doesn't happen, so I thought that was strange."

"Right," I say, letting out a deep sigh. "So what are we gonna do?"

He shrugs. "Nothing?"

"What do you mean, *nothing*?"

"What do you want to do?" he says, his eyes still glued to the screen. "It's out there. Even if you make your brother delete the video, it won't go away because people have already copied and shared it."

"Yeah, but even so, shouldn't we have some strategy for dealing with it or something?"

Shrugging again, he says, "Ignore it or own it."

"Goddamnit!" I kick a wastebasket across the room.

Startled, Phil briefly looks at me, then he looks back at the phone.

"You can hardly see my cleft," he says, almost sounding pleased. "Do you think I should wear lipstick more often?"

"Give me that!" I snatch the phone from his hand and switch it off. "Not everything is about your stupid lip, okay?"

He stares at me with a hurt look in his eyes. "Maybe for you it's not."

His words hit me like a blow to the stomach, and a well deserved one. Phil is not the enemy here. I hate that I dragged him into this, but what I hate even more is that he doesn't even seem to care. Anyway, the way he wants to deal with it isn't working for me. I don't want to shun him, but maybe it's best if we're not seen together until the dust has settled.

"All right, you know what?" I say, sliding my phone into my pocket. "If you want to own it, go ahead and own it. Because I sure as hell don't want it."

I turn on my heel and stomp out of the restroom, feeling miserable.

More miserable and lonely than ever before.

* * *

I step out into the hallway, and for a moment I have no idea which way to turn—right toward the cafeteria where a blood-thirsty mob is waiting for me so they can point their fingers at me and laugh and feed on my misery, or left toward the exit. Part of me just wants to run, run, run away, leave it all behind, leave this school behind, this city, this country, this life, and settle in Guatemala or Belize and grow yams or something. Another part of me wants to entertain a more sensible approach.

Walk, not run.

Go home, not to Belize.

Ambush Greg before *he* can flee the country and become a yams farmer. Make him feel miserable, so maybe I can feel less miserable myself.

But then my growling stomach reminds me that I have track practice later and that I better eat something so I don't get hypoglycemic and pass out before I pass the baton to Chris.

Speak of the devil, I turn the corner and the last person I want to see right now is walking straight toward me, hands in his pockets, wearing an annoyingly smug T-shirt reading *#fabulous*. Maybe I should have run to Belize after all, but it's too late for that now.

"Oh, hi," he says, stopping in front of me. "I've been looking for you."

"Why?"

He looks at me with his piercing blue eyes, smiling, but it's not his usual boisterous, cheeky, easy-going smile. It's more subtle and sympathetic and even a little sad.

"You seem to be having quite a day, huh?"

I feel a lump in my throat and I avert my gaze, looking at the floor, at the ceiling, at the message board to the left and the endless row of classroom doors to the right because I don't want him to see my eyes glazing over.

"Come here," he says, and without giving me enough time to comply he makes a step forward, wraps his arms around me and pulls me into a tight hug. The warmth of his body, the gentle force of his arms, and his deep, soothing breaths allow me to finally let go and burst into tears. As the world around me sways, my shaky legs give way and I collapse. Chris's grip around my trembling, convulsing body tightens and he keeps me from sinking to the floor and sliding into the abyss.

Chapter Twenty

Hugging my knees, I wipe my nose on the sleeve of my sweater. The big, wet spot on the sleeve keeps getting bigger and looks disgusting, but a less than immaculate wardrobe is probably the least of my problems today. While occasional sobs still rock my body, my tears are finally subsiding.

"Want one?" Chris asks, holding a pack of cigarettes under my runny nose. When I shake my head, he shrugs and pulls a cigarette out for himself.

We're sitting in the bushes behind the gym, the secret spot where Chris and Jack and Steve go to smoke cigarettes between classes. Lunch break is already over and we should be sitting in class, but Chris convinced me to skip the last two periods to get me out of the firing line and give me a chance to calm down while the dust settles.

"Why?" I say. "Why does shit keep happening to me?"

"Because that's life, and you're alive?"

"But what have I done? Why can't I just live my life and be left alone? Why can't I just be happy?"

Chris lights his cigarette and exhales the smoke away from me because he's considerate like that. "I don't think that's how it works," he says.

I look at him. "What do you mean?"

"The universe doesn't owe you happiness or justice or a good life. These are all things you have to fight for. We all do. And not just once or twice but all the time, for the rest of your life. It's like food and drink, you know? No matter how much you eat today, you're gonna have to eat again tomorrow and the day after and so on, or you will die."

"But in the end we all have to die anyway," I say, tapping into the darkest corners of my soul. "So why even bother?"

"Don't be stupid now, Matthew."

"Seriously, though. Sometimes I wonder if it's all worth it. If there's a point to all fighting, all the struggle. All the death and disease and destruction in the world."

There is no immediate reply. Chris takes a couple of drags from his cigarette and picks a scab on his elbow, the only blemish on his otherwise immaculate body. I wipe my nose again, and he finally asks me, "Have you ever felt happy? I mean, genuinely happy?"

I snort. "I guess. But that was a long time ago, when I was a little kid."

"Why?"

"Why?"

"Yeah, why were you happy as a little kid?"

"Jeez, I don't know," I say. "Because I was young and free I didn't care about all the crap that's happening in the world?"

Chris nods. "See? You didn't care, and I put it to you that you didn't care because you didn't know. The world wasn't any better when you were young. You were simply ignorant about it. Ignorance is not a bad thing, you know? I think in a crazy world, ignorance might be the only thing that'll keep you sane."

I look at him. "What are you saying?"

"I'm saying brave adversity by embracing ignorance. Forget about what all these people out there think about you. Most of them are jerks anyway, so why would you even care about what they think? It's the people you matter to that should matter to you."

Resting my head on my knees, I mull over his words. He makes it sound so reasonable, so simple, like it's such an easy solution to shrug it all off and laugh those bullies and homophobes in the face. But it's an easy thing to say for a boy of his stature, for someone with his unnatural level of self-confidence, and it probably helps a lot if you're handsome and popular and everybody's darling and not an awkward, mousy wallflower like me. And if that strategy of wanton ignorance that seems to be working so well for Chris isn't bound to work nearly half as well for me, then how is it supposed to work for someone like Phil? Maybe Phil doesn't care about anyone because nobody seems to care about him, but I very much doubt that this kind of arrangement is making him happy. It might help him deal with life, but at what cost?

We sit in silence for a few minutes while Chris finishes his cigarette and I keep wiping my nose on my sleeve. The first period we're skipping is almost half over, and a shadow of guilt is rising in the back of my mind. It's probably a good sign, because it means my emotions are slowly simmering down to normal levels, yet at the same time I feel a great sense of relief because it's been—I look at my watch—more than half an hour since the last person laughed at me and blew me a kiss.

"So," Chris finally says, stretching out his sun-tanned legs beside me. "You and Phil, huh?"

"Yeah, well." I shrug, unsure what to say.

"It's okay," Chris says with a wide grin and nudging me with his knee. "No need to be embarrassed."

"I'm not."

"I mean, you were just messing around, right?"

I look at him, making sure to remove the last trace of a smile from my lips. "Is that your excuse for everything?"

He frowns. "What do you mean?"

"Just messing around. That's what you said after you made out with me and looked on while I was basically sexually assaulted by Jack."

He shrugs it off, his grin returning. "Hey, we're hormone-driven sexually active gay teenagers. It's what we do."

"You're also a cliché, apparently. And speak for yourself. I hope by we you mean yourself and Jack, and not me."

"Dude, why are you so angry?"

"I'm not angry," I say, trying not to sound angry. "It's just difficult to keep the emotion out of my voice when I'm being ... emotional."

He chuckles. "See, that's exactly what your problem is, Matt. You're too emotional, and you worry too much. Loosen up! You're a teenager. Try to be young and wild and free."

"I'm a teenager all right, but I'm not like you, and not everything that works for you will also work for me. And I'm sure as hell not *just messing around* when it comes to these things."

He looks at me with a big, wide grin, and it annoys the hell out of me because I don't know what it means.

"What?" I say.

"You have a crush on Phil, don't you?"

"No, I don't!"

"Of course you do," he says and ruffles my hair. "Because you're not messing around when it comes to these things, right?"

I swat his hand away. "Stop that!"

"That is so cute," he says, his grin widening. "So tell me, is he a good kisser?"

"He's a great kisser. And his mouth doesn't reek of nicotine, so that's a plus."

For a brief moment he looks stunned and I fear he's going to blow up in my face, but then he laughs out loud, gently punches my arm and says, "Touché, Matthew."

"Sorry, but you had that one coming."

He nods. "I sure did. So, next stop second base, yeah?"

"What?"

"You and Phil."

I sigh. "Oh, I don't know. It's ... complicated."

"More complicated than us?" He winks at me.

"Hell yeah. He's carrying around his very own flavor of emotional baggage, you know? And it's very special."

"Just like he is."

"I guess."

"You guys will figure it out," Chris says. "And maybe you guys are meant to be together. I've been watching you, you know." When I frown at him, he explains, "In most classes I'm sitting right behind you guys, remember? You had a thing for him from day one."

"No, I didn't!"

"You did, too. And it's okay. You're a sweet couple, so go for it."

I snort, not quite sure what to make of this assessment. Sure, it's always nice to have someone—especially someone you like—encourage you and support you in what you're doing. Then again, 'You and that really ugly person are really a great fit' is not exactly the kind of thing you want to hear, especially not from the person who's been making out with you less than a week ago. He's probably just trying to be nice, but the sneaking suspicion that Chris can't retire me as his love interest soon enough puts a sting in my heart. How can a person be so sweet and kind and cruel and inconsiderate at the same time? I'm grateful that he's sitting here with me, listening to me, shielding me from more classroom cruelty by having talked me into skipping class, yet at the same time he's so talented at riling me up with his rash, imprudent remarks and his just-messing-around attitude as if everything is just fun and games and nothing really means anything.

Chris nudges me with his knee again.

"Hm?"

"A penny for your thoughts."

"Please," I say in mock indignation. "A penny? You think I'm that cheap? Make it a dollar and we'll talk."

He chortles. "Aren't you cute, Matthew Dunstan." Then he leans into me and plants a kiss on my cheek. A week ago that would have been enough to send the butterflies in my stomach into a frenzy. Today I find this plump display of undetermined affection annoying and almost offensive, but I don't say anything.

Because hey, he's just messing around, right?

* * *

As we exit the tunnel that connects the locker room with the track, we're met with an angry rant in a familiar, high-pitched voice coming from the bleachers. Sandy is standing by the fence at the top of the bleachers, shouting abuse at four sophomores on the sidewalk below. They've surround-ed a miserable looking little figure and keep pushing him around, taunting and ridiculing him. One of them takes away his umbrella and abuses the next lamp post with a pathetically inept Gene Kelly impression while the other three keep pummeling Phil.

"Sissy boy!"

"Where's your boyfriend, Ching Chong?"

"Not Ching Chong! His name is Chop Suey!"

Sneers and laughter.

"Your lips are so pretty, Chop Suey!"

"What's in your purse, little geisha? Tampons?"

"Tampons and lipstick!"

"And a vibrator!"

"Let's have a look, sissy boy!"

"Yeah, let's get your lipstick out and make you pretty!"

The guy tosses away Phil's umbrella and joins his three friends as they tug on Phil's bag. He clutches it with both arms, trying to shield it from the attackers with his skinny body as they keep pushing him and pulling on the bag.

"Hey! Stop it!" Chris shouts, rattling the chain link fence that separates the track from the sidewalk. "Leave him alone, you assholes!"

As they keep pummeling Phil, one of them turns to Chris and flips him the bird.

"Come on," Chris says and runs back towards the tunnel. Jason, Jack and I follow him. Through the tunnel and locker room, we make our way outside. As we turn the corner and approach the crime scene, Phil is on the ground, surrounded by the bullies. He's still desperately holding on to his bag as two of the guys are pulling on the handles, continuing their laughter and verbal abuse. When they see us coming, the cowards finally let go of Phil and make a run for it.

While Chris and Jack chase after the bullies, Jason and I tend to Phil. When we get to him, he's still lying on the ground, clasping his handbag, his eyes closed, his body motionless. His shirt and pants are dirty from the dusty sidewalk. One of his sleeves is torn, and there are bruises and abrasions on his face and hands. When I kneel next to him and put my hand on his shoulder, his body twitches and he tightens his grip around his bag.

"Phil," I say. "It's me, Matt."

He slowly opens his eyes and finally begins to relax. Jason and I both grab one of his arms and carefully help him sit up. He coughs and shakes his head, blinking rapidly, trying to remove dust particles from his teary eyes. When he lifts his hand to his eyes, I hold it back.

"Don't touch your eyes," I say. "Your fingers are all dirty."

I sit on the ground, putting one arm around Phil's shoulders to hold him steady while I use my other hand to carefully wipe the dust from his face and his blinking eyes. I turn my head, looking up and down the street. There's not a single Tesla in sight. Where the hell are the feds when you need them?

As Chris and Jack come walking back to us, Sandy joins us from the other direction.

"Did you guys get them?" Sandy asks.

Chris shakes his head. "No, but I've seen these guys before. I'll recognize them, next time I see them, and then ..."

Sandy squats in front of Phil, putting one hand on his knee. "Are you all right, Phil?"

Phil nods, blinking slower now as his silent tears wash the remaining dust from his eyes.

Pulling a bottle of water from her bag and unscrewing the cap, Sandy says, "Those stupid assholes! Should we call the police?"

Taking the bottle and having a few sips of water, Phil shakes his head.

"Or at least take you to the school nurse, and let the principal know what happened?"

Shaking his head more emphatically, Phil hands the bottle back to her. "It's nothing. I'm fine."

"Like I said," Chris says, "I know these guys, and I'll report them to the principal first thing in the morning."

"Can you stand up?" Jason asks Phil.

Phil nods. As Jason and I help him to his feet, Sandy takes his handbag from him. It looks mangled, the shiny surface scratched and dirty, and one of the handles has been torn off. As soon as Phil is standing, he takes his bag back and examines it closely as I dust off his shirt.

"I'm so sorry about your bag," Sandy says. "It must have been expensive."

I shake my head. "It's just a cheap knockoff, Sandy."

"Well, even so." She looks past my shoulder. "Here comes your dad."

Frowning I turn and look down the street.

She was of course talking about Phil's dad, not mine.

Mr. Thongrivong pulls up in his clunker and gets out. Looking serious but not overly concerned, he approaches us and asks, "What happen?"

As I bring his dad up to speed, I see the look in Phil's eyes, begging me to not make it sound too dramatic, so I just give a quick roundup, leaving out delicate details like lipsticks and homophobic taunts.

When I'm finished, Mr. Thongrivong just nods, looking strangely indifferent, almost apathetic. He doesn't ask any questions, nor does he do anything to comfort Phil. In the end, he shakes everyone's hands, saying, "Thank you helping guys." Then he pushes Phil toward the car. They both get in, and as I'm standing on the curb, Phil keeps looking at me with his big, brown fawn eyes until the car finally pulls out into the traffic.

* * *

I'm about to put my key into the lock when the front door swings open and Zoey pulls me inside. She must have been standing by the window, waiting for me to return home.

"Where is the little turd?" I demand.

"They're in the dining room," she whispers, putting her hand on my chest. "Mom and Dad already know. It's a major drama. It looks like he didn't do it on purpose, so try to remain calm, okay?"

"Not on purpose my ass," I say, dropping my bag and pushing past her. I have no intentions to remain calm. I have no reason to remain calm. If anything, the fact that Zoey seems to be defending Greg riles me up even more.

They're sitting at the table, Greg sandwiched between Mom and Dad, and none of them are looking happy. Mom's eyes are red, and in her hand she's holding a crumpled Kleenex. When Greg sees me appear in the doorway, he jumps to his feet and raises his hands in defense.

"I'm sorry, Matt!" he says in a pathetically whiny voice. "I didn't do it. I didn't want this to happen. I'm so sorry!"

His words don't even register with me. As I make a few strides in his direction, he hides behind Mom like a coward, and Dad stands up to block my way.

"You little piece of vermin!"

"Matthew!" Mom scolds me, as if I'm the villain here.

Dad puts his hands on my shoulders to keep me from charging at Greg. "Buddy, you need to calm down!"

"I'm so sorry, Matthew," Greg says again, almost on the verge of tears now, his voice cracking.

Half-heartedly, I try to shake off Dad's hands and make my way past him, but of course I don't stand a chance against him. Tightening his grip and raising his voice, he says, "Matthew, I mean it! Let's sit down and talk about this."

Letting out a deep breath through my nose, I take a step back. As Dad lets go of me, I grab a chair and sit down.

"Sit down, Gregory," Mom says, her hand on his arm because clearly he's the one in need of moral support.

Dad and Greg both sit back down, Dad acting as a human shield between me and Greg.

"All right," he says. "Now let's all take a deep breath and deal with this thing like adults, okay?"

A derisive snort escapes me, but being the prudent, discreet person that I am, I refrain from addressing our little Model UN peace conference with a few extremely adult remarks.

"Matthew," Mom says, "I think your brother would like to tell you something."

Oh, I'm sure he would. He's so excited to talk to me, he can't even look me in the eyes.

"I'm listening," I say.

Mom gives Greg an encouraging nod. "Gregory?"

His head bent, his eyes fixed on his fingers that are nervously playing with each other, Greg starts his testimony in a low, miserable voice.

"I showed the video to Luke, nobody else. Just for shits and giggles. And I didn't want to show it to anyone else, honestly. But then Luke told Gary and Michael about it, and they wanted to see it too, so I told them they couldn't. Then they jumped on me and wrestled the phone out of my hands, and while Michael was holding me in a headlock, Gary posted the video on Vine. And Instagram and YouTube."

Oh great, we're on Instagram and YouTube, too.

"And Facebook."

Facebook. Of course!

Where else? MySpace?

IC-freaking-Q?

"I hope you understand," Mom says, "that it was very stupid of you to show that video around in the first place."

"Yes, Mom."

"And couldn't you have deleted the video?"

"I probably could have, if I'd gotten my phone back. But they kept it."

"They still have your phone now?"

Greg shrugs. "I guess." He looks at me. "I'm really sorry, Matt. I didn't want this to happen."

"You don't even know what you did, do you?" I say. "Do you know what happened at school today when the video went viral? A bunch of bullies pounced on Phil. At first they only pushed him around. Then they beat him and kicked him. They tore his clothes, broke his umbrella and his bag, and then they left him lying in the gutter like a dead rat. All thanks to *you!*"

Greg averts his gaze, looking at his fingers again. His eyes are filled with tears, which is kind of heartbreaking to look at because I actually believe his account of what happened, but if he's feeling miserable now then only because he deserves it. Besides, I've been on the verge of tears myself the whole day, so my compassion for Greg is pretty limited.

"Who's got your phone now?" Dad asks him. "Gary or Michael?"

"I don't know. Michael, I think. I'm not sure."

While Dad gets up and disappears into the kitchen, Mom looks at Greg and says, "All right, I think we've heard enough. As you can imagine, we cannot let you go unpunished. It may not have been your fault that these guys posted the video online, but you had no business shooting that video in the first place, and you definitely shouldn't have shown it to anyone, you understand?"

Greg just nods, tears running down his face now.

I hate him for tapping into my most primal brotherly urges that make me revel in his misery.

As Dad returns from the kitchen with a notepad and pen, Mom continues, "You're grounded indefinitely. In addition to your own, you will do Matthew's chores for a month. No Internet, no TV, no phone privileges. Do you understand?"

"Yes," he says in a low, croaking voice.

I'm enjoying this way too much.

Dad puts the pen and notebook in front of Greg. "Write down their addresses so I can go and get your phone back."

When Greg has finished scribbling down his friends' addresses, which takes a while because he has to keep wiping away his tears, Mom says, "All right, off to your room."

He pushes his chair back and gets up. When he passes me, he stops and says, "I'm sorry, Matt."

I don't acknowledge him. My arms crossed, I don't even grace him with a look.

"Give him some time, Gregory," Mom says. "Go to your room."

As he turns to leave, I say, "Yeah, give me a couple of *years*."

Mom raises an eyebrow at me. "Matt, please."

"All right, all right," I say, getting up.

"Hey, buddy," Dad says, "where do you think you're going?"

"Shower," I say. "I'm all sweaty and sticky."

"Nice try, bud, but I think your shower can wait a couple of minutes. Come on, sit back down. Let's have a little chat."

Dang! I thought with all the focus on my evil little brother I could avoid the inevitable talk about the elephant in the China shop that caused this whole mess in the first place.

I guess it was worth a try.

As I take my seat again, Mom and Dad look at me expectantly, but hey, let's play *Jeopardy!* Since they already know the answer, let them try and come up with the right question.

"Well?" I say.

They exchange awkward looks, as if neither of them wants to go first. Eventually, Mom clears her throat and plucks up all her courage. "Is there anything you'd like to tell us, Matthew?"

"Oh yeah," I say. "We set a new personal best in the hundred-meter relay today, and the coach thinks we got a really good chance to win the Schoolympics next month."

"That's awesome, buddy!" Dad says and raises his hand to high-five me. When Mom casts him a disapproving look, he clears his throat and puts on his being-a-father-is-serious-business face. "However, that's not what we mean. Anything about your recent use of lipstick, maybe?"

"Oh, that," I say with a deliberately camp wave of my hand. "You see, that wasn't *my* lipstick. It was Zoey's, so yeah, no worries."

More awkward looks. Coming out to my parents was never going to be easy, so given today's events, who can blame me for trying to share some of the burden?

"It's okay, Matthew," Mom says. "You can tell us."

"Tell you what?"

One final moment of hesitation before she finally takes the leap. "Matthew, are you gay?"

I've been enjoying this little skirmish up until this very moment, but now that the word *gay* is out and circling over my head like a military drone, hiding under a rock is no longer helping. It's time to face the music.

Let's hope it's a show tune.

"Yes?" I say with a voice as steady as I can muster, finally daring to look my parents in the eyes.

That's it. It's out. *I'm* out. It's as if a huge weight has been lifted off of my shoulders, and not only my shoulders, apparently. Mom and Dad both exhale deep breaths, and a diffuse tension seems to depart their bodies. Dad reclines in his chair. First he crosses his arms, then he uncrosses them and holds the open palm of his hand under Mom's nose.

"Oh for crying out loud," Mom says, pulls a ten-dollar bill out of her pocket and slaps it into Dad's hand.

Stumped, I look at them both. "You've got to be kidding me. You had a bet going on?"

Dad leans forward and pats me on the shoulder. "Sorry, buddy."

"How long?" I ask.

He looks at Mom. "How long's it been, honey? Five years? Six?"

"Five," Mom says, wiping her nose. "We were sitting here and you said, 'Honey,' you said, 'I bet you ten dollars that one day we'll be sitting at this very table listening to our son coming out to us.'"

I facepalm. "You are literally the worst parents ever."

"Nah," Dad says. "I think we're pretty awesome. Right, honey?"

Mom responds with a wry smile.

I'm at a loss for words. Apparently I was indeed the last person to find out I'm gay.

And the only one bothered by it.

My life is so freaking ridiculous.

"All right," I say, "you've had your fun with me. Can I go now?"

Mom looks at me. "Actually, honey, can we talk about your … boyfriend for a minute?"

"My—" I shake my head emphatically. "Oh, no, no. That's not … Phil is not my boyfriend!"

"Oh," Mom says, looking puzzled. "That's …"

"You kissed him, but he's not your boyfriend?" Dad asks.

"Okay, look," I say. "We were talking about his cleft lip and I asked him if he'd ever tried covering it up. He said no, so I went to Zoey's room to borrow one of her lipsticks because I wanted to see if we could, you know, cover it up. But he wouldn't let me do it unless I put it on too, and then one thing led to another and … then we kissed. It was our first kiss. There's nothing going on between us. We were just … messing around."

I can't believe I just said that.

Casting glances at each other, Mom and Dad both seem kind of relieved.

"Why?" I ask, alerted by their looks. "Would that be a problem if he were my boyfriend?"

"Oh, no," Mom hurries to say. "No, honey. Not at all. I mean ... no."

"Good."

"Yeah."

"But he's not, so ..."

"Okay."

Now move in for the kill.

"Well, in that case I'm sure you won't mind if I invite Phil over for a sleepover on Saturday. We're lagging behind with our English papers. We need some time without distractions so we can catch up."

As expected, this is a bombshell.

"Whoa, whoa, whoa," Dad says very eloquently, and Mom looks at me as if I'd just announced I'm leaving home to live in a hippie commune.

"Honey," she says, "I'm not sure that's such a good idea."

"Why not?"

"Well ..." She turns to Dad for help.

"This is all going a bit fast," he says, "don't you think?"

"It has to," I say. "We need to get our papers done. We have a deadline."

Dad shakes his head. "Yeah, that's not what I meant, buddy."

"It's not?"

"No. We think that given the circumstances, having a sleepover with Phil maybe isn't the best idea."

"Oh, I see, the circumstances," I say, hardly able to conceal the snark in my voice. My heart is beating fast now, and I interlock my fingers to keep my hands from shaking. "But if I wanted to have Alfonso over for a sleepover, that would be okay, wouldn't it?"

"Yes, but—"

"And if I had told you yesterday that I wanted to invite Phil for a sleepover, that would have been okay too, wouldn't it?"

"Buddy—"

"No, hear me out," I interrupt him. I'm high on adrenaline, and I barely know what I'm doing. "I'll tell you what the circumstances are: Phil got beaten up today. He got beaten up bad because of Greg. We owe him. This family owes him. The only reason that what would have been okay yesterday is no longer okay today is because today you know I'm gay, and I'm not having you discriminate against Phil—or me, for that matter—simply because we're gay. I've had enough of that at school today, and I'm not having it in my own home. The last time I checked, gays were a protected class in California, so if I can't have Phil over for a sleepover, this discrimination will become a matter for the courts."

Dad pinches the bridge of his nose, then he covers his mouth with his hand, glancing at Mom. "Is that what they teach them in school these days?" he asks through his fingers.

Mom sighs. "Matthew—"

"I mean it, Mom."

"Matthew, I want you to know that you'll always be our son and we will always love you, no matter what. We just want you to be happy, that's all."

To be honest, I didn't expect anything less. "Thanks, Mom. I appreciate that. I'll be super happy if I can have that sleepover and we move on."

Dad motions his hand toward Mom, shaking his head. "You go argue with that, Claire, because I can't."

"Joe—"

He shrugs. "I mean, seriously."

"I'm not discriminating against anyone. We don't allow Zoey to have random guys sleeping over, do we?"

"You know why that is, Claire."

"Yes, because we don't want them to have random sex with random guys."

"No," Dad says, shaking his head. "You know that didn't stop us when we were young, and it's not stopping anyone today. The reason we—like every other set of parents in the world—don't want our kids to sleep in the same room with a potential sexual partner is because we don't want them to get knocked up or knock someone else up. Unless I'm completely missing something here, I don't see that happening with Matt and his boyfriend."

"Not my boyfriend," I say.

"See, they're not even boyfriends."

He pushes back his chair and gets up.

"Where do you think you're going?" Mom asks.

Picking up the notepad, Dad says, "I think I'm going to go and get Greg's phone back." He turns to me and opens his arms. "Come here."

I get up and he wraps his arms around me for a tight hug.

"I'm proud of you, son," he says. "Just don't do anything stupid, all right? And if you do, make sure you don't get filmed again."

"Yes, Dad."

Mom gets up too, walks around the table, and pries me out of Dad's arms. Pushing him aside, she says, "Go away, you!" Then she gives me a hug, almost crushing me. "My little baby boy. Mommy loves you much more than Daddy does. You know that, don't you?"

Standing behind her and looking at me, Dad shakes his head, mouthing 'no.'

I wink at him and say, "Yes, Mom."

She lets go of me, wiping away one last tear. Then she turns to Dad and pokes his chest with her finger. "This conversation is not over yet."

"Our conversations never quite are, are they?"

"Get out!"

Chapter Twenty-one

Philip arrives in the afternoon. His dad, who drops him off at my place, doesn't bother to get out of the car and say hi to my parents. I assume this is just as fine with Phil as it is with me, although my mom seems to find it curious, to say the least. She's polite enough not to mention it in front of Phil, but I can see the bemused look on her face when between the moment she watches from behind the curtains how Phil gets out of the car and the moment she opens the door, the car has disappeared into thin air.

Dad notices it too, but he's one who is easily distracted by shiny objects.

"A Tesla!" his inner twelve-year-old automophile exclaims with glowing eyes as Special Agent Nicole Tesla cruises past our house pretending to have her eyes on the road when she is undoubtedly continuing to spy on me from the corner of her eye.

Once Phil is inside, Mom summons Greg from the solitary confinement cell formerly known as his bedroom.

"Philip," she says, "Gregory would like to say something to you."

Upon her nod, Greg steps forward like a trained dog and recites his carefully memorized speech.

"I'm sorry I filmed you and Matt with my phone and I showed it to one of my friends. He told some of his friends about it, and they stole my phone and posted the video online. I didn't mean for any of this to happen, and I'm sorry for anything that happened to you because of me."

In his very own unique deadpan style, Phil says, "Okay," as if he really couldn't care less, with no sense of anger or bitterness in his voice. The guy is basically a saint, and Greg doesn't have much experience in dealing with saints. The glance he casts Mom after a few moments of awkward silence is almost a silent cry for help.

"Looks like you got off easy," she says with a shrug. "Back to your room. We'll call you down for supper."

"Sorry," Greg utters under his breath as he passes Phil and makes his way to the stairs.

"All right," Mom says, turning to Phil and me. "I guess you guys have work to do, and so do I. I'm trying this new recipe today. It's Thai. I'm sorry I couldn't find anything Laotian, but I figured Thai will be close enough. Anyway, the dish is called Tom Yum Gai. It's some kind of chicken soup, apparently. I hope you like it, Philip."

"Yes."

"Oh, good," Mom says, visibly relieved.

"But it's pronounced *guy*, not *gay*."

As Zoey bursts out laughing, Mom's head turns the color of a ripe strawberry. Dad takes pity on her, putting his arm around her shoulder and planting a kiss on her glowing cheek.

"No matter what it's called," he says, "I'm sure it'll be delicious."

Sharing some of Mom's embarrassment, I grab Phil's arm and say, "Let's go to my room before somebody gets hurt."

* * *

We enter my room, and Phil stands there like a hotel guest who's being shown to his room by a bellboy, looking around as if he's never been here before and waiting for me to tell him where he can drop his stuff. Since his fake Louis Vuitton bag got badly damaged by those bullies the other day, Phil is carrying his clothes and books in a big, white plastic bag from Walmart. When I indicate the loveseat, he doesn't drop his bag like a normal person would. He lays it down carefully, almost ceremonially as if the print on it didn't say *Walmart* but *Louis Vuitton*.

As he unpacks his study material, which basically consists of his notepad and a pencil, I ask, "So I guess you haven't fixed your handbag yet, have you?"

He shakes his head. "I don't think it can be fixed."

"That bad, huh?"

"One of the handles came off. I can probably sew it back on, but when they stomped on the bag and dragged it across the ground the leather surface got damaged permanently. It's all scratched and scraped."

"Right," I say. "Well, listen, I feel kinda semi-responsible for what happened, so I was thinking maybe I can get you a new bag?"

"Thanks, but I don't think you can afford it."

Everybody else I know would have at least appreciated the gesture and said, 'Thanks, but you don't have to,' or something similarly gracious instead of insinuating that I can't afford a cheap knockoff LV bag that they sell at the local Asia market for twenty bucks.

I know, because I already checked.

Trying not to sound offended, I say, "They have it at the Asia market downtown. Same model, as far as I can tell, and it's not that expensive, actually."

"It's not that genuine either," he says with a wry smile.

I frown. "But yours ... wait, you're not telling me your bag is the real deal, are you?"

"Of course."

"What? How? I mean, a genuine LV bag must cost hundreds of dollars, no?"

"Yes?"

"How could you afford it then?"

"It was a gift," he says. "From my godmother."

"The lady in the photo! Phyllis, was it?"

Phil nods.

"Wow," I say. "So is she, like, rich or something?"

"I guess?"

I sit on my bed, leaning my back against the wall. "Tell me about her."

He shakes his head. "I wouldn't know where to start."

"As a budding literary genius I can assure you it's never a bad idea to start a story at the beginning."

"Okay," he says. He sits on the edge of the bed, putting his hands in his lap. "Her parents owned a factory up in Irwindale. They manufactured leather goods. Shoes, belts, bags and things. They were doing pretty well for themselves. Sometime in the 90s, when Phyllis was just out of college—she studied fashion design—her parents had a car accident. They both died. Phyllis was an only child, so she inherited the family business. Except, she didn't want it. Not anymore. She had studied fashion design because she was supposed to take over the family business one day, but when her parents died she got all depressed and started questioning everything, her life, her future, everything. She didn't want to carry on the way her parents had, so she sold the factory for a small fortune."

"Wow," I say. "Good for her. I mean, it's terrible that her parents died, but ... you know."

"Anyway, with her parents dead and the family business sold, Phyllis started traveling. She wanted to see the world and experience different cultures and everything. So that's what she did."

"Let me guess, she went to Laos."

Philip shakes his head. "Not right away. First she went to the Philippines, I think, then Vietnam. But she wasn't, like, a regular tourist or anything. She tried to live like the locals. She even took on odd jobs here and there, even though she didn't have to. Waiting tables in Manila, gutting fish in Bangkok, things like that. Anyway, at some point she worked as an English teacher in Vientiane. That's the capital of Laos, you know?"

I know.

I've secretly been reading up on Laos.

"She taught adults who wanted to learn English so they could get better jobs. That's how she met my dad. He always says he was one of her most talented students, although his English is still pretty awful today." He laughs. "Anyway, one day he invited her over for supper so she could meet my mom.

They got along great, and she and my mom became friends too. In fact, when my mom was pregnant with me, it was her idea that Phyllis became my godmother. And that's what happened. My parents didn't even know at the time how rich she was."

"That is one cool story," I say.

"I guess," Phil says, shrugging.

"So have you told her what happened? I'm sure she'll be happy to get you a new handbag, no?"

He looks at me and shakes his head. "I haven't seen her in seven or eight years. I don't even know where she is right now."

A good story wouldn't be a good story without an unexpected twist.

"Really?" I ask, raising my eyebrows. "What happened?"

"I was born," he says, followed by a dramatic pause. "And my parents eventually decided to move to America because I could get better medical treatment here. Phyllis helped us with some of the immigration paperwork and whatnot, and so we came here and she got on with her own life, traveling from one place to another like she's done before."

"And you've never seen her again?"

"She visited us once when I was six or seven. She stayed with us for a week. That was the first time I really got to know her, because before that, when we were still in Laos, I was still a baby and I don't remember any of that. One day, I drew a picture for her. She loved it, and she said I'm going to be a great artist one day. It made me so proud because it was the first time anyone ever said something nice to me. And the last, I think."

I frown. Surely he must be exaggerating. "What about your parents, though?"

"What about them?"

"I mean, aren't they proud of your talent?"

"No?" he says with a bitter laugh. "They think it's a waste of time. Anyway, then one night something happened. They got into an argument, my parents and Phyllis. My brother later told me it was about money. Phyllis wanted to support us financially, but my dad categorically rejected her offer. He got very upset, my mom started crying, and in the end Phyllis just left. That was the last time I've seen her. She calls me every year for my birthday, though, and asks me if I want anything for my birthday. I always tell her I want her to visit us again, and then she comes up with some excuse how she's in Australia or Europe or wherever and she can't make it, and then she asks again what else I would like, and last year I said I wanted the bag. I got it in the mail a week later. But I feel stupid about telling her that in less than a year, I managed to get the bag destroyed, so ..."

"But that was not your fault, though."

He shrugs. "Even so."

I look at him. He's still sitting there on the edge of my bed, his shoulders slumped forward, his hands in his lap. It's such a familiar sight by now, but something has changed. The flat, dull surface is beginning to show cracks, and where I used to see nothing but a blank stare I'm now seeing hints of a whole universe of emotions.

It's almost as if he were a real human.

"What?" he says as he catches me staring at him.

"Nothing." I get up and walk over to my desk. "Come on, we should try and get some work done before supper."

* * *

During supper, everyone is trying to present themselves from their best side. Greg is doing it by limiting his utterances to *please*, *thank you*, and an assortment of smarmy compliments on Mom's cooking. Phil is unusually talkative as he volunteers to introduce us to the finer details on how to properly eat Tom Yum soup.

"You're not supposed to eat everything that's in the bowl," he says, much to my delight. "You just pick the bits and pieces you like, and have the broth with your rice. You can eat the chili peppers if you like, but like the other herbs and spices they're just in there for flavor, and in Laos most people don't eat them."

Mom looks confused, bordering on shock. "So what do you do with the leftovers then?"

Phil shrugs. "Compost them, or feed them to the pigs."

As Mom, Dad, and Zoey exchanged amused looks, I look at Greg. He glares back at me, knowing I'm tempted to liken him to a pig, but in a goodwill attempt to keep the peace at least for tonight I turn my head to Phil and announce, "I shall honor the proud heritage of your country and eat only the meat and rice with some broth."

Mom casts me an unambiguous look to let me know that I'm only getting away with this because we have a guest, but that's fine with me, as long as I can get away with it.

When we're done eating, with Greg back in solitary and Zoey heading out to hang out with friends, Phil volunteers to help Mom load the dishwasher, and since I don't want to stand idly by, I help as well. Through Mom's cunning questioning we learn that Phil's family doesn't own a dishwasher, or a washing machine for that matter. Phil does the washing-up by hand every day, while his older brother Ricky is responsible for doing the laundry.

Once the dishwasher is loaded, we're excused and retreat to my bedroom.

"So, about your brother," I say. "Do you get along with him?"

Shaking his head, he says, "I don't get along with anyone."

"Jeez, I wonder why that is," I tease him.

"I don't know?"

"Yeah, it's a complete mystery," I say, slumping on my bed.

Phil joins me, sitting awkwardly on the edge of the bed. "Ricky hates me because we had to leave Laos because of me."

I frown. "What?"

"We came to America because I could get better medical—"

"Yeah, no, I got that," I interrupt him. "Why would your brother hate you for that, though? I mean, no offense, but aren't you guys better off here? I've been reading up on Laos. It's still a pretty poor country, right?"

He nods. "Laos is poor, but we were doing all right. My parents owned a bit of land and employed a handful of people, harvesting and selling tea. Then I came along, and they sold everything so we could come to America. Fourteen years later we have two mortgages on a tiny, run-down house that isn't really worth anything, all our savings are gone, we barely get by on the fifty or sixty hours my dad works on his minimum-wage job as a security guard, and I …" He swallows. "… I still look shit."

The brutal honesty of his words sucks all the air out of my lungs, and I'm daunted by the incredible amount of guilt he must be feeling, no matter if that guilt may be justified or not.

"Ricky was only two when we left Laos, so he doesn't even remember what it was like, but he compares the life we have here with the life he thinks he may have had in Laos not only if we had stayed there but if I had never even been born or if my parents had abandoned me or given me to an orphanage or something."

Struggling to come up with a response, I finally say, "I'm sorry," but it feels shamefully inadequate.

"It's not your fault."

"It was not an apology."

"Oh," he says. "Thank you, then."

We sit in silence for a while, then I say, "So what do you wanna do?"

"I don't know? We still have work to do, no?"

"Dude, I have never in my entire life done schoolwork on a Saturday night, and I'm definitely not gonna start today. Let's just watch some TV or something."

"If you say so."

"I say so. But first let's make your bed."

"Why?"

"Because it's more comfortable," I say, and I honestly have no shady agenda. I just enjoy watching TV better when I'm lying down instead of sitting up, and since my loveseat is wider than my bed it'll probably be less awkward.

Once we're done converting the loveseat into a futon-style bed, Phil takes a look at my books-and-random-junk shelf. As he bends his head to read the spines, I join him in case I need to provide information on my favorite books. The first thing that catches his attention, though, is a six-inch E.T. doll that I've called my own almost my entire life. He takes it in his hand, examines it, and asks, "What's that?"

"Seriously?"

He looks at me, his face sporting a look of innocent ignorance. "Yes?"

"You don't know E.T.?"

He quickly puts the doll back on the shelf, as if it's suddenly become toxic.

"What's wrong?"

"I don't like E.T.," he says.

I'm puzzled. "You don't like E.T. but you don't even recognize him when you see him? How does that even work?"

It's obvious the question makes him feel uncomfortable, which makes me want to know the answer even more.

"Well?" I say, poking his ribs with my finger.

He twitches, the external stimulus producing a brief smile on his face. Then he says, "When I was little, the other kids used to call me E.T. because of how I look."

"And that's why you don't like E.T.?"

He nods.

"And you've never even seen the movie?"

He shakes his head.

"Dude," I say, "I think you're under a terrible misconception about extraterrestrials. Everyone *loves* E.T."

He looks at me as if I'd just told him the sky is green and clouds are unicorn farts. He wants to believe it, but it simply sounds too fantastic.

As I walk over to my laptop and open my movies folder, he asks, "What are you doing?"

"We're going to watch *E.T.*," I say. "Haven't seen it myself in a while."

"Thanks, but I'd rather not."

"I know," I say, turning to look at him. "But I don't care. Nobody can be my friend if they haven't seen *E.T.* House rules. So make yourself comfortable and get ready to face your demons."

I grab my laptop and sit down on Phil's bed. As I mirror my computer screen on the TV and start the video, Phil sits down next to me. I put the laptop down and pull the bed sheet over our knees.

"I still can't believe you've never seen *E. T.*"

"Sorry," he says.

"I forgive you."

"Thank you."

Our eyes meet, and it's one of those strange moments where we both seem to be trying to figure out what's going on in the other's mind. I keep wondering if he's for real. Does he mean everything he says, or is he just a master of deadpan humor? Does he even have a sense of humor at all, or does he take everything I say at face value even if I'm obviously joking? And what does he make of me and my clumsy attempts to be nice and friendly when nobody else is ever nice and friendly to him?

"You're so weird," I say.

He shrugs. "When being normal is not an option, being weird is not a choice."

I let his words linger for a moment, then I snap my fingers in front of his face to catch his attention, even though he's still looking at me.

"What?"

Without averting my eyes I point at the TV and say, "Look, a movie."

He holds my glare for another two or three seconds before he finally says, "You're weird, too."

We focus our attention on the movie. Or at least he does, while I keep watching him from the corner of my eye. A few minutes into the movie he's mesmerized. His eyes are glued to the screen, his mouth half open, taking long, calm breaths. He laughs and flinches and frowns at the right moments, and he seems so fascinated by the experience that I wonder if he's seen any movie before, ever. Who knows, if he doesn't have Internet access at home, maybe his family doesn't even own a TV. Very occasionally he catches me staring at him, and then I pretend I was only checking if he's still awake, but he is. He's wide awake. At one point when E.T. burps because he's had too much beer, Phil chuckles, so I take a couple of big swigs of Coke and burp too, which makes him chuckle more. He's easily amused by bodily noises, like a seven-year-old, which is rather endearing, and I enjoy sharing those chuckles with him.

When he picks up on the deep, even telepathic connection between E.T. and Elliot, he says, "I wonder if there's a word for it."

"For what?"

"A romantic relationship between a human and an alien."

I look at him, frowning. "You think they're in love?"

"I don't know about E.T.," he says, shrugging, "but the boy sure feels a deep, personal connection that goes beyond friendship."

"Not sure that's love, though."

"I didn't say love. I said romantic relationship."

"What's the difference?"

He shrugs. "I wouldn't know."

We turn our attention back to the movie. Things aren't going well for E.T., and when he almost dies, Phil's eyes glaze over. It makes me think he might be human after all.

Phil, I mean, not E.T.

Anyway, all is well that ends well, and when the movie is over and the credits start to roll, he keeps his eyes glued to the TV, which I take as a good sign.

"So what do you make of it?" I ask.

"That could never happen."

What surprises me is that even though his response is classic Phil, it still manages to baffle me. "What?"

"Aliens from three million light-years away could never visit the earth because even if they could travel at the speed of light it would take them three million years to get here. And even if they could, the military would kill them right away. And they would kill the human family too, because they could be infected with alien diseases. And a bunch of kids would never be able to assemble a machine that could contact the alien spaceship from the junk they find in their garage. And—"

"All right, stop it!" I interrupt him. "You realize it's just a movie, right?"

"Yes?"

"Then stop analyzing it as if any of it could be real."

He shrugs. "I'm just saying."

"Have you ever been a child?" I ask, looking at him. "I mean, a real child?"

"No," he says. His reply is so casual and blunt that I'm at a loss for words. "I didn't have time to be a child. I had to fight for my life from the first day. My earliest childhood memory is being in hospital. Most of my childhood memories are about getting ready for surgery, having surgery, or recovering from surgery. I didn't have any friends I could play with, because nobody wanted to be friends with a freak. I didn't even have any toys or anything."

I frown at him. "You didn't have any toys?"

This sob story is getting way too fantastic, yet somehow I know for some wicked reason it has to be true.

"My parents don't believe in toys, or that toys contribute to anything. They think toys are just a waste of time and money. My dad says the only toys he had as a child were sticks and empty tin cans."

"Even when you were at the hospital all the time? Heck, I got my appendix removed when I was ten, and while I was at the hospital I got more toys than I did for Christmas that year."

"Lucky you," he says with no hint of sarcasm. "I was always left to my own devices. I remember once when I was in hospital I made my own doll. I would take a towel and roll it up and bend it in half, and then I would tie it in the middle with a piece of string so that one end would become the head and the other end would be the legs. Anyway, my parents didn't like it. They're very conservative and don't think boys should play with dolls, but I didn't know how to turn a towel into a car."

"That is the saddest story I have ever heard," I say, but it turns out I haven't even heard the punchline yet.

"By the way, regardless of what my parents think about toys, socially they would buy toys for other people's kids, and I never understood why they never bought anything for me."

I feel miserable, and since I don't know what else to do or say, I get up, grab the E.T. doll off my shelf and hand it to Phil. He looks at me, not quite sure what to do with it.

"I want you to have it," I say, sitting back down.

"Thanks, but you don't have to do that."

He obviously lacks the experience to know that rejecting a gift is considered rude.

"But I want to. Take it as a souvenir from your first ever sleepover. Unless you still hate the movie, now that you've seen it."

"No," he says.

"No what? No, you don't want the doll, or no, you don't hate the movie?"

"I don't hate the movie. And thank you for the doll."

"You're welcome."

I look at him looking at the doll. At first he's handling it clumsily as if he isn't quite sure what to do with it, but then, slowly, his movements become more graceful, gentler, even loving, and when he finally cradles the doll in his arm, his eyes glaze over.

"Sorry," I say in a low voice. "I didn't mean to upset you."

He just shakes his head.

We sit in silence for a while. I don't know what else to say, and I want to give him a few moments to collect himself. I even avoid staring at him any longer, because at this point it feels like an inappropriate invasion of his privacy. I wonder if I should leave him alone for a few minutes and go to the bathroom, but then, from the corner of my eye, I notice a movement of his hand. When I turn my head to look, I see him raising his hand to my face, his index finger extended. He moves his finger closer until it very gently touches my cheek, and in a croaky E.T.-style voice he says, "Elliot."

The level of dorkiness is off the chart, but his acting like a silly little boy is such a rare and unexpected event that I don't want to spoil it, so I hold my laughter.

"Hey," I say, "who told you my middle name?"

"Elliot is your middle name?"

"Yeah."

"I didn't know that."

"Do you have a middle name?"

"Yes."

"What is it?"

"Viengkhone."

"Is that Laotian?"

"No," he says, "it's Swedish," and when he sees my puzzled face, he grins.

"Stupid question, stupid answer," I say, scratching my head. "I probably deserved that."

"You sure did. Of course it's Laotian."

"What does it mean? Does it mean anything?"

"I don't know. Does Elliot mean anything?"

"Yes."

"What does it mean?"

"It's derived of Elijah, and it means 'The Lord is my God.'"

"And does Matthew mean anything?"

"Yes, it means 'the dude who wrote the first book in the New Testament.'"

"Your parents must be very religious."

"No," I say, "they're not religious at all. They just liked the names."

He shakes his head. "No, they're religious. You're religious, too."

"No, I'm not."

"Of course you are."

"No, I'm not. Jesus Christ!"

"See?"

"Shut up!"

"Make me," he teases me.

So I make him shut up by leaning into him and pressing my lips on his. He flinches, presumably because he hasn't seen this type of physical assault coming, and he moves his head back to look me in the eyes as if in search of an explanation. But when I put my hand on his neck and gently pull his head towards mine, I'm met with little resistance.

"What are you doing?" he whispers.

"Picking up where we left off," I say and kiss him again, my tongue entering his welcoming mouth. I gently roll Phil on his back, my left hand caught between the pillow and the back of his head while my right hand is touching his glowing, fiery cheek. While our passionate kiss continues, I let my hand wander down his neck and to his chest, rubbing it gently. I lift my leg and force it between his legs, although not much force is required as he puts his hand on my back and pulls me on top of him, welcoming my vanguard leg like a liberating soldier, embracing it, entwining it with his own. Then, as our bodies react in that awkward, embarrassing way, that physical manifestation of teenage lust that is impossible to ignore, we end our kiss. I put my head next to his, our glowing cheeks touching. My hand stroking his head, his hand rubbing my back, gently as if he were afraid to burst a bubble, we just lie there, silently breathing into each other's ears, allowing ourselves to savor a sweet, delicious tenderness that neither of us has ever experienced before.

* * *

The warm sensation of Phil's long, deep breaths on my neck tickles me awake. When I open my eyes and turn my head to the left, I find his waxy face next to mine. He is lying on his belly, his face half buried in his pillow. His wet lips glistening in the gleaming morning sun, his mouth is half open, feeding the drool stain on the pillow next to my neck which is gross and adorable. His limbs sprawled in all directions, bent and twisted as if he'd hit the ground after a ten-thousand-foot drop from the skies, his left arm is resting heavily on my belly. The smell of his sweet, warm breath mixes with the musty scent of teenage sleep and triggers memories of the night we very nearly lost our innocence in exchange for ... for what? Some kind of bond that comes with shared intimacy? I guess that will depend on how Phil will react when he wakes up from what was not just a dream.

If he doesn't end up running down the street in his undies, screaming, we'll probably be fine.

Accompanied by a big yawn I stretch my arms and legs. Phil's body twitches. He licks his lips like a baby that's just had his bottle, then he slowly opens his eyes. As his gaze falls upon my torso, he moves his arm and repositions it so that his hand comes to rest on my chest, just above my heart. With a hint of a smile on his lips, he closes his eyes again. Trying not to disturb our peaceful tranquility I watch him in silence for a while, enjoying the warmth of his hand on my chest.

Sadly, it isn't meant to last.

Of course it's not.

After a minute or two he rolls on his back, removing his hand from my chest. Stretching his limbs, he moans. Then he turns his head, his tired eyes blinking, and when he catches me staring at him, his moan grows louder, less content, more disapproving, and he pulls the sheets over his face. Such behavior being entirely unacceptable, I pull the sheets away, prompting him to avert his face while failing miserably at his half-hearted attempt to conceal a bashful smile.

"Good morning," I whisper because it's early in the morning and the walls in this house are thin.

Sitting up and scratching his head, he replies, "Morning."

While I look at him, he rubs his elbows, scratches his knees, and does everything humanly possible to avoid my gaze. We sit like that in silence for a while, and I wonder what the socially accepted standard for this kind of situation is. Given the events of the night, would it be okay for me to just lean into him for a good-morning kiss?

Would it even be expected?

What about bad morning breath, though?

Or are we supposed to pretend that nothing out of the ordinary happened, in order to provide an easy, graceful way out in case either one of us should come to the conclusion that this is all but a terrible mistake? What baffles me is the thought that I couldn't be any more confused if our close encounter had been the result of an alcohol-induced loss of self-control.

But it wasn't.

We knew exactly what we were doing. Or, in fact, not doing.

"This is awkward," I say.

"I know," he says, offering no further insight into his state of mind. Instead, he keeps playing with his fingers. In a reckless act of boldness I finally reach out, force his hands apart and insert my own, interlocking the fingers of my right hand with his. His soft, warm hand gently squeezes mine, which is comforting and reassuring. Then he turns on his side, away from me, pulling my arm across his chest and inviting me to spoon. I snuggle my chest against his back and put my nose in the thick, black hair on the back of his head so I can inhale the beautiful, fragrant scent of his scalp.

Motionless and silent, we just lie there, listening to our long, deep breaths, his hand on mine, my hand feeling the beating of his heart in his scrawny chest. Still sleepy, I close my eyes, enjoying the silence, the coziness, and the unfamiliar yet unspeakably comforting sensation of another body nestled against mine. As I let my thoughts meander through the twisted valley my life has been in those first few weeks of high school, I can't help but wonder how I got where I am and what I am doing here.

Somehow, I'm a pillar of the Brookhurst High School track team that will compete at the Brookhurst County Schoolympics in a few weeks.

Me!

It's kind of ridiculous.

It's also incredibly well deserved.

Somehow, I'm officially out and proud.

My coming out didn't go any way I would have done it, had the choice been mine.

Then again, it's easy to argue that I had plenty of opportunities to do it my way before the decision was taken out of my hand.

And somehow, I'm finding myself in bed on a Sunday morning, cuddling with someone who only a few weeks ago was just a random stranger I've met on the freaking Internet.

Don't try this at home.

I just got lucky.

But lucky I got.

I have no idea how this is supposed to work and how things will pan out in the next couple of days and weeks, but right now I don't want to be anywhere else or do anything else but hold Phil in my arms, and I wish this moment would never end.

Then, of course, it ends.

Abruptly.

I'm on the verge of dozing off again when a knock on the door startles me out of my dreamy thoughts. Before I even know what's happening, I'm on my feet, shedding the sheets and scrambling toward my own bed that's pristinely untouched apart from its missing pillow. As I jump into it and pull the sheets over my body, I flounder and wriggle like a fish out of water to mess up my bed and make it look like I actually slept in it. Phil is sitting up, staring at me with his eyes wide open, looking terrified and guilty as he messes down his bed and hurls my pillow at me. I catch it, hug it, and press my face into it as I assume my typical sleeping position.

There is another knock on the door, a little louder this time.

"Matthew?" I hear Mom say.

Trying to sound as if I've only just woken up, I reply with a groan.

The door opens and Mom steps inside. As I put on my best I'm-so-tired act, blinking and moaning, she looks at me, she looks at Phil, and she's smiling like sunshine.

"Good morning, sleepyheads."

"Mornin'," I mumble back, and Phil twangs, "Good morning, Mrs. Dunstan."

"Did you sleep well?" she asks him.

"Yes, thank you."

"Good." She looks at me. "Anyway, breakfast is ready. Surely you don't want to spend all day in bed, so I'll see you guys downstairs in a few minutes, okay?"

It's not a question, it's a request, so I dutifully say, "Yes, Mom."

Satisfied, she is about to leave when my phone chimes to notify me of an incoming text message. Turning her head to look where the sound came from, Mom sees my phone lying on the floor next to Phil's makeshift bed where I put it last night, just before he fell asleep in my arms. Mom looks at me, then at Phil, then back at me. She knows he doesn't have a phone.

Trying to act casual, although my ears must be glowing bright red, I reach out my arm in Phil's direction.

"Can you hand me that?"

He rolls over, grabs my phone, and hands it to me.

"Thanks."

Mom glares at me for an excruciatingly long moment. She knows what's going on. What she doesn't know is if she should say something. Before she makes up her mind, I look at her and say, "We'll be right down, Mom."

"All right." She casts me one last suspicious look and leaves.

Once Mom has closed the door behind her, I look at my phone. The text message is from Zoey.

Zoey

Pull up your undies, Mom's on her way up.

I get up, make my way back to Phil and slide under his sheets. I hold the phone in front of his face so he can read the message. He looks at me, and after a moment of awkward silence we both burst into silly schoolboy giggles.

CHAPTER TWENTY-TWO

I spend the rest of my weekend skipping from cloud seven to cloud nine and back, happy like a first grader on her way to school, silly giggles and bouncing pigtails and all. I keep talking on the phone with Sandy and El Niño, freely answering all their unasked questions about my new and improved relationship status. Sandy is thrilled for me. I know it because she tells me so.

"I'm thrilled for you, Matt!"

"Thanks, Sandy."

Alfonso is thrilled for me too.

"So, are you a top or a bottom?" he asks unabashedly.

"To quote a president," I say, "I did not. Have. Sexual. Relations with that boy. We made it to third base, no further, so technically I'm still a virgin."

"You're not one of those no-sex-before-marriage guys, are you, Guapo?"

"No, but I'm not one of those sex-with-anyone-at-any-time guys either. I don't know that I'm even ready for sex yet."

He chuckles. "You're such a prude."

"You're just jealous because I never came on to you when we had sleepovers."

"About that," he says. "Why *did* you never come on to me?"

"Oh, I don't know," I say. "I mean, you're really nice and all, but you're just so ugly."

Alfonso laughs, because he knows me well enough to know when I'm trolling him, and I love him for it. How could I not?

I love Zoey, too, and the way she admires my audacity to make out with Phil in our parents' house with Mom and Dad peacefully sleeping in the room below.

Speaking of Mom and Dad, they've been acting all weird recently. They whisper to each other when they think nobody's looking, and they stop talking whenever they see me coming. You don't need a Ph.D. in psychology to guess that they're probably talking about their homosexual son and how he's turned their once honorable home into a bottomless pit of lecherous debauchery, but I don't care. For once I choose not to care, because for the first time in ages I'm seriously, genuinely happy.

Of course it isn't meant to last.

I'm starting to feel nervous when on Monday morning Mrs. Spelczik enters the room and Phil's desk is still empty. He's never late. He's often aloof in class, drawing sketches in his sketchbook, or simply zoning out instead of paying attention, but he's never late. Maybe he overslept. Of course. He must have overslept, because why else wouldn't he be here? That's what I keep telling myself for the entire first period.

When he doesn't show for our next class, I'm seriously freaking out because I know something terrible must have happened.

"I'm scared," I say to Alfonso as we're standing out in the hall and I'm scanning the crowds for any signs of Phil.

He nudges me with his elbow. "Don't be stupid. I'm sure he's fine."

"If he were fine, he would be here, Alfonso!"

"Maybe he caught a sexually transmitted disease over the weekend. You should get yourself checked."

I glare at him.

"Dude," he says, "you need to chillax."

"What if he's had an accident? What if he got hit by a car on his way to school?"

Alfonso nods emphatically. "Yeah. Or what if he joined a cult? Sweet Jesus, Matt, I don't know what you think you're doing, but it's not helping. Stop torturing yourself. Make it through the day somehow, and after school you drop by his place and check in on him. Everything's gonna be okay, you'll see."

"I have Track after school," I say. "I won't be able to make it to his place until, I don't know, five or something."

Alfonso sighs. "You want me to do it?"

"Nah," I say, shaking my head. Then I look at him with puppy eyes. "Would you?"

"Aw, shoot, I was so looking forward to watching you stare at Chris's butt and drool while you chase him down the track, but I guess I'm gonna have to heed a higher calling now, huh? All right, I'll do it, but only if you pull yourself together and snap out of that mother goose mode. Like, right now."

That's easy for him to say, but I'm not gonna argue with him. "Fine," I say like a sulky little child.

The next two periods I try not to imagine any of the horrendous things that might have prevented Phil from coming to school, but of course I fail, and come lunchtime I feel the way the mashed potatoes look that the lunch lady slops on my plate.

"Matt," Alfonso says, standing behind me, and when I turn to look at him he flicks his head at the outcast table under the stairs across the room. I follow his gaze, and my heart skips a beat when I see Phil sitting there, sucking on a juice box, his shoulders slumped forward. My initial relief to see him alive and unscathed quickly gives way to a rush of anxiety and panic, because if he's been at school all morning without coming to class it can only mean something's terribly, terribly wrong.

Without taking my eyes off him I pay for my lunch and walk over to his table. He doesn't notice me until I stand right in front of him.

"Oh, hello," he says when he finally sees me.

His casual voice and demeanor as if nothing's wrong makes me want to bitch slap his face with my lunch tray, but I just say, "Where have you been all morning?"

"In class?" he says.

"No, you haven't."

"I'm not attending regular classes anymore."

I hear his words, but their meaning must have gone missing somewhere along the way.

"What?" I say, sitting down next to him. "I ... what?"

"Mr. Mills called my dad in last week," he finally explains. "There have been complaints from teachers because I don't engage enough in class. They think I keep zoning out because I lack the intellectual capacity to follow the curriculum. Also, I don't speak loud enough, and even when I do they still can't understand a word I say, apparently. So Mr. Mills and my dad agreed that it'll be best if I attend special ed classes from here on in. So I can learn, you know, how to do handicraft work without using scissors and things like that, and not slow down everyone else in regular classes."

I lean into him, frowning. "That doesn't even make any sense," I say, exasperated. "If you're zoning out in class then only because you're bored and under-challenged. You're one of the most intelligent people I know!"

"No, I'm not."

"Shut up. Of course, you are."

"Thank you for saying that. But it's obviously not what the teachers think."

"Well, screw the teachers. They don't know what they're talking about."

Sucking on his juice box again, Phil shrugs.

"So," I say, "what are you gonna do about it?"

"Nothing?" he says. Of course that's what he says. He wouldn't be Phil if he said something like, 'This gross injustice won't stand! I will fight for my right to get a proper education!'

And I wouldn't be me if I didn't.

"What do you mean, *nothing*? You don't belong in special ed, Phil. This is outrageous. They can't do this to you. It's not right."

"It doesn't matter," he says.

"I mean, I'm not a lawyer or anything, but I'm pretty sure they can't do this without your parents' consent. So what do they make of it?"

"My parents grew up in communist Laos, remember? They believe in authority. If someone in a position of power tells them what to do, it's what they'll do, even if they have no idea what's actually going on because they don't understand English properly."

Feeling the anger rise in me, I say, "And that's okay with you?"

"What am I supposed to do?" he asks, shrugging.

"How about *not nothing*? You can't let them push you around like that. We should stage some kind of protest or something."

"No," Phil says, shaking his head, but I'm not even listening to him.

"First we need to talk to your parents."

"No!"

The fierceness in his voice stumps me. Finally there's some kind of emotional response, a sign of fighting spirit, but it seems to be directed at the wrong person.

"Why not?" I ask.

"Having you talk to my parents would only make things worse."

Leaning back in my chair, disappointed and hurt, I say, "Why would you even say that?"

He sighs, averting his gaze. "My parents know about us."

"What? I mean, why? I mean … *how*?"

"Your mom. After I got home yesterday, she called my mom and told her."

"No. What? No!" I shake my head and cover my face with my hands. "Oh my God, I'm so sorry."

"It's not your fault, so don't worry," he says. "But my parents aren't too happy about it, so I don't think you talking to them would do us any good."

I close my eyes and pinch the bridge of my nose. Phil is right, me talking to his parents wouldn't do us any good at this point, and that's mainly because I'd shout abuse at them for letting their own son down like that. But since we don't have the resources to fight a two-front war—three fronts, if you count my mom whom I clearly need to have a word with for ratting us out to Phil's parents—we have to focus on the bigger problem at hand.

"All right," I say, "listen to me. You. Do. Not. Belong. In. Special. Edu. Cation. You hear me? I'm not gonna let that happen to you. It's not right."

He looks at me for a long time, his face rigid but his eyes filled with sadness, until he finally says, "Let it go, Matthew. It's okay."

"How can you—" I slam my hand on the table, drawing attention from the people sitting nearby, so I lower my voice. "How can you be such a lemming, for heaven's sake? How can you let people push you around like that?"

He shrugs. "People have been pushing me around my whole life. It's no big deal. Not anymore."

"Well, maybe for you it's not, but it is for me, and I'm not having it. I'm not gonna let you go down without a fight."

"Please," he says, getting slightly annoyed which is something I've never seen before, "let it go already. Why do you even care?"

Am I losing this battle?

"Because I do," I say, half-heartedly because I don't know that I really do.

With a cold stare, he says, "Don't."

I'm losing this battle.

I feel a lump in my throat. Having a potential boyfriend reject you is one thing. Being rejected by your actual boyfriend—if that's really who Phil is—feels a million times worse, and I don't know if I can deal with it. Or if I even want to.

"Fine," I say in a low voice. "Suit yourself then."

I grab my lunch tray and start walking away.

Phil is right: why do I even care? Especially if he clearly doesn't. I don't have time for this. I don't have the energy for this. And it's probably not even worth it, because everything that happened between me and Phil in the last couple of weeks, all the conversations we've had online and off, the awkward moments, the giggles, the bonding over a stupid, childish movie, and the physical intimacy were obviously all worth shit to him. It was all a terrible mistake and a complete waste of time. I hated Phil from the moment he stepped into Mrs. Spelczik's classroom, and the reason I hate him even more now is because he's making me think all these silly, superficial, awful things about him as if I'm no better than any other person who's ever let him down.

Screw you.

Screw you, Philip Viengkhone Thongrivong!

You're not gonna make me treat you like everyone else has been treating you your entire life because it's so convenient.

After a few steps I stop and turn around. "Are you coming?"

He looks at me, puzzled. "Coming where?"

"This is not your table," I say. Then I flick my head at our regular table where the others are sitting and pretending they haven't been staring in our direction the whole time. "That's your table over there."

He hesitates, probably trying to come up with some silly reason why he should just stay there at his table under the stairs like some petulant little child, but no such reason exists, so he finally gets up and follows me.

"You're a nasty piece of work, Philip Thongrivong," I say as we make our way across the cafeteria to our table.

"I know."

Well, it's a start.

* * *

"So how did it go?" Chris asks, lighting his pre-training cigarette. He's wearing a T-shirt depicting two unicorns engaging in explicit sexual conduct under a rainbow. We're standing behind the gym in the secret smokers' retreat, just the two of us, which is rare, because Jack and Steve are picking up litter in the schoolyard, which is their punishment for creating a mess in the cafeteria during lunch that involved hurling dollops of mashed potato at each other or something. I don't even know—or care—because I haven't been paying much attention to whatever's been going on around me since I've had that conversation with Phil. I'm so out of it, I don't even know what Chris is talking about, although that might be because there have been so many *it*s happening in my life recently that I can't be entirely sure which *it* Chris is referring to.

"Hm?"

"Your sleepover," he says.

"Oh, that," I say. "Yeah, good."

He looks at me with a subtle, inquisitive smile, obviously waiting for me to elaborate and share some raunchy details, and when I don't, he asks, "Good?"

"Yeah," I say. It's not that thinking about that night I spent with Phil no longer sends thrilling shivers down my spine and that I don't want to tell the whole world about it, but Chris ... I don't know, it just doesn't seem appropriate to tell him how Phil is so much more pure and authentic and honest than he is. But I don't want to lie to him either, so I don't say anything at all.

"Good," he says, getting the message and not prying any further. He takes a drag from his cigarette and exhales the smoke through his nose. "So listen, I've been thinking about what happened last week. I mean with the video of you and Phil, and especially Phil getting roughed up by those bullies and whatnot. It's a shame that this kind of stuff still happens in this day and age. It makes me angry and sad. Mostly angry, though. So I was thinking we should probably do something about it. You know, do something to raise awareness."

"Uh," I say, having no idea what he's talking about.

"Do you know what Spirit Day is?"

It sounds vaguely familiar. Something to do with LGBTQ rights or something, but I'm not sure, so before he asks me to explain what it is and I make a fool of myself, I shake my head and say, "Not exactly."

"On Spirit Day people wear purple to show their support for LGBTQ youth who are the victims of bullying. You know, like what happened to you and Phil."

I don't like where this is going.

"So I was thinking," he continues, "we should do something to observe Spirit Day here at our school. I mean, nothing huge or anything. Just put up a couple of posters and hand out leaflets in the next ten days, and ask people to show their support of LGBTQ youth by wearing something purple on October 20. So what do you think?"

He looks at me with a wide grin and big, twinkly eyes as if he's just told me he figured out how to reverse climate change, end world hunger, and cure cancer all at once.

"Oh, I don't know," I say.

He was obviously expecting me to fling my arms around his neck and thank him for his willingness to fight the good fight on behalf of all LGBTQ people. Now that this isn't happening, he eyes me suspiciously.

"What do you mean, you don't know?" he says, and without giving me the chance to reply, he drones on. "You've seen what happened when that video of you and Phil went around, right? I mean, you suffered a bit of abuse and ridicule, but you're a big boy. You can handle it. But look what they did to Phil. He's vulnerable, more so than you or me, and you've seen what they did to him. I really think the good and decent people of this school—the majority, no doubt—should stand up against bullying and ... I don't know, make a difference. I really want to do this for Phil, you know?"

"Good luck with that," I say with a wry smile.

"What's that supposed to mean?"

"Nothing," I say, waving my hand dismissively. I really don't want to go into the details how Phil clearly doesn't want other people to fight his fights for him, or explain to Chris how I know this, because I'm still trying to come to terms with Phil's stupid stubbornness myself. "I just think Phil and I received enough attention last week, and to be honest, we're both kinda glad that after the weekend people seem to have moved on. I really don't know that we should put ourselves out there again and remind people why everyone made fun of us in the first place. We want to move on too, rather than revisit last week, you know?""

"I see," he says, visibly disappointed. "Look, nobody's expecting you to be the poster boys of a campaign or anything. I just thought you'd appreciate the effort, that's all. Because I think it's a really important issue, you know?"

"I know."

"Anyway, I think I'm gonna go through with it. It's a good thing. Give a voice to people who can't make themselves heard." Taking another drag from his cigarette, he looks at me. "Or don't want to."

I ignore the obvious jab at me and look at my watch. "We ought to be going. We don't want Coach Gutierrez yelling at us again."

Without a word, Chris drops his cigarette on the floor, grinds it out with his shoe, and we start moving.

* * *

I can hear their voices before I even open the front door. They're familiar and female, both of them, and from the sounds of it, there is no love lost between them. When I enter the house, Greg is coming down the stairs. I look at him quizzically, but he raises his eyebrows and his hands, shaking his head and mouthing, 'I don't know.'

"I honestly can't believe you would stoop so low, Mom!" Zoey says. "You should be ashamed of yourself!"

"Now wait a minute, young lady," Mom shouts back. "You are not gonna talk to me like that. I'm your mother. And I'm *his* mother, and it's my job to protect my children. Now, I'm terribly sorry you don't like the way I'm doing it, but excuse me, you don't know the first thing about the pressure and responsibility that comes with being a parent!"

"What's going on?" I say as I enter the kitchen, the tone in my voice making it clear I'm not merely asking out of curiosity. I'm demanding to know, because I'm obviously the topic of this heated debate.

As their heads turn, Mom says, "Matt!" as if she's surprised to see me in my own home.

"Your mother," Zoey says with disdain in her voice, "just tried to hire my services as a spy. She wants me to keep an eye on you and Phil and tell her whenever one of you farts or something, I don't even know."

I look at Mom. "What?"

Greg whistles through his teeth as he opens the fridge to get something to drink.

"Gregory, go to your room," Mom says.

Looking at Greg, I say, "You will stay right here."

Greg is visibly confused as to why I'm taking his side, although that's not exactly what I'm doing, but right now my mom's enemy is my friend.

"Greg has nothing to do with this." She looks at him. "Gregory, get something to drink and then go back to your room. I mean it."

"Greg has everything to do with it," I say. "Because right now you are using him as a pawn in your perfidious game to distract from the real issue here."

"Matthew Elliot Dunstan, I'm not having you talk to me like—"

"And I'm not having you call one of my friends' parents and tell them their son is gay! How is this even any of your business?"

Her eyes wide open, Zoey looks at Mom and says, "You did *what*?"

"She called Phil's parents yesterday and told them about us. They had no idea of course."

"Wow," Zoey says. "Just wow, Mom."

Meanwhile, Greg grabs a bag of popcorn from the snacks cupboard, sits down at the table and starts munching, looking back and forth between Zoey, Mom, and me. Greg hates popcorn. He's making a point, silently, brilliantly, and it almost makes me like him again.

"They have a right to know," Mom tries to justify herself.

"No, they don't," I say. "Remember when Zoey had her first boyfriend sleeping over? That Marvin guy?"

"Martin," Zoey corrects me.

"Whatever. I don't remember you calling *his* parents to discuss their relationship."

Mom shakes her head in despair. "That was completely different."

"How?" I ask. "How was it different? Other than the fact that they weren't, you know, gay."

"Matthew," Mom says quietly, "I really think we should discuss this in private when your father gets home."

"Oh, now you're concerned about privacy all of a sudden? Give me a break, Mom! Nobody's been giving a rat's ass about anybody's privacy in the last couple of days, so why start now?"

Mom turns away, speechless and on the verge of tears.

"I can't believe you did that, Mom," Zoey says. "Remember that chat we had after that video of Matt and Phil went viral? How you told me that nobody should be denied the right to come out of the closet on their own terms and when they're ready for it? What happened to that?"

Slamming her hand on the counter top, Mom says, "This is not about anyone being gay!" She turns back around and looks at Zoey and me. "Do you really think Phil's parents didn't already know he's gay? I mean, come on, a blind person can see that."

"So what was it about then?" I ask.

"Look, Matthew," Mom says, "we only want the best for you, don't you understand?"

I look at her, and suddenly my linguistic instinct kicks in, that innate primal urge to pick people's sentences apart and to strip away all the smoke and mirrors to see what they're really saying, and then it strikes me.

We only want your best is one thing.

We only want the best for you is quite another.

Most people probably wouldn't even notice the difference, but I'm not most people.

Words matter to me.

"Oh, I understand," I say. "I understand perfectly well. You think Phil is not good enough for me because he's weird and Asian and not the kind of immaculate, handsome Prince Charming you've secretly been dreaming of. You're worried what people will think when you have to tell them, 'This is my son's boyfriend.' You're afraid that they'll think, 'Oh my, couldn't Matthew do any better for himself?' Well, screw them, and screw you. Whom I choose to be or not to be my boyfriend is none of your business, just like it wasn't grandma and grandpa's business to decide if Dad was good enough for you. They hated him when you first brought him home, but you didn't care. Just like I don't care what you think about Phil, so here's my advice for you: Get. Off. My. Back!"

You could hear a pin drop if it weren't for Greg noisily munching away on his popcorn. In Mom's concrete face cracks are beginning to show, and she's either going to blow up in my face or burst into tears any moment now. I'm not sure I can handle either, so I turn around, ready to stomp out of the kitchen, but Dad is standing in the doorway, blocking my way. I'm not sure how long he's been standing there or how much he's heard, and at this point I don't even care.

"Excuse me," I say as I squeeze my way past him and head toward the stairs.

* * *

Dad gives me about half an hour to cool down before he comes knocking. "Hey, buddy," he says, sticking his head in the door. "You got a couple of minutes? I need help with the car."

Lying on my bed, I frown at him. "What?"

"I have to change the timing belt on the Highlander, and I need a hand."

"Are you sure you got the right room? Greg's one door down."

"Greg is busy helping your mother in the garden," Dad says.

"Should I help Mom instead? Greg's much better with cars and everything."

Dad rolls his eyes and sighs. "Look, Matthew, the car is a false pretense so I can have an innocuous chat with you about awkward topics, all right?"

"Oh," I say.

"You might want to put on an old shirt, this could get messy, and you don't want a lecture from your mom about the difficulties of removing oil stains. I've already heard it, and trust me, it's not pretty. Anyway, I'll see you down in the garage."

He closes the door, leaving me with a smile. I appreciate his effort to sound casual. Nevertheless, I feel apprehensive about the impending conversation. I put on a plain black T-shirt because I figure no one will even notice any oil stains on it, and I make my way down to the garage where the hood of Dad's Highlander is propped open and Dad is bending over what I assume is the engine. Unsure what else to do, I put my head under the hood as well to see what Dad is doing.

"So what's a timing belt?" I ask.

"The timing belt," he points at a rubber belt with teeth on its inside surface, "synchronizes the crankshaft and the camshaft to make sure the engine's valves open and close at the proper times."

I have no idea what the man is talking about. Feeling completely inadequate in my role as my dad's firstborn son, I say, "Right, I knew that."

"It's a rubber belt, as you can see, so it doesn't last forever. If and when it fails, the engine will shut off, and we don't want that."

"Nope," I say, shaking my head in agreement.

"So we change the timing belt every thirty thousand miles. Hand me the wrench, will you?"

Relieved he's not asking for a more obscure type of tool, I turn to the work bench and confidently pick the wrench from among a million other tools whose names I don't even know.

"Thanks," Dad says as I put the wrench in his hand, and he starts ... wrenching. He removes a nut and hands it to me. It's black and greasy, and now so are my fingers.

"You want me to hold on to it or ... ?"

"Put it on the bench," he says, "it's gonna be a while. But make sure you'll find it again."

"Okay."

I place the nut on the bottom right corner of the workbench. When I turn back to Dad, he hands me the wrench and a second nut and plunges his hands back into the depths of the engine compartment. As I put the nut next to the first one and the wrench back where I picked it up, Dad says, "You know your mom and I love you, right?"

So here we go. The innocuous chat about awkward topics is off to an easy start because there aren't really that many options to answer this presumably rhetoric question.

"I guess?" I say, shrugging my shoulders which Dad can't see because he's focused on getting the old timing belt out.

"We want you to be happy," he continues, "but we also want you to be safe." His voice is sounding strained because apparently that timing belt is being stubborn. "And by safe I mean not just safe from physical harm but also from mocking and ridicule and whatnot. You know, bullying, basically."

"I know."

The removed timing belt in his hand, he comes crawling from under the hood and looks at me. "Your mom and I never had a problem with gay people, you know? I mean, we have gay friends, and we support gay marriage and everything. Having a generally very liberal attitude like that is one thing, but as it turns out, when your own kids come into play, things suddenly look different. Look, if you're gay, you're gay, and that's fine. Sexual orientation is not a choice, so there's nothing anyone can—or should—do about it. But for your mom it's a bit much all at once."

"A bit much of what?" I ask.

"Of everything," he says as he discards the timing belt in the trash and wipes his hands on a dirty old rag. "Come on, buddy, you know your mom. She was hoping for a beautiful fairy tale wedding for you one day, with a beautiful princess, and now it turns out the princess is a prince—"

"And he's not even beautiful, is that it?"

"Look, buddy, as far as I'm concerned Philip seems to be a perfectly decent guy, and it's not his fault that he looks the way he does. But your mom ... just give her some time, okay? She'll come around."

My hands buried deep in my pockets I just nod.

"Your mom's scared, you know?"

I frown at him. "What, scared of Phil?"

"No, not scared of Phil," he says, shaking his head. "She's scared of how people respond to him. After what happened last week ... how Phil got roughed up after school, I mean ... this kind of thing is pretty worrying, you know? Gay marriage may be legal, but that doesn't mean everyone loves gay people now. It's a rough world, and there are some pretty disagreeable people out there. Like it or not, but people like Phil are easy targets. Easier than most. Your mom, I think, is afraid that what happened to Phil will happen to you when you and Phil are together."

"That's very nice and all," I say almost defiantly, "but I think I can take care of myself."

He moves a step closer and puts his arm around my shoulders. "You know that, and I know that, but your mom ... to her you'll always be her little baby that she needs to protect. It's what moms do. I know it must feel awkward or maybe even embarrassing when you're trying to grow up and be your own person, but you have to understand she's not doing it out of spite or to make your life more difficult or because she doesn't have anything else to do. She's doing it because she loves you and because she cares about you."

I sigh. "I know. But asking Zoey to spy on me is just out of line."

"About that," Dad says, "I think this was a bit blown out of proportion by your sister. Spying is a big word. After you told us what happened to Philip the other day, your mom was worried that something similar might happen to you and that you wouldn't tell us. But if you get bullied or assaulted, we have a right to know, Matthew. All your mom asked of Zoey was to let us know when something happens to you. It doesn't even have anything to do with you and Phil being ... what are you, actually? Boyfriends? Friends with benefits? Fuck buddies?"

Shocked, I writhe out of Dad's embrace. "Dad!"

"Hey!" he says, raising his hands. "I'm making an effort here. Just trying to be open minded."

I shiver in mock disgust, and covering my face with my hands to conceal an embarrassed smile, I say, "Please ... don't."

Chuckling, Dad reaches out his arm and hauls me back in. "Come here, you," he says, ruffling my hair with his grease-stained hand. "Your mom and I, we both love you, you know?"

"I know. I love you too."

He ruffles my hair some more and kisses me on the head. Then he puts his hands on my shoulders, looks me in the eyes and says, "You should go and tell your mom. She kind of thinks you hate her right now."

"Yeah, I guess. But first—"

I turn around and grab the new timing belt from the work-bench. When I turn back, I shriek at the sight of Mom standing in the back of the garage, leaning against the door frame, her arms crossed, her eyes glazed over. "Jesus!" I say. "How long have you been standing there?"

"Long enough," she says, her voice cracking.

"Honestly," I say, "all this sneaking up on people in this house needs to stop."

CHAPTER TWENTY-THREE

When I enter the Korova, the place is nearly empty but for three hipster students hovering over their laptops and sipping their lattes as they sit at the small tables lining the shop front facing Madison, and a lesbian couple feeding each other cheesecake in—of all places—what used to be our regular booth. Or maybe it still is, I don't know. It's been a while since I've found myself enjoying company at the Korova. My friendship with Chris has been going through a considerable cooling-off period, and outside the school cafeteria and the track we haven't been spending a whole lot of time together in the last two weeks. I'm not sure if it's because he's disappointed by my lack of active support of his Spirit Day campaign or because he's trying to give me some space so I can develop my relationship with Phil. Not that there have been any significant developments. We no longer have any classes together, but it might be just a matter of time until they put me in special ed, too, because I keep zoning out in class more and more often, and since Phil's term paper in Mrs. Spelczik's English class has become obsolete, we don't really have a reason to hang out outside of school anymore.

Unless you consider being boyfriends a reason, but really, who does that?

Nevertheless, Phil is the sweetest guy I can imagine. He keeps surreptitiously sliding little love notes into my backpack that put a smile on my face whenever I accidentally find them, and he never leaves my side during lunch at the school cafeteria. Two days ago, overcome by our lascivious desires, we spent our lunch break in a stall in the second-floor restroom, kissing and touching each other in inappropriate places. But when it comes to meeting outside of school, Phil keeps using his suspicious parents as a convenient excuse to not see me. It's driving me insane, but I try not to be pushy. And so, with the semester in full swing and everyone being busy one way or the other, today I'm being a loner boy in search of a place where I can have a milkshake and put the finishing touches on my *Romeo and Juliet* term paper, which was in large parts written by Phil.

"Why, hello there, handsome."

"Hi, Milo," I say with a sigh as I climb a stool by the counter next to the cake display and drop my backpack on the stool next to me.

He raises an eyebrow at me. "Oh my, aren't we cheerful today."

"Don't ask."

"Moi? Asking nosy questions? Never!" he says. "What can I get you, darling?"

"Chocolate shake, please."

"Why do I even ask? Coming right up."

As Milo busies himself preparing my milkshake, I open my backpack and pull out my notebook, a pen, and Phil's tattered copy of *Romeo and Juliet*. I've finished reading it a while back, but I like carrying it around with me because it's the only thing I have that reminds me of Phil. Well, that and Greg's video that I still have on my phone.

I place the book on the counter, open my notebook, and start reading Phil's draft term paper. It's written in Phil's very own distinct voice, including his typical spelling and grammar mistakes and his linguistic quirks. As endearing as they may be, they have to go. With Phil no longer in Mrs. Spelczik's class, I can't pass off his work as my own, so I pick up my pen and start editing.

"There you are, sweetheart," Milo says, placing my milkshake in front of me.

"Thanks, Milo."

"His gaze falls upon my book. "So where's your Romeo today?"

Absentmindedly, I say, "At home with his homophobic parents, I guess."

"Whaaaat?"

I look at Milo, his jaw dropping to the floor, when I realize he was probably talking about a different Romeo.

"Oh," I say, "you were talking about Chris. Yeah, he's not my Romeo. Not anymore. More like Benvolio or Mercutio or whatever, I don't even know. I can't tell all these people apart."

Covering his mouth with his hand, Milo says, "Oh dear, I'm so sorry to hear that. About you and Chris, I mean. You were such a cute couple."

"Yeah well, so were Mowgli and Baloo, but it wasn't meant to be, I guess."

"God, you're so adorable, little man-cub," Milo says. "So who's the new one? He must be quite a hottie if you dump a guy like Chris for him, huh?"

For a moment I'm tempted to tell Milo that this is none of his business, but suddenly I find myself pulling my phone out of my pocket and looking up the video of Phil and me. I show it to Milo, and I'm not even embarrassed about the lipstick. Of all the people in the world, Milo is probably the one least likely to mock me for wearing lipstick. I keep a close eye on Milo, curious to see how he'll react when expectation meets reality. He watches the video a couple of times, smiling.

"That is so sweet," he finally says. "So who's doing the filming?"

"My little brother."

Milo rolls his eyes. "Urgh! Little brothers are a pest, aren't they?"

"Tell me about it."

"Tell me about him."

"About my brother?"

"No, silly," Milo says, still looking at the video. "About your sweetheart."

I shrug. "Nothing much to tell. His name is Philip. He's sweet but pretty shy. Pretty weird, too. And … well, as you can see …" I awkwardly point at my lip.

"Oh please, honey, don't be so stereotypically superficial just because you're gay. What use is the hottest, sexiest guy in the world if he's dumb as a rock? Trust me, I know what I'm talking about. Hans is as ugly as they come, but I love him dearly because he's the kindest and most caring guy you can imagine." He hands me back my phone and turns his head toward the kitchen door. "Hans. Hans! Get your ugly face out here for a minute so we can stare at you!"

A moment later, Hans appears in the doorway. He's a proper Teutonic giant, tall and muscular under his white T-shirt, with slicked back platinum blond hair, an armor-piercing jawline, and super-tight jeans that don't leave anything to the imagination.

"Vhat you vant?" he says in a thunderous voice.

"Hans, meet Matt. Matt, meet my punishment for whatever barbaric atrocity I must have committed in my previous life."

"Hi," I say, trying not to sound too intimidated, and making sure to not leave my mouth open in awe.

Hans nods at me. "Hallo."

"Little Matty here thinks his boyfriend doesn't meet standard beauty requirements, so I wanted to show him how he could do so much worse."

Hans slowly walks up to Milo. Then he grabs him and forces his tongue down Milo's throat—and I mean *literally* down his throat. It's the most violent, primeval kiss I have ever seen, and it leaves Milo gasping for air.

"Oh my," he says, taking a few deep breaths. He slaps Hans on the butt. "Go get your ass back into the kitchen. This is a quality establishment, I can't have you scare away my customers."

Hans nods at me and makes his way back into the kitchen. When he's gone, I lean into Milo and whisper, "Milo, what are you talking about? He looks stunning!"

"Yeah well," he says, waving his hand dismissively, "if you're into that brutish gladiator type. My dream guy would be a petite Latino, but I have yet to find one with a heart as big as that of Hans and a soul as kind. So what is one to do, right? Love trumps everything. Money, looks, everything."

Looking at the screen of my phone where the video is still looping, I say, "Yeah, I guess."

"Listen, why don't you bring Phil over some time? I'm sure he's a lovely guy, but if what you said about his parents is true, he should probably get out more."

"No kidding," I say. "I'll see what I can do."

Milo turns away to greet a new customer who comes walking through the front door, so I turn back to my term paper.

"Why, hello there, stranger," Milo says. "What can I get you?"

"I think," she says as she climbs the stool next to my backpack, "I'm gonna have a beer."

Milo raises an eyebrow. "I'm afraid I'm going to have to see some ID."

The woman laughs out loud, so I turn my head and look at her, and when I see her face I'm so startled that I lose my balance, toppling over my stool and crash-landing on the floor.

As Special Agent Nicole Tesla slides off her stool and rushes toward me to inject me with some undetectable toxin to make my premature death look like a freak accident or a heart attack or something, I try to get up and run for my life, but I fell so hard on my tailbone that I collapse under excruciating pain.

"Are you okay?" she asks sanctimoniously as she kneels down next to me, helping me to sit up, but I shy away from her poisonous touch and flee into Milo's arms who is kneeling on my other side now.

"What are *you* doing here?" I ask, exasperated.

Milo looks at me, then at her, then back at me. "You know her?"

"She's been following me, Milo!"

"The other night," Nicole says, "this kid walked right in front of my car when he was drunk and tried to cross the street without looking."

"She's been following me around for weeks!"

"Who are you, lady?" Milo asks, eying her suspiciously.

"I'm no one. I'm in town to visit old friends, that's all. Our paths may have crossed a couple of times before, but honestly, Brookhurst is not that big a place."

"Right. Let's get you up," Milo says, helping me back on my feet. "You okay, darling?"

"Yeah, yeah," I say, climbing back on my stool, my butt hurting as hell.

"Now, let's see that ID …"

Nicole pulls her driver's license out of her pocket and hands it to Milo. He looks at it and shakes his head. "Now that is clearly a fake. There's no way in the world you are forty-five, darling."

She sighs. "I get that a lot."

"I bet you do," Milo says, returning her license. He makes his way back behind the counter and grabs a bottle of Budweiser from the fridge. "Glass?"

Sitting back down, Nicole shakes her head. "I'm a big girl."

As she takes a swig from her bottle, Milo asks. "So, first time in town? I've never seen you around here."

"I used to live up in Irwindale, but that was a million years ago. I moved around a lot in the last few years. I'm just passing through. As I said, visiting old friends."

"I see. I moved down here from the Bay Area with my husband five years ago. Compared to the Bay Area this place is Dullsville, USA, but good Lord, everything is so much cheaper down here, and when the opportunity to buy this beautiful establishment came along we simply couldn't pass it up. Best decision we ever made, apart from getting married."

The woman nods. "It's funny how life sometimes deals you a hand that you didn't ask for, and then when you play it you realize it's the best thing that ever happened to you."

"Right on, sister," Milo says.

I look at her.

I look at her for a long time until she finally turns her head and looks back at me.

"You're not FBI, are you," I say.

Frowning at me, she says, "No."

"CIA? NSA? Homeland Security?"

She slowly shakes her head. "Why would you even think that?"

"Never mind," I say, feeling like the stupid little boy that I probably am.

Behind the woman, whose name is very likely not Nicole, the door opens, and much to my delight I see Sandy walking in.

"Why, hello there," Milo says, leaning across the counter to give her a quick hug. "So nice to see you, darling. What can I get you?"

"Diet Coke, please," she says. Then she turns in my direction, which also happens to be Not Nicole's direction. "Oh, hi! Good to see you again. What are you doing here?"

Clearly, she's not talking to me.

"Just popped in for a drink, when I accidentally ran into your boyfriend here."

Sandy laughs as she takes my backpack off the stool next to me, dumps it in my lap without even acknowledging me, and sits down. "Oh, he's not my boyfriend. He's gay."

"Thanks, Sandy," I say, putting my backpack on the floor.

"Urgh," Not Nicole says, "the cute ones always are, aren't they?"

"I know, right?" Sandy finally turns to me and gives me a hug. "Hey, I didn't know you were here."

"Yeah, I have to go over my term paper with a pair of fresh eyes. My eyes aren't fresh at home. So what are you doing here?"

"Right, I am here," she says, pulling a stack of fliers out of her bag, "in my official function as a member of the Brookhurst High School Sadie Hawkins Dance committee. We made fliers, and I just picked them up from the printer's. I was on my way home when I saw you sit here, so I figured I say hi real quick. Anyway, here, look."

She hands me one of the fliers. It reads, *Catch his eye. Catch his smile. Make him dance. Join us for the Brookhurst High School's Sadie Hawkins Dance on November 11 at 7pm.*

"November 11?" I say. "That's when the Schoolympics are taking place."

Sandy nods. "I know. But they end in the afternoon, so you guys can basically collect your medals, take a shower, change into your tuxedos, and then get all sweaty again at the dance."

"Awesome," I say with little enthusiasm.

"I know! Anyway, I was going to ask you to be my date for the dance, but then I figured—"

"That I'm a terrible dancer?"

"This is high school, Matt. Everyone's a terrible dancer. No, I figured that you will probably want to ask Phil to go to the dance with you, won't you?"

I look at her, surprised, because that's about the last thing that would ever occur to me, not only because Phil would in all likelihood say no, but also because, well, I'm a terrible dancer. Then again, there probably isn't a law that says you actually have to dance at a school dance.

"Oh, I don't know," I say. "The whole school has seen that video. How do you think they will react if Phil and I show up at the dance together?"

"That probably depends on whether or not you guys choose to put on make-up."

"Funny," I say with a wry smile.

"No, seriously. Look, tomorrow is Spirit Day, and almost everyone I know is going to wear something purple to show their support. I've talked to a lot of people, and honestly, nobody cares about you guys being gay one way or the other. They just thought it was hilarious that you guys were wearing lipstick, that's all. So as long as you're not showing up to the dance in a dress ..."

"Right."

"There you are, sweetheart," Milo says, placing Sandy's Coke in front of her. He eyes the fliers in her hand. "What's that?"

"Sadie Hawkins Dance," Sandy says, handing him a flier.

"Sadie Hawkins Dance!" Milo looks at the flier, his face full of nostalgia and surprise. "Is that still a thing?"

"Of course. Wanna come? Tickets for non-students are ten dollars."

"That's okay, sweetheart," Milo says, handing back the flyer. "Hans and I are terrible dancers. And besides ..." His voice trails off.

"Besides what?" I ask.

He waves his hand dismissively. "I don't want to ruin the fun for you guys, so never mind."

"No, come on," Sandy insists. "Don't be shy. We're your friends, you can tell us."

"Okay then. Do you know how Sadie Hawkins Dances came about?"

"Not exactly," Sandy says. "All I know is that for Sadie Hawkins Dance it's the girls asking the guys out whereas usually it's the other way around. So I guess it's to do with feminism and empowerment of women and equality and ... such."

"That's adorable," Milo says, "and I hate to burst your bubble, but let me tell you a bit about poor old Sadie. First of all, she was not a real person. She was a character in a comic strip, back in the 1930s when men still knew how to dress. Anyway, she was so ugly, she couldn't find herself a husband. So her father declared it Sadie Hawkins Day and ordered a race in which Sadie would chase after the town's bachelors, and the one who got caught would have to marry her."

"Wow," I say.

Next to me, Sandy nods. "I did not know that."

"See?" Milo says. "I'm not sure that's the kind of empowerment twenty-first-century women want to go for if it implies they're too ugly to get a date otherwise."

"Oh please!" Not Nicole chimes in. She takes another swig from her bottle and says, "Sorry to butt in, but that kind of politically correct bullshit always riles me up."

"Oh is that so?" Milo says, putting his hands on his hips.

"You bet it is, honey. The unraveling of beloved, age-old traditions in the name of political correctness is turning into an all-consuming cancer that nobody wants or needs. What are we gonna get rid of next, Thanksgiving because of how it led to the genocide of Native Americans? I mean, don't get me wrong, the genocide of Native Americans was a terrible atrocity that we as a country should be ashamed of, but getting rid of Thanksgiving is not the solution. If anything, we should use Thanksgiving to commemorate it. You know what I mean?"

Shaking his head slowly, Milo says, "I have no idea what you're talking about, sister."

"Look, nobody *needs* Sadie Hawkins dances anymore. In this day and age girls ask guys out all the time and it's no longer a big deal. But holding on to old traditions is a great way to remember how things used to be different and to celebrate how far we've come." She turns to Sandy and me. "So don't you kids let this spoilsport spoil your sport for you. He's just a grumpy old man bemoaning the loss of his innocence."

"Why, aren't you feisty, Missy," Milo says. He grabs a rag and starts wiping the counter top. "I'm nowhere near as old as you are, and one man's innocence is another man's ignorance."

"Yeah, I don't even know what that means," the woman says and takes another swig.

"It means way to commemorate something if you don't even know what you're commemorating or that you're commemorating something at all."

"Except these kids do know." She looks at us again. "Don't you, guys?"

"Yup," I say, and Sandy adds, "We sure do. You see, Milo, there once was this comic strip about a girl named Sadie Hawkins, and she was really ugly and—"

Milo throws up his hands, exasperated. "I told you that!"

"I know!" Sandy says. "And I'll be sure to pass it on." She looks at me. "You know what, we should actually make an announcement during the dance or something. You know, to let people know about Sadie Hawkins and how we have a Sadie Hawkins Dance to celebrate the fact that we don't even need it anymore."

"Sounds awesome," I say. "Go for it."

"Yeah, more power to you, girl," Not Nicole says. "Making the world a better place through education, one Sadie Hawkins Dance at a time."

As she and Sandy fist-bump, Milo looks at me, perplexed. "I don't even know what just happened."

I shrug and say, "Welcome to my world."

* * *

"Would you like to go to the Sadie Hawkins Dance with me?"

"What?" Phil says, sheer terror in his eyes.

We're sitting on the lawn outside the school cafeteria enjoying the October sun and sharing a burrito for lunch. And by sharing I mean I let Phil have most of it because as always, he was too broke to buy his own and too proud to let me buy one for him. Just like he outright refused to let me buy him a purple T-shirt to wear on Spirit Day, which is today. So I had to trick him by buying a plain purple five-dollar T-shirt for myself and giving him my purple *Huntington Beach - Surf City California* T-shirt to wear that I bought as a souvenir during a family trip to the beach last summer. He stuffed it in his plastic Walmart bag when I gave it to him yesterday, and that's where it still was when he showed up for school this morning, wearing the same old frilly button-down shirt he's wearing every day. I dragged him into the next restroom and made him change, and I think he only complied because he realized I was on the verge of getting really mad at him. So, if it took that much effort to make him wear something purple for Spirit Day, I don't have very high hopes of convincing him to go to a dance with me, but even a tiny bit of hope is better than no hope at all, so I repeat my question.

"Would you like to go to the Sadie Hawkins Dance with me?"

"I heard you," he says. "What's a Sadie Hawkins Dance?"

I pull one of Sandy's fliers out of my pocket and hand it to him. While he looks at it, I tell him everything I know about Sadie Hawkins, or at least everything I remember from Milo's lecture. Phil listens intently, but without any discernible reaction.

"So what do you say?" I ask when I'm finished.

He hands me back the flier. "So does that mean you're the girl in this relationship?"

"There is no girl in this relationship," I say, glaring at him. "That lipstick thing was a one-off. Stop holding it against me."

"Right." He looks at me, squinting against the gleaming sunlight. "But shouldn't I be the one asking you out to the dance? With me being the ugly one and everything?"

"That's cute, but I wasn't gonna take a chance on this one. Are you gonna ask me out to the dance then?"

"No?"

"See? I knew it, that's why *I'm* asking *you* out."

"Thanks," he says, picking a scab on his elbow, a remnant of that incident two weeks back. "But I'm not a good dancer."

"Yeah, I'm not a good dancer either. Who cares? Dancing isn't mandatory, even at a dance. We can just mingle and hang out with our friends, and look at other people who are not good dancers either but who don't give a damn and dance anyway."

"I don't have any friends, though."

"Jeez, I wonder why that is," I say, rolling my eyes. Then I nudge him with my elbow maybe a little harder than necessary. "Anyway, I'm your friend. And my other friends are your friends by proxy, kind of. So stop making up silly excuses."

"Sorry. But do you really want to go to a school dance with a guy like me? After everything that happened? Do you really want to spend an evening having people make even more fun of us?"

As if on cue, two guys and a girl from my math class walk by, all wearing purple. One of the guys says, "Hey, Matt." The other guy nods at us and smiles, and the girl says, "Hi, guys."

"Hey," I say and wave. Then I turn to Phil. "See?"

"What?"

I flick my head at them. "See how these bullies just made fun of us? It almost made me want to run home to my mom and cry. And they're wearing purple, too! Probably ironically, to ridicule the whole concept of Spirit Day. It's hopeless, Philip. The whole world is against us, so we should probably just crawl under a rock and die."

"Maybe?" Phil says in a low voice, still picking his scab and working hard to avoid my gaze.

"I'll give you maybe!" I say and give him a friendly but determined push with both hands so he almost topples over on his side. "I was being sarcastic, you idiot!"

I bite my tongue and immediately regret what I said. People have been calling him a retard his entire life, so maybe calling him an idiot—even if it was meant as friendly banter—wasn't exactly considerate. To my relief I notice a subtle smirk on his face because apparently he was being sarcastic too. Nevertheless, to make sure he knows I didn't mean it, I lean into him and plant a quick peck on his cheek.

"Get a room, you two!" a voice sounds from behind us. When we turn to look, El Niño and Hurricane Sandy come walking towards us. He slumps on the ground next to me while Sandy sits on the other side of Phil. She's wearing purple shorts. Alfonso has two purple ribbons pinned to his T-shirt, one over each nipple. Chris has been passing ribbons out all morning to people who couldn't find any suitably colored garments in their wardrobe.

"Are we interrupting something?" Alfonso asks.

"Nothing," I say, shaking my head, "except my boyfriend here giving me the brush-off. He says he isn't coming to the Sadie Hawkins Dance with me." I nudge Phil with my knee. "Isn't that right?"

"Yes?"

"Matthew," Sandy says as if she were talking to a seven-year-old. "Phil is just teasing you. Of course he's coming to the dance."

"No, I'm not."

"Of course you are. We're all coming."

"Well," Alfonso says, "nobody's asked me yet, so I don't know about that."

"Wanna go to the dance with me, Alfonso?" Sandy asks.

"Wait," he says, "don't you want to ask Jason first?"

"Too late. Kishana already asked him and he said yes."

"Oh. Sorry to hear that."

Sandy shakes her head. "No, it's fine. It's not like I've called dibs on him or anything."

"Right," Alfonso says. "All right then, let's do it."

"Awesome." Sandy turns to Phil. "See? Everyone's going."

"I'm not," Phil insists.

"Yes, you are. We're all friends, we're all going. What are people supposed to think of us of you're not coming? It'll make us all look bad, and it'll be your fault, and I will be mad at you forever. You don't want that, do you?"

"No?"

"There you go then, it's settled. I'm sure you look great in a tuxedo."

Phil wants to protest, I can see it in his face, but he knows Sandy is not going to let him off the hook, so he keeps quiet. I have no illusions. This matter is far from settled, and I know I will have a lot more convincing to do once I'm alone with him again. But it's a start, and if he remains stubborn I can always sic Sandy on him again.

"Guys, guys!"

We turn our heads to see Chris run towards us like an excited middle-schooler who just found his dad's secret stash of porn. He's wearing a purple T-shirt reading *#spiritday* in white lettering.

"Isn't this awesome?" He says with a sweep of his arm indicating the entire campus.

Alfonso nods. "That is one beautiful campus for sure."

"Not the campus, you idiot! The people. Spirit Day! Everyone is taking part, and I don't mean that hyperbolically. I'm talking about e-ve-ry-one. Every single person in this school is wearing something purple today, even if it's just socks or hair bands or whatever. Even the teachers. Mr. Mills is wearing a purple tie! Some people didn't have any purple garments in their wardrobe, or at least that's what they claimed." He arches an eyebrow at Alfonso. "But I bullied them all into sticking on our Spirit Day ribbons."

"That's kinda ironic, isn't it?" Alfonso says.

Chris frowns. "What?"

"Bullying people into supporting an anti-bullying event?"

Next to me, Phil opens his mouth, presumably to share how he was bullied into wearing a purple T-shirt by his boyfriend, but I put my finger on my lips and say, "Shhh!"

"Yeah, well," Chris says with a grin, "it's for a good cause, so the end justifies the means."

Alfonso throws me a surreptitious look over this bold statement. Every end clearly doesn't justify any means, but basically having bullied Phil into wearing a purple T-shirt today doesn't exactly put me in a position where I should be overly self-righteous, so I just shrug.

Hey, I'm only human.

Meanwhile, Sandy is getting on her feet and gives Chris a big hug.

"Great job, Chris," she says. "I'm very proud of you."

"Aw, that's so sweet, Sandy. Thank you!" He rubs her back and kisses her on the cheek. "But you know what's best? You're never gonna guess."

"What is it?"

He looks at his watch. "In a few minutes I'll be meeting with a reporter from the *Brookhurst Sentinel*. They heard about our event, and they want to interview me. How awesome is that?"

We clap and cheer, and Chris takes a bow, visibly pleased by our acknowledgment of his achievement. Behind him, Jack is walking across the lawn, making his way toward us.

He's wearing a purple T-shirt.

"Look at you!" Sandy says. "You should wear purple more often, Jack. It suits you."

"You think?" he replies with a wide grin. He's still closeted, and he probably will be for a long time, but today he couldn't be prouder to support a cause that is supposed to protect people from the kind of person he used to be.

That's a good thing, I suppose.

"Absolutely!" Sandy says, giving him a hug. "Anyway, I have to get to class."

"I'm coming with you," Alfonso says.

Chris looks at his watch again. "And I have to go talk to the press. Care to join me, Jack?"

"Sure thing. Wouldn't wanna miss it for the world."

As our little gathering disperses, I look at Phil. He's been quiet, even quieter than usual. Something is clearly bothering him.

"What's wrong?" I ask.

Looking almost distraught, he says, "I don't have a tuxedo."

Chapter Twenty-four

I'm sitting in my third period World History class, pretending to be listening to Mrs. Beitz droning on and on about the political, economic, and social institutions of feudal Western Europe and the Byzantine Empire during the Middle Ages. There are few times and places I'd less rather be than medieval Europe or a twenty-first-century high school class about it, so I'm not paying attention to anything around me but the clock on the wall above the door. The moment the clock hits 9:55, I raise my hand to catch Mrs. Beitz's attention.

"Yes, Matthew?"

"I need to go to the restroom, please," I say.

With a small sigh, because no teacher will ever not display their annoyance when nature calls a student out of their classroom, Mrs. Beitz looks at her watch and writes down the time on a hall pass. As I get out of my chair, Alfonso looks at me, squinting. He knows me too well not to realize I'm up to something, and I wouldn't put it past him to even remember that exactly one week ago I raised my hand at exactly 9:55 to ask Mrs. Beitz if I could go to the restroom. I shrug at him with a subtle smile.

At a leisurely pace I pick up my hall pass and leave the class-room. The moment I've closed the door behind me, I start sprinting down the hallway. While the school handbook states that students shall be given 'ample time to conduct essential restroom business,' there is an ongoing debate as to what exactly constitutes 'ample time.' Five minutes seems to be the lowest common denominator. Most teachers will raise an eyebrow but let you get away with seven minutes, whereas ten minutes will be pushing your luck very hard with just about everyone. So I'm gonna try to be back in Mrs. Beitz's classroom in seven minutes, and seven minutes is preciously little time for what I want to do.

At the end of the hallway I turn right and make my way down to the second floor, taking three steps at a time and taking a five-step leap holding on to the handrail to reach the second-floor landing. Turn left, and run another thirty feet to the restroom door. The moment I push it open I see Phil step out of his classroom at the other end of the hall. My feet inside the restroom, my head sticking out in the hallway, I watch him jog towards me. When he comes within my reach I grab his arm, pull him inside and use his body to push the door shut as I move in and press my lips on his.

After a passionate half-minute kiss, we take a break to catch our breaths. His eyes closed, his lips glistening with our saliva, Phil tilts his head back against the restroom door and smiles, his chest heaving. He opens his eyes, wraps his arms around my waist and pulls me in. We kiss again, our crotches grinding against each other, both of us physically aroused.

"Naughty Matty," Phil whispers in my ear.

Putting one of my hands on his scrawny butt, I let my other hand wander and feel up the bulge in his crotch. "Look who's talking."

He chuckles adorably, which makes me chuckle back.

I put my hands on his shoulders, pull him away from the door so I can wrap my arms around his neck. Squeezing him and rubbing his back, I whisper, "I miss you so much."

"But I'm right here."

"I meant I miss you so much throughout the day, every day. I miss just sitting next to you in class, staring at you."

"I'm sorry."

"Listen," I say, cupping his face with my hands, "can you make it to my place today? Everyone will be out."

"What about your brother, though? Isn't he still grounded?"

I shake my head. "Yeah, but my mom is taking him to a dentist appointment. I hope they'll make it hurt real good."

"Don't say that," Phil scolds me. "No one deserves to suffer physical pain."

I hate when he's acting all saintly like that, but I'm not going to argue with him. "So, can you make it over to my place in the afternoon?"

"I guess?" he says, moving in to kiss me again, but I lean back my head, annoyed by his apparent lack of commitment.

"Do you *want* to come over?"

"Yes?"

That's good enough for me, it has to be, so we exchange another very wet kiss until my gaze falls upon my watch again. I have ninety seconds to get back to class.

"I have to go," I say. "We have to go."

"Okay."

"Okay."

I open the door to the hallway and stick my head out to make sure no one's around. "I'm gonna go. You wait ten seconds, then you go."

"Yes, ma'am."

I glare at him. "Don't get cute with me now."

"Me? Never."

A quick final kiss, and then I run back down the hallway. When I reach the door to Mrs. Beitz's classroom I pause for a few seconds and take a few deep breaths. I look at my watch. It's been six minutes and forty-five seconds since I left when I open the door and get back inside. As I return my hall pass, Mrs. Beitz looks at her watch and clears her throat theatrically, but I ignore her and make my way back to my desk. Alfonso glares at me, squinting again and slowly shaking his head.

* * *

After picking my dirty socks off the floor and tossing them in the hamper, I comb my hair, brush my teeth, and take a shower—in that order. I make sure we have Coke in the fridge, and I place a bowl of M&Ms on my coffee table. I know Phil pays great attention to detail, so I, too, pay great attention to detail in preparation of his secret visit, not because I aspire to be like him but because I want him to show I care.

The one detail Phil doesn't seem to pay all that much attention to today is punctuality. He's never late to school, which is amazing in and by itself, given the condition of his dad's old clunker of a car, but since today's conjugal visit is officially off the record, I can only assume Phil underestimated the time it takes him to get from his place to mine on foot, and he will be here any minute now, so I just wait patiently.

And I wait.

And wait.

When he's ten minutes late, I'm mildly annoyed.

Fifteen minutes late, I'm mad as hell.

Twenty minutes late, I'm getting worried.

Half an hour late, I'm freaking out, trying—with little success—to dismiss a growing number of horror scenarios that might have led to Phil's continued absence as paranoid nonsense: maybe he crossed the road without looking and got run over by a car. Maybe he got abducted by a child-molesting ax murderer. Maybe he got crushed by an airplane that fell out of the sky—although, to be fair, I probably would have heard that last one, the explosion, police sirens and all that. Or maybe, much more likely, there has been some kind of domestic incident. Maybe a pipe burst and Phil has to help clean up the mess. Maybe their microwave exploded and set the house on fire. Or maybe his parents threw a fit because Phil is gay, and so they locked them up in the basement and threw away the key.

Whatever the reason Phil skipped our foreplay date may be, it can't be a good one, and given the anxiety I've been experiencing in the last half hour, I can't see myself simply shrugging it off and waiting until I see him at school tomorrow to find out what the heck is going on. What if he doesn't even show up at school? Then I won't be back at square one, I won't even have left it in the first place, and square one is a miserable place to spend the night.

There's no point in waiting any longer. He's not gonna show up, and I'm not gonna feel better any time soon, so I grab my phone and my keys, and I make my way over to Phil's place, a fifteen-minute walk away from my house. When I get there I immediately feel depressed. The area looks like the ugly stepsister of the street Jack lives in, and that one is already pretty ugly.

Phil's house, if you want to call it that, is a better shack, a one story house with outside walls that look sad and gray. There is no porch, no garage, no driveway. A two-hundred-square-foot patch of wilted grass separates the house from the street where Mr. Thongrivong's old clunker is parked—and right behind it a shiny black car. And it's not just any old car.

It's a freaking Tesla.

It's *the* Tesla.

First my heart explodes.

Then my head, as my mind is assaulted by a fireworks display of gruesome imagery of Phil and his family lying in their own blood on the kitchen floor, Special Agent Nicole Tesla towering over them with bloody hands after she has slain them all for being communist Laotian spies.

Which means she must have lied to me when I asked her if she's a law enforcement agent and she said no.

That bitch!

Despite my fear, I run toward the house, drunk on adrenaline, and the closer I get to the house, the more clearly I can hear the voices coming from the inside. There at least two or three of them, both male and female, shouting at each other and over each other, and I can understand only fragments of a female one—she seems to be the only one speaking English. The one thing that keeps me from ringing the doorbell is the fact that there is no doorbell, so I pull open the screen door with a creak and I knock. Loudly. Then I quickly close the screen door again, getting ready to run for my life, should the necessity arise.

After a few seconds the front door opens, and a seventeen-ish Asian boy—Phil's brother Ricky, I presume—stares at me. He doesn't say a word. No 'Yes', no 'Hello', no 'What do you want'. He just stares while in the background the English-Laotian shouting match continues.

"Hi," I say, panting heavily, my right hand nervously scratching my left elbow. "Is Philip there?"

He stares at me a moment longer, then he turns around, and the door falls shut.

Well, nice to meet you too, I'm thinking, fairly embarrassed. Unsure how to proceed, I just stand there for a moment, my hands in my pockets, the noise from inside dying down. Should I just leave? No, that would be stupid. Should I knock again? That seems importunate and rude. Luckily, I'm quickly being put out of my misery when the door opens again. When he sees me, Phil is aghast.

"What are you doing here?" he hisses, keeping the door open just a crack so no one can see me and I can't look inside. Behind him, people are still arguing, though no longer yelling.

"Well, excuse you," I say, "but I was worried about you! I've been waiting for you, and when you didn't show up I thought something's happened to you."

"I'm sorry. Something came up."

That excuse is pretty much useless. I wasn't assuming he simply decided not to come for no reason at all, so obviously something must have come up, but he's not volunteering any information on what *something* means. I stretch my neck and try to catch a glimpse of what is happening inside the house as people are still fighting, but Phil is continuing to block my line of sight.

"Is everything okay?"

"Yes?"

"Are you sure?"

"Yes."

"You could have just called, you know?"

He looks at me with an expression of guilt and … what is it? Embarrassment? Shame?

"I'm sorry. Our phone … it's …"

"Oh my God, you don't have a phone, do you?"

He shakes his head. "No, no, we do have a phone. But it got disconnected because we forgot to pay the bill."

"Oh," I say, and deep down inside I know he's not being entirely truthful. They didn't *forget* to pay the bill. They simply didn't have the money.

"Philip," a strangely familiar sounding voice says behind him, "I need you back here. Who are you talking to?"

"Nobody. I'm coming," he says over his shoulder. Then he turns back to me. "I have to go."

Before he manages to shut the door in my face, a hand appears and forces it open. I almost stumble over my own feet as I take a step back in shock.

"Oh my God!" I blurt out when the truth finally dawns on me.

"Oh, it's you," Special Agent Nicole Tesla says, reaching out her hand. "I'm Phyllis. I'm Philip's godmother."

* * *

"You were not supposed to hit on my underage customers, lady," Milo says as he places our beverages in front of us, a milkshake for me, green tea for Phil and Phyllis. "That kind of thing can get you into big trouble. You know that, right?"

Phyllis looks at me. "Don't listen to him. He's just jealous because he looks twice my age even though he's younger."

I chuckle because I know it's the kind of thing that riles Milo up.

"Excuse me," he says, putting his hands on his hips, "it's not my fault I lost my hair at a very young age. It's genetic. If I still had a full head of hair I'd put you to shame, darling."

"Yeah, but you don't, do you, Kojak?"

"That's Pontius Pilate to you," Milo says with an indignant smile, "and FYI, sister, Telly Savalas was a very fine man, and very sexy. You, on the other hand, are one of the rudest people I have ever met, second only to Jennifer Rizzuto whom I had the misfortune of sitting next to in fifth grade. Arrogant and mean, she was. And she had cooties. To this day I refuse to eat risotto, just because of the name."

I watch Philip as he follows the exchange with big eyes. He's definitely not feeling comfortable, although I'm not sure if it's the banter between his long lost godmother and that weirdly peculiar bald man that irritates him, or the fact that I walked in on a situation that he was feeling overwhelmed by. All I can tell is that he'd rather be elsewhere right now.

"What a character," Phylis says when Milo has left us alone to serve other customers, "I love him. But don't tell him that, it'll only go to his head."

"Right," I say and suck on my milkshake because, in Phil's defense, I'm overwhelmed too and I have no idea what the heck is going on.

Phyllis looks at me. "So you're Philip's boyfriend, huh?"

As Phil looks down at the table, mildly embarrassed, I nod. There's no point in denying it, because it was a rhetorical question. When we walked in, Milo blurted out, "Oh, there's your sweetheart!" before he started bantering with Phyllis, and by now she must have figured out that his customers are predominantly gay. She also must have overheard Sandy encouraging me to ask Phil out to the Sadie Hawkins Dance the other day. I wonder if at that point she realized that the Phil in question was no other than her own godson. After all, she has been following him around for weeks now, and she's seen us together more than just a few times.

"That's sweet." She turns to Phil. "I had no idea you two were an item."

Staring at his tea, Phil says, "You had no idea about a lot of things."

Phyllis winces. "Ouch! I guess I walked right into that one. It's true, I haven't been in touch a lot, have I? And I clearly misjudged the reaction my surprise visit would provoke. I'm sorry."

"Don't apologize to me," Phil says, shaking his head. "I've been walking around with that face for fourteen years, I'm used to embarrassment. Mom and Dad and Ricky are not."

"They have no reason to be embarrassed, though. Not in front of me."

"Really? Are you telling me you weren't shocked to see how we live in the dirt, in a place other people would be embarrassed to call their garden shed?"

Her silence is telling. She obviously was shocked, in spite of herself. She takes a sip of tea and asks, "What happened, Philip?"

He looks at her as earnest as I've ever seen him. "Life happened. The economy happened. Medical bills happened.

Dad is moonlighting at five dollars an hour. Ricky dropped out of high school and hauls crates of vegetables at the warehouse at four a.m. to help my parents put food on the table. America is what happened to us. Nothing more, but it's quite enough for us to deal with."

Amazed at how he delivers the ugly truth with blunt honesty but no discernible sign of bitterness in his voice, I look at Phyllis. She stares at her cup of tea, takes a sip, then stares at it again. Then she leans back, rubs her eyes, and says, "I'm so sorry. I don't know what I was thinking. Maybe I shouldn't have come."

"Maybe you shouldn't have left."

A bitter smile creeps across Phyllis's face, her blue eyes a sea of pain. She stares at the table for a long time. Then she takes a deep breath and says, "When you guys moved to America, I decided to keep my distance. Back in Laos I'd almost become part of your family, and I think your mother didn't like it much. She never said anything, of course, but I felt she thought your dad and I were growing too close. So when you left, it was time for me to carry on with my own life. But then I went from one extreme to the next. The sad truth is I'm terrible at maintaining friendships, especially at a distance. I'll never understand how people make long distance relationships work. I need to see, touch, feel." She looks at Phil. "Whenever I called and I had your dad on the line, I could tell he was feeling awkward. He always kept telling me things were fine, but I knew he wasn't being honest. I could tell from the tone in his voice and his awkward laughs. But I never pried. I figured if there was something he wanted to tell me, he'd tell me."

"He didn't tell you because he was ashamed," Phil says. "Ashamed he couldn't make the American Dream work for us. He feels he let everyone down."

"That is such nonsense, although I can see why he would think that. But to be fair, Philip, you never mentioned any problems either. Not on the phone and not in your letters. Your letters were always so wonderful, cheerful, full of spirit the way you talked about your hopes and dreams and plans for the future. How was I supposed to know things weren't going so well? And then, like you said, life happens. I was busy chasing my own demons, or getting chased by them or whatever, and before I even knew it, ten years had passed and suddenly I realizes that all this time I've just been running away. I know it's not an excuse, but … well, I guess it's an explanation. I'm sorry, Philip. I'm a terrible godmother."

Phil shakes his head. "No, you're not."

"I haven't been there for you. Or for your family. Not the way I should have."

"Well, you're here now."

"At least one person who seems to appreciate it," she says with a wry smile. "Your parents didn't seem too thrilled."

"Mom and Dad adore you, and so does Ricky. But when you showed up on our doorstep unannounced, they felt ambushed. You should have called ahead and at least given them a chance to clean and tidy the place. Instead you just walked in on the mess we're living in. Of course they were upset, because you made them feel embarrassed and ashamed. We're Asians, you know? To us, embarrassment feels worse than physical pain."

Phyllis shakes her head, wringing her hands. "I was so naïve. I thought I could just barge in on you guys and you'd be just as excited as I was. But when I stood in front of your house and saw how you lived, I had second thoughts. This was a stupid idea, I thought, and I just wanted to run and never come back. But that was a stupid idea too. To come here all this way and after all these years and then just run away without even coming to see you. I didn't know what to do, so I took a step back and tried to figure things out."

"And that's when you started spying on Phil," I say. "All this time I thought you were spying on me, but you were just following Phil around, weren't you?"

Phyllis nods. Looking at Phil, she says, "I was going back and forth, back and forth, wondering if I should come and see you guys or not, until I finally thought, I'm not running away! Not again, not this time. So I finally plucked up all my courage and showed up on your doorstep. Now I almost wish I hadn't because of the way the whole situation blew up in my face. I'm so sorry, Philip."

"It's okay. I'm glad you're here. The others will come around. Just give them a little time."

"You think I could redeem myself by taking you guys out to dinner? I mean, the whole family?"

Philip sighs, his shoulders slumping forward. "And remind us that we haven't eaten out in ages because we're poor?"

Phyllis winces. "Urgh, I'm such an idiot."

"You could cook dinner for us, though. I'm sure Mom and Dad would love that. I know I would."

Phyllis slams her hand on the table. "That's a great idea! Let's do it."

"Maybe not today though."

"No, I was thinking tomorrow because of your—"

"Yeah," Phil interrupts. "Give Mom and Dad a night to get used to the idea."

"Right." She looks at me. "You should come, too."

"Who, me?" I say. "Oh no. No, no no. Thanks, but … no. The last time I wanted to meet Phil's parents, he didn't seem to like the idea all that much."

"What? Why not?" Phyllis says with a frown. Meanwhile, Phil glares at me, clearly not very happy I brought this up, and Phyllis is too attentive not to pick up on it. "What's going on?"

I look at Phil. He stares back at me, silently pleading to shut the hell up. There's a fear in his eyes, the fear that I might go where he doesn't want me to go, because despite his best efforts to pretend it didn't bother and embarrass him to be demoted to special ed classes, he hasn't been able to convince me, and he knows he won't be able to convince Phyllis. Suddenly I feel drunk with the power I'm wielding over Phil, and maybe that power rush is clouding my judgment when I turn to Phyllis and tell her the truth. When I'm finished she looks at Phil.

"Please tell me this is a bad joke."

Phil shakes his head.

"And your father is okay with this?"

"I guess?"

"Are *you* okay with it?"

Phil shrugs. "What am I supposed to do?"

Phyllis has no immediate answer to that question. She finishes her tea, and after a long silence she finally says, "Let me make a few calls."

CHAPTER TWENTY-FIVE

"You must be Matthew," Mrs. Thongrivong says with a heavy but charming Laotian accent as she shakes my hand. "Welcome to our house. Please come."

"Thank you." I step inside and offer her the flowers I brought.

"For me?"

"Yes," I say, slightly flummoxed by her question. I hope she didn't think I brought them for Phil. "Of course."

"Thank you. Very pretty flower."

"Oh, there you are," Phyllis says, coming out of the kitchen and wiping her hands on her apron before she shakes my hand. "Come on through."

When I enter the kitchen in her wake it's like I stepped through a magic portal that led me right into the middle of a bustling alley in Bangkok—or rather Vientiane, I suppose, because that's the capital of Laos, and I only know that because I googled it. The small kitchen is hot and cramped, the air ripe with exotic smells. And it's loud. Mr. Thongrivong, who is stooping over the kitchen sink and rinsing a whole chicken, is shouting at Ricky, who is standing by the stove, caramelizing sugar in a large pot and shouting back. Mrs. Thongrivong is adding to the noise, shouting, like the others, in Laotian. For all I know, she might be telling them, 'Look, that gay American kid is here, and he smells funny.' Then again, maybe she's just saying, 'Guys, please be polite and say hi to Phil's friend, and where the hell do I find a vase in this mess?' I like to think it's the latter, because she opens one of the cupboards and gets out a vase while Mr. Thongrivong turns his head, and when he sees me he drops the chicken in the sink and starts looking for a towel to dry his hands. When he doesn't immediately find one, he shakes the water off his hands, wipes them on his pants and walks up to me to greet me.

"Ah! Welcome, welcome!" he says. His hand is still wet as he shakes mine with a nervous grin, and his awkwardness immediately makes me feel … if not more comfortable then at least less uncomfortable, if that makes any sense. Ricky, on the other hand, makes no attempts to make me feel welcome. He briefly looks at me with no discernible expression on his face, then he turns back to his pot and continues stirring his sugar while adding chopped garlic and ginger. Meanwhile Mrs. Thongrivong puts her flowers in the vase and proudly shows them off to her husband. He raises his eyebrows and smiles as if they're the prettiest flowers he's ever seen, which puts me even more at ease.

"Hello," a familiar voice twangs behind me, and when I turn around, Phil is standing in front of me, holding a bowl with two coconuts—or rather four half coconuts—and a meat cleaver in it, and another, smaller bowl with coconut milk.

"Oh, there you are," I say. "I thought you were hiding away in your room or something."

"No, I had to crack these coconuts open. They don't want me messing about with the meat cleaver here in the kitchen with so many people around, so I had to do it in the backyard."

"Probably a good idea. So what are we having?"

Stepping between Phil and me, Phyllis says, "We're having Tom Khem with sticky rice, and Khao Pahd for dessert."

I have no idea what any of that means, so I say, "Mmmmh, rice," prompting Phyllis to laugh.

"Tom Khem is caramelized chicken stew. It's usually pork belly, but that's pretty fatty and not everyone likes that, so we're making it with chicken today. And Khao Pahd is made of rice flour flavored with pandan leaves and shredded coconuts on top."

"Sounds yummy."

"It is, you'll see. Anyway, as you can probably tell, in Laos cooking is pretty much a family affair. No loitering in the kitchen!" She passes me a bowl full of hardboiled eggs. "You wanna peel these for me?"

"Sure," I say, happy to make myself useful instead of just standing in everyone's way.

As I peel the eggs and Phil scrapes his coconuts at the opposite end of the table, Mr. Thongrivong is standing between us, chopping up the chicken with the meat cleaver he grabbed off of Phil. Mrs. Thongrivong is brewing green tea, and Phyllis is cutting the Khao Pahd she's taken out of the fridge into bite-sized pieces that looks like opaque, pale green Jell-o. Among all the shouting, partly in Laotian, partly in English, Phil and I keep exchanging furtive smiles. Eventually, the chopped up chicken goes into the pot with the caramelized sugar and added water. The shredded coconuts are mixed with the Khao Pahd, and before I know it, we're almost done.

"So what do I do with the eggs?" I ask.

"Just leave them there," Phyllis says. "They go into the chicken stew later, but first we let it simmer for an hour or so."

We retreat to the small living room, and over green tea Phyllis and Phil's parents exchange fond memories of their time together back in Laos, a time both Ricky and Phil are too young to remember, so most of these stories are just as new to them as they are to me. Phyllis is a gifted storyteller, the kind of person you could listen to for hours on end, and she is clearly in charge of her audience, which becomes most notable whenever she leaves the room for a minute to check on the Tom Khem, leaving us behind in awkward silence. While Phil's brother continues to ignore me to the best of his abilities, his parents treat me with reserved politeness, and I'm hoping it's their limited English skills that holds them back rather than the fact that I'm a stranger, and a gay one at that.

Our lively conversation continues throughout dinner. The food is flavorful and spicy—perhaps a bit too spicy for me. After a few bites of the otherwise extremely delicious Tom Khem, I'm sweating like a pig and I have to use my paper napkin to dab my face dry, much to everyone's amusement.

By the time the dessert is served, I'm beginning to notice a strange pattern. As with the main course earlier, Mrs. Thongrivong is making sure that Phil ends up with the biggest portion, and throughout the evening, a disproportional amount of the conversation has been revolving around Phil. A strange suspicion creeping up on me, I lean into him and ask, "It's not your birthday today, is it?"

He responds with a sheepish smile.

"Oh you gotta be kidding me!" I whisper pointlessly because everyone is sitting so close they can hear me anyway. "Why didn't you tell me?"

"I don't know?"

"I would have got you something."

He shakes his head. "You already got me the E.T. doll, remember?"

'That wasn't for your birthday,' I want to protest, but then I realize how much it meant to him—how much it still means to him—so I just say, "Well, Happy Birthday."

"Thank you."

Everyone else is still staring at us. It's awkward, and I feel compelled to say something—anything—so I laugh and say, "I had a feeling we were celebrating something, but I didn't know what it was."

"We're celebrating something else as well, actually," Phyllis says. She puts down her fork, puts her elbows on the table, and entwines her fingers. "Well, kind of, I guess. As you know, Matthew, when I arrived here a few weeks ago, I was shocked, to say the least. And even now, I'm still not sure what upset me more, to see these wonderful people live in poverty like that, or the fact that all these years I was too blind to see. So yeah, it got a little loud yesterday, and that's what you walked in on. I apologize for that. It wasn't as bad as it sounded."

I shake my head. "It's okay."

"So anyway," Phyllis continues, "then I spent a wonderful afternoon with you and Philip at the Korova, and I calmed down a bit, but when I heard about Phil's situation at school and I got all upset again."

"The special ed classes?" I say.

Phyllis nods. "I think it's an outrage. You know Philip, and you know he doesn't belong in special ed."

"Yeah, I know."

"But what we do?" Mrs. Thongrivong says, and I can tell she's feeling helpless. "When school say Philip has to take special class, what we do? They say is better for Philip. If we fight school, how school will treat Philip then? Better? No, not better."

Phyllis puts her hand on Mrs. Thongrivong's arm. "And you know what, I perfectly understand that. We've been through this. If this is what the school recommends, who are you to argue with them? And if you were to argue with them, it probably wouldn't make Philip's life at school any easier, I get that. But the important point here is, the school shouldn't have recommended that in the first place, not for a kid like Philip. He is very special, but not in a way that the term *special education* implies. I think he's not made for the kind of public school he's going to at the moment, nor do I think your school is qualified to deal with him in a way that suits him best. Do you understand what I'm saying, Matthew?"

I don't like where this is going.

"I guess?"

"And I can't even blame the school, to be honest. They're simply not equipped to recognize Philip's extraordinary talent, or to deal with his unconventional personality. You've seen his amazing artwork, and I understand you've been exchanging emails with him before you've even met him at school, right?"

"Yes," I say. Phil's parents and his brother look at me curiously, clearly unaware of the nature of our written conversations or of how they came about, and I hope we don't have to get into the details.

"Right, so you know that the Philip you see on public display at school is not the real Philip, the Philip that comes through in his art and his emails. He acts differently, and he expresses himself differently, so it's true, in a way, that he is a special needs child. But those needs are so special, they can't be met by a school like Brookhurst High School that just puts him in a class with people with all sorts of learning disabilities."

I'm torn between pride, anger, and fear. Pride, because my boyfriend is such an awesome person, an unrecognized genius, apparently. Anger, because nobody ever noticed it until now. And fear of what it all means. Deep down inside, I know what's coming next.

"I know a school," Phyllis says, "that would be perfectly suited to accommodate Philip's needs. Small classes. Highly trained experts. And a curriculum tailored to the individual, with a strong focus on the arts."

"That's ... great," I say. I look at Phil. He looks proud. Proud and sad.

"The school is a boarding school," Phyllis continues. "It's in Maine. I lived there for a while. I know some of the staff."

"Maine?"

"They don't take on everyone, of course."

Please don't let them take Phil, I'm thinking, feeling ashamed for being so incredibly selfish.

"Of course," I say in a low voice.

"I already talked with one of my contacts at the school. They're willing to have Phil over for a trial week. He'd stay at the school and attend classes, to see if the school is right for him and if he's right for the school. And after that week, if both sides agree, he could enroll in the school for the next semester."

"Wow," I say, looking at Phil. "Way to go, you."

He smiles at me awkwardly.

"So how do you like this idea?" I ask.

"I don't know?" He shrugs. "I haven't seen the school yet."

"No, I mean, how do you like the idea of going there to check it out?"

Again, he shrugs. "It's worth a try. It can't be much worse than here, can it?"

"Right." I'm being told there are people who are able to withstand the most horrendous torture techniques and never reveal they're a Russian spy or an Islamist terrorist or whatever it is we're torturing people for these days, so I'm channeling my inner Russian-Islamist terrorist-spy and try to prevent the sting in my heart from making itself visible on my face. To hear that living three thousand miles away from me couldn't be much worse for him than staying here hurts, even if he probably didn't mean it that way.

I look at Phil's parents. His dad smiles at me awkwardly—it's the only way how he knows to smile.

"Is good school," he says. "Good school. Maybe good for Philip. Maybe better school make him happier."

"We want Philip be happy," his mom adds. "But what we can do? Nothing we can do."

"I understand." Turning to Phyllis, I say, "But won't this cost a fortune?"

"Well," she says, "there are scholarships and half-scholarships for exceptionally gifted students. And then there's still me, you know?"

"I see." I look back at Phil. "I guess we'll still have the school holidays, right?"

Without a reply, he looks at his plate, his Khao Pahd untouched.

"What?" I say.

"Look, Matthew," Phyllis says, "There's something else we need to tell you. This family isn't doing well here in Brookhurst, as you know. Sure, I could buy them a house and give them enough money so they would never have to work a day in their lives. Except they don't want me to. Of course they don't. They want to stand on their own feet. Philip's dad wants to support his family all by himself, and I understand that. He wants a proper job, but he can't get a foot on the ground around here. So I got him a job, a good job. It'll allow them to rent a decent home, and Ricky will be able to go back to school and at least get a high school degree. But ... well, that job is up in San Dimas."

"That's ... great."

No, it isn't, you idiot, I'm thinking to myself. *It's awful.*

"It's only an hour up the interstate," Phyllis says. "And you'll be able to drive in a little over a year."

"Yeah, no," I say, trying to sound as cheerful as possible, "it's fine. It's great. I mean, it just comes as a bit of a surprise. It's a lot to take in all at once. But ... it's all good. It's great.

I'm happy for you." I look at Phil, then at his brother and his parents. "For all of you."

"Thank you," Phil says.

"All right," Phyllis says, "now that we got that out of the way, let's enjoy our dessert, shall we?"

I pick up a piece of Khao Pahd and put it in my mouth.

It's delicious.

It's sweet.

It puts the sweet in bittersweet tonight.

Chapter Twenty-six

It's autumn proper now. The days are still warm, but with the sun rising later and setting earlier the nights get chilly, and that chilliness seeps into the days like autumn's inherent melancholy keeps slowly seeping into my soul.

Meanwhile, my life has turned into a dream.

That's not a metaphor for something exceptionally gratifying or some wild fancy or unrealistic hope. My life has literally turned into a dream, a series of images and emotions and sights and sounds occurring in a seemingly random manner, disconnected, wild and raw and scary. It doesn't have to be an actual nightmare to make you toss and turn and sweat in your sleep, to make you feel anxious and confused. All it takes is the nagging question what it all means and the disconcerting feeling that it might not mean anything at all, that whoever is behind it all has no plan.

Everything just happens.

Life just happens.

And there's nothing anyone can do about it.

My relationship with Chris is back to where it was on the first day of school. He's being all nice and smiley and friendly, acting as if nothing good or bad ever happened between us, and it annoys the hell out of me because I have no idea what to make of it. But I never say anything. I don't want to create any tension, because we do have one common goal left after all, and that is winning the Schoolympics relay race. Once that's over and done with, I might never even look at him ever again.

One Monday morning I hand in my *Romeo and Juliet* term paper. Mrs. Spelczik is so happy I've done it with weeks to spare that she doesn't waste any time and returns it to me two days later with a big, fat B+ on the front page.

"Good job," she says.

"Good job," I say to Phil an hour later between kisses, sitting on his lap on a toilet seat in a stall in the second-floor restroom.

"Thank you," he says, visibly proud.

"Not bad for someone who's in special ed."

We both chuckle, and then we kiss again.

Our secret restroom meet-ups continue. We try to have them at least once a day, in alternating periods as to not raise any suspicions. Nevertheless, one day as I'm picking up my hall pass, Mrs. Spelczik says, "You should see a doctor about your bladder."

"I already have," I say. "He said it's my prostate."

Under the roaring laughter of the entire class Mrs. Spelczik pinches the bridge of her nose while motioning me out of the room with her other hand.

Later that day we're having lunch in the cafeteria—the guys and I, not Mrs. Spelczik, obviously—and Sandy says, "So, only ten more days until the Sadie Hawkins Dance. Are you guys excited?"

The question isn't directed at anyone in particular, but Phil is the first to reply.

"About that," he says, looking at me sheepishly, "I can't make it to the dance after all."

"What?" I say, feeling deflated.

Sandy shares my sentiment. "Oh no! Why not?"

"The school in Maine confirmed my trial week. It's next week. I'll be leaving this Sunday and I won't be back until Friday."

"Oh," I say. "When on Friday?"

"I'll be landing in Santa Ana in the afternoon. Three-thirty, I think."

"Right," I say. "That sucks because you'll be missing the Schoolympics, but the dance isn't until what, seven p.m.?"

Sandy nods. "Yeah, seven."

"There you go. Plenty of time to get home from the airport, throw your scrawny butt into your tux and make it to the dance. You have no excuse."

"I have no tuxedo, either."

"Oh please," I say, rolling my eyes. "Do I look like I have a tuxedo?"

"No?"

"Exactly. And that's why we're gonna rent one. Or two, actually. I was gonna talk to you about that anyway. Are you free this afternoon?"

Phil shrugs. "I guess?"

"Good. I'll pick you up at three."

So I pick him up at three to take him to that place on Madison that rents out tuxedos. Phyllis is tagging along which is perfectly fine with me because it means we don't have to walk, and also—more importantly—because I suspect with her help it will be much easier to pick an outfit. Turns out I'm right. She makes us try on two, and it's the second that wins her unreserved approval.

"My," she says, clasping her hands in front of her chest like a proud mother, standing behind us as we admire ourselves in the mirror, "if that isn't the most adorable thing I've ever seen!"

We do look pretty awesome, if I do say so myself. I look at Phil's reflection in the mirror and he looks back at mine, and we both have to grin.

"What are you grinning at?" I say.

"Nothing? What are you grinning at?"

"Nothing? You look sexy."

His awkward grin mellows into a contented smile. "Thank you. You look pretty."

"Thank you."

As we keep standing there for another few moments, looking at each other, smiling at each other, I realize that for the first time since the summer, I'm genuinely happy. I've finally adjusted to high school life, my grades are all right, I'm openly gay and proud, and I have a boyfriend who may defy conventional standards of attractiveness but who is very special in the best possible meaning of the word. Not yet two months ago I would have been embarrassed to be seen with him in public, or to be associated with him in any way. Now it fills me with pride to call him my boyfriend.

Phil, for reasons I can't coherently explain, makes me want to be a better person. I have never met anyone who had that effect on me, not in my family, not in my small circle of friends. Sure, there are some issues that need to be resolved. I find it difficult to deal with the dichotomy between his breathtaking private displays of affection in the confines of a school restroom and his pretty much non-existent public ones. Sometimes I wish we could just sit in a park and kiss, or walk down a busy street holding hands, but as long as we're in public, Phil seems to be happy to be just friends and nothing more. It's a less than perfect situation, but I can deal with it as long as I at least get to spend some time with him every day.

In a few days he'll be heading off to Maine, though, for a trial week of living three thousand miles away from me. It might as well be three million light years. Occasionally, I catch myself secretly hoping that he'll hate the school or that the school will turn him down so he'll come back after that one week and stay for good, even if the family will move up north after New Year's. Fifty miles is still a lot better than three thousand. But whenever I have these thoughts, I feel like a despicable, selfish jerk because if you love someone you should root for them, not against them. And I do love him, I think, even if I haven't said the magic words to him yet. I don't want to put any pressure on him or create an awkward situation if I tell him I love him and he's not ready to say it back to me. Anyway, I'd hate to see him go to school in Maine and only get to see him once or twice a year, but I'd hate it even more to stand in his way, because if anyone ever deserved a break, it's Phil, even if his break may lead to my breakdown.

I'm trying not to let any of this get to me. With my mind focused on the Schoolympics and the Sadie Hawkins Dance, all I care about is that at this point in time I feel happy, and I want to cherish that happiness as long as I can. I know it's not gonna last. Nothing is ever gonna last. There will always be ups and downs, highs and lows. Right now I'm on a high. I'm on a high at last, and I'm not going to let the future drag me down before it's here.

It's autumn proper now, and that's all right.

I love autumn, even though it means that winter is coming soon.

* * *

Chris and Jack wrap their arms around me, Jack his right, Chris his left. Not too long ago the mere thought of finding myself wedged between these two would have sent me running or, more likely, made me crawl under a rock and hide in shame, and even now their touch makes me feel awkward. But it's all good. Today I'm exactly where I want to be, standing in a huddle with Chris, Jack, and Jason. Our arms wrapped around each other's shoulders, we're standing on the lawn of Lincoln High School's sports ground. Lincoln High is one of five high schools in Brookhurst County that take part in the annual *Brookhurst County Schoolympics* and this year's host school. We've been at Lincoln all day, since eight-thirty in the morning. It's mid-afternoon now, and the competition is drawing to a close. In the bleachers some six or seven hundred spectators, most of them schoolmates, friends, and family members of the competing athletes, are eagerly awaiting the final event of the day, the 4 x 100-meter relay final. And we're in it. We've dominated our preliminary and semi-final heats with resounding wins, but we're not taking anything for granted, because in their semi-final, the Lincoln team was almost a second faster than we were in ours. They're our biggest rivals, and beating them is a steep mountain to climb, but that doesn't mean we're not gonna try.

"All right, guys, this is it," Chris says. "This is what we've been working for, so let's make it count. The Lincoln guys are strong, but their anchor's got nothing on me, so as long as we're at least even with them by the time Matt passes the baton to me, this will be ours."

Pumped up, we all say, "Yeah!" because there isn't really anything else to say. We all want this. As we break up to get on our positions Jack slaps my butt, but he's doing the same with Jason and Chris so I'm not taking it personal.

The second leg runners need a minute to reach their starting positions at the opposite end of the track, so I jog over to the bleachers for a quick chat with Zoey.

"Anything yet?" I ask.

She looks at my phone in her hand and shakes her head. "Not yet."

"Maybe the plane got delayed?"

Still shaking her head, she says, "Airport website says they landed twenty-five minutes ago. They're probably still waiting to pick up their luggage or something."

"Right," I say, but I'm not convinced. I imagine waiting by the luggage belt in the arrivals hall of an airport to be a pretty boring affair and a perfect opportunity to send a text message. Phyllis texted me last night, promising me to check in with me as soon as they land. It was only the second text she sent since she and Phil arrived in Maine on Sunday night, and it was all she said, so I have no idea how the week went for Phil and I'm dying to find out.

"You want me to text her?" Zoey asks.

"No!" I say. "It'll make me look desperate. Just keep your eye on it and let me know when you hear something."

"All right then."

I look back at the track. Almost everyone is in position now. "I have to go," I say. "My school needs me."

She gives me a tight hug. "Run, Forrest, run. You guys got this in the bag."

"Thanks, Zoey."

The moment I turn to leave, my phone chimes. I look back at Zoey as she reads the incoming message. "Is it them?"

She looks at me, and her face augurs nothing good. Whatever it is, I can tell she doesn't want to say. She wants me to go and concentrate on the race.

Behind me, a referee is calling out my name.

"Zoey, what is it?"

"Nothing, just go, Matthew! They're calling for you."

The referee is calling my name again, and from fifty meters away I can hear Coach Gutierrez shout, "Get your ass on your position, Dunstan, or I'll get it there for you!"

I make a step forward and grab my phone from Zoey's hand. On the screen is a text message from Phyllis.

There's been an emergency. We're at Orange County Global Medical.

Phyllis

That's all. No further explanation. I feel my heart beating in my throat, my knees trembling.

"This is your final call, Mr. Dunstan. If you don't get on your starting block now, your team will be disqualified!"

"Matthew, you have to go!"

I drop the phone back in Zoey's hand and say, "I'll meet you at the car. Go!"

As Zoey turns on her heel, I make my way onto the track. The referee is scowling at me, but I don't even care. All I can think about is one word: emergency. Way to be vague, Phyllis!

Did the plane have to make an emergency landing, and they had to be pulled out of a flaming inferno?

Did Phil's stomach not tolerate the airline food and he fell ill?

Were they in a car accident on their way home from the airport?

A million nagging questions torment my mind, but one question dwarfs them all, and that question is: what the hell am I still doing here? The sports ground of Lincoln High is the last place on earth I want to be right now.

"On your marks!"

I don't have to be told twice. I'm on my mark at the end of the back straight, looking across the field at Jason cowering in his starting block. A hundred meters behind me, at the beginning of the back straight, Jack is also looking at Jason, shaking his arms and legs. Over at the start of the home stretch Chris is not looking at Jason. He's looking at me. Even from across the field I can see he's worried, and it's that look on his face that finally makes me snap out of it. Chris is our anchor runner, we can't have him worried. He needs to concentrate. I need to concentrate, just for the next sixty seconds, so I nod at Chris and give him a thumbs up. Relieved and reassured, he nods back and raises his thumb at me.

"Get set!"

I'm all set, so let's get on with it already!

I'm so concentrated that at the sound of the starting pistol, my body twitches and I almost dash off. Three meters behind me in the second lane, the Lincoln runner cackles at my amateurish near faux pas. He looks reasonably handsome with his boyish face, his dark brown, wavy hair, and his long, skinny legs, but his sophomoric sense of humor destroys it all. You can look handsome all you want, pal, but if your personality sucks, you suck.

But whatever. Pride goes before a fall.

I rub my sweaty hands on my thighs and look across the field where Jason is catching up to the Lincoln runner stride by stride. The beauty of running on the inside lane is that even if the second-lane runner is slightly faster than you, it still looks like you're catching up. It's a priceless psychological advantage, and sometimes it's psychology that makes all the difference.

At the end of his stretch, Jason has made up nearly half the distance to the Lincoln runner, and he passes the baton to Jack perfectly, as if the two have never done anything else in their entire life. The Lincoln guys almost mess up their exchange, so Jack quickly makes up another two meters, and with powerful strides he manages to keep the distance to Lincoln small. By the time the runners approach the end of the back straight, the audience is on their feet, their cheering and shouting reaching deafening levels.

"Come on!" I shout at Jack and start running, maybe a moment too early, but we're doing great. Jack is doing great, and I trust he can catch up with me before I reach the end of the exchange zone. I get my legs pumping at full speed, and without looking back, I stretch out my arm in anticipation of the baton. As I approach the end of the exchange zone, I glance back. Jack is close, but not close enough to pass the baton, and I can't afford to slow down and lose valuable fractions of a second. He makes three more strides, then he thrusts his arm forward, sending the baton flying through the air. It's only two or three inches, and I'm thinking it's probably against the rules to have the baton airborne for the tiniest moment, but then I remember the coach's advice.

It's not my job to observe or interpret the rules.

My job is to run, so the moment the baton touches my hand, the moment I pass the check mark, I clasp my fingers around it and I run. I run like I've never run before, my legs cutting through the noise-filled air, catching up with Lincoln inch by inch.

At the end of the curve, I'm neck and neck with the Lincoln runner, leading the other teams by several meters. As I enter the home stretch, I catch Chris's glance. He nods at me, claps his hands three times, and then he's off. My legs are burning now, but I just keep going. I have to keep going. When I've almost caught up with Chris I shout, "Stick!"

Without looking back he stretches out his left arm, and with a downward swipe I place the baton securely in his hand. From the corner of my eye I see the Lincoln guys pass their baton almost simultaneously, but Chris is already half a meter ahead, still increasing his speed.

And I?

I just keep on running.

My legs keep pounding the track, not slowing down. For me the race and, in fact, the Schoolympics are over, and I need to get out of here. I need to get to the parking lot where Zoey is hopefully waiting for me in the car, the engine running, ready to take me to the hospital. The shortest way out is the tunnel at the end of the home stretch, so I keep going at top speed, hardly losing any ground on Chris two meters in front of me and keeping up with the Lincoln anchor to my right. When the crowds in the bleachers realize I'm not slowing down, the already deafening noise rises to a thundering roar lashing me on like a whip, making me forget the fire in my thighs and the stinging pain in my lungs. Stride by stride the noise gets louder, the pain harder to bear as I take deep breaths through my nose and exhale hot air through gritted teeth, spewing droplets of saliva. And then, suddenly, Chris slows down and the Lincoln runner next to me falls behind, but I keep on running.

"What the hell?" I hear Chris say as he turns around and I run past him and almost make him stumble backward over his feet.

As I enter the tunnel, the noise behind me slowly subsides. At the end of a long hallway I push the door open, and in the parking lot I see Zoey leaning against the car, her head bent over my phone.

"Get in the damn car!" I shout at her.

Startled, she stares at me for a second, her eyes wide open. Then she opens the door and jumps into the driver's seat just as I open the passenger door.

"Any news?" I say, panting heavily.

She shakes her head and turns over the engine. "No."

"Give me that!" I say and grab my phone from her lap as she pulls out of the parking space. "Do you know the way?"

"O.C. Global Medical?"

"Yes!"

"Yeah, I know," she says, making her way to the exit of the parking lot.

"All right, then go!"

"I am going, Matthew!"

"Go faster!"

"All righty!" She steps on the accelerator and pulls into the moving traffic with screeching tires, causing cars behind us to brake and honk their horns at us.

"So how'd the race go?"

"Fast," I say. "I think we won."

"Hey, congratulations!"

"Thank you. Turn right onto Harbor Boulevard."

"I know the way, Matthew!"

"I'm just saying," I say, frantically tapping the screen of my phone. "Nothing on Twitter."

Taking a right turn, Zoey says, "Twitter? What on earth do expect to find on Twitter? The airport's website said—"

"Look, if a plane were to make an emergency landing, the website would still list it as landed, not as *emergency landed* or something. But passengers on that plane would most likely take to Twitter and, you know, tweet about it and post pictures of their burning plane or whatever."

Zoey sighs. "You need to get your imagination under control, Matthew."

"Well, I don't have very much to go on, do I? I mean, that text was so vague. *Emergency*. It could be anything."

"You could simply text her back and ask," Zoey says.

I look at her. "I could. But what if she didn't get more specific because it's the kind of news you don't want to find out via text message?"

Zoey doesn't reply. I'm grateful she doesn't make me spell out what kind of news that might be.

My phone chimes. My heart skips a beat, but it's just a text from Alfonso.

El Niño

Dude, what happened? :o

Phil's in hospital. Some kind of emergency is all I know. Talk later.

Me

El Niño

Shit! D: Good luck!

Some twenty-five minutes after I've crossed the finish line at the Schoolympics we pull into the parking lot of Orange County Global Medical Center, and not a moment too soon, because apparently Zoey learned how to drive by playing *Grand Theft Auto*. She parks the car, and we run inside.

"Can I help you?" a young nurse asks as I approach the information counter.

"We're here to see Philip Thongrivong," I say. "Some kind of emergency, I don't know."

The nurse arches her eyebrows. "Philip *who?*"

I spell the name for her, and she checks the computer.

"He's in the ER," she says pointing over her shoulder. "Down this hallway, turn right at the end."

"Thank you."

As we make our way down the hallway, I look at Zoey. "He's in the emergency room! This can't be good."

"Relax," she says. "If it's an emergency, where else would you want him to be?"

"I don't know! Do I look like a doctor?"

"I'm sure he's going to be fine, Matthew."

I appreciate her attempts to calm me down, but I find her continuing use of my full name alarming rather than soothing.

We find Phyllis waiting outside the ER, together with Phil's family. I don't take it as a good sign to see them all here, but then again, they don't seem all that upset. Worried, yes, but not upset. At least not as upset as I feel.

"Matt!" Phyllis says as she sees us coming.

"What happened? Where's Phil?"

"He's getting an MRI scan at the moment."

"What happened?" I ask again.

"About an hour before we landed, Phil started not feeling well. He said he had a headache and blurred vision. So I gave him an aspirin and some water, but then his speech got slurred, and all of a sudden he had a seizure."

"Oh my God," Zoey says.

"Luckily, there was a doctor sitting in the row behind us. He checked on Philip and said it was probably a thrombosis."

Shaking my head, I say, "I don't know what that means."

"A blood clot," she says.

The term blood clot sends a shiver down my spine as I remember Phil telling me how he's always at risk of developing a blood clot due to his many surgeries, and that a blood clot can actually kill you.

"When we got here," Phyllis continues, "the doctors examined him, and they think it might be somewhere in his head, so they're scanning him now to see if they can find anything."

"Is he gonna be okay?" I ask.

"I don't know. Sorry." She looks at Zoey. "Are you Matt's friend?"

"I'm his sister. Zoey."

"Very nice to meet you, Zoey. I'm Phyllis. I'm Philip's godmother."

As Zoey introduces herself to Phil's family, I take a seat on one of the chairs lining the walls in the waiting area. Resting my elbows on my knees and putting my hands on my head, I close my eyes, trying not to burst into tears.

Why? I'm asking myself. *Why Phil? After all the shit he's already been through in his life, what has he done to deserve this? What have I done?*

Phyllis sits down next to me and puts her hand on my back. "He's going to be fine, I'm sure. He may not look like it, but he's strong. He'll pull through this. Somehow."

I slowly shake my head. I want to believe her, but what does she know? She's not a doctor. She's doing what every adult would do in this situation: comfort a scared kid by assuring them of something nobody can be sure of.

"I'm so scared," I whisper.

Her hand rubs my back. "I know."

My phone chimes. It's a text from Chris. Attached is a picture of Jason, Jack, and himself, all of them wearing a Schoolympics gold medal around their necks and grinning into the camera. Chris is holding a second medal in his hand.

Chris

No idea where you're at but I picked this up for you. You okay?

Thanks! Can't talk right now. Check with Alfonso.

Me

I pick my phone back in my pocket and rub my eyes when Zoey alerts me with some urgency in her voice.

"Matt!"

When I look up I see a handsome young doctor of Asian descent approach Phil's parents, and it's funny how I find his ethnicity comforting because he probably won't be racist toward Asian patients. In the blink of an eye, Phyllis and I are on our feet to join Zoey and Phil's family.

"How is he?" Phyllis asks.

The doctor looks at her. "I'm sorry, you are?"

"I'm Philip's godmother. This is his family."

"Right, okay," the doctor says. "So, we ran an MRI scan on Philip's head, and it confirmed our suspicion that he suffers from a cerebral venous sinus thrombosis. In layman's terms that's a blood clot in the veins that drain blood from his brain. When the blood can't drain properly, it will increase the pressure on his brain, giving him a headache, blurred vision, and seizures, all of which is consistent with his symptoms. If not treated, the clot could break off and migrate to the lungs, causing a pulmonary embolism and, in the worst case, death. But fortunately he made it to the hospital just in time."

"Is he gonna be okay?" Phyllis asks.

The doctor looks at her. "He's stable now. We're administering heparin. It's a blood thinner that will dissolve the clot, and within a few days he should make a full recovery."

"Oh thank God," Zoey says, grabbing and squeezing my hand.

"However …," the doctor continues, and I feel my heart sinking because however is never a good thing. "… given Philip's medical history—I understand he's had several facial surgeries and he's bound to have more—he's always at an increased risk to develop blood clots, so once we're done with the initial treatment, we want to put him on warfarin—a different type of blood thinner—to reduce that risk. It's just a pill a day, nothing too dramatic, but he'll have to take it at least for several months, maybe indefinitely."

"Doctor," I say, "is that why he got a blood clot now? His recent surgery?"

"How recent was it?"

I look at Phil's parents. They think about it for a moment, then his mom says, "Three month? Yes, August. Three month."

The doctor tilts his head. "Not impossible, but unlikely. The risk his high in the first few weeks after surgery. Three months seems a bit long."

"What about air travel?" Phyllis asks. "People can develop thrombosis on long-haul flights, no?"

"Not this kind of thrombosis. The problem with long-haul flights is that people sit cramped in their seats for too long and they don't move their legs, so that's where a blood clot would form. In the legs. A more likely cause would be trauma to the head. Did he take a fall recently? Or hit his head?"

Zoey gasps and squeezes my hand so hard it hurts. "Oh God."

"He got beaten up in school the other week," I say. "It didn't seem that bad at the time, although he did get a bloody nose."

The doctor looks at me. "Did he see a doctor?"

I shake my head. "We wanted to take him to the school nurse, but he didn't want to go. He said he was fine."

"I see." He strokes his chin. "Well, it's impossible to say for sure, but it may have contributed to his current condition."

I take a deep breath, trying to fight two competing emotions in my stomach, anger and guilt. Anger at the four assholes who have beaten up Phil and, as it now seems, nearly caused his death, and guilt because I didn't insist on taking him to the school nurse to have her take a look at his bleeding nose. All right, she's not a doctor, but maybe she would have told Phil to go see a doctor, and maybe he would have done it and maybe then none of this would have happened.

"Can we see him?" I beg. "Please?"

"He's resting now," the doctor says. "But yes, you can see him. Maybe not all of you at once, though. No more than two people at a time, and only for a few minutes."

I look at Phil's parents, and they look back at me. "Go on, you're his parents. I'll wait my turn," I say even though I'm dying to see him. They both nod and smile at me before they follow the doctor behind the glass door into the ER. I turn to

Zoey, and when I look in her eyes a dam breaks and tears start running down my face. She puts her arms around me and holds me tight.

"I was so scared," I sob into her shoulder.

She pats my back. "I know. He's gonna be fine, though."

I let her hold me for a while as I dry my tears on her shoulder. Behind us, Phyllis is sitting next to Ricky, her arms around his shoulders. They talk quietly. Nurses keep scurrying around, their sneakers squeaking on the linoleum floor as the intercom keeps calling doctors to their stations.

After a few minutes, Phil's parents return.

"Matthew," his mom says, "you want see Philip, you can go in now."

"Thank you."

I look at Phyllis. Reading my mind, she asks, "You want a few minutes alone with him?"

"Would you mind?"

She shakes her head. "Go on."

"Zoey, can you text Alfonso? Let him know Phil's okay?"

"Sure," she says. "Now go. Tell Phil I said hi."

"Thanks."

I walk through the glass door and down the hallway along a long line of windows, behind each of them beds with people in varying degrees of sickness, until I reach Phil's room. He's lying in his bed, his eyes closed. He looks fragile and pale. When I open the door, he turns his head and opens his eyes. The hint of a smile crosses his lips. It turns into a frown when he realizes I'm still in my sweaty track kit.

"Hey," I say as I walk up to him.

"Hey," he says. His voice sounds weak.

I grab his hand as I bend over him and kiss his forehead.

"You smell."

"Well, excuse you," I say, "but I ran all the way from Lincoln High."

"No you didn't."

"But I could have."

He looks me in the eyes. "Have you been crying?"

"No?" I pull up a chair and sit down, still holding his hand.

"Liar."

I swallow to get rid of the lump in my throat.

"I thought you were gonna die," I say with a shaky voice.

Arching his eyebrows, he slowly shakes his head. "Why would I do that?"

"Because you're Philip Thongrivong and you do all sorts of silly stuff."

"Sorry about that."

"I was so scared I was gonna lose you."

"Now look who's being silly."

"I know," I say. "I'm an idiot for loving you, but here we are."

He looks at me with big fawn-in-the-headlights eyes. "What did you just say?"

I replay my words in my head, and only then do I realize what I have indeed just said. I didn't mean to say it but I've meant what I've said, and since there's no point in denying it, I say it again. "I love you, Philip Thongrivong."

He swallows hard, averting his gaze.

"I mean it," I say.

After a few moments he looks at me again, his eyes glazing over. Squeezing my hand, he says. "I love you too, Matthew Dunstan."

Overcome with relief and joy, I lean into Phil and we kiss.

Then I lean back and say, "Now don't you ever scare me like that again!"

"I can't make any promises. Due to my condition and my medical history I'll always be at risk." When he sees that his response isn't going down well with me, he adds. "But I'll try not to."

"God, I hate when you're being so reasonable."

"I can't help it," he says with a sheepish smile.

"Yeah, I know."

"So how did the Schoolympics go?"

"Good. We won the relay final. Or at least I think we did. I didn't stay. After I passed the baton to Chris, I just kept on running because I had to get here."

"You're such a dork. But I'm very proud of you."

"Thanks," I say. "But enough about me. How did your trip go? I mean, apart from nearly dying on me and everything."

He shrugs. "Good."

"You like the school?"

"I guess?"

My heart sinks because *I guess?* is philspeak for *It was freaking amazing and I loved it!*

"It's a small school. Only forty or fifty students per year. And they have lots of arts and design classes and whatnot."

"That's great," I say.

"Yeah, and they have twenty teachers. That's one teacher for every ten students, so every teacher has more time for individual students. And the building the school is at is, like, a hundred and fifty years old and by a lake in the middle of a forest. It's really beautiful and inspiring and—"

"All right, all right, I get it," I say. "You want to go, don't you?"

"I guess?"

"Oh for crying out loud, stop guessing already! If you want to go, just say it."

He avoids my glare. "It's a great place. A really great place. And the people ... they made me feel welcome. They didn't just stare at my face. I mean, some of them did, but it wasn't as bad as here. Some even asked about my condition and actually listened with genuine interest when I told them about it. I don't get that a lot."

I'm trying not to be offended. It's not like I have never asked him about his condition and shown genuine interest. But I don't want to rain on his parade, so I swallow my pride.

"Go for it then," I finally say.

He looks at me. "You think?"

"Of course! This is a once-in-a-lifetime opportunity. I don't even know what you're waiting for."

"I'd miss my family," he says in a low voice. Then he looks me in the eyes. "I'd miss you."

I smile a bittersweet smile. "I know. I mean, I'd hate to see you go and live three million light-years away from me, but ... look, you'll be home for the school holidays and I'll visit you up in San Dimas. And high school doesn't last forever, it only feels that way."

"It's three thousand miles, not three million—"

"Oh shut up," I say and press my lips on his mouth.

* * *

I don't have much time to get ready for the dance. When we return home from the hospital, I take a quick shower, put on my tux, and bring Mom and Dad up to speed on Phil's situation while I'm waiting for Zoey to throw on her dress and do her hair. By the time we make it to school, I feel relatively calm and collected. I knew I was going to raise quite a number of eyebrows if I was going to show up at the Sadie Hawkins Dance holding hands with my facially-deformed, special-education-classes-attending, lipstick-wearing weirdo boyfriend whereas surely not single soul will give a single shit about me, now that I'll attend the dance with Zoey as my emergency escort, no matter how great I may look in my tuxedo.

Then again, maybe I'm just not very good at predicting what people are gonna say or do.

The moment I step into our high-school-gym-turned-dance-hall, heads turn and faces brighten up. Animated conversations cease, giving way to whispers and murmurs that slowly swell up to cheers, and from all sides hands of acquaintances and strangers are coming down on my shoulders. As word of my arrival spreads, a spotlight finds me and triggers people's natural response to encountering even the most superficial, temporary instances of fame: they burst into spontaneous applause. At first it's just a few people nearby, then it quickly eats its way through the crowd like wildfire until the whole place is roaring with thunder and somewhere across the gym a bunch of jocks start chanting, "USA! USA!" as if I'd just personally and single-handedly killed Osama bin Laden.

I turn to Zoey, her eyes as wide open as her mouth.

"Oh my God, what is going on?" she says.

I shrug. "Damned if I know."

Through the euphoric crowd, parting the masses like a triumvirate passing through the Roman Forum, three familiar faces make their way toward us.

"There's my boy!" Chris says, flinging his arms around my waist, lifting me up and swirling me around. When he puts me down, Jack takes over. He throws himself around me, putting one hand on my back and squeezing my butt with the other.

"I love you, Maddie!" he slurs into my ear. "I've always loved you, you know that, don't you?"

I pull out of his embrace, gently because I don't want to offend him, and I look in his glazed-over eyes. "Are you drunk again, Jack?"

He puts an arm around my shoulder and pats me on the chest. "Hell yeah! You betcha I am! Why wouldn't I be? I'm in the presence of a freaking hero! I've never seen anyone run like that, Maddie!"

"Thanks, Jack. That means a lot coming from you."

Taking pity on me, Chris pulls Jack away from me. "Okay, I think that's enough, Jack. Let the poor boy breathe."

Next up is Jason, giving me a good old-fashioned bro hug and patting me on the back. "That was awesome, Matt."

"Thanks," I say, "but … I'm not even sure what exactly is going on here."

"Dude," Chris says, "haven't you seen the video?"

"Video? What video? Sorry, but things have been kinda hectic."

He pulls his phone out of his pocket. Zoey and I bend our heads over it to watch a cellphone video of our relay final that was shot from high up in the bleachers of Lincoln High. The video is titled *Watch my awesome brother kick ass at the Schoolympics*. It's up on Greg's YouTube channel and it shows how after passing the baton to Chris, I kept on running and I actually beat the Lincoln anchor runner to the finish line by the length of a nose. It must be the first time in the history of the sport that a single team came in first *and* second in a race.

"Wow," I say when the video finishes.

Chris nods. "Jack may be drunk as a skunk, but he's right: you are a freaking hero today. The medal ceremony was delayed by half an hour because Lincoln challenged our victory, but the judges couldn't find any rule in the book that says you can't keep running after you pass the baton, so ..."

"That's just crazy."

"By the way," he says, "I think this belongs to you." He pulls a gold medal out of his pocket and places it around my neck under the continuing applause of the people surrounding us.

"Thanks," I say.

"You're welcome. And forgive me, but I think as the person awarding you this medal I'm entitled to do this ..." He leans into me, placing two pecks on my cheeks, one left, one right, followed by another hug.

I still like his smell. Minus the nicotine.

"Now come on and let's get you some punch to celebrate."

Chris leads me through the crowd, and after a thousand handshakes and pats on my back we finally make it to the bar where Sandy and Alfonso are waiting for us.

"Matt, oh Matt!" Sandy squeals as she throws herself around my neck. After a quick hug her face turns serious and she asks, "How's Phil?"

"Thank you for asking that," I say. "He's gonna be fine. He'll have to stay in hospital for a few days, but he'll be fine."

"Oh thank God!"

Alfonso steps up to me, also giving me a hug. "That was crazy, dude!"

"Honestly," I say, "I wasn't even aware of what happened. I just wanted to get out of there and get to the hospital."

"Yeah, I know. I'm glad Phil is doing okay."

"Me too."

Chris hands me a glass of punch. "There you are, champ. Enjoy."

"There's no booze in it, is there?"

"Of course not."

"Good," I say and take a swig.

"Listen," Chris says, "I'm gonna take Jack outside for a minute. He needs a bit of fresh air, and I need a cigarette. Wanna come?"

I shake my head, forcing a smile. "I'm good."

"All right, then. We'll celebrate later, okay?"

"Yeah, sure."

As Chris and Jack head for the door, we mingle with the crowd. People keep congratulating me, patting me on the back and having selfies taken with me, their hero for the day. A million times I have to recount the race and tell everyone how it happened, how after I passed the baton to Chris I just kept on running. Few people ask me why I did it. They don't need to know I did it out of love, so I just tell them, "I had to go somewhere."

"When you gotta go, you gotta go," someone says to me, sowing the seeds of a meme that quickly spreads, and within a few minutes it's common consensus that I kept running because I had to go pee. It's the birth of a myth I'm not gonna bother to refute. The people who matter to me know the truth, and that's good enough for me.

As the night grows older, we stay young just a little while longer as we drink and dance and celebrate our youth. Everything is perfect, save for the fact that the one person I most wanted to be here is not.

"Matt?" Sandy suddenly says, looking past my shoulder. "I think there's someone here to see you."

My heart skips a beat, and for a brief moment I'm hoping that by some miraculous healing process Phil has recovered and made it to the dance after all, but when I turn around I look straight into the face of Greg.

I've never been so disappointed, yet at the same time so happy. It's very confusing.

Of course, being his brother, I can't let him know how glad I am to see him here. It's a natural law.

"What the hell are *you* doing here?"

"Sorry," Greg says, his feisty grin turning sheepish. "Mom and Dad wanted to play Scrabble with me. My only way out was having them come here."

"Mom and Dad are here too?"

"They're parking the car. They'll be here in a minute."

"Right," I say. "Hey listen, thanks for posting that video."

"Dude," he says, "that was so freaking awesome! And guess what, the video is already going viral. Eighteen thousand views, last time I checked. Some sports magazine with half a million followers posted it on Twitter or something."

"Wow," I say, "that's crazy."

"Uh-huh. Great job, bro. Really awesome."

"Thanks."

"So how's Phil?"

His question makes me smile. "Thanks for asking. He's still in hospital, but he's gonna be okay."

"I'm glad to hear that. Really."

I believe him.

And I forgive him. Greg is not a bad person. The only reason he's been acting up against me is because he's my brother. That's not his fault. It's the fault of the two figures who are making their way through the crowd toward me now, but I'm not blaming them either.

"I see you've come to bask in my glory," I say as Mom hugs me and Dad pats me on the back.

"Don't be so full of yourself," she says. "Although we are very proud of you, aren't we, honey?"

"Of course we are," Dad says, and I can see in his eyes he really means it. No dad has ever not been proud to see his son win a gold medal.

"Let me get you something to drink," I offer.

"White wine for me, please."

"Mom, this is a school dance. We have punch and orange juice."

"Really?" she says. "I could have sworn I've just seen Jack Antonelli throw up in the parking lot."

"He brought his own," I say.

"Oh well, punch it is then, I guess."

"Coming right up."

When I return with a tray full of glasses, Mom and Dad have found a table where they're standing with Zoey and Greg. We sip our drinks, and I tell them all about Phil's new school, feigning enthusiasm like a used-car salesman selling Mr. Thongrivong's old clunker to an unsuspecting customer. My parents see through my spiel, but they're kind enough not to say anything. They know the person I'm trying to convince is me.

I'll be getting there, somehow.

After a while, Sandy and Alfonso come walking off the dance floor and join us at our bar table. They're holding hands which is an odd but endearing sight. Also, it's making me feel strangely jealous.

The DJ puts on some song that must have meant something to Mom and Dad in the eighties or nineties or whenever it was they were still young, so Dad grabs Mom's hand and pulls her onto the dance floor.

"God, how embarrassing," Greg moans.

With a twinkle in her eyes, Zoey grabs Greg's hand, and without putting up much of a fight, Greg follows her onto the dance floor.

Sandy says, "I don't know about you guys, but I could use a bit of fresh air."

Alfonso and I both nod, so we leave the hot and steamy air of the gymnasium behind and make our way outside into the balmy night where we find Chris and Jack sitting on the floor. Jack is hugging his legs, his head resting on his knees, his eyes closed. He's sleeping. Chris is leaning against the gymnasium wall, smoking a cigarette.

"Oh," Sandy says in surprise as she sees them. "You guys need some privacy?"

He shakes his head, exhaling smoke from the corner of his mouth. "I could use some company. He's been out of it for nearly half an hour. This is the most boring high school dance I've ever been to."

"How many high school dances have you been to before?" Alfonso asks.

"Just this one," Chris says with a melancholy smirk.

We sit down next to him, and Sandy leans her head against Chris's shoulder.

"Your hair smells nice," he says.

"Thank you," Sandy says, and after a pause she adds, "You reek of cigarettes."

Chris chuckles. "Sorry about that."

"It's okay."

"Thanks," he says and kisses her head.

We sit in silence for a while, listening to the muffled sound of music from inside the gymnasium and looking at the waxing crescent moon hovering over the horizon. For the first time today I have time to catch my breath and let it all sink in—everything, not just what happened today. It's hard to believe it's only been a little over two months since I've started high school. In those two months I've been through more highs and lows than I would have imagined to encounter all the way through my graduation that's still the better part of four years away. The thought of all that's yet to come scares me, but it doesn't scare me quite as much as it used to. I feel like I've finally arrived somewhere. It's not yet where I want to be, nor will I stay here very long, but for now it's exactly where I'm supposed to be—among friends, feeling appreciated, accepted, even loved.

My phone chimes twice in rapid succession. It's two incoming text messages from an unknown number.

Unknown

Hello, Mr. Handsome! You're probably busy shaking your booty on the dance floor, being admired by ecstatic crowds and being all sweaty, your shirt soaked, making you look like a handsome Latino lover in some music video or something. I'll let you get back to it, right after telling you that I wish I could be there to share the moment with you. I miss you very much. I have missed you all week and will do so in the weeks and months to come, always longing for the next time you'll hold me in your skinny arms again. Now back on the dance floor with you! Continue shaking that scrawny booty! Love you! <3

Unknown

Oh, this is me, by the way. Philip. Phyllis just bought me a brand new FancyPhone so I can stay in touch with you and her and my family when I'm in Maine. I have no idea how to use this thing, haha. ^^;

351

Me

> Haha, no booty-shaking because I'm a terrible dancer. Still having a good time, though, except I wish you could be here, too, my silly baby! And congrats on your new phone, Mr. Fancypants. But anyway, it's late and you've had a rough day, so you should go and get some sleep now. I'll pay you a visit at the hospital tomorrow, k?
> Love you too! <3

As I hit send and put my phone away, a near silent sigh escapes me, prompting Alfonso to turn his head and look at me.

"You all right?" he asks.

"I am, actually," I say and lean my head against his shoulder.

"Hey, are you coming on to me?"

I snort. "You wish."

"No, I don't."

"Although …," I say, "you are kinda sexy sometimes."

"I didn't need to know that."

"Nah, I was just kidding. You're ugly."

"Guys, be nice," Sandy says, and after a pause she adds, "Fánshì dōu yǒu měinǚ, dàn bùshì měi gèrén dōu kěyǐ kàn dào tā."

We look at her.

"What's that mean?" Alfonso asks.

"It means 'everything has beauty, but not everyone can see it.'"

Alfonso nudges me. "How about that?"

"I know," I say, and it's the truth. I know.

I put my head back on his shoulder, he rests his head on mine, and it's okay. For now, for this brief, fleeting moment in time, everything is perfectly okay.

I'll worry about the future tomorrow.

Thank you for reading *Cupid Painted Blind*. If you enjoyed it, a quick review over at Amazon and/or Goodreads would be greatly appreciated. Reviews help authors make a living and write more books.

Older versions of Chris and Jack appear in the novel *Never Do a Wrong Thing*. You may want to check it out if you haven't already done so.

About the Author

Marcus Herzig, future bestselling author and professional cynic, was born in 1970 and studied Law, English, Educational Science, and Physics, albeit none of them with any tenacity or ambition. After dropping out of university he held various positions in banking, utilities, and Big Oil that bore no responsibility or decision-making power whatsoever.

Always destined to be a demiurge, Marcus has been inventing characters and telling stories since the age of five. His favorite genre, both as a reader and a writer, is Young Adult literature, but he also very much enjoys science- and literary fiction.

Marcus, who finds it very peculiar to talk about himself in the third person, prefers sunsets over sunrises, white wine over red, beer over wine, pizza over pasta, and humanity over humans. His favorite person is his future husband. Their favorite place is the beach.

Also by Marcus Herzig

Never Do a Wrong Thing
Instafamous
Counterparts
Eschaton - The Beginning
Idolism

www.marcus-herzig.com
Follow the author on Twitter @Marcus_Herzig

Coming out is hard enough on its own, but when you have a crush on your best buddy, things get really complicated.

Best friends since kindergarten, best friends forever. That was the plan. High school sophomores Tim and Tom know everything there is to know about each other ... or at least they should, but Tim has a secret that could change everything he doesn't want to see changed.

Tim is gay and almost ready to be out and proud. Tom is already proud—a proud homophobe, that is.

As if the stakes were not high enough already, things get even more complicated when Tom talks his friend into double-dating a pair of girls. But sometimes unwanted challenges offer unexpected opportunities, and after the most embarrassing night of his life, Tim knows he can no longer avoid the inevitable. The question is, how will his best friend take it?

From the author of *Cupid Painted Blind* comes a captivating new Young Adult LGBTQ novel that provides insight into the conflicted soul of a teenage boy who finds himself torn between honesty and friendship.

ISBN: 978-1726616317

54588362R00214

Made in the USA
Columbia, SC
02 April 2019